THE SILVER SORCERESS

Book 2 of The Raveling

ALEC HUTSON

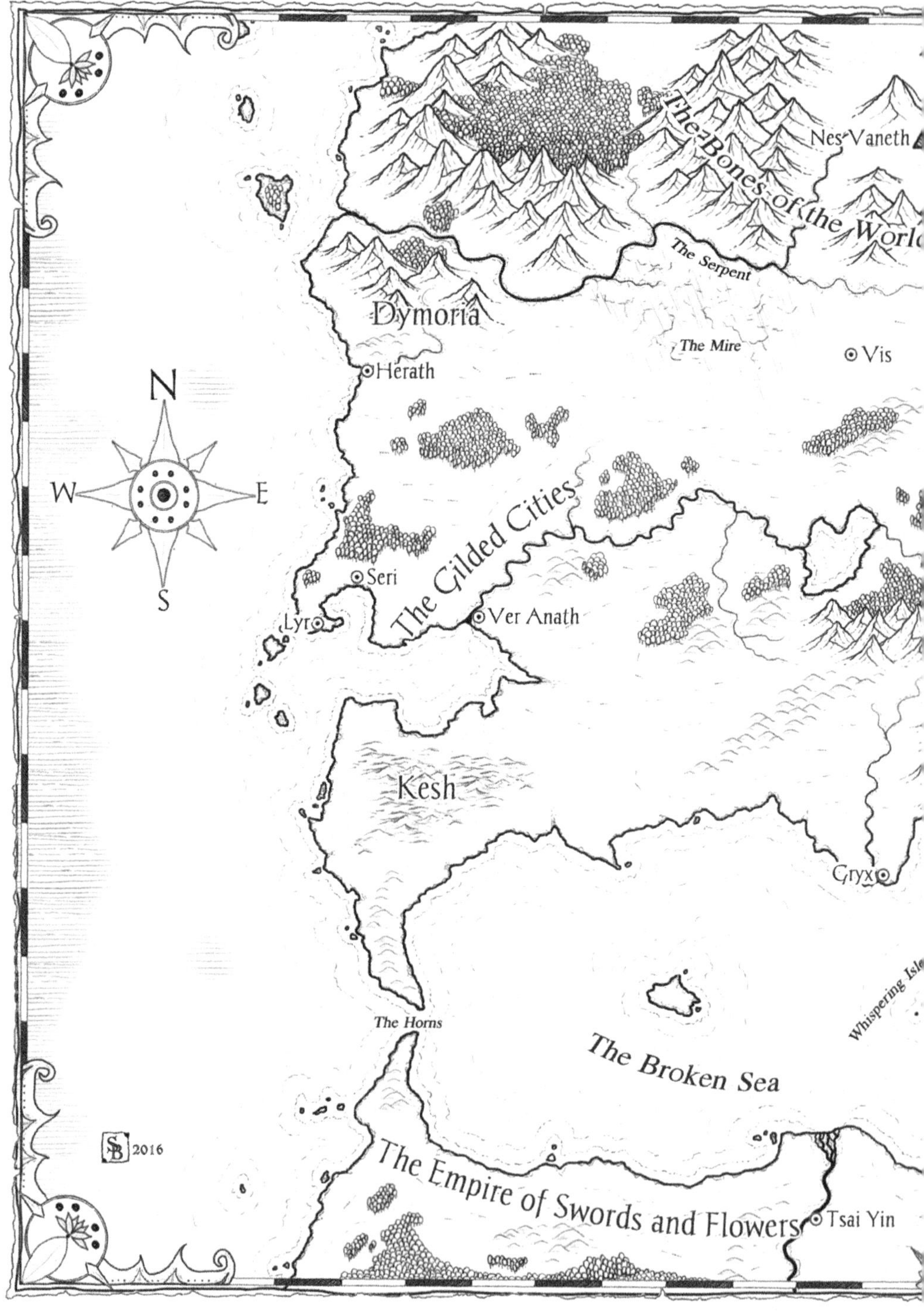
The Bones of the Worl
Nes Vaneth
The Serpent
Dymoria
The Mire
Vis
Herath
N
W
E
S
The Gilded Cities
Seri
Lyr
Ver Anath
Kesh
Gryx
The Horns
Whispering Isl
The Broken Sea
SB 2016
The Empire of Swords and Flowers
Tsai Yin

ARAEN
The Frostlands
Telemach
Menekar
The Menekarian Empire
The Fens
The Blightwood
The Spine
Theris
The Shattered Kingdoms
Uthmala
Palimport
Whispering Isles
The Thread
The Eversummer Isles
SB 2016

Published by Alec Hutson

Cover art by John Anthony di Giovanni
Typography by Shawn King
Map by Sebastian Breit

Edited by Laura Hughes
Interior layout and design by Colleen Sheehan

First Edition

ISBN: 978-0-9982276-4-1 (paperback)
978-0-9982276-5-8 (ebook)

Please visit Alec's website at
WWW.AUTHORALECHUTSON.COM

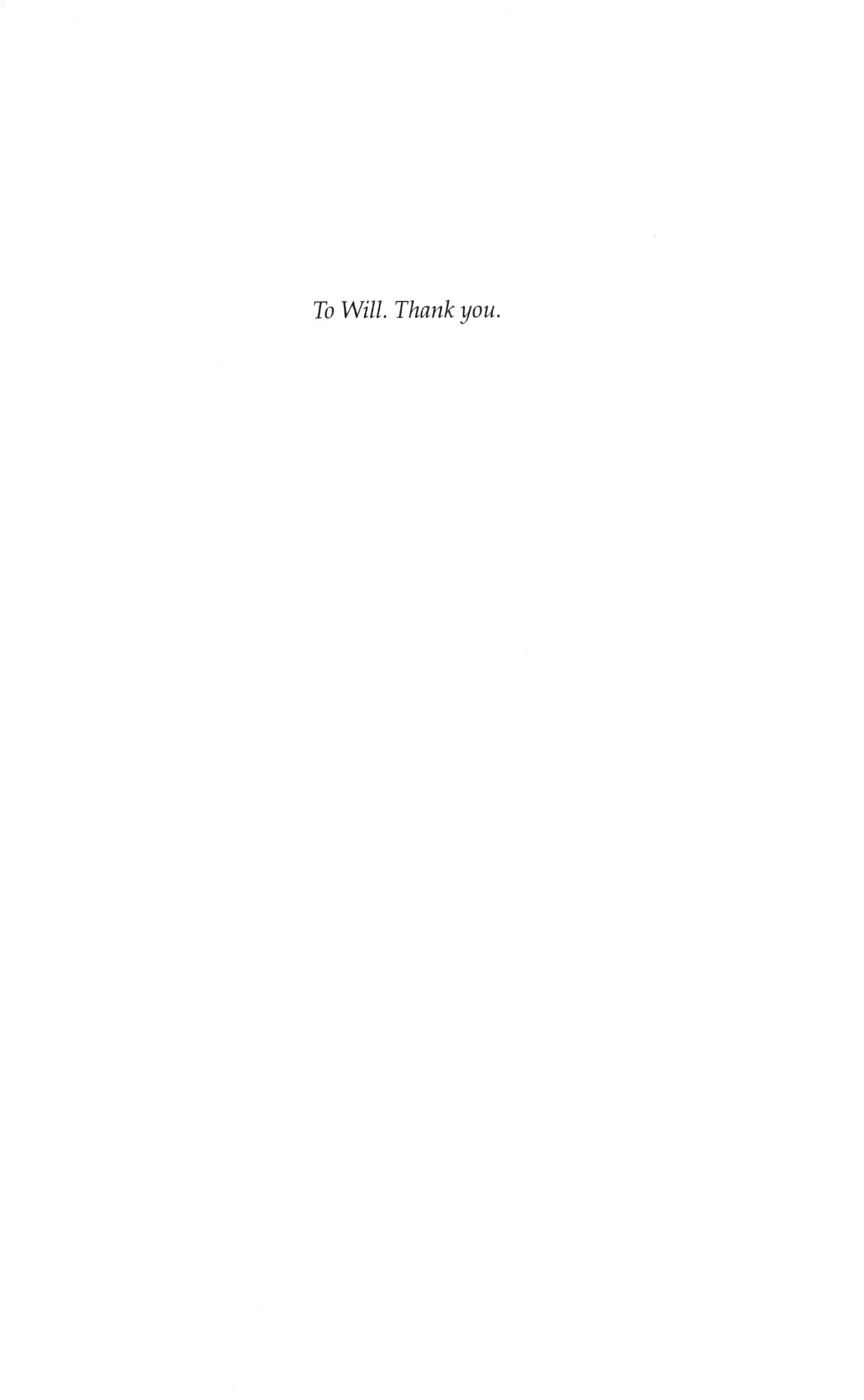

To Will. Thank you.

WHAT CAME BEFORE:

THE HISTORY OF sorcery is scribed in blood.

The seekers of the Reliquary say that the first men to draw power from the beyond were born in ancient Menekar, the Mother of Cities, in the years that its armies swept across the white plains. Most tribes knelt in fear before their glittering power, awed by this sign of the god Ama's favor. Those who dared resist were consumed and left as ash to be trampled beneath the boots of the marching legions.

For a time, the first sorcerers were content to serve Ama and the emperor. But the hunger for power that comes with a mastery of sorcery is insatiable, and when no more cities remained to conquer the sorcerers turned back towards Menekar. The emperor was cast down from the alabaster throne, his broken body hung above the Malachen Gates, and the Warlock King rose in terrible glory. In his court, those touched by sorcery were venerated as holy and those without the gift seen as barely more than animals. All manner of depravity was condoned.

Ama was not so easily ousted, however. There arose during the darkest time a champion infused with the divine light of his lord – the monk Tethys, first of the Pure, bearer of a white-metal sword. Immune to the ravages of sorcery, he led a crusade that destroyed the Warlock King and his monstrous court and returned Menekar and her empire to the sheltering radiance of Ama.

But the knowledge of sorcery could not be suppressed. Across the mountains of the Spine, in the shadow of the decaying wraith kingdoms, walls were being raised against the wilderness. In the fertile lowlands Kalyuni was founded, and soon the first Star Towers thrust towards the sky. Sorcerers now had a new sanctuary to pursue their art, and one by one the Mosaic Cities of the south were bound into a great Imperium. At the same time, in the far north, the holdfasts of Min-Ceruth emerged deep within the towering peaks of the Bones of the World. The wraiths were beaten back into their mountain sanctuaries, and the queens of Nes Vaneth ruled with a merciless splendor.

For centuries the history of Araen was shaped by the rivalry between these three great powers: the holdfasts of Min-Ceruth, the Mosaic Cities of the Kalyuni Imperium, and the vast and etiolated empire of Menekar. The Pure – the paladins of Ama – had taken as their divine task the liberation of man from sorcery and all the evil it brought into the world, but the power of sorcerers was great as well, and for an age the strength of these three realms remained in balance.

The Pure were right to warn against sorcery. When the princess of Nes Vaneth was murdered by a diplomat from Kalyuni, her grieving mother set in motion an ancient spell the sorcerers of the north had long ago constructed as a final devastating strike upon their rivals to the south. The waters of the Derravin Ocean surged over the western mountains and flooded the lands of the Mosaic Cities, creating the Broken Sea. Yet even as the churning water climbed the gleaming walls of their Star

Towers, the wizards of the Kalyuni Imperium unleashed their own cataclysmic spell, bringing black ice and endless winter to the Min-Ceruthans.

Two great empires perished that day, entombed within ice or drowned beneath the waves. Menekar wasted no time, dispatching its shining legions and the Pure over the Spine to restore order in the devastation and cleanse what remnants of sorcery remained. Treaties were signed at the point of a white-metal sword between Menekar and the kings and archons and padarashas of the western realms. Sorcery was renounced and any surviving practitioners given over to the paladins of Ama for swift and brutal judgment.

Menekar was not long without a rival, however. For decades the Shan and their Empire of Wind and Salt had wandered upon the waves, fleeing a devastation in their own lost homeland. Now, even as the north convulsed in the aftermath of the cataclysms, the Shan set about recreating their glorious empire in the lands south of the newly formed Broken Sea. They erected towers for their warlocks from the bones of the turtles that had ferried them across the ocean, built mighty cities in the ruins of the Imperium, and once again their brilliant culture flourished as they sought to forget the Raveling that had devoured their ancient lands. An age ended for the Shan, and the Empire of Wind and Salt gave way to the Empire of Swords and Flowers.

For a thousand years afterwards the pulse of magic faded like the heartbeat of a dying man. Until once more it began to quicken . . .

THE STORY SO FAR: THE CRIMSON QUEEN

KEILAN IS THE son of a fisherman from a tiny village on the shore of the Broken Sea. His mother, who had been plucked from the sea during a storm, was accused of sorcery and put to death by the frightened villagers. His father was nearly broken by this tragedy, numbing his sorrow and rage with drink. Keilan's own power begins to awaken during this time, and while using his sorcery to hunt for fish he accidentally brushes against a vast and terrible presence slumbering beneath the waves. His brief disturbance of this creature brings him to the attention of Dymoria's Crimson Queen, who is the first great sorceress born since the cataclysms. She dispatches her servants to claim him, but a paladin of Ama, Senacus, discovers Keilan first and takes him from his village. Like all children found with the taint of sorcery, Keilan will be brought to Menekar to be cleansed, in the hope that he will rise again filled with the holy light of Ama.

But the queen's magister, Vhelan, and his knife, Nel, rescue Keilan from the Pure and flee. After a harrowing escape from dark sorceries that still lurk in one of Kalyuni's ruined cities, they join a caravan traveling along the ancient northern road. Among their fellow travelers is the seeker Garmond, a scholar of the Reliquary, and his Fist guardsmen. One of the Fist brothers, Xin, becomes friends with Nel and Keilan, and begins to teach them the secrets of his swordfighting. Also among the caravan is a Shan by the name of Cho Yuan. He claims to be searching for something important that was recently stolen from the Empire of Swords and Flowers.

The caravan is attacked by wraiths under the command of a shape-changing monster. Cho Yuan is slain, and Keilan unleashes sorcery that wounds the monster badly enough that it is forced to flee. In order to discover more about the demon that attacked them they descend into the Barrow of Vis, one of the world's great libraries. There the spirit of the Barrow bequeaths several ancient tomes to Keilan, though at the time he does not understand their importance.

With a Visani escort they soon arrive in Herath, the largest city of Dymoria and the seat of Cein d'Kara, the Crimson Queen. Keilan pledges himself to her and joins the Scholia, her school for sorcery. When the queen realizes the depth of Keilan's power she enlists his aid in unlocking the memories of the sorcerer Jan, who has recently arrived in her court and claims to be the last of the vanished Min-Ceruthans. With Keilan's help, Cein passes through the barriers in Jan's mind and discovers he was part of a mysterious cabal of sorcerers who orchestrated the cataclysms that destroyed the old world – all so they could use these deaths to power a spell that would render them immortal.

Even as these truths are laid bare a trap nested by the sorceress Alyanna within Jan's mind is tripped, and a surge of sorcery nearly kills Keilan and the queen. When Keilan awakens soon after, he discovers the queen barely alive and goes to find aid, only to be captured by another of the ancient sorcerers, the swordsinger Demian, and Senacus, the paladin who first took him from his village. While Demian stays behind to interrogate Xin and Nel, Senacus takes Keilan from the palace. Before they can flee the city, however, Keilan reveals that he saw Demian in the memories of Jan, and that the swordsinger is in fact a sorcerer. Shaken by this revelation – though it does confirm his own suspicions about Demian – Senacus abandons Keilan at the gates of Herath.

The next day Keilan discovers that Xin is dead, slain by Demian, who has now disappeared. Nel and Keilan intend to chase after the paladin in the hopes that Senacus can lead them to the vanished swordsinger.

Jan is a farmer in the Shattered Kingdoms. He is plunged into grief after his wife dies of a sickness, and in the depths of his sorrow something happens that awakens long-suppressed memories. To his shock, he realizes he is in fact an immortal sorcerer, though most of his past still remains lost. The incident that triggered this revelation was a murder committed by some sort of supernatural creature near his farm, and Jan comes to believe this was done to wake him. He follows the creature's trail, until he arrives in the pleasure gardens of the Menekarian Empire. There he meets Alyanna, who claims to know him, though his own memories of her are indistinct. She tells him magic is returning to the world, and that a great sorceress has arisen in the far west: Cein d'Kara of Dymoria. Alyanna promises to restore his lost memories if he investigates this Crimson Queen for her. Jan asks about the creatures he has chased across the plains, and Alyanna tells him they are her new servants, recently freed from imprisonment in Shan. Despite his wariness, Alyanna convinces him that they are firmly under her control.

Jan travels to the kingdom of Dymoria, and Cein d'Kara quickly unmasks him as a powerful sorcerer. Curious about his missing past, she agrees to try and break through the barriers in Jan's mind. During the ceremony, a magical trap laid by Alyanna is triggered and the queen and Keilan are nearly killed. In her anger, Cein decides to imprison Jan until she can be sure that he is no longer a pawn of Alyanna.

Alyanna is an immortal sorceress who has lurked in the shadows for over a thousand years. It was her magical brilliance that crafted the spell that rendered a secret group of wizards immortal, including Jan and Demian. To her distress, she finds that the potency of this spell is fading, and she has begun to age again.

In recent years, Alyanna has posed as a concubine in the pleasure gardens of the Menekarian emperor, hoping to unravel the mysteries of the Pure, though she has become intrigued by her new servants, the Shan demon-children that call themselves the Chosen. She heard them calling from their prison inside the bone-shard towers of Tsai Yin and freed them in return for their servitude. Alyanna learns from the Chosen that a demon hunter from Shan is searching for them, and that he wields a weapon capable of imprisoning their spirits again. She dispatches another of her servants, the shape-changing genthyaki, to slay the demon hunter Cho Yuan. He is traveling with a merchant caravan to Dymoria because he believes it was Cein d'Kara who liberated the demons. During an assault on the caravan Cho Yuan is slain, but the genthyaki is badly wounded by the sorcery of the boy Keilan. Alyanna learns from the dying genthyaki that Keilan is a Talent, a rare and powerful breed of sorcerer. Hoping to use Keilan to recreate the spell that granted her immortality she sends Demian west to capture the boy.

Meanwhile, Alyanna forges an alliance with the dreaded kith'ketan shadowblades, enlisting their aid to destroy the Crimson Queen before Cein can become a true rival to her power. Alyanna's web of plots comes together on a single night, as the trap she laid within Jan's mind is triggered by Cein just as Demian and the shadowblades invade the queen's fortress in search of Keilan. Alyanna transports herself inside the palace and challenges the weakened queen, but is defeated when the Chosen refuse to obey her commands. She is forced to flee back to Menekar, where she is captured by the genthyaki she thought had perished. Now the creature serves the Chosen, having been succored back to health through their dark magics. He is consumed by the desire to inflict suffering upon his former mistress.

The land of Araen is poised to enter a new age of sorcery, but darkness gathers . . .

THE SILVER SORCERESS

1: CHO LIN

"YOUR FATHER IS dead."

– self my nothing the self my nothing the self my nothing the self my nothing the self my nothing the self my nothing the –

"Your father is dead, Mistress."

It was a voice from a distant peak, cast across a chasm plunging down into unimaginable depths.

– self my nothing the self my nothing the self my nothing the self my nothing the self my nothing –

"Mistress, your father –"

Cho Lin's eyes snapped open. "Is dead," she finished.

A single melted candle guttered in the small chamber. The light burned her eyes, and she forced herself to stare into it.

– the self –

Kan Xia huddled before her, forehead pressed against the stone, his arms outstretched in supplication.

Cho Lin unclasped her hands from the *chigreum* mudra. Her fingers felt stiff, unresponsive.

"How long?" she asked, swallowing away the rawness in her throat.

Kan Xia spoke into the floor, his words muffled. "The disciple outside said two months . . . He said you –"

"No. How long has my father been dead?"

A pause. Kan Xia's hands scrabbled at the chamber's stone floor, as if trying to find purchase. "We . . . we are not sure, Mistress. One month, we think."

"You think?"

"Y-yes. He was across the Sea of Solace, in distant realms. Word travels slowly in the barbarian lands. They have no couriers on fast horses or arrow-straight roads."

He was across the Sea of Solace. "Kan Xia, what has happened while I've been away?"

"Much has happened, Mistress," the servant murmured, trembling. "Much has happened."

She swept from the chamber, Kan Xia trailing behind her. A disciple stood outside, his eyes averted, her clothes folded across his arms. Cho Lin undid her robes and pulled on the silken breeches and embroidered *yi* shirt she had arrived at Red Fang Mountain in many months ago. She gathered her long hair back and secured it with a jade pin.

"Where is Master Ren?"

The disciple did not look at her. "Master Ren is secluded within Gold Leaf Temple. He is expecting you."

Cho Lin frowned. *How long have they known?*

She walked the twisting underground corridors, past other cells containing monks, the ground slanting upward until she came to an ancient wooden door painted with a picture of the Enlightenment. She pushed through it, and her vision was consumed by dazzling blue. Clouds were piled to the horizon. Swallows flitted between the eaves of pagodas. Sunlight. For a brief moment everything seemed to tilt and spin, and she had to close her eyes.

– the self my nothing –

The world righted itself. Cho Lin breathed deep, savoring the many smells of the world above. Someone was cooking braised pork, and her jaw ached at the thought of eating real food. Between the temple's paths lilies were blooming; when she had retreated into her trance the delicate shoots of those flowers had just been starting to emerge.

She crossed the courtyard, enjoying the feel of crushed stones beneath her bare feet. Disciples in red tunics hurried past her, eyes downcast. There, a familiar face coming towards her.

"Master Gu," she said, inclining her head.

If the saffron-robed monk was surprised to see her outside, he did not show it. He mirrored her gesture and pressed his hands together in the mudra of greeting. "Mistress Lin. My heart soars to see you this day. But my mind is curious to know why you have abandoned your meditations."

"My family's servant brings notice that my father has died."

The monk pursed his lips and bowed his head slightly. "Lord Cho has died? A great loss for Shan. I shall remember his name in my prayers."

"My ancestors thank you," Cho Lin said, her fingers steepling in the mudra of respect. Master Gu nodded in reply and walked on.

She came to Gold Leaf Temple, blazing in the day's brilliance. The roof of the pagoda, it was said, had been forged from the melted jewelry ripped from the bodies of the Third False Emperor's concubines. It had taken a dozen wagons to carry the metal to the top of Red Fang Mountain, and a hundred craftsmen many years to shape the *rythenki* spirits and *malachen* demons that now cavorted across it in flashing gold.

"Wait here," she told Kan Xia, and the servant drew back.

She climbed the steps and entered the temple. Inside, a thousand votive candles had been lit among the forest of red pillars, their flickering flames marching in rows towards the great golden statue at the temple's center: Sagewa Tain, first among mortals to reach an understanding of the Self. Incense spiced the air, and the faint chime of devotional bells echoed in the distance.

Master Ren was seated cross-legged before the looming statue, his eyes closed and his hands shaping the mudra of understanding.

Cho Lin's bare feet made no sound on the gleaming stone floor, but Master Ren spoke without opening his eyes before she had approached to within fifty paces.

"Mistress Lin. Welcome, child. You have attained perfection far sooner than we dared hope."

She halted, taking a deep breath to master herself. "Enlightened One, I must admit failure in my quest for the Self. I come here because I have been called away from Red Fang Mountain."

Now Master Ren looked at her. His eyes were the piercing black of a desert hawk's, windows to the Nothing within his Self.

"Truly, a pity." His expression of calm detachment did not waver.

Cho Lin couldn't contain herself any longer. "Master, how long have you known that my father is dead?"

Five heartbeats of silence. The candle flames seemed to bend away from her, as if disturbed by her agitation.

"There were rumors, brought to us by pilgrims."

"And how trustworthy were these rumors?"

The abbot's fingers shifted to the mudra of sympathy. "Very."

Cho Lin concentrated on the Nothing, willing herself to tranquility. "And you did not see fit to inform me?"

Was that a tightness at the corner of his mouth? Such a loss of control was almost as surprising as the news of her father's death.

"You were on a quest for the Self. The first step on such a journey is to abandon your ties to this world, as you well know. To disturb your meditations would be a betrayal of our most fundamental principles. The Cho Lin who came to us would agree with my words. She knew that this world is merely a realm of ghosts and mirrors, a pale reflection of the Self."

"Yet you allowed my family's servant to enter my cell."

The faint lines on the abbot's face vanished, like ripples fading away after a stone had sunk to the bottom of a pond. "He came to us bearing a writ from Lord Cho. In this world, we cannot deny one such as he."

"That's impossible. Lord Cho is –" *My brother*. A cold fist clutched at her heart. Her brother was now Lord Cho.

The abbot watched her carefully. "Mistress Lin, rarely does Red Fang Mountain admit disciples such as yourself. Most who arrive at our temple are orphans, lacking ties to any place or people. Thus, it is easier for them to embark on their quest for the Self and shed the memories of this world. You were a special case. From one of the greatest families of Shan, first daughter of a lord listened to by many among the Thousand Voices, a child raised in the Jade Court. And far more advanced in her martial training than should have been possible by anyone outside of this mountain."

"My father hired a Tainted Sword to train me when I was very young. But I had reached the limits of what he could teach me."

"Yes. So you came to us. And I saw in you someone who could forsake her name and achieve immortality for her soul through a mastery of the Self."

Cho Lin turned from the abbot, watching the dancing flames. "My father believed something different. He thought true immortality could only be attained through the family. Someday you must pass into the spirit realm, he once told me, but the glory your descendants bring to your name will sustain you in the afterlife. The body might die, but the family is truly eternal."

Another pause. Master Ren's fingers formed a mudra she did not know. "So the question you must ask yourself is this: are you Mistress Lin, disciple of Red Fang Mountain, or the Lady Cho, sister of a Jade Court mandarin?"

She met the abbot's placid stare and matched it. "Neither. I am Cho Lin."

After several months sequestered away in meditation, Cho Lin's body was not happy to return to the saddle. She shifted uncomfortably, trying to find a spot where she wasn't already chafed raw.

"Would you like to stop for a while, Mistress?"

Cho Lin waved away Kan Xia's words, annoyed that the servant had noticed her discomfort. She had ridden for three days straight when she first passed through this forest on her way to Red Fang Mountain, and now after only a half-day on horseback she was already yearning for the goose-down bed and pillows that awaited her at her family's estate outside Tsai Yin. Had her twenty months among the monks made her stronger, or weaker? Was she like a sword kept too long in the forge, tempered to brittleness by the fire's heat? She twisted around in her saddle, trying to catch through a gap in the trees the glint of Gold Leaf Temple high up on the mountain's slopes. What foolishness. That crucible had produced some of the world's most legendary warriors. Any weakness was her own.

Well, even if riding still seemed strange at least *something* felt like it had finally been returned to her after too long. She almost felt guilty about how much she had missed the weight of the short butterfly swords strapped to her waist. The ancient blades had been given back to her when she left the temple, and despite her months of training to forsake just these kinds of worldly possessions, she hadn't been able to resist a little thrill of pleasure when the carved ivory handles had again slipped into her hands.

The forest they rode through was darker than she remembered. Probably because she had first come to Red Fang Mountain in the waning days of winter, when the cold daylight filtering between empty branches had blazed upon bone-white trunks stripped bare by hungry deer. Now a full canopy arched overhead, serpentine vines wrapped the trees, and bright yellow flowers spotted the trail. And yet, the forest was just as silent as before. Just as silent; not even a note of birdsong, how strange –

A sharp hiss sliced the air. The Cho warrior who had accompanied Kan Xia toppled from his mare, his hands scrabbling at the arrow through his neck. Cho Lin threw herself from her horse, knocking Kan Xia from his saddle. Together they tumbled to the ground, her family's servant emitting a strangled yelp of surprise that was cut short when he hit the grass hard. Cho Lin rolled away and came up in a low crouch, her butterfly swords already in her hands.

"Stay down," she said to Kan Xia as she scanned the undergrowth for their ambushers. In response, he made a whimpering sound and buried his face in the grass. The horses stamped their feet and milled nervously as the Cho warrior thrashed between them in his death throes, his legs and arms drumming the earth.

Farther up the path four men had appeared. Cho Lin quickly moved so that her horse was between her and the ambushers. They did not have the look of bandits, that sense of frightened desperation which clung to men who had turned to thievery when their crops had failed or their livestock had been taken by the yellow-ear disease. Quiet competence was evident in the way they held themselves, in their tightly controlled movements as they approached with their weapons at the ready. And those weapons were too fine by far, city-forged or fletched. No, these were assassins.

Luckily, only one carried a bow. That might just save her life.

Cho Lin thrust her swords into the soft earth and slipped one of the shuriken that studded her belt into her hand.

"P-please," she stammered, forcing fear into her voice. "M-my name is Cho Lin, of the clan Cho. My brother is rich and powerful. Anything you desire could be yours if you let me live!"

As she had hoped, some of the wary tension leaked from the three foremost warriors, including the bowman. Knowing smirks passed between them.

"Don't listen to her!" commanded the fourth, who had stayed behind, standing on the path where they had first emerged from among the trees. "She is a Red Fang warrior. Lies drip from her lips like venom from a snake. Kill her quickly!"

But it was too late. They were close enough now.

From between her horse's legs, Cho Lin threw her shuriken at the bowman. Without watching to see where it struck, she surged to her feet, pulling her butterfly swords from the ground and leaping forward in one smooth motion. Her slippered foot touched lightly upon the saddle of her startled horse, then she gathered herself and jumped once more before the shocked assassins could even finish raising their swords. Time seemed to stretch and slow, the Nothing opening up within her. She took in everything before she'd even touched the ground again.

The bowman was down, his crossed eyes staring at the metal spike of the shuriken buried in his forehead. The assassin on the left held his broad-bladed beidao sword awkwardly – he was used to a lighter weapon. The one on the right appeared more balanced, and he reacted faster as Cho Lin hurtled closer. He was the greater threat.

She lashed out with both butterfly blades, batting aside the second assassin's sword with one as she sliced open his shoulder with the other. He snarled and thrust at her and she twisted away, using the last bit of momentum from her jump to slip past him. She went to one knee, completing her motion by slashing backwards, and felt the slight resistance as her sword severed his hamstring. He collapsed, screaming, and she quickly rolled away and back to her feet, sensing the other assassin's approach. Bellowing something unintelligible, he charged at her, hacking with his heavy sword; she easily turned aside each swing, and when he had overcommitted to a lunge she calmly stepped inside his guard and slipped her thin blade between his ribs, piercing his heart. His shocked eyes stared into hers for a brief moment, and then they fluttered closed as he slid to the ground.

Sparing a glance at the final assassin, still standing motionless some ways up the path, Cho Lin moved over to where the maimed warrior lay moaning, his bloodied fingers reaching desperately for the sword hilt just beyond his reach. She knelt beside him and cut his throat.

Cho Lin stood, sheathing her blades, and faced the last assassin. "Tell me who sent you."

The fourth warrior chuckled, strolling closer. He pulled from his scabbard a curving sword and held it up, showing her what was carved upon the bronze hilt.

"You have a lotus blade," she remarked, shifting her weight to the balls of her feet.

As he approached, she noticed how curiously flat and dead his eyes were. Like the corpses of the men at her feet.

"I do, girl."

"Did you earn it fairly?"

The assassin seemed to consider her words. "In a manner of speaking. It belonged to my master. I killed him."

"You are a Tainted Sword."

He shrugged. "My master was a Tainted Sword, cast down from Red Fang for violating one of their ridiculous rules. I'm not sure what that makes me."

Cho Lin put as much disdain as she could into her smile. "It makes you less than nothing."

He laughed, but his eyes stayed cold and distant. "I suppose it would to a rich little lady like yourself."

"Who sent you?"

He started working his lotus blade through some basic patterns. His movements were crisp, skilled.

"I am instructed not to say."

She sighed. "You are dead anyway. Tell me, and I promise to burn an offering for your spirit at the Moon Stone Temple in Tsai Yin."

Now he sneered. "So confident, little girl? You think you can measure my worth by these three fools? I have killed two masters of Red Fang in single combat, and a dozen members of the Jade Court. I am an assassin of the ninth circle in the Brotherhood of White Knives."

Cho Lin snapped her blades into her hands. She noted absently that the ivory handle of one of her butterfly swords had been stained black by blood. She would have to clean it later. "Enough. I must return home. Let us finish this."

They came together with a clash of steel.

Cho Lin arrived five days later at her family's estate outside Tsai Yin, far from happy with the time she had made. The wound in her side was bothering her and had kept her from pushing her horse too hard – that, and Kan Xia in his awkward mothering had insisted they stop at almost every inn and guesthouse along the road, even if she could have easily ridden on. The lotus blade was wrapped in a blanket buried among her saddlebags, but all through their journey she had felt a heavy malignancy pulsing from where she had stored it, sending a cold prickling up her spine. It was a cursed blade, the tool for many black deeds. She would donate it to one of the temples here, hoping the prayers of monks could cleanse the darkness from its past, and perhaps even allow for a rebirth of the sword in the hands of a true warrior.

They rode past peasants sunk to their waists in the ponds ringing the Cho estate, bent-back old men and women with lined brown skin pulling rice from stalks as they sang ancient songs extolling the virtues of the common people. Mulberry trees pressed against the compound's walls, and the season's harvest must have been nearly finished as Cho Lin saw only a few children scurrying among the branches, pulling cocoons from the damp, dark places where the moths had hidden them in the boles of the trees. The orchards here, at the Tsai Yin estate, were barely a grove compared to the vast plantations her family owned to the west. Much of the Cho wealth was founded in silk production – Cho Lin's distant ancestor, Cho Tzin, was even credited as the first to discover that the unspooled cocoon of the silk moth could be woven into luxuriant, shimmering cloth.

Cho Lin and Kan Xia passed through the Turtle Gate, the great stone portal carved with images ranging from the common painted-shell denizens of quiet streams and ponds to the sea-spanning titans that could cross the world with an army on their backs. The Cho warriors flanking the gate's pillars gaped at her when she nodded at them, then snapped to attention. Within the outer walls the compound was a riot of activity: hammers rang upon the forges set up in a corner of the courtyard, grooms were leading horses to and from the stables, and servants rushed back and forth on tasks.

Cho Lin smiled, imagining what Min Min and Cook Po's reactions would be when she sauntered into their kitchen. They would cry out and clap their hands and hurry to make her favorite dumplings, lamenting loudly about how thin she was.

But first she had to see her brother.

He waited for her within the innermost garden, a carefully sculpted labyrinth of twisting rock and shadowy paths which led to a small lake spotted with lily pads and lotus blossoms. Fragments of color, white and orange and black, flashed just beneath the surface of the water as the great schools of koi swarmed closer to where Cho Lin walked, hoping for a scattering of rice. She crossed the arching bridge that led to the small pavilion at the lake's center. Her brother sat at the round stone table where their father had often spent his mornings reading, watching her approach.

He was not alone. Kneeling beside his bench was a beautiful young girl in a green dress, her long black hair unbound. Her eyes were downcast, and she held upraised in her hands a delicate porcelain tea cup decorated by cranes in flight.

Cranes. The symbols of fidelity. Of course.

Cho Jun smiled at her when she entered the pavilion, gesturing with a trembling hand for her to sit across from him.

"First brother," Cho Lin said, taking her seat.

"First sister," he replied.

They stared at each other. He was wearing their father's imperial vestments, a long red-and-blue silk robe with a golden phoenix unfurling along its length. He also wore the scholar's circular black cap, though Cho Lin knew he had never studied with any real diligence the Master's teachings.

"Have you eaten?"

"I have. Some biscuits on the road. I'm not hungry."

"Tea, then?"

"Yes, thank you."

Her brother snapped his fingers, and the girl rose gracefully to pour her a cup from the pot on the table. Cho Lin breathed deep as the tea's flavor reached her. Petals from the jasmine flower, her favorite, and a drink she hadn't enjoyed since she'd left two years ago for Red Fang Mountain. Her brother wanted something.

She sipped her tea. The girl picked up her brother's cup and brought it to his lips. He drank, watching Cho Lin over the rim.

She set down her cup. "You seem better."

Her brother swallowed his tea and the girl returned to her knees, holding his cup aloft. "Do I? Life grows easier, certainly. I have learned to live with my weaknesses. It is a very important skill to c-c-cultivate."

It would be almost ten years to the day, she suddenly realized, since someone in this very compound had slipped poison into her brother's wine. It had not killed him, but the poison had so damaged his body that he had been rendered incapable of performing even the most basic of actions by himself. Unsure who the poisoner had been, Lord Cho had decided to execute all the servants who had touched his son's cup that night.

No further poisonings had occurred.

"Our father is dead."

"He is."

"What happened? Kan Xia would not tell me."

Her brother lifted something from the bench beside him and placed it on the table. It resembled very closely the wrapped sword she had stored among her saddle bags. Her heart began to beat faster.

"Our father," Cho Jun began, running his fingers along the length of the bundle, "was a man of honor."

"Of course."

"While you were away, in the east, something happened, something momentous. An intruder snuck inside the w-w-warlock's tower, pierced the ancient wards, and stole something."

Coldness filled her. "What was stolen?"

"The chest."

Cho Lin was having trouble staring at anything except the wrapped object on the table. "Was it the Raveling?"

"The warlocks think not. They think . . . they think it was a barbarian from the north. He or she used sorceries they had never f-felt before to slip past their wards."

"And whoever it was, they opened the chest?"

"They d-did. The warlocks have sensed the Betrayers since th-then, moving in the n-north."

"And what would you have me do about it? Why did you recall me from Red Fang Mountain?"

He reached out a trembling hand and clutched at her wrist. "I n-need you, Lin. I cannot fulfill our family's sacred duty. Only you can satisfy our ancestors. Our father."

"What would you have me do?" she repeated, barely whispering.

Her brother peeled away the cloth from the object on the table. Tapering steel glimmered in the sunlight as the legendary Sword of Cho was revealed.

"When I heard he had died in far-off lands, I feared it had been lost." Her own voice sounded distant to her ears.

Her brother's shaking hand closed around the black dragon-bone hilt. "No. A p-prince of a city near where our father died sent the sword south when he realized who our father was. With it was a letter describing our father's death, at the hands of a d-demon that wore the skin of a man like a cloak."

A new demon? An ally of the Betrayers?

He watched her carefully. "The warlocks say it sounds like a demon from Shan's lost past. But they were all thought to be d-dead thousands of years ago, long before the Raveling."

"Has the emperor bestirred himself after hearing of this new threat?"

Her brother choked back a laugh. "He is consumed with his own p-petty interests, and cares not for what happens outside the palace walls. The w-warlocks suspect the Raveling's servants have penetrated even the heart of the Jade Court. Before they move openly, they wish for us to try once more to recover the chest or destroy the Betrayers. Our family has always been first among the d-demon-hunters of Shan."

"Assassins were waiting for me when I descended from Red Fang Mountain. Did the Raveling send them, or another house?"

Her brother shrugged, stirring his tea with a long nail. "House Cao, I would suspect. But perhaps another lurks in the shadows. It is a d-dangerous time. We have few friends, and with father gone, our enemies think us weak."

"Us? So I am a Cho again? I thought you disapproved of me."

Her brother looked out over the lake's tranquil waters. "I did, first sister. But with father dead only you are left who c-can bring honor to our house. Only you can finish what he started, and what our ancestor began a th-thousand years ago when Cho Xin first bound the Betrayers."

"And if I refuse?"

"Then the Cho are finished, and the ghosts of our ancestors will howl in sorrow and rage."

"Do they have any suspicions about who stole away the Betrayers?"

He told her. When he finished, Cho Lin rose, searching his eyes for any hint of falseness. The Nothing within the Self she had been so tantalizingly close to reaching seemed to be tumbling farther and farther away as she stood motionless within that tiny pavilion in the middle of the lake.

Her brother smiled to himself as he watched her walk back across the curving bridge, carrying their father's sword.

2: KEILAN

"WE REST!"

With a relieved sigh Keilan slid from Storm, his fingers tangling in her sweat-damp mane. His poor horse must be exhausted, as his own legs felt like jelly, and all *he'd* done the past day and a half was try to stay in his saddle while Storm struggled to keep up with the rangers' long-legged mounts. He stroked her lathered flank, feeling the muscles trembling beneath her blotchy coat.

"Empty your bladders and your food bags," barked the scarred captain. "We won't be stopping again until we've caught the paladin."

Keilan uncorked his water skin and took a long swallow. They had halted outside a squat stone building flying the dragon banner of Dymoria, and a plump soldier was at that moment rushing down the path from the fort to the road, his face red and his arms flailing comically. It looked like he had just donned his mail shirt and surcoat for the first time in several years, as both were several sizes too small, revealing a protruding bulge of pasty white belly. Behind him a pair of soldiers were hurrying to catch up.

The ranger captain watched the officer approach with barely-concealed disdain.

"God's blood . . . what is going on?" gasped the soldier when he reached the rangers. "Rangers of Dymoria, riding south in strength?" The man's mouth shaped numbers as he made a quick calculation. "Twenty! And you've worked your horses hard getting here. You must have ridden through the night!"

One of the rangers near Keilan leaned over to his companion and said, "Not as hard as he worked to get off his arse." A snort of laughter followed, cut short by a sharp glance from the captain.

"Commander. We are chasing a fugitive who has committed crimes against the crown. We require fresh mounts and supplies at once. Time is precious; the longer we delay, the more chance our quarry has of slipping away."

The fort commander's eyes widened. "A fugitive," he repeated, squinting down the road, as if he could catch sight of whoever it was they were pursuing.

With an annoyed sigh, the captain rummaged in his saddle bag and drew forth a roll of parchment bound by a red ribbon.

"This is a writ from the queen herself. It gives me authority to requisition whatever I need to fulfill my duty. Hurry up and bring me what I asked for, or I'll be forced to inform Her Majesty of your lack of quick cooperation."

The officer's face blanched, and he seemed to emerge from his fog of bewildered surprise. He turned to the soldiers behind him, both of whom had watched this exchange with wide-eyed amazement. "Ghervis! Empty the stables! Bring every horse down here *at once*! Farin, tell Cook to gather up all the hardtack and cured meat we have in the larder and put it in some travel bags for these men!" The soldiers hesitated for a moment, and the officer's face flushed crimson. "Now, or I'll have both your hides tanned!"

The leader of the rangers twisted in his saddle, turning to Nel. "We'll be on our way soon, my lady."

The captain had barely blinked when Keilan and Nel caught up with the hunters a few leagues outside of Herath. He had recognized Nel, and knew that she was in the service of one of the most senior magisters. Keilan he'd barely spared a glance, probably assuming he was her servant. Even still, Nel had flashed an amulet with Vhelan's personal crest to allay any suspicions the captain might have. Keilan suspected that she had 'borrowed' this without asking. He doubted very much that anyone else knew they had taken it upon themselves to join the hunting party.

Nel slid from her saddle and began working at the straps securing her bags. "Captain d'Belin, do you think we've gained any ground on the paladin?"

The Dymorian frowned. "We should have, Lady Nel. At least a little. But from here is when we'll start closing. His horse should be exhausted, and we'll be riding fresh mounts – unless, of course, he's seized a new one along the way."

"And that doesn't sound like something the Pure would do."

Captain d'Belin nodded, rubbing at the scar on his cheek. "Aye. But sneaking into a castle to assassinate a queen isn't what I'd expect from one of those paladins, either. So I'm not assuming anything right now. We ride as hard as we can for Lyr, and if the Pure gets there first then we'll come up with a new plan. I swore an oath to the queen I'd bring him back to Dymoria, and I will do that."

Nel glanced over at Keilan. "I like that kind of confidence."

A soldier reappeared from behind the fort leading a line of horses. Keilan laid his hand on Storm's side protectively. "What will happen to ours?"

Nel unlashed one of her saddle bags and tossed it on the ground. "Don't worry, they'll be waiting for us when we return. The soldiers here will want their own horses as well when we come back. But the captain's right – there's no way we're catching the Pure unless we get on some fresh legs. He'll have to rest eventually, or his horse will give out."

Keilan stroked Storm's face affectionately. "I'll see you soon, girl," he whispered. His horse whickered and tossed her head, as if trying to argue with him that she still had the strength to continue the chase.

The old coastal road that bound the kingdom of Dymoria with the Gilded Cities was well-trafficked, and on occasion they passed strings of wagons heading north. Captain d'Belin halted briefly each time to ask if they had seen a man matching the paladin's description. Most of the merchants only blinked in surprise, taking in the score of grim-faced rangers, and muttered that they had not. But one grizzled old man laid down his reins and pointed at a magnificent white stallion that towered over his other two nags and told them that not long ago he had traded horses with a man who might have been the one they were chasing. The man's hood had been drawn up, but the old merchant had glimpsed a few stray strands of hair, and yes indeed good sir, may Garazon steal away his soul if he lied, it'd looked to be silver.

The captain had cursed and urged them to ride faster.

Evening stole into the sky, and unlike the previous night the moon was now hidden behind a veil of clouds, plunging the road into darkness. The captain called a halt when his horse stumbled and nearly fell, his frustration evident.

"Enough. We stop until first light. These damned horses will lame themselves if we continue."

"We could light torches, sir," suggested another ranger, but the captain shook his head curtly.

"If we still had our mounts I would. But these horses haven't been trained to ride at night."

"What if the paladin reaches Lyr before us?"

Keilan could hear the edge of exhaustion in Nel's voice. She needed rest, even if she would never admit as much.

The captain slid from his horse. "I still don't think he will. You saw the other two nags that old merchant had yoked to his cart. The Pure must have slowed down since he traded away his horse, and he'd be foolish to press on through the night."

"I hope you're right, Captain," Nel replied, still astride her horse. "The temple of Ama in Lyr is a veritable fortress. And there's no way the archons will countenance any action within their walls that might risk Menekar's wrath. He'll be lost to us if he passes through those gates."

"The only way he's reaching Lyr, Lady Nel, is if our horses break their legs in the dark. If you want to order us on tonight, you know I can't countermand your wishes. But I hope you'll listen to reason. A few hours' rest will do us all some good." The captain's last words were almost pleading. They were exhausted, Keilan realized, glancing at the shadows slumped in their saddles. Surely none had slept more than a few hours since the assassins had invaded Saltstone three nights ago, which meant most were going on four days without rest. They were like pieces of frayed rope, close to breaking.

Nel muttered something under her breath, but still she swung herself down from her saddle. Keilan did the same, the anticipation of throwing himself onto the grass and sleeping for a few hours pushing aside his desire to catch up with the Pure.

Yet even though he could feel the heaviness pressing behind his eyes he knew he wouldn't be able to rest well tonight. His thoughts were scattered – so much had happened in the last few days, and he felt that if he could just concentrate a little harder the larger pattern he sensed would finally resolve. A mysterious sect of assassins thought by most to be legend had allied themselves with ancient, immortal sorcerers to try and steal him away from the Scholia. Why? He was special, or so the queen had said, a powerful natural sorcerer. But surely that man in black, Demian, was even stronger. Keilan had seen him before, in the memories of the sorcerer Jan, when the queen had tried to help him recover his lost past. Keilan remembered Demian practicing his swordsinger routines in that great empty mountain hall a thousand years ago, his blade flashing silver in the light of hanging mistglobes. Then Demian had been standing across the table from Jan during the terrible ceremony as the crystal drew the souls from the uncountable dead and thrust them into the gathered sorcerers. What use did such a man – or his accomplice Alyanna, the sorceress who had challenged the queen herself – have for him?

And then there was the other mystery, the woman he had glimpsed in Jan's memories. How could she look so much like his mother? Since leaving his village last summer Keilan had visited three great cities and many villages and towns, and never had he seen anyone with the same silver hair or cast of face. The closest might actually be the Pure, but the paladin's hair was more a pale white, while his mother and the mysterious sorceress shared hair that shimmered like polished silver. The thought that there might be some thread connecting them seemed beyond all reason, and yet Keilan could not shake the sense that if he could find out who this woman was he might discover something about his mother. If she had been there during the ceremony to make them all immortal, could she still be alive? His skin prickled as he considered this, staring into the darkness spread above him.

He did not remember falling asleep, but suddenly Nel's boot was in his ribs, prodding him awake. He opened his eyes to find a crescent moon still etched sharp against the gray dawn sky.

"Up, Keilan. This is the day. Either we'll catch him before he reaches Lyr, or he'll make it to the city before us."

Keilan slowly climbed to his feet, wincing at the pain in his back. The ground here was stony, yet still his sleep had been deep and dreamless.

"Already used to the Scholia's featherbeds? You look like an old man . . . or a spoiled prince."

Keilan quickly rolled his sleeping mat and lashed it across the back of his new stallion. "I'm ready," he said to Nel, swinging himself into the saddle.

"Have some breakfast," Nel said, handing a strip of dried jerky up to him. "We ride hard today."

Captain d'Belin set a brutal pace, and before the sun had fully emerged from the horizon they were thundering south, the horses misting the air with their labored panting. The stunted forests hemming the road gradually disappeared, until they followed a narrow path which clung to the side of a cliff, the ocean spreading westward like an endless dark plain. Keilan urged his stallion as close to the edge as he dared and peered down, to where gray seals clustered on rocks draped with seaweed. He was glad Captain d'Belin had decided not to brave this road at night, as the image of a horse and rider tumbling off the cliff in a tangle of flailing limbs refused to leave his thoughts.

Once, he saw a sail in the distance, a square of white stamped with a lidless black eye. Nel saw it as well and pointed.

"The black eye of Lyr!" she yelled over the pounding of hooves. "We're close to the city!"

The road rose and fell with the ragged coastline. Sometimes they could actually feel the spray rising up from where the waves crashed against the cliff, and then the way would ascend again until the basking seals were just tiny splotches of color speckling the black rocks below. Keilan stroked his horse's neck, whispering encouragement as they labored to climb these stony paths.

It was well past midday when they finally caught sight of the paladin. The ranger at the front of their column saw him first, giving a shout of triumph as he crested a hill. Keilan urged his horse forward, jostling with the others as they all strained to glimpse the one they hunted.

The road descended sharply before them into a low, wide plain that was empty save for an occasional tree or watchtower, and in the far distance soared the gray walls of a great city. Towards the gate a white rider galloped, his armor flashing in the sun. Keilan remembered dimly that Senacus had been wearing leather and mail when the Pure had brought him out of Saltstone; he must have donned his white-scale armor sometime along the way.

Captain d'Belin cursed. "He's too far."

It was true, and Keilan's heart fell. The paladin was nearly halfway across the plain and riding hard.

Nel snarled something unintelligible and spurred her horse down the slope. The rangers glanced at their captain, and this seemed to wake him from his stupor.

"With me!" he cried, and his horse surged forward. "H'yah!"

They charged down the hill, but Keilan knew they would be too late, that the paladin would find sanctuary behind the walls long before they could reach him.

Then the unthinkable happened. Far ahead of them the paladin's horse stumbled and fell; the white rider rolled into the grass, but he was up in moments, pulling on his mount's reins. The horse stayed unmoving, and Nel let out a triumphant cry.

To Keilan's surprise, the paladin did not turn and flee. Instead, he reached up and unclasped something he had been wearing around his neck. Keilan gasped as the radiance of Ama suddenly filled his eyes, blazing even in the light of day. The paladin drew his white-metal sword and waited as the Dymorians thundered closer.

"Behind him!" one of the rangers cried, pointing beyond the paladin.

A line of riders had appeared, issuing out of Lyr's gates. They held long spears, and as Keilan neared he could see Lyr's black eye emblazoned upon their dark blue tabards.

The Lyrish warriors arrived shortly before the Dymorians, forming a half-circle with the Pure and his fallen horse in the middle. Captain d'Belin held up his hand, and the rangers slowed and halted, mirroring the Lyrish formation. The paladin turned slowly, his calm gaze taking in the warriors surrounding him. He did not raise his sword, but he also did not return it to its sheath.

For a long moment, no one spoke. The wind strengthened, rippling the paladin's white cloak and bending the long grass.

Finally, one of the Lyrish warriors nudged his horse forward. His helm was shaped differently than those of the other soldiers, a plume of purple horsehair falling from its crest, and the dark blue cloak he wore was clasped by a brooch shaped into a lidless eye.

"Welcome to Lyr, strangers."

Captain d'Belin nodded respectfully towards the leader of the gate guards. "Greetings, Lyrishmen. My deep apologies for bringing our pursuit to your doorstep. This paladin was involved in an assault on Saltstone and an assassination attempt on Queen d'Kara herself. I have a royal writ calling for his arrest and immediate return to Herath."

The Lyrish captain removed his plumed helmet and tucked it under his arm, then rubbed at his bald head. Keilan could tell by his pained expression that this was a position he did not want to be in. The captain was quiet for a long moment, as if trying to decide what to do next.

Finally, he sighed. "It is rare the rangers of Dymoria leave the northern forests, and rarer still when they hunt the holy men of Ama."

"Our tracking skills were needed. I warn you, we will not be denied."

The Lyrish captain raised his eyes to the sky, as if hoping for a miracle. "Surely you see the predicament you've put me in, Captain. If I refuse you, I will anger our neighbor to the north. But if I let you have the paladin, and the emperor discovers what

I have done, then I will have made an enemy of Menekar." The captain of the gate shrugged. "Truly, such a decision is not one I can make, at least if I want to keep my head attached to my shoulders. You will all come with me and present yourselves before the council, and the archons will decide your fates."

The paladin, who had remained silent during this exchange, slid his sword back into its sheath with a sharp clang. Then his blazing eyes finally found Keilan among the rangers, and he flinched as if he had been struck.

3: KEILAN

HARSH RAPPING ON the chamber door dragged Keilan from a deep and dreamless sleep. He surfaced groggily, feeling as if his head was stuffed with straw, and pushed himself into a sitting position. He winced as his muscles protested – his legs and back were not about to let him forget about the days recently spent on horseback.

Blinking away the last remnants of sleep he glanced around the room. He had been so exhausted when he was brought here that he had barely noticed anything before collapsing. The chamber was low-ceilinged and windowless, the only furniture his small lumpy cot, a rickety-looking wooden table, and a partially shuttered lantern that hung beside the door.

Clearly, he was not an honored guest.

Someone else had been here since the Lyrish guardsmen had led him inside and instructed him to rest; a wooden bucket had been placed on the table, along with a ladle and a small ceramic cup. Licking his dry lips, Keilan slid from the cot, shivering as his bare feet touched cold stone. The gray cloth shoes he had been wearing since leaving Saltstone were nowhere to be found, but a pair of leather boots that looked to be about his size had been arranged beside the bed, and he quickly slipped them on, then dipped the ladle into the water bucket.

The rapping came again just as he was taking a sip, and he spilled half of the water down his spider-silk shirt, soaking his chest and deepening the chill he already felt.

"Lad! Are you awake?"

It was a woman's voice, cracked by age but still powerful. Not a servant – Keilan could hear the edge of authority in her tone.

"Yes," he called back warily.

"Good. We've waited a fair long time, and I'm certainly not getting any younger. Better make sure your breeches are on. We're coming in."

A key clanked in a lock, and then the chamber's door creaked open. A bald giant of a man sauntered into the room first, his gaze sliding over everything but lingering on nothing, not even Keilan. He was wearing an unadorned gray tunic and simple brown trousers, the kind of clothing men wore in Keilan's own small village, but jutting over his shoulders were a pair of ornate silver sword hilts fashioned into the shape of twining serpents. He spat out something he'd been chewing on and leaned back against the wall, crossing his arms over his chest.

"Just the boy," he said gruffly, his eyes heavy-lidded.

"Of course it's just the boy," snapped an old woman as she stepped inside, frowning. She was dressed in rich robes, red and purple flowers picked out in glimmering thread, and her gray hair had been gathered back in a severe bun. Her hand clutched the arm of another woman, this one tall and thin and wrapped in a dark shawl. This second woman was somewhere in her middle years, Keilan thought, because though her skin was smooth and unlined, her long black hair was streaked with silver. At first Keilan thought the old lady was leaning on her for support, but then he noticed the blindfold the younger woman was wearing and her tentative, shuffling steps as she was led into the room. A tingle of unease crept up his spine. There was something odd about the blindfolded woman, something almost familiar.

The old woman's frown deepened as she regarded Keilan. "Well, you're not as impressive as I'd hoped. Any young man that can bring two great kingdoms to the brink of war should at least have a look about him. Either tall and handsome or brooding and dark." She waved her hand dismissively towards the man leaning up against the wall. "By the Silver Lady, you're as unremarkable as Telion here."

The man in gray chuckled. "Sorry we're so disappointing."

Keilan swallowed, trying to find his voice.

"Wait, he's about to say something," said the old woman, leaning in and raising her eyebrows expectantly.

"Who . . . who are you?"

She scowled. "As ignorant as he is unimpressive. What do they teach you up at that Scholia? I am Lady Willa ri Numil, the eyes and ears of the archon council."

The man in gray spat again. "Known as the Crone in some parts of Lyr."

"You know I don't like that name," the old woman said crossly, narrowing her eyes. "Stop trying to annoy me."

"Some parts?" Keilan said, trying to remember what he knew about Lyr. "Like the Warrens?"

The man in gray's humorless grin failed to touch his hard eyes. "See, mistress, the boy's not completely ignorant."

The old woman sighed and studied the ceiling. "And to think this lad's only knowledge of our great city comes filtered through that ruffian girl."

"She's not a ruffian," Keilan said, feeling his anger start to rise from being talked down to like a fool. "In Saltstone they call Nel a lady."

The Crone snorted. "I could dress a pig in silk and damask, but that wouldn't make it a noble. Boy, I'm not here to discuss what *she* is; I know that well enough. I want to know what *you* are."

She snapped her fingers and the blindfolded woman shuffled closer. Keilan couldn't help drawing back a step as she leaned towards him. The air seemed to shimmer faintly, and the light from the lantern flared brighter. He held his breath, his body tensing.

The woman straightened. "It's as the paladin said. The dark flame burns inside him, and it is brighter than anything I've seen before. But he's completely untrained."

"I could have told you that," said the man in gray. "Even I can feel the boy's power. The first thing any sorcerer is taught is how to hide his gift from others. He's learned nothing from the magisters."

"Is there any danger here?" the Crone asked. Indignation filled Keilan as they continued to discuss him as if he wasn't even present.

The blindfolded woman shrugged. "I've never dealt with natural ability like this before. I'm not sure what he could summon forth if he felt threatened. I doubt he even knows himself."

The old woman plucked at a loose thread on her sleeve. "What would you suggest, Telion?"

The man in gray's response was shriven of emotion. "He's a threat to the city. We court war with Menekar or Dymoria if we decide to give him up to one or the other, and if he stays here then they'll both come knocking at our gate sooner or later. I'd suggest putting a sword through his belly now, dumping his body in the bay, and saying he choked on a fishbone."

Coldness spread through Keilan at the man in gray's words, but the old woman clucked her tongue, shaking her head. "That's a rather inelegant solution to our problem. And I have a strong suspicion there's more going on here than we realize. Simply wiping our hands clean of the whole mess will only leave us with more questions than answers." She turned to the blindfolded woman. "Philias – as you said, we cannot predict what sorcery he might summon. You'll have to stay here until the council meets, and then accompany him when he's called before the archons."

The woman sighed. "I feared you might say that. Very well, but I refuse to wear this anymore. I entered your service so I wouldn't have to hide." She reached up and undid the knot securing her blindfold.

Keilan gasped as she unwound the black cloth and let it flutter to the stone floor.

Beneath the blindfold, her eyes blazed with the holy radiance of the Pure.

After the Crone and the man in gray had left the room, the woman pulled one of the stools from beneath the table and sat heavily, letting out a long sigh. She regarded Keilan with a slight frown as he stood beside the bed, and he couldn't stop himself from squirming beneath her shining gaze.

"Well, sit down," she said, motioning towards another of the stools. "The Silver Lady herself couldn't make the archons move their fat arses any faster, so I think it'll be a while yet before the council is finally called to session and a summons is sent."

Keilan slowly lowered himself onto a stool, trying to avoid staring into her glowing eyes. Was she Pure? In all the stories from the Tractate he'd heard while sitting before the Speaker's Rock in his village there had never been any mention of female paladins. Sella had even remarked upon it once, her face twisted up in annoyance, and the mendicant that day had smiled down and claimed something about how only men could become Pure, since they alone were fashioned in the divine image of Ama.

Certainly, she did not look like Senacus. While the paladin was tall and broad-shouldered, radiating strength and vitality along with Ama's holy light, this woman was thin and frail and slightly stooped, her silver-threaded hair hanging limp. But her eyes blazed similarly, and now that he looked for it Keilan could see the same faint shimmering aura that limned the Pure.

"I know what you want to ask," she said. "So out with it."

Keilan swallowed. "Are you a paladin of Ama?"

She snorted. "All right, not what I was expecting. No. In fact, if given the chance I'd love to stab that shining arse with one of his own white swords."

Keilan's jaw dropped. He'd never heard anyone dare insult a god like that before, not even the bitter old men who used to mutter into their grog when the mendicants preached in his village – and Ama wasn't just any minor spirit, but the blazing heart of the most powerful empire in Araen.

"But you're . . . I mean, your eyes . . ."

One side of her mouth quirked. "Since I can sit here cursing him, I don't think the light inside me comes from Ama's favor."

She cocked her head, as if listening for something, then smiled when there was a faint knock on the door. "Enter," she called out loudly, and a timid-looking servant slipped inside carrying a large rosewood box. "Put it here," she said, motioning at the table, and the boy scurried over and gently laid his burden down. Then he hurriedly retreated, flashing a final terrified look at them both before vanishing.

Upon the side of the box, lines of breaking waves had been carved, each one slightly different, until suddenly they more resembled tongues of flame than cresting water. A tzalik set.

The woman snapped open the lid and removed a gameboard of polished white stone. "You know how to play, yes?"

Keilan nodded as she pulled two cloth bags from the box, one red and one blue, then dropped the box on the ground beside her chair with a clatter.

"Good. I don't want us to sit here ogling each other like a couple of halfwits until the archons finally decide to see you. I'm Philias, by the way. Just Philias, so don't go calling me 'lady'. Grew up on the docks of Palimport, and I don't have much respect for those who lord over other folk, especially when it's all just some coin flip by Chance that they were born in a big house with golden chamber pots."

Not a lady. Keilan thought he wouldn't have much trouble remembering that.

"You prefer fire or water?"

"Ah, water, I suppose." He felt dizzy: days of chasing the Pure, half-dead from exhaustion while clinging to his saddle, and now he was sitting down for a leisurely game of tzalik.

Philias handed him the blue bag and Keilan carefully dumped its contents onto the table. He hadn't played very much, as tzalik was considered a pastime suitable only for the old men of the village, but his father had sometimes enjoyed setting up a board outside when the weather was nice in the evenings. Keilan remembered crouching in the grass across from his father as they both studied their pieces, a cool breeze carrying away the heat of the day as the smell of his mother's cooking wafted from their hut.

They had never played again after her death.

Philias placed her fortress – in this set, intricately carved to look like a castle clinging to the side of a volcano – in the middle of her side of the gameboard. Then she began to build out her army, arranging ranks of imps and mephits, while also occasionally sprinkling in her more powerful pieces: gaunt efreets brandishing scimitars, fanged cherufe, squat, toad-like kaliza, and finally the general of her forces, a rearing dragon with wings outspread.

"This set was once used by the veiled ladies of the Cinnabar Palace," Philias murmured, distracted by the task of arranging her side. "It was a gift to Lady Numil from the padarasha himself. The Crone doesn't play, though, so she gave it to me. My pieces are made of pumice, a volcanic rock. Yours are carved from sea-stones rounded smooth by the waves." Philias surveyed her army, resting her chin on laced fingers. "You were asking whether I was a paladin of Ama."

"And you're not, you said," Keilan replied, busy deploying a phalanx of serpentine naga around his fortress.

"I am Pure, though. I can feel the heat of your gift."

Keilan swallowed, remembering the ease with which Senacus had sent him spiraling into darkness when he tried to summon forth sorcery in his village. Philias could probably do the same to him, if she so wished. "I didn't know women could become Pure."

Philias snorted. "Aren't there girls born with the gift? Garazon's black balls, look at your Crimson Queen. The mendicants strap just as many girls as they do boys to that damned altar."

"But you're not allowed to become paladins?"

Her mouth twisted. "No, we're not. Instead, we're hidden away in nunneries to spend our lives kneeling on stone pews and mumbling prayers."

"I don't think you'd make a very good nun."

"Ha! Yes, for some reason, unlike most others who are Cleansed, I could recall most of my childhood on the docks. My new life of rubbing a copper sunburst and intoning the Effulgent Prayer ten thousand times a day was just deathly dull in comparison. So one day, I fled."

"And Ama did not take back your powers?"

She frowned. "You're not listening, boy. Ama doesn't make us Pure – otherwise he'd have withdrawn his damned light from me when I first escaped the nunnery. Believe me, I wish he had. I can't leave these halls, or else a Menekarian assassin will find me. Years ago, when I first came to Lyr, I served a powerful merchant. But then the mendicants heard of me and sent a knife in the darkness. The Pure are not supposed to slip their leashes, don't you know." She drummed her finger on the stone board, then slid one of her efreets forward. "Have you heard of the Blackson Rebellion?"

The name tickled at Keilan's memory. "Yes," he said, moving a naga forward to block the efreet's path. "I read about it in one of my mother's books – the second son of the Menekarian emperor rose up against his father, I think. Nearly tore the empire apart."

"Well, what you don't know – what almost no one knows, since the mendicants have tried to strike it from the records – is that the rebellion began with the greatest of the Pure turning against his faith. The emperor's son only joined later, when it seemed the revolt might actually succeed in overthrowing the alabaster throne."

"Truly?"

"Aye. Melekaith was his name, and the light of the Pure burned more strongly in him than in any paladin since Tethys. But then the unthinkable happened – while hunting for those with the gift, Melekaith fell in love with a sorceress. Now, while children are returned to Menekar and sacrificed upon the Radiant Altar in the hope that they will rise again as Pure, adults are given no such mercy. According to the Tractate, they must be put to death . . . but Melekaith could not do this, and so he rebelled. More than a few of his brothers joined him, accompanied by several legions, and dozens of sorcerers also emerged from where they had hidden. They flocked to his standard, hoping to free themselves forever of Ama's scourge. Can you imagine? The Pure fighting alongside sorcerers against the armies of Menekar? They lost in the end, of course, and Melekaith and his sorceress lover were strapped side by side on thorned wheels and left to die above the Melichan Gate. The mendicants made sure to pluck out his eyes before he was displayed to the people, as even then they still shone with the mark of their lord."

Philias deliberated for a moment, and then brought out her dragon from the back of her ranked pieces. "And that is how I know the light inside me does not come from that bastard Ama – Melekaith's power should have deserted him when he turned against his lord, yet it did not. No, the Pure are not the creations of a god. We are something else entirely."

Keilan imagined he could feel his skin growing warm under her blazing gaze.

"Your move, boy."

He was well on his way to losing his third straight game when the door banged open and four pikemen in ornate ceremonial garb entered. They quickly arrayed themselves on either side of the door, facing each other in pairs. Their black-metal helms were shaped to resemble the heads of demons, and no two were alike: one had pointed ears like a cat, while the ears of another hung pendulous, as if stretched by an invisible weight; one had spines like a sea-creature, others sported webbed crests, or random barbs, or hooked noses. All had open, roaring mouths, out of which the faces of the guards stared without expression. After a long, drawn-out moment they raised their pikes in unison and struck the stone floor twice.

Keilan glanced at Philias uncertainly as the sound faded away. She rolled her eyes and sighed, crossing her arms. "Take note, Keilan. No matter where you go in the world, those with a little authority – but no real power – are all the same."

As if summoned by her words, a small man in a white damask tunic stamped with the black eye of Lyr strode inside, his back straight and his chin held high. He surveyed Keilan and Philias with disdain. "You are summoned before the Council of Black and White. Follow me."

Keilan hurried to stand, but Philias laid a hand on his arm. "Perhaps a simple 'please' is in order, Demarchus? The boy was a personal guest of Dymoria's queen, you know."

The man's lip curled. "Quiet, creature. The Crone isn't here."

"Oh, she isn't?" came a familiar voice from behind the man. His face instantly drained of color, and he whirled around, dropping to his knees.

"Lady Numil!"

The old woman stumped inside the chamber, leaning heavily on an ebonwood cane. Behind her came the man in gray, smiling like a cat who had just caught a bird after endless hours of watching it flutter just out of reach.

Keilan thought he saw a few of the pikemen struggling to hold back grins.

When she reached the groveling servant, the old woman rapped him sharply on the shoulder with her cane. "Idiot. Boy, please excuse his rudeness. His master is an old rival of mine, though while his duties to Lyr could be done by a troupe of trained monkeys – such as this fool here – my own require very unique talents. And the council knows that." Her gaze settled on the half-finished game. "Roped him into playing, Philias? Does he show any skill?"

Philias shrugged. "The boy's not about to become padarasha, but he has some ability."

"That's good," the old woman said, turning to him. "You swim in dangerous waters, Keilan. Queens and shadowblades and paladins – the sharks will feast on you sooner or later, unless you have a decent head on your shoulders." She thrust backwards with her cane, spearing the prostrate servant in his side, and he shrieked in pain. "Which Demarchus does not. But he is correct: the summons has come, and the archons are waiting. Let us go."

Without another word she turned and hobbled from the room, the man in gray falling in behind her. As she passed the man splayed out on the floor, she paused. "Stay like this until the tenth bell and I just might forget that vile name I heard you call me." Then she leaned in closer. "And you know I'll be watching, Demarchus. This is my home, and the walls have eyes."

With a grin, Philias pushed herself from her stool, beckoning for Keilan to follow.

The Crone snapped her fingers and two of the demon-helmed guardsmen turned sharply on their heels. The other pair waited until Keilan and Philias had stepped across the threshold, then moved behind them. Keilan caught a final glimpse of the servant, still on his knees with his head lowered, before one of the guards drew the door closed.

"Come along, boy. No dawdling."

Keilan found his legs moving faster at the whip-crack of command in the Crone's voice. She reminded him in many ways of the queen: when she spoke, it was never a request, and he couldn't imagine what her reaction would be if he failed to respond quickly. He didn't want to find out.

The shadowy corridors twisted oddly, and the scrape of their footsteps echoed. They passed through no large rooms or galleries, just endless branching corridors lined with iron-banded doors.

"What is this place?" whispered Keilan. His memories of being ushered inside the great doors to this fortress were clouded by the fog of exhaustion, but still he hadn't thought the building was this large. Much of it must have been hidden underground.

Philias didn't bother keeping her own voice low. "The lower levels of the archon's palace. We call it a palace, but really the archons only meet here – they all have their own manses on the Hill or in the Bright. It's somewhere to put important people they don't want wandering about that's at least a bit nicer than the pits."

"Then it's a prison?"

"Well, you can consider yourself an honored guest who is not allowed to leave."

"Certainly sounds like a prison," Telion said from in front of them.

"Come to think of it, it does."

After many twists and turns the corridor emptied into a large chamber. Its high ceiling was painted with a series of images of Lyrish daily life: men in white masks presiding over some dispute between two finely-dressed nobles, a boat laden with fish returning to the city's docks, and a cloth merchant hawking bolts of his wares in a market square. The far wall was dominated by an arched entrance; the space beyond was dark, but Keilan sensed its vastness. Deep within this chamber a pillar of light stabbed down from above – its brightness did not illuminate much else, and the rest of the room remained draped in shadow.

The Crone turned to him. "We'll leave you now, boy. You must pass beyond and stand within the circle of light. Do not worry overmuch: if you answer the archon's questions truthfully, I doubt any harm will come to you or your friends. The archons do not have the courage to anger Cein d'Kara."

Philias gave him a gentle push towards the entrance. "I'll be watching from the balconies. Don't try to use any sorcery, or things could get messy."

Keilan swallowed and stepped into the chamber. He approached the falling light, passing through a forest of dark pillars, blinking as his eyes traveled to the distant ceiling and the circle of blue sky cut out of the soaring dome.

Shapes resolved from the dimness: to his left was a long, curving table of black stone, and on his right its twin, though carved of some strange material so white it gleamed almost nacreous in the semi-darkness. A dozen men sat behind each table, and their murmuring conversations quieted as Keilan moved into the circle of light. Their faces were hidden: the archons behind the black table wore featureless white masks, while those seated at the white table had donned black masks.

Keilan shifted nervously, acutely aware that he was the center of the room's attention. He felt almost naked, standing in a puddle of light while the archons gazed at him from out of the gloom. A thought came to him as he stood there, clenching and unclenching his sweaty hands – if someone could stand at the lip of the hole cut into the roof, the scene below would resemble an eye: the two tables would shape its outline, and the spot of light he stood in would be the gleaming pupil. He glanced up, narrowing his gaze against the brightness, and noticed there was a second floor to the chamber, well above their heads, a gallery within which moved more dark shapes. Keilan glimpsed two burning embers hovering in the shadows. Philias's eyes, he supposed. For some reason, knowing she was there gave him a small measure of comfort.

One of the white-masked men rose from behind the black table, and the last lingering whispers died away. "Keilan Ferrisorn," the man said, his fingers splayed on the gleaming dark stone in front of him. "You come before the Council of Black and White. We welcome you to Lyr."

"Thank you, my lords," Keilan stammered, ducking his head respectfully.

Another man stood, this time from the middle of the white table and wearing a black mask. He was slightly stooped, and even before he spoke Keilan knew his voice would quaver with the weight of many years. "Tell us, Keilan, how you came to be outside our gates."

"I . . . I . . . came with a troop of rangers. From Dymoria. We were chasing a paladin of Ama."

"Why?"

"He had been involved in a plot against the queen. Assassins tried to murder her."

"And he tried to steal you away," said the man in the black mask.

"Y-yes," Keilan stuttered, surprised that they would know this.

"And why did he take you? The Pure are not known to abduct boys. Not unless they are tainted by dark sorcery."

Keilan cast a quick glance at the gallery above, meeting Philias's burning eyes. She must have already told the archons that he was indeed gifted – nothing could be gained from trying to evade the question. "I am not a trained sorcerer, but I could become one. Or that's what they told me."

Whispers rippled the length of the tables. The man in the black mask waved for quiet. "You admit to being a sorcerer. The paladin has already come before us and explained how he was on a holy mission to bring you back to the High Mendicant. By the ancient treaties signed by the elders of our city long ago, we are obligated to give you up to the servants of Menekar."

Louder mutterings followed this pronouncement. Another archon in a white mask rose. "Old pieces of paper signed at the point of a sword. They have little relevance in this changing world."

"But if the emperor or the High Mendicant knew we harbored a sorcerer," the black-masked archon countered, "and had taken him from the Pure, they could use this transgression as a justification for war."

"You heard what that thief, the Lyrish girl, said – the paladin slipped inside Saltstone in the company of shadowblades. Shadowblades! How could the chosen of Ama consort with those creatures? Perhaps other powers employ the sullied Pure."

"You saw his armor and his white-metal blade. And he carries an artifact from the hand of Tethys himself!"

"I saw a paladin so uncertain of himself he struggled to admit what he had done without wilting in shame!"

Keilan's head whirled as he tried to follow this argument. More archons were rising to their feet as the council deteriorated into chaos, but whatever they said was lost in the surging tumult of voices. He wished there was something he could lean against.

Keilan blinked in surprise. From the small gap where the curving tables nearly touched a small girl, perhaps nine or ten years old, was walking calmly towards him. She was dressed in a simple white robe, and her golden hair was coiled in a long plaited braid atop her head. Gradually, the archons noticed her arrival and fell quiet. By the time she stopped a few span from Keilan, the audience chamber was completely silent. She searched his face for a long moment, as if making sure of something. Then she turned back to the council.

"The Lady has seen this boy," she said, her voice so soft a few of the archons leaned forward to hear her better.

The black-masked archon who had spoken first cleared his throat respectfully. "Priestess, what does the Oracle say?"

"That he and the paladin must come at once to the House of Many Streams. She awaits them with great anticipation."

A stunned silence followed this pronouncement, broken by the sound of Philias's laughter echoing down from the gallery above.

4: SENACUS

DURING HIS TIME in the archon's palace, a storm had come raging out of the Derravin, transforming Lyr into a city of ghosts. Black clouds writhed in the slate-gray sky, their edges occasionally lit by the flicker of distant lightning, and tendrils of fog slithered like blind serpents through the empty streets, coiling around shuttered merchant stalls and the columns of elaborately carved porticos.

Any residents of the city sheltering inside their houses who happened to glance out their windows would no doubt be surprised by the procession fighting its way through the freezing wind and rain. A troop of the archon's demon-helmed guardsmen escorting a finely-wrought carriage stamped with the black eye of Lyr was surely not so uncommon a sight, but at the head of the column a young girl sat cross-legged and straight-backed on a litter carried by four tonsured monks in sodden white robes, seemingly unaffected by the lashing rain.

Senacus adjusted the straps of the ill-fitting cuirass that had been given to him – the archons had insisted he don the armor of a Lyrish guardsman when he ventured outside the palace, as having a paladin of Ama marched through the city to see the Oracle could give life to all sorts of rumors. He wished he'd kept the sellsword garb he'd worn while traveling to Dymoria, but he had cast that armor aside soon after fleeing Herath in an attempt to lighten the burden for his horse. The boots they'd pressed on him were at least more suited to sloshing through the streams now running through the streets, and were doing an admirable job of keeping his feet dry, despite the terrible weather.

This district seemed more prosperous than the little of the city Senacus had glimpsed yesterday as he was ushered through the streets to the palace. The buildings here soared several stories and were constructed of some sea-green stone which glistened wetly in the dampness. Many of these manses were crowned by cupolas or towers, and Senacus guessed this was so those within could watch the harbor for the sails of their family's boats returning to port. Lyr was the hub of a vast merchant empire, its sleek, black-hulled ships famous in every port in the known world. And because their commercial interests were so widespread, Senacus did understand why the archons had been so hesitant to choose between Menekar and Dymoria. Whatever decision they made would be bad for business. He'd been worried about which side the archons would choose, but also curious what they would do. And then, to his great surprise – and apparently the surprise of everyone else – this summons had come.

The Oracle of Lyr. Ancient and mysterious, its prophecies and pronouncements had toppled empires and changed the fates of kingdoms. Even High Mendicants had made the long pilgrimage to its temple to ask for counsel. One of the later books of the Tractate included a tale that Tethys himself had come before the Oracle, though what he had asked and if he had been given an answer were not revealed.

In any of the stories about Lyr's Oracle, Senacus had never heard of someone being summoned to the temple. Supplicants begged for an audience, and if granted the Oracle would dispense cryptic hints about what it had glimpsed in the future. Sometimes those glimpses were true, sometimes not, and sometimes the Oracle's words could only be understood after many years.

Senacus lifted the heavy demon-helm from his head, wiping away the water from his eyes. Each of the helmets was fashioned differently, and he had suffered the bad luck of being given one that had strange jutting horns that seemed perfectly shaped to funnel the rain down onto his face. Terrible design in a city where it rained all the time – perhaps that was why none of the other guardsmen had claimed this helm.

He caught a glimpse of the boy up ahead, closer to the front of their procession. His cowl had been drawn up and he was hunched against the storm, but Senacus knew it was him. Even though he wore the relic of Tethys he could feel the sorcery emanating from the child, curdling the very air. The slight figure beside him in a dark hooded cloak must be the girl who had become his companion since that day she had stolen Keilan away from him. Senacus felt a stab of relief seeing her alive and unharmed. He had begged Demian not to kill her when she had surprised them in the corridors of Saltstone, and the shadowblade had apparently kept his word. Or she had slain him instead, but that seemed impossible. Senacus remembered how helpless she had been as she strained against the invisible chains binding her. And there had been someone else in that passageway, a man with the look of a warrior about him, but Senacus couldn't see him up ahead. Perhaps he'd stayed behind in Herath.

Their procession passed down narrow, twisting streets, the dark stone buildings rising up like canyon walls. Rain hissed upon the slanted tiled roofs and was channeled into the gutters feeding the squat stone goblins crouched upon the eaves. Those leering creatures in turn spat or urinated upon those passing below.

Senacus's thoughts returned to Keilan. His world had been shattered in the months since the boy had come into his life. First had come the embarrassment of having him stolen away by a Dymorian sorcerer, but that paled when compared to the shame Senacus had felt when he returned to Menekar and the High Seneschal confronted him about his decision to save the life of the same sorcerer beneath the cursed city of Uthmala. He had hoped to absolve himself before Ama by recapturing the boy and bringing him back to be Cleansed, only to discover that his companion on that quest, a man personally chosen by the High Mendicant, was almost certainly a sorcerer himself.

The thought that the leaders of his faith were being manipulated by powerful sorcerers – or were perhaps even in league with them – had shaken Senacus to his core. How could this be possible?

They emerged onto the city's docks, a great wooden expanse cluttered with crates and sacks and the skeletons of half-built boats. Skiffs and dhows bobbed in the churning waters beyond the low seawall, tied to long quays. One of these jetties was very different than the rest, a ribbon of black stone that extended far out into the water, quickly vanishing within the curtain of rain. The litter-bearers did not pause for even a moment before they started upon this span, and Senacus noticed the priestess had pressed her palms together in front of her and bowed her head, as if praying.

Keilan and the girl followed soon after, stepping carefully upon the darkly glistening bridge, and then came a detachment of the Lyrish guardsmen. It was very obvious to Senacus that the soldiers had been positioned so that they separated him from the boy – was that because they feared he would snatch Keilan away? As if in answer to this question, the girl suddenly twisted around. Her gaze found him, and her face hardened in anger. He could see the venom in her eyes even from this distance, and he felt a chill that was separate from the cold rain. He glanced away from her, and when he looked back after a few long moments she had gripped Keilan by the arm and leaned in closer to confide something. She hated Senacus, that was clear.

The carriage halted where the gleaming black stone of the bridge disappeared into the wood of the dock. A guardsman hurried to open the door, and then moved to help the same elderly woman who had questioned him earlier step down. She was one of several archons who had visited him before he had gone before the council. The Lady Numil. All the Pure who were sent out into the world to hunt sorcerers were given a firm grounding in the powers that controlled every city and kingdom, and Senacus knew she was a great power in Lyr, one of the handful who actually wielded influence behind the vain and ineffectual archon council.

A large man in hardened leather armor, the hilts of two swords visible over his shoulders, appeared beside her holding a strange device. It was long and stick-like, flaring out into a flat circle of what looked like dyed leather, the rain running off its edges and keeping the space directly beneath it dry. The Lady Numil saw Senacus staring and motioned for him to come closer.

"Ingenious, wouldn't you say? They've spread like wildfire here in Lyr, since it rains nearly every other day."

"What is it, my lady?"

"The merchant who first brought them in called them parasols, because their original name is unpronounceable. They're from Shan. Apparently, in the Empire of Swords and Flowers the noblewomen carry them around to keep the sun from browning their skin." The old woman squinted up at the gray sky. "I can't even remember what the sun looks like. But they do a fine enough job of keeping the rain off as well. You see, I'm quite dry standing under here."

"Very dry," repeated the man beside her who was holding out the parasol, the water running in rivulets off his great bald head.

The old woman ignored her servant. "Come closer, paladin." She studied him, her dark eyes shrewd. "Remarkable. If it wasn't for your white hair there would be nothing to mark you as a warrior of Ama."

"It is a blessing of Tethys," he said, touching where the amulet of bone lay beneath his cuirass.

"A powerful artifact, and quite the gamble to send you into Dymoria bearing it. And this lends credence to the claim that you were dispatched by the very highest among the faithful in Menekar."

"I would not lie."

The Lady Numil quirked a smile. "Yes, yes. You paladins pride yourselves on your adherence to the truth. But even if you do not lie, I've – how should I say it? – I've known the Pure to withhold certain facts so that others will arrive at mistaken conclusions."

She paused, as if expecting Senacus to say something, then continued when he did not.

"I'm curious what you think of this summons to see the Oracle."

Senacus shrugged. "I am . . . surprised. I've never heard of anything like this happening."

"And yet it has, for the first time in two hundred years. The question is: why has she requested to see you and the boy? He has the potential to become a great sorcerer, I've been told, and you are a paladin of Ama who allied himself with the kith'ketan to steal him away from Dymoria's sorceress queen. That alone is a story beyond belief. But there must be more to come. The Oracle is concerned with the future, not the past." She reached out and grabbed his wrist, her grip surprisingly strong. "There is more you did not tell me. What is it?"

Senacus met her gaze calmly. She was right, there was more. It was the reason he had abandoned Keilan at the gates of Herath, rather than attempt to return him to Menekar. Powerful sorcerers had somehow infiltrated the faith of Ama and were positioned highly enough in the temple back in Menekar that they could influence the actions of the High Mendicant himself. Such a thought was chilling. Ama's faithful were the only defense against the terrible danger that could be brought down upon the lands, and now it seemed they had been subverted.

But this was not something he could share with the infamous Crone of Lyr. He needed to return to Menekar and help draw out this corruption from the faith before the disasters of the past could come again.

The old woman sighed. "Fine, keep your secrets, paladin. The Oracle will lay some things bare, I'm sure." She started to turn away from him and then paused, looking back. "You know, you do have beautiful eyes. It's a shame no one can ever see them."

That caught him off guard, and he was left blinking in mild surprise as she hobbled onto the soaring bridge, her bald man-at-arms keeping pace to continue shielding her from the rain. The sound of a throat clearing brought him back, and he turned to find the batch of guardsmen who had brought up the rear of their procession watching him expectantly, their hands on the hilts of their weapons.

When the Oracle requested someone to attend her, their presence was clearly not voluntary.

Senacus kept to the middle of the black stone bridge as he began the crossing, but every strong gust of wind still made his heart leap. The rain had made the stone so slick it was almost like trying to walk across a frozen pond, and he was forced to edge along slowly in order to keep himself balanced. He wasn't the strongest swimmer, and if he slipped over the side and fell into the churning black water he didn't like his chances of making it back to the docks.

After what seemed like an eternity, he passed the bridge's midpoint and something emerged from the gloom ahead, a great shape bulked within the fog. Gradually it resolved into an island of bleached white stone. The ground there seemed to undulate strangely, barren of any grass or trees, sloping precipitously upwards into a series of small, lumpy hills. The guardsmen were clustered near where the black stone of the bridge disappeared into the island's white rock, as if nervous to venture too far. The Crone and her servant, however, were a ways off, and the child-priestess had left her litter-bearers behind and was picking her way over the rugged landscape.

"The temple of the Oracle," he heard the girl say as she stepped off the bridge. "I always wondered what it looked like." She was turned away from him, standing beside Keilan as he crouched over a pool of seawater.

"Is the whole island one giant piece of coral?" Keilan asked, running his hand along the ground's pitted surface.

That's what it was, Senacus realized. He had seen bits of this sea-substance before, washed up on beaches. An old fisherman had told him once that the brittle little shards were the bones of the fish-men who lived beneath the waves, but he had suspected that to be just an old fabler's tales. Here, though, the thought that this great bleached expanse might be the remains of some dead leviathan made him shiver. He kicked at the ground with his boot, breaking off a chunk of the strange substance. It certainly wasn't rock.

"Aye, it is," the girl said. She looked uneasy, her hand playing with her sleeve as she squinted at the rippling hills.

The Crone stumped closer, leaning heavily on her ebonwood cane. "The island changes," she said. "It is alive, always growing, though slowly." She grunted and turned away. "Let's get out of the wind and rain, eh? If a chill like this seeps into my old bones, it will stay for half the winter. Keilan, Nel, come with me."

Nel. That was her name. Senacus had heard it when he'd been half delirious as she'd cared for him after Uthmala, but he'd forgotten until now.

"And you too, paladin. She asked for you as well."

They turned to him then, just now realizing that he stood only a few paces away. Nel's gaze could have soured milk, and for a moment Senacus thought she might reach for one of her daggers. He didn't see anger in Keilan's face, to his surprise.

The boy would have had every right to hate him. Senacus had taken him from his family, then tried to kidnap him again from his new home. What was he thinking? Senacus saw wariness . . . and something else. Curiosity? Keilan opened his mouth as though to ask Senacus something, but before he could begin Nel interrupted.

"Where is the temple?" she asked.

Senacus glanced around, wondering the same thing. There were no buildings secreted in the folds of the coral mounds; just a barren white expanse.

"We're standing on it, girl. The entrance is over there." Senacus's gaze followed the old woman's outstretched hand towards a rent in the side of the white hill barely large enough for a man to enter. "It's in a different place every time I come here. But that looks like it, and the girl seems to think so as well."

The child-priestess had almost reached the cave's mouth, picking her way carefully over the jagged ground, and as Senacus watched she vanished inside the opening.

The demon-helmed guardsmen and the Oracle's servants stayed behind as their small band followed the priestess across the shattered landscape. They skirted the edge of several deep basins filled with seawater, tidal pools where brilliant ecologies flourished. The coral beneath the surface was not the bleached white of bone but instead vibrant shades of brown and green and blue. Small fish skittered among drifting fronds, hiding within the swaying tentacles of things that resembled purple flowers. The contrast between the dead world outside and the riot of life just below the surface was striking.

Soon they stood on the cave's threshold. "Should we light a torch?" Keilan asked hopefully, peering into the darkness within.

"No," the Crone said. "The Oracle does not permit fire in her temple. There will be light inside." She ducked her head to avoid the low-hanging coral and stepped into the dark, disappearing almost immediately.

Keilan and Nel hesitated at the entrance, and a moment later the old woman's voice came from inside, slightly muffled as if she'd already descended a ways. "Quickly now. She's waiting for you."

"It's harder to take that first step when we're not following Vhelan, eh?" Nel muttered, then took a handful of Keilan's sleeve and pulled him along into the cave.

Before the boy vanished he turned to look at Senacus. "Come on," he said, and these simple words, spoken without hate or anger, hit the paladin like a blow to the stomach. *Have I been forgiven?*

Senacus stepped into the cave. The blackness in front of him was seamless, and he was tempted to remove the relic of Tethys and allow his holy radiance to push back the dark. But he did not. Instead, he groped blindly until his hand brushed the rough, jagged coral, and then he moved forward, stumbling slightly on the uneven ground. Keeping his other arm extended so he wouldn't walk into a wall Senacus moved down the passage, hoping there was only the one leading away from the cave's entrance. He felt a small stab of relief when he heard a thump from up ahead, and then a torrent of colorful curses from Nel.

Slowly the tunnel began to lighten, and Senacus emerged with the others into a vast, soaring chamber. Part of the ceiling had been hacked away, and the wan light filtering in from outside through the falling rain painted the coral walls in shades of gray. It was not the only source of illumination in the space: a vast pool filled most of the chamber, swarming with blue lights. Senacus stepped closer to get a better look, his boots nearly touching the dark water, and gasped. The pool seethed with spectral jellyfish, shards of blue within a darkness plunging down so deep the creatures within dwindled into tiny glimmering specks.

"Gods," he heard Nel breathe, and he tore his gaze from the swirling, hypnotic patterns of the drifting jellyfish.

His companions were all staring at the far wall of the chamber, which bulged oddly and hung over the pool like some tumescent growth. There were things embedded in the coral; the color was nearly the same, so they almost blended with the wall, but the texture was different, smoother, not rough and pitted.

Bones. The coral was festooned with bones. A skull leered down at them, only its grinning mouth and eye sockets visible – the rest had vanished into the coral. A skeletal arm dangled from the wall, its fingers missing. The shattered remnants of ribs emerged elsewhere, above a pair of feet that still stood upon a narrow ledge carved from the living rock.

A sense of unease was rising within Senacus. He saw a dozen skeletons, at least, each to a varying degree in the process of being swallowed. One was not yet even reduced to bones. The pale, emaciated corpse of a woman stood on another small ledge, her right arm vanishing into the wall. The coral was creeping over her other limbs, fusing with the flesh until Senacus wasn't sure where the body ended and the wall began. A long, snarled cascade of yellow hair obscured most of her unclothed body, but Senacus could see that the corpse's skin was scabrous and covered with festering sores.

The child-priestess knelt by the edge of the dark pool and raised her hands towards the body embedded in the coral. Sickening dread stole over Senacus as realization slowly dawned.

The woman in the wall lifted her head and turned to look at them with empty eye sockets.

"They come," she rasped. Her voice was soft, but it echoed in the vast chamber.

A chill filled Senacus as he stared into that sightless gaze. She saw him, he was sure of it. She saw *into* him.

He let out a shuddering breath. It felt like spiders were crawling inside his head, skittering along his skull on countless prickling legs. Her presence was there, within him. Watching and measuring. Senacus swallowed, his hand going instinctively to the hilt of his sword, even though he knew it would do no good. The spiders were picking their way through his memories, and at times they paused to examine moments from his past –

Crying out from the burning pain in his legs as Nel crouched over him, the dark forest blurring as they fled the ruined city –

He and Demian riding along the Wending together, mist clotting the gray waste as the Mire unraveled into the distance –

An old man with kind eyes plunging a shining knife into his chest as he screamed for his mother –

It was like he was experiencing those times again, and all the emotions he had felt crashed down on him in a single great wave. Beyond that last memory was nothing but blinding light, yet the presence inside him pushed closer, peering into what he had been before his rebirth as Pure . . . Senacus groaned, nearly falling to his knees.

"Get out of my head!" cried Nel, and the sound of her ragged voice pulled him back to the cavern of dead coral.

From the look of it, the presence had imposed itself on everyone save the child-priestess, who still knelt motionless at the edge of the pool. Keilan looked stricken, like he had been forced to witness again something terrible. Nel's face was pale and drawn but her eyes flashed angrily as she glared at the Oracle. Even the old woman had been affected, as she leaned heavily on her cane, her eyes closed and her mouth set in a thin line.

The child extended her arms out towards the woman in the wall, her palms upraised. "Blessed lady, I bring before you the boy and the paladin, as you desired."

The woman's bony shoulders slumped, and her head fell so her face was veiled by tangled hair. For a long moment, the only sound was the whisper of rain falling onto the slice of the pool beneath the gash in the cavern's ceiling.

"I gorge," she finally said, her voice cracking from disuse. "Too long since others have come. Too long since I have tasted what *was* instead of what *might be*."

"What do you know, Oracle?" asked the Crone, wiping at her face with an embroidered cloth. "Why did you send the summons?"

The gaunt woman raised her empty gaze again. "Lady Numil. Many years have you visited the House of Many Streams. We welcome you for the last time."

The old woman blinked in surprise. "Last time? Oracle –"

"I see a great threat."

"To Lyr?"

The Oracle shook her head, her snarled blond hair swinging. "Not just to Lyr. To Menekar. To Shan. To small villages on the shores of distant seas."

"Can you tell us what shape this danger will take?"

"Step forward," the Oracle commanded. "All of you. Senacus, Keilan, Nel. Look into the water."

Senacus edged closer to the pool, staring down into the abyss. Out of the corner of his eye he saw Keilan and Nel do the same, and then his attention was drawn to the swirling blue jellyfish as they pulsed in the darkness. There was a pattern to their movement that slowly resolved the longer he concentrated; they spiraled down into the deep in undulating circles, creating a shaft of black water untouched by their luminescence, and from within this emptiness something was rising from the depths. At first it was just a smear of white, then gradually it became more distinct: pale flesh marred by swollen black veins, dark hair slowly writhing in whatever currents moved within the pool, tattered clothes. It was a corpse, a child's corpse, although it was so wasted he couldn't be sure if it had been a boy or a girl. Its ascent slowed as it approached, until it drifted motionless a few span from the surface. Had some poor urchin fallen off the city docks in the storm? How had it come here, to the Oracle's pool? He leaned out over the water and studied the child's body, looking for some clue.

The corpse's eyes opened, and it saw him.

"Radiant Father!" Senacus cried, stumbling back a step. Then he lunged forward to confront this creature, his hand gripping the holy relic around his neck, poised to pull off the amulet and let the full power of Ama flow through him once again.

But the corpse was gone, no trace of it remaining. The shimmering blue jellyfish had abandoned their strange dance, filling the space where it had floated.

"What was that?" Nel asked hoarsely, and a glance at her face showed Senacus that she must have seen the same vision in the pool.

"Death," the Oracle replied, her voice hollow. "The end of all."

"The child will bring about that?" the Crone asked. "How?"

"I do not know. I am only a rock in the river of time. I cannot see the future, save in tattered glimpses. Nor the past. Only this moment is clear and sharp; all else is shrouded by mist. What has come before is a mighty torrent surging towards me; it dashes upon this moment and breaks into endless possibilities. Now many of these streams tumble into darkness. This has never happened before to me, so I have sifted through the memories of past Oracles searching for anything similar. And I found it – for when the empires of old cracked the world open with their sorceries, it was the same. Something terrible is approaching.

"I have stared into the future, and I have been given a vision. Look again into the depths, and I will show you."

Senacus willed himself to tear his eyes from the Oracle and stare again into the pool. He gasped when he saw that all the blue jellyfish had vanished in the few moments since he'd last looked; now it was a darkness so pure it seemed to swallow the cavern's dim light, a hole cut into the fabric of the world.

It was pulling him, drawing him down into the depths. The oily water filled his mouth, his nose, and he was drowning, sinking into oblivion . . .

5: KEILAN

KEILAN EMERGED FROM the darkness.

He was on his hands and knees, retching, trying to expel the darkness clotting in his lungs; nothing was coming out, yet the pressure he had felt in his chest – that terrible, suffocating weight – was lessening. He drew in a deep, shuddering breath.

His fingers clutched at the red dirt beneath him, but even though it looked to be loose, the ground was hard as stone. Dirt? Where was the coral of the Oracle's cavern? What had happened? He'd looked into the dark water, as the Oracle had commanded, and then he'd felt something rush over him, dragging him away . . .

To where?

Keilan pushed himself to his knees, his head spinning, and shielded his eyes from the harsh daylight. He blinked away the spots in his vision as the world around him slowly resolved.

The first thing he noticed was the sky. It was a dull white, like during the coldest days of winter, without a cloud to be seen. But it was not empty. A gash of deep red resembling an open wound spread across the sky, as if the dawn itself had been smeared across the heavens. And from this stain more red was trickling, a lighter shade but still vivid.

The sky was bleeding.

Keilan stumbled to his feet, swaying. He saw the paladin standing with his back to him a few paces away at the edge of a cliff, staring at something below. With great effort Keilan took two staggering steps, and when he stood beside the Pure he steadied himself by laying his hand on the taller man's shoulder.

Senacus turned. Ever since the paladin had abandoned him at the gates of Herath, Keilan had seen guilt and pain when the Pure looked at him; now, though, his face was empty of those emotions. Empty of all emotion. Something had shaken him greatly.

"It's Menekar," the paladin said softly, inclining his head slightly to indicate what was before them.

Keilan looked. They stood on the lip of a rocky cliff that plunged down a thousand span or more. Spread before them were the ruins of a vast city, an expanse of tumbled white stone that gleamed like bleached bone in the light of the broken sky. Keilan couldn't see a single intact building among the devastation – everything had been reduced to rubble, even the walls. Beyond these low mounds stretched an endless sea of white grass.

"The city is gone," said Senacus, his voice hollow.

Keilan tightened his grip on the paladin's shoulder. "It's not real. It can't be. The Oracle is showing us something."

"But what could do this?" Senacus said softly. "An army wouldn't destroy everything. This isn't a sack by a Qell horde, or a great fire. It's like the city has been wiped away."

Keilan pulled at Senacus's arm, and the paladin allowed himself to be led from the edge. "We need to find the others."

He saw them immediately: Nel was helping the Lady Numil to her feet, while a young woman with long golden hair stood nearby, watching them. The Oracle, Keilan realized, although she looked different: her skin was unblemished, and she was dressed in robes similar to what the child-priestess in the temple had worn. Behind them was another tumbled pile of white stone, the shattered remains of some great building. Unlike the city below, though, there seemed to be something still standing deeper within the ruin, a twisted dark spire stabbing at the sky.

"The Selthari Palace," Senacus murmured as they moved towards their companions. "The empire has fallen."

"Where are we?" Nel was asking the Oracle as Keilan and Senacus approached. She glanced over and saw them standing side by side, and her face tightened.

"Menekar. This is a moment that came to me etched clearly. It is one possibility that might be, though how far downstream I do not know."

"Then we are not truly here?" the Crone asked, jabbing the red dirt with the butt of her cane. It left no indentation.

The Oracle shook her head. "No. I am sharing with you my vision. You cannot affect this place, or what will come."

"What happened?" Senacus asked, his voice still heavy with shock. "There are a million people in the city. They cannot . . . they cannot all be dead."

The Oracle turned to him. In her coral temple she had been blinded, her sockets empty, but here she had been restored. Her eyes were a beautiful shade of pale green, glimmering with flecks of gold. "They are all dead."

"Then where are the bodies?"

At Senacus's question the Oracle raised her arm, indicating the structure rising from deeper within the destroyed palace. "Some are there. Come, I will show you."

They picked their way through the debris, following the Oracle as she seemed to glide across the toppled pillars and tumbled slabs of stone. Senacus was right, Keilan realized – this kind of devastation could not have been caused by men. Perhaps the earth had shaken the city to pieces? But if so, where were the dead?

When finally they emerged from the ruin, they found themselves at the edge of what once must have been a lush garden.

Cracked ceramic paths twisted between copses of dead trees, and from a few of their skeletal branches hung broken wind-chimes or blackened, gnarled fruit. Beneath the trees the rust-colored dirt was mostly bare, though here and there the withered remnants of flowers were scattered. Recessed within the garden was the strange building; it was not so large, Keilan realized, but with the rest of the palace so utterly destroyed it loomed over everything.

"This was the emperor's pleasure garden," Senacus said, reaching up to try and pick a rotten fruit from a low-hanging branch. His hand passed through it, as if he was a spirit. "What is causing this corruption?"

No one answered, but Keilan found his eyes drawn to the twisted structure. There was something wrong about it, something unnatural. They were still too far away to see it clearly, but it didn't seem to have the clean lines of buildings made of stone or wood – it bulged strangely in places, as if something was bubbling up from within.

The Oracle started on the ceramic paths, and they fell in behind her. The silence was unnatural: there was no birdsong, no rustle of animals moving through the dry grass. Even the chimes hung motionless, as if the wind itself had perished.

Details became clearer as they neared the building. Its surface was black and oddly ridged, though the color was not uniform. In some places it shaded to gray or was speckled with scraps of white.

The path they followed emptied into a large clearing; trees must have grown here once, but now the ground was pockmarked with holes where they had been uprooted. They had been removed to make space for the building, which hunched brutal and monstrous. There was no symmetry to it, no reason: part of it slithered almost organically deeper into the garden, while another section bulked partway up the height of the spire at its center, its top studded with oddly bent crenellations. Strange, those battlements almost looked like . . .

Keilan gasped, and beside him Nel cursed, her voice raw.

"What is it?" Senacus asked, striding forward, his hand on his sword. "What – oh, by the Father."

The building was made of corpses. Twisted, their flesh blackened, twined together like reeds or stacked like stones. Dozens were contorted unnaturally to form an arched entrance, beyond which was darkness. Some of the bodies were turned inward; others stared out sightlessly. In places, limbs or hair had slipped free to dangle down. What Keilan had thought were battlements above were actually arms, clawing at the sky.

"This can't be," Nel whispered.

"Why have they not rotted away?" asked Lady Numil, taking a few shuffling steps closer to examine one of the many faces in the closest wall: it was a man, his mouth open in endless frozen agony, his eyes wide and glassy.

"Sorcery," Senacus muttered, his voice seething with anger. "This is worse than the cataclysms. Something terrible was unleashed here. Something monstrous." He whirled on Nel, his fists clenched. "Your queen must have done this. This is her revenge."

"She would not do this," Nel retorted, her eyes flashing. "Nor would those who follow her!"

Senacus turned to Keilan. "You see? You see what horrors sorcery can bring into the world? A city . . . a people, dead by the hand of the Crimson Queen."

"No," interrupted the Oracle calmly. "Sorcery this is, but not from her. What did this came from the Empire of Swords and Flowers."

"The Shan?" Senacus exclaimed in surprise, and then his face hardened. "Those cowardly dogs. They could not defeat Menekar on the field of battle, so they resorted to this?"

The Oracle shook her head. "If I was to bring you to their land, it would look the same. A dead waste. As would Lyr. The archon's palace has fallen, my own temple ground to dust."

Lady Numil sucked in her breath.

Senacus blinked, confusion in his face. "What? Then who –"

"Look," interrupted the Oracle, pointing at the shadowed archway. "This is what you must see."

Keilan sensed some movement deep within the darkness, coming closer, and fear tightened his chest. What was it? What horror could have done this?

It emerged into the light, a small child with unnaturally pale skin veined with spidery black lines. Its dark hair was tangled and matted, falling nearly to its waist and covering more of its body than the torn gray rags it wore.

Such malice and dread emanated from the creature that Keilan wanted to turn and flee. He was rooted to the ground, though, his legs frozen as the child's empty gaze passed over them without stopping.

Relief flooded Keilan, making his legs weak. It couldn't see them!

Senacus drew his sword and started forward, but the Oracle held up her hand. "You can do nothing except watch."

Three more of the ragged children filed from the darkness after the first. They all looked similar, but Keilan noticed small differences: two of the children's hair was shorter, though still unkempt, and the others had been blinded, their eyes removed so that only gaping black holes remained. They arrayed themselves into a line perhaps two dozen paces across, standing what looked to be an equal distance apart.

With eerie precision they lifted their faces in unison, staring into the sky.

Keilan followed their gazes, but saw nothing. They seemed to be concentrating on a slice of sky that was merely a wash of white, far removed from where the scarlet lesion leaked blood into the heavens.

As the moments dragged out the unnatural children remained motionless.

Something glinted in the sky, a momentary flash.

A sibilance that made the hairs on Keilan's arms rise started among the creatures, swelling as the light in the distance grew larger. The hiss was like the sound a coiled snake might make before it struck . . . when it felt threatened.

Something was coming.

No, not something. Someone.

It was a woman in blue robes, limned with crackling power, her long silver hair streaming behind her as she descended.

Keilan's breath caught in his throat. It was her. The sorceress he had seen in the memories of that ancient bard, Jan. He remembered her face, contorted with the pain of channeling the surging energy from a million doomed souls into the crystal that would unlock immortality, her cheeks flushed from the tremendous effort.

A face that looked like an echo of his mother's. And the hair . . . never had he seen its like anywhere else, in all the places he had visited.

But that ceremony beneath the mountain had happened a thousand years ago, and this was a glimpse of the future. She had survived as well, then, down through the centuries.

The sorceress alighted in the clearing, her blue robes swirling. She gazed contemptuously at the monstrous children before her and the twisted building looming behind them.

"Why did this happen?" she asked, her voice high and clear.

revenge

The word was a hoarse whisper, many voices speaking as one.

The sorceress narrowed her eyes. "The Weaver is not here. This is not her doing."

In response the children took a step forward, the black veins beneath their pallid skin beginning to twitch and writhe.

you came to your death, old one

The sorceress sneered, reaching inside her robes. "I came to end you, abominations." She pulled something forth and tossed it onto the withered grass.

It was a head, a child's head framed by tangled black hair, its mouth opening and closing like a fish out of water. "You sent only one to kill me. That was foolish arrogance. I have studied you; I know your weaknesses." A dagger was suddenly in the sorceress's hands, long and black and curving. Runes glimmered, carved in red fire down its blade.

The monstrous children drew back, as if frightened.

Then they struck.

Oily black lines of glistening power erupted from the children's outstretched arms, flashing towards the sorceress. With a crack the sorcery struck the silver-haired woman's wards, which flared around her, a shield of shimmering golden energy. Light exploded, blinding Keilan, and he threw up his arm as he stumbled backwards. The radiance did not subside, but strengthened, consuming everything around him, and he felt something pulling him away with terrible force . . .

Keilan surfaced, spluttering.

He kicked out frantically, keeping his head above the dark water. For a panicked moment he did not know where he was, and then it all came rushing back. Lyr. The Oracle's temple. The demon children. He must have slipped into the pool . . .

Something thrashed awkwardly in the water beside him – Nel, struggling to stay afloat. With the sure strokes of a boy who had spent countless evenings practicing for his Night Dive, Keilan swam closer to the knife and reached one arm around her. "Nel, relax."

"I can't swim," she managed between mouthfuls of water.

"Relax," Keilan repeated, drawing her closer. "If you keep struggling, you'll pull us both under."

At that, she tried her best to stop; he could still feel the tension in her body, but at least she was no longer splashing about wildly.

Keeping her head above water, he brought her to the side of the pool, then gave her a push to help her haul herself out. The sharpness of the coral didn't seem to bother her at all as she scrambled over the edge and collapsed on her stomach, panting.

Keilan pulled himself out after her, laying his hand on her back. "Did you swallow any water? Cough if you have to; try to get it out."

"No," she said, rolling onto her back. Her eyes found his. "Thank you. I have terrible dreams about drowning."

Keilan shook his head to dismiss her thanks, hoping she couldn't see his blush in the temple's wan light.

A few dozen paces away the paladin was helping the Lady Numil from the pool, lifting her like a babe from the water. She clutched at him, and with her sodden robes clinging to her Keilan could see how thin and frail she truly was.

"Lady Numil, are you all right?" Keilan asked as he hurried to her side. She was shivering violently, and it made him realize how cold he was in his own wet clothes.

He glanced around wildly and found the child-priestess who had led them to the temple sitting calmly beside the pool, watching them. "Fire," he said to her. "She needs to get warm."

The girl shook her head. "There can be no flame here."

"She's an old woman! She could die from the chill!"

"I'm f-fine," Lady Numil tried to say, but she stumbled on the words, her teeth chattering.

"Some clothes, at least?" Keilan continued, and again the child priestess shook her head.

"We have none."

"I can help," Senacus said, and with his free hand he pulled off the amulet of bone he wore around his neck. Light flared in his eyes, and the aura of warmth around the paladin appeared again. The rush of power flooding the Pure made Keilan dizzy.

"Stay close to me, Lady Numil. My light will burn away the chill."

She patted his chest with her hand, her shivers starting to subside. "Thank you, lad."

"Look," Nel said, and Keilan turned to her. She was pointing up to where the Oracle hung suspended over the pool.

Her knees had buckled and she sagged forward, her tangled blond hair veiling her face, and only her arm sunk into the coral kept her from toppling into the pool below.

"Is she . . ."

"She is dead," the child priestess said without a shred of emotion in her voice. She rose from where she sat and shrugged free of her vestments, then turned and dove smoothly into the dark water. Keilan watched in stunned silence as she swam across the pool and pulled herself up onto the far side. She did not glance at the body of the old Oracle hanging above her as she climbed the wall, using the ancient bones jutting from the coral for purchase. When she had found a ledge where she could stand, she faced them again from across the water.

"She knew the strain of showing you what she had seen would kill her. Value her sacrifice, and act to forestall the doom rushing towards us all." The girl reached out and gripped a knob of coral hanging beside her. For a moment, some emotion passed across her face, and then it was gone. "Leave. And tell the elders of this city to send a new child here."

6: THE MANDARIN

BAE LING STARED into the open jaws of a dragon.

It was Shalagan, he guessed, the servant of the South Wind. He thought that because the Hall of Celestial Tranquility had been built along the traditional north-south axis, in order to better channel the harmonious energies into the emperor seated upon his throne, and the huge dragon of wrought gold that coiled down the red pillar near where Bae Ling performed his ritual obeisance was most certainly located in the hall's southern quadrant. A good omen, to be placed here while he waited for the emperor to see him, as Shalagan had always been the most benevolent of the four sacred dragons. Centuries ago, when the great fleet had found itself becalmed on an ocean smooth as glass, it had been Shalagan who swooped down from the clouds and filled their sails with the South Wind, pushing them towards these shores.

Bae Ling squinted into the dragon's mouth, which almost brushed the hall's floor of polished jade, looking past the curled lips fringed by writhing tendrils. He frowned. A few of the golden teeth had been snapped off, he realized, near the back, deep enough down the statue's gullet that only a careful inspection would reveal the crime. What brazen courtier or guard had risked the emperor's wrath by stealing some of the dragon's teeth?

Bae Ling was so lost in his consideration of this nefarious deed that he did not stir when the heavy tolling of a gong sounded and his name was announced into the silence that followed. It took the sharp elbow of the mandarin kneeling beside him for Bae Ling to realize he had finally been summoned before the Phoenix Throne. He stood stiffly, his heart climbing up into his throat as he raised his head and turned towards the gleaming steps that led to the dais where the emperor waited.

Dai Feng, beloved of Heaven, ruler of the Empire of Swords and Flowers, struggled to lift himself from the depths of his vast chair when he noticed Bae Ling approaching. His small head, hairless as an egg, seemed to float above a rippling sea of yellow brocade and silk. Bae Ling knew the emperor had recently celebrated his eighteenth year, but his face still retained the smooth plumpness of a much younger boy.

And that would never change. Like the phoenix that gave the throne of Shan its name, Dai Feng had been reborn when he had donned the imperial vestments. He had given up his manhood but gained the favor of Heaven. His only desire now was to rule the empire wisely and well.

At the base of the gilded steps Bae Ling threw himself down, pressing his face to the cool floor.

"Rise," the emperor murmured.

Bae Ling stood, still keeping his head respectfully lowered. "Son of Heaven," he said, "you called for me, and I have come. My heart bursts with the honor you have shown me today."

The emperor perched on the edge of his throne. "Scholar Bae. You may kneel upon the fifth step."

"Such kindness," Bae Ling said, his voice nearly cracking with emotion. Slowly, he put his silken slipper upon the first step, savoring the sensation, then the second, the third, and then the fourth. Finally, on the fifth he sank to his knees, only a dozen paces away from the emperor. This was a great moment for his house; he could almost hear the excited mutterings of his ancestors' ghosts as they peered between the veil that separated the worlds.

"You deserve no less, Scholar Bae. Do you know why I have summoned you?"

"No, Son of Heaven."

"It is because I have been brought news of an eating house that has recently opened in Tsai Yin. Not an eating house that serves delicacies to rich merchants and lords – no, an eating house where the poorest may dine even if they do not have a single tin shaerling in their pocket. Do you know this house, Scholar Bae?"

"I do, Son of Heaven."

"Of course you do. For it is your wealth that keeps its pantry stocked. Your generous nature has not gone unnoticed."

Bae Ling felt his cheeks redden at the praise.

The emperor clapped his hands and a black-robed man suddenly appeared beside Bae Ling, holding out a small scroll.

"You may read it now," the emperor said, and Bae Ling reverently accepted the gift with both hands. He undid the yellow ribbon and carefully unrolled the delicate rice-paper. It was a poem, the characters written in what he surmised was the emperor's own thin, graceful hand.

Beyond the red lacquered door
Rice rots and wine is left to sour
While outside are scattered the bones of the starved
A man is measured
Not by whether he must knock
But if he opens the gate

A pale imitation of one of the ancient masters, Scholar Bae would have said if an apprentice had shown this to him. Derivative and formulaic. But this was not the fumbling attempt of just any child with delusions of profundity – this had sprung from the stylus of the emperor of Shan. Bae Ling found his hands were shaking as he rolled up the scroll and bound it again with its yellow ribbon.

"My descendants will treasure this forever, Son of Heaven."

The emperor favored him with a smile. "Scholar Bae, I hope your actions will inspire others among the Thousand Voices to help the poorest and least fortunate. You have pleased me."

The emperor sank back into his chair and Bae Ling knew he was dismissed. With a final deep bow, he turned from the Phoenix Throne and descended the steps, then strode across the cavernous hall, his slippers whispering upon the jade floor. He did not look to either side, but he felt eyes following him, envious glances from the supplicants who still lay prostrate beside each of the four pillars.

A gong sounded behind him, but again Bae Ling did not hear it.

The carriage ride back to his manse passed in a daze. It seemed to last only a few heartbeats: one moment he was settling into the velvet seat-cushions, and then the next his steward, Gu Wan, was swinging open the carriage door and helping him to climb down.

The street outside the ancestral house of the Bae family was unusually quiet for this early in the evening; there was only a single lamp-lighter raising his copper pole high to hang a lantern back on its post, and a russet-scaled galagen lizard waddling down the road on stubby legs, delivery bags piled upon its back.

Bae Ling patted the cheek of the stone dog-dragon standing guard beside the gate to his manse, as he had done every day since he was a small boy. Behind him he heard Gu Wan leading the horse back to the stables, hooves clattering upon the wide stone path.

He passed through his flourishing gardens, noting that the orange and purple blossoms of the elioch thorn flower had finally opened, despite the season's unusual coolness. He pushed through the heavy wooden door to his manse.

At once he knew something was wrong. Nothing looked out of place: the ancestor shrine across from the entrance was undisturbed, the painted face of his father regarding him with the same lack of affection he had maintained when he was alive. The celadon cups and bowls of his mother's collection were still arrayed on low benches along the hallway, each worth a laborer's yearly wage. The thick fur of the brightly patterned Keshian carpet did not hold the indentation of any intruder's steps.

It was the silence. It filled the house like incense in a temple, oppressive and choking. "May?" he called out into the stillness. "Where are you? Why do you not greet me?"

A sob came from an adjoining room. Tingling with unease, Bae Ling stepped through a threshold, into another of the foyers where he often received his guests. A small girl was crouched against the wall, her knees drawn up almost to her chin; in her hand she clutched a long curving knife from the kitchens. Her round green eyes filled with relief when she caught sight of him.

"M-Master Bae," she stammered in her broken Shan, climbing to her feet.

Bae Ling frowned and crossed his arms. "May. What is this? Why are you frightened?"

His barbarian slave girl from the north swallowed. "Something in the house, master." She pointed the wavering knife towards the staircase that led to the second floor. "Up. I hear sounds."

Bae Ling held out his hand, and after a moment's hesitation she passed him the knife. "Where are the other servants?"

"Chala went market, Gu Wen with you. Only me here now."

"May, we've had problems with your racing imagination before. Remember when you thought spirits were haunting the well? And it turned out just to be the echo of croaking frogs."

"This not echo, master."

Bae Ling adjusted his grip on the kitchen knife. He had never been a warrior, but he also doubted very much that he would be called upon to fight. Burglaries here in the Tiandan District, where most of the Thousand Voices lived, were almost unheard of. Most likely some stray cat or monkey had found its way through an open window and into the rooms upstairs.

"Come with me, May."

Her face paled, but she quickly mastered her fear and nodded meekly. "Yes, master."

She followed him as he climbed the stairs to the second-floor landing. The corridor here was decorated by one of the paintings his father had done before his death: a small red bird, bright as a jewel, perched upon the bare spidery limb of a tree in winter. A poem about the changing seasons was written in his father's austere hand. There were three doors set in this corridor, but two were always locked. The third led to Bae Ling's own bedroom.

He heard muffled sobbing coming from behind that door. May whimpered, her fingers tangling in his robes.

Brandishing the knife in front of him, its handle slick in his sweaty palm, Bae Ling pushed open the door to his bedroom. Slowly, it creaked wide, and he edged closer, peering within.

The room was darkened, but enough of the wan early-evening light filtered through the latticed windows that Bae Ling could see the strange scene laid out before him. Upon his bed, behind the silken curtains stirring in the breeze, a naked man had been tied, ropes running from his wrists and ankles to each of the four curving columns that supported the wooden canopy. He was gagged by a gray cloth, and his eyes were panicked. Panicked, and round like May's. He was a northern barbarian as well, from across the Sea of Solace.

The man thrashed frantically in the bed when he caught sight of the knife in Bae Ling's hand, but his bonds held and he soon subsided again, chest heaving.

Bae Ling stepped into the room, his gaze flickering to the shadowed corners. He felt May's presence behind him, and her hand clinging fiercely to his robes.

From the darkness, something stepped. A small boy, dressed in ragged clothes like a beggar child might wear, tangled black hair covering his face.

May gave a sharp intake of breath when she caught sight of it as well. Without hesitating, Bae Ling turned and plunged the knife into her chest, slipping the point between her ribs and piercing her heart. May's brilliant green eyes widened in surprise, and her mouth fell open.

"Oh," she managed, and then she slid to the floor, lifeless.

Bae Ling let the knife fall. Then for the second time that day he knelt in obeisance.

"Master, you have returned," he whispered hoarsely, joy swelling in his chest.

slave

The word echoed strangely, spoken in the rasping voices of many children.

it is good you remember us

"We never forgot, master," he stammered, the words tumbling out too quick. "We have kept the dream alive for a thousand years." Bae Ling's pulse thundered in his ears. He was talking to a god! How he wished his father had lived to see this day!

your ancestor was bae fan

Bae Ling nodded, his head still lowered. Out of the corner of his eye he noticed May's blood creeping towards him across the wooden floor. "He was, master."

the one who first cut us

Bae Ling's mouth was suddenly dry. "Yes. And my family has been trying to atone for that sin ever since."

Small, cold fingers brushed his cheek. *have you kept it*

"Yes."

bring it to me

Bae Ling stood, averting his gaze from the Chosen, and slowly backed out of the room. Outside in the hallway, he pulled a black iron key from his pocket and with shaking hands unlocked one of the other doors. The fetid smell of stale blood washed over him as he passed into the small shrine where his family had worshipped the Raveling for all these centuries, ever since the first Shan had settled in these lands. The walls were covered in black cloth without any markings, and the room was empty save for a white stone altar. Russet stains covered its scratched surface and reached with red fingers down its sides.

An ancient glass container shaped to look like a cavorting demon had been placed in the center of the altar, clouded black from its contents. How many times had Bae Ling prayed here for this very moment to arrive, when the Chosen were again free to work their will in the world?

Reverentially, he lifted the container and retreated from the shrine, locking the door behind him. Gu Wan was also of the faithful, but the new cook Chala – like May – knew nothing of his family's secrets. She would have to die as well if she returned while the Chosen were in the house.

Or if she found May's body, Bae Ling thought, carefully stepping over the sprawled corpse of his servant. As a northern barbarian she would not have known what the Chosen were, but if she had described what she'd seen an educated Shan would have realized at once of what she spoke.

And then they would have come to his home with fire and swords.

In his bedroom the child-god had clambered up onto his bed and now crouched on a satin pillow beside the head of the bound man. Pale fingers tangled in the barbarian's brown hair, brushing aside a stray strand that had fallen across his face. Sweat glistened on the man's forehead, and he watched the Chosen with wide, terrified eyes. He was not struggling anymore; it seemed like his will had melted away, like a mouse trapped in the gaze of a Keshian hooded serpent.

we have returned to this city of our imprisonment looking for the sword of cho

Of course.

"Master, I had heard Lord Cho was slain in the north, hunting for you."

his sword accompanied his body south, to his estate near tsai yin

"And there it will stay. There is no one left to wield it, master. My father had the only son of Lord Cho poisoned; the boy survived, but he can barely lift his hand, let alone bear the sword."

there is another. a daughter

Bae Ling suppressed a smile. "A girl?"

she has taken the blade. our other servants tell us she trained with the daisun monks, in the place called red fang

"But certainly a woman –"

Searing pain shot through Bae Ling. He cried out, writhing in agony, the container falling from his fingers. The Chosen appeared beside him – he hadn't seen it move. It held the bottle in its small hand, stroking the dark glass.

so long as the blood of cho carries the sword we are not safe

"Yes, master," Bae Ling gasped.

The child-god returned to the side of the bound man. Gently, it unwound the cloth covering his mouth. The man watched him, his chest heaving, but he did not cry out. His eyes were glazed now. Empty.

The Chosen unstoppered the container and held it up, seeming to consider its contents. Bae Ling's breath quickened.

this man we found at the docks. he can travel in the barbarian lands with ease. he will find the cho girl and kill her and return to us with her heart

The child-god tipped the bottle and a thick black liquid poured out, slipping between the man's parted lips.

The blood of gods, drained in their last mortal moment.

The man spasmed, straining against the ropes that held him. The wood of the posts creaked and began to buckle with the force of his thrashing.

Something rippled beneath the man's skin, like an eel sliding along the water's surface. It flickered down his throat, pressed against his ribs and then dove deeper into his body. He coughed violently, blood flecking his bare chest. His eyes rolled back into his skull and his back arched as he flung himself back and forth.

Then, as quickly as it had begun, the fit passed, and the man sagged once more into the bed. The Chosen leaned close, whispering in its chorus of lost voices.

kill the cho girl

Pale blue eyes found the child-god, and the man nodded.

7: KEILAN

KEILAN CROUCHED BESIDE the hearth, enjoying the rolling waves of warmth coming from the blazing fire. The damp and cold that had seeped into his bones was finally being drawn out, and he rolled up the sleeves of the dry shirt he'd been given, enjoying the prickle of the heat crawling along his arms.

The chamber door opened behind him, and he twisted around to see who had come. It was a servant girl, carrying a silver tray laden with steaming cups and strange foods. She set her burden down on the low, wide table in front of the ornate velvet couch where Nel was swaddled in a thick blanket, then glanced shyly at Keilan and went to stand in the corner, her face lowered.

Nel leaned forward to better see what had been brought. Keilan rose and approached as well, suddenly aware of the hollow ache in his belly. On the tray was a ring of honey-glazed pastries speckled with small red fruit, and in the center a bird carved from spun sugar looked almost ready to take flight.

Keilan chose one of the pastries and tried a tentative bite, unsure what was inside, but he was pleasantly surprised when he found the filling to be sweet jam. Nel extricated her arm from the blanket, then plucked the sugar bird from the tray and popped it into her mouth. She sank back into the couch, chewing blissfully.

"Delicious," she sighed after swallowing. "Even in Herath, where the trade ships from the Sunset Lands unload their holds, sugar is expensive. I think we've become honored guests of the archons."

Their accommodations had certainly improved greatly. Keilan remembered the barren cell in the palace where he'd first been brought before his audience with the Council of Black and White, and it was a far cry from the chamber they were in now: rich Keshian rugs covered the stone floor, the gilded furniture was carved from gleaming black and red wood, and the fireplace was large enough to roast a sheep, for which Keilan was especially grateful.

Keilan sipped from one of the steaming cups and found it to be hot apple cider laced with honey, a drink he'd had before while traveling across the north. Perfect for banishing a chill.

"What happened in the Oracle's temple?"

Nel took up another of the cups and cradled it to her chest, the rising warmth turning her cheeks pink. "I don't know. I've been Vhelan's knife for many years. I've seen sorcery before, but nothing ever like that. We were *there*. In Menekar."

"Do you think . . . do you think that could be the future? That horror?"

Nel chewed on her lower lip, staring into the fire. "It felt real. Didn't she say that she saw possibilities – what *might* be? Not what *will* be?"

"So we can change what happens."

"And maybe that's why she showed us what she did. Even though she must have known it would kill her."

Keilan was silent for a long moment, watching the crackling flames. "But what can we do?"

A troubled look passed across Nel's face. "Keilan, there's something else. In Lyr, we grow up on stories of the Oracle. And some are cautionary tales. The Oracles . . . they all go mad, eventually." She sighed, and then shuddered. "I mean, can you blame them? But what I'm saying is that at some point the Oracle's visions lose their power. They start imagining the future, instead of getting real glimpses. Kingdoms have fallen because of these false prophecies."

"I don't think this was false."

"Why?"

"Because I've seen that sorceress before."

Nel's eyes widened in surprise. "The silver hair . . . god's blood, Keilan, could it be?"

The chamber door swung open again and the large bald servant of Lady Numil entered. He nodded at Keilan and Nel, and then stood against the wall as the old woman followed him inside, leaning heavily on her ebonwood cane. She looked much better than she had in the Oracle's temple – even after being warmed by the paladin, her skin had been so cold and waxy Keilan had feared she'd die – but the exhaustion was clear on her face. Keilan bowed to her as she stumped across the room to a cushioned chair and sank into it.

"Ah. Much better. It feels so good to finally get off my feet." She snapped her fingers at her servant. "Telion, bring me my sweet bird."

The bald giant strode over to the couch and stared down at the tray of delicacies. "It's gone."

Lady Numil gasped. "Blackguards! I bet it was the thief." She glared at Nel, who stared back innocently.

"Should I fetch another?" Telion asked, but the old woman held up her hand. "Not you. Girl!" she shouted at the servant waiting in the corner – she'd been so quiet Keilan had forgotten she was even there. "Run down to the kitchens and get someone to make me another sweet bird." The girl hesitated for the briefest of moments, as if unsure what she should do. "Now!" Lady Numil yelled, and the girl blanched and scurried for the door.

When the sound of her running footsteps had vanished, Telion chuckled. "Not one you trust?"

The old woman smoothed her robes. "I think she belongs to Belimis. In any case, I don't want anyone else hearing what's said in here. Would you mind standing outside, Telion, and making sure no little mice are listening?"

"You'll be all right? You're not fully recovered –"

"Go. I'm fine."

Her servant nodded and left the chamber, drawing the door shut behind him.

Lady Numil sighed and shook her head. "He blames himself for what happened in the temple, though of course it was I who insisted he wait with the guardsmen. Loyal fellow." She twisted one of the jeweled rings on her finger. "A lesson there, ducklings. Loyalty and honesty are what you should look for in your friends and servants. The fawning and groveling types might burnish the image of yourself you keep in your head, and that is certainly pleasurable, but in the end it only leaves you more likely to make mistakes."

She gestured at Keilan. "Boy, bring me the tray. I could eat an aurochs right now."

The old woman deliberated for a moment after Keilan had done as she asked, then chose a lemon tart and waved him away. "Now sit. We have much to discuss."

Keilan returned the tray to the table and found a spot on the couch as Lady Numil finished the tart in three quick bites. After brushing her hands clean, she set them in her lap and turned her full attention to Keilan and Nel.

"When I woke up this morning I had no idea what the day would bring. Usually I can see these things coming, you know. Wars and plots and assassinations take time to develop, and somewhere along the way someone will spill a secret. I'm very rarely caught unprepared." She picked at the embroidered hem of her sleeve, frowning. "So imagine my surprise to find out I would end up taking a swim in the Oracle's pool. Or, for that matter, that the Oracle of Lyr would sacrifice herself to allow me a glimpse of the world's end."

Nel shared a glance with Keilan. "Lady Numil, do you think the Oracle might have been . . . mad?"

The old woman dismissed Nel's question with a wave of her hand. "I've seen Oracles spiral down into madness before. That one seemed as clear as crystalwine. No, I believe we must accept what she showed us. What I want to know is why she showed it to *you*?"

Keilan glanced furtively over at Nel, but she wasn't looking at him. Should he share that he had seen that silver-haired sorceress before? Could they trust Lady Numil?

"Did she want you to carry a message to Cein d'Kara? If so, why not send a summons to Herath so the queen could come to the coral temple herself? Cein's no fool. She would not have refused."

Keilan swallowed. Would the queen be angry if he spoke to Lady Numil before her?

"Or do you have some insight into this coming doom? Something to help avoid it?" The old woman eyed him shrewdly.

Perhaps he should wait and tell Vhelan first when they returned to Herath. He was wise and knew much about these sorts of things. Perhaps –

"Out with it, boy!" she barked, and Keilan jumped in surprise. "I can see you know something. By the Silver Lady, you're as easy to read as an unrolled scroll."

Keilan felt a hot flush of guilt. "I . . . I . . . "

Lady Numil's eyes narrowed. "I have less savory ways of making you speak than plying you with pastries, boy. And don't think I won't do it when my city's fate hangs in the balance."

"Tell her, Keilan," Nel said. "You won't be able to hide anything from her."

"That wasn't the first time I'd seen that sorceress," he said in a rush. "The one with the silver hair."

The old woman settled back, lacing her hands in her lap. "Interesting. She's from the Scholia, then?"

"No, no. I helped Queen d'Kara with a great sorcery the same night the assassins came to Saltstone. I saw that sorceress in a vision from long ago. A thousand years in the past."

The old woman's brow arched, but she did not interrupt.

"She was part of a ceremony that granted immortality to a secret group of powerful sorcerers. They had somehow orchestrated events so that the old sorcerous empires in the north and south would destroy each other . . . and then through dark magic captured the souls of those killed in the cataclysms to fuel their spell."

This was the first time he had told Nel the whole story of what he had seen in Jan's memories, and she was staring at him with a strange expression. "She sounds monstrous. They all do."

Keilan licked his lips. "Yes . . . but one of the sorceresses, Alyanna – she was the leader of them – she tricked some into participating. Jan didn't know what he was doing. She might have fooled others, or not told them what was necessary for the ceremony to succeed."

"So you have seen this sorceress before," said Lady Numil. "We know she's alive now, I suppose. And that she can kill the demons that seemed to be what brought down this doom. But that doesn't tell us where to find her."

"She looked like my mother," Keilan said, and the old woman blinked in surprise.

"She's your mother?"

"No. She looked like my mother. So similar. They had the same hair, and the face . . . it was just a little different. They could have been sisters."

"And where is your mother now?"

"She died. And she never told me where she came from. My father was a fisherman and he found her in the sea after a storm had sunk her ship."

Lady Numil shook her head. "Boy, have *you* fallen into madness?"

"No. It all seems like a strange dream, I know. But that sorceress was the reason I followed the Pure to Lyr. In that vision of the past I saw a man with her, another sorcerer. And that man was a companion of the paladin when they tried to take me from Saltstone. I thought the Pure might know something about these ancient sorcerers, and where I could find the woman who reminded me so much of my mother."

"Any other time I would consider this to be nonsense," Lady Numil muttered. "But . . . the Oracle requested you come to her temple. She let you glimpse the future she'd seen for a reason. She killed herself to do it."

The old woman wiped her face with her age-spotted hand, and Keilan saw again how utterly exhausted she was. "And she shared this vision with me. I must have some part in what is coming."

"What will you do?" Keilan asked quietly.

"What I have always done," Lady Numil fairly snapped. "Protect my city however I can. The Oracle claimed these . . . children . . . were from Shan. Perhaps they were summoned by the warlocks of the bone-shard towers, some kind of weapon to use in a coming invasion. Or not. Despite what the Menekarians would have us believe, the Shan are a peaceful people. I've heard no rumblings that they are planning to cross the Broken Sea. But these creatures . . . someone must know what they are, and I will wring it from them."

Her gaze suddenly sharpened, and a prickling crawled up Keilan's back. "And I know what you must do as well, boy."

"What's that?"

"You must find this sorceress. She has the power to slay these demons. You must enlist her aid before they unleash this doom upon the lands."

"But I don't even know if my mother truly had any connection to her!"

The old woman's voice softened. "The Oracle shared what she saw for a reason, and I believe it must be because she thinks you can find her. There can be no other explanation. Believe me, boy, I'd rather not entrust the fate of my city to someone who's never even had to put a razor to his neck!"

"And how is he supposed to find this sorceress?" Nel asked, her voice hardening. "Whoever she is, she's managed to hide for a thousand years."

Lady Numil ignored the challenge in Nel's tone. "You said she reminded you of your mother," she said to Keilan. "Return to your village and find out where she came from."

Return to his village? A numbness spread through Keilan at the thought. He remembered faces twisted in hate and fear as the Pure loomed over him, Sella screaming as she flailed helplessly at the paladin, his father bellowing, straining to reach him through the swirling chaos . . .

"No," Nel said flatly. "We must return to the queen. She's the only one who can make sense of this madness and has the power to forestall it."

"We don't know how much time we have," retorted the old woman. "We could be well into the last watch before the storm. And what if the queen refuses to let Keilan search for this sorceress?"

"As well she should!" Nel cried, flinging her blanket aside and coming to her feet. "Because it's madness! You would send him *back* to the Shattered Kingdoms, just a stone's throw from Menekar's shadow? The Pure have tried to take him twice already!"

"The boy is the key. Now sit down," said Lady Numil firmly, gesturing for Nel to return to her seat on the couch. The knife was trembling, and Keilan suspected it wasn't because of a lingering chill.

"I'll send him with protection. The Iron Road from the Gilded Cities to Gryx teems with merchants and other travelers; there's not a safer way to travel to the east. From the city of the Fettered it's only a few days of riding to get to the western edge of the Kingdoms."

Keilan shook his head. "My apologies, Lady Numil. You don't understand – my mother never told me about her past and where her family had come from."

The old woman snorted. "Ha! Boy, there's a clue somewhere back there, if you search hard enough for it. No one could live for so many years and not reveal something. Perhaps she confided in a friend in a moment of homesickness. Maybe there's a clue to be found in some object that washed up on shore after your father plucked her from the waves. There must be a way to find her – otherwise why would the Oracle set you to this task?"

Nel had sunk back down on the couch, but still she glared daggers at Lady Numil. "The queen will have our heads on spikes if we go haring off on this quest instead of bringing back the paladin in chains."

Keilan glanced sharply at Nel, and she sighed.

"Yes, 'we'. I'm not letting you out of my sight. There's probably bands of paladins and shadowblades and shape-changing monsters roaming around looking for you."

The old woman clapped her hands. "Then it's agreed. You're off to find this sorceress."

"We said no such thing!" Nel cried, exasperated. "We're returning to Saltstone!"

"What do you think, boy?" Lady Numil asked suddenly, turning to Keilan.

"Don't ask him," Nel said. "This is not his decision. He's just a –"

"Boy?" Keilan finished for her. He stood, nearly upsetting the silver tray. "I'd be a man in my village if the Pure and the queen hadn't come hunting for me. I've been pulled by my ear across half the world." He was surprised at the anger he heard in his voice. "With no say in any of it. Nel, I think Lady Numil is right. The Oracle wanted me to find this sorceress – she killed herself to tell us that – and the only place to start would be where my mother lived for so long. That's where I have to go."

Nel flushed crimson, but she said nothing.

Across from her, the old woman smiled like a cat who had just swallowed a mouse, lacing her fingers in her lap. "Very good, Keilan. You'll leave on the morrow."

8: CHO LIN

CHO LIN SAT in the courtyard of her family's compound in Ras Ami and watched the moths dance. They swarmed the copper lanterns the servants had hung from the eaves when the sky began to darken, pale white wings as large as her palm fluttering like falling leaves. Her finger traced the rim of the cup set before her on the small stone table, slicked by the steam rising from the freshly poured tea.

It was a beautiful night, a poet's night. The Cho compound was set far enough back from the busy streets of the port that the sounds of revelry from the eating houses near the docks were drowned out by the hum of the cicadas crouching in the branches of the small, gnarled trees scattered about the courtyard. She would miss moments like this, she suspected, when she journeyed into the barbarian lands.

She would certainly miss the tea. Almost two years atop Red Fang with only water from the mountain streams to drink, yet she had fallen back into her old habit immediately. A servant had started following her in the compound, a container brimming with hot water ready to be poured into her teapot whenever she refilled her own cup. She sipped her drink, savoring the slight taste of honey imparted from the dried and crushed jasmine petals.

The buzzing conversations of the cicadas abated as the sound of hurrying sandals disturbed the night. Cho Lin motioned for the servant waiting silently in the shadows to approach, and the slight girl stepped forward to place another teacup on the table and fill it from the spouted copper flask she carried.

Kan Xia entered the courtyard in his usual state of dishevelment, his robes flapping and his sash half-untied. "Mistress," he said, pressing his hands together and bowing.

Cho Lin gestured for him to sit, and he slid onto the stone bench across from her, wiping his flushed face with his sleeve.

"Good evening, Kan Xia. Have you eaten?"

Her family's servant bobbed his head. "Yes, Mistress."

"Have some tea, then. It's delicious."

Kan Xia smiled gratefully and picked up his cup, blowing on the tea to cool it.

"You have news?" she asked as he drank. The worry lines on his brow and at the corners of his eyes smoothed away as the tea worked its sorcery. How was she going to survive in the north without tea in the evenings to wash away the day's troubles?

With a satisfied sigh, he set down the cup. "I do. I've just come from our office down on the docks. None of our ships are in port, but there's a captain who has worked with us before who plans on setting off for the Gilded Cities tomorrow morning on the early tide. He's agreed to continue with us to Herath after he delivers his goods to Lyr. The ship's name is the *Loyal Gull*, and the captain and his crew have a good reputation."

"A fast ship?"

"Our contacts at the dock assure me it is. Built with an ice-hold to bring fresh-picked winter melon and dragon fruit into the barbarian lands without any spoilage. We can be in Herath in a fortnight."

We. Cho Lin swallowed away a small frown, not wanting to start this argument again. Kan Xia was insisting that he accompany her to Dymoria, along with a squad of elite Cho warriors. But Cho Lin was quite certain it would be impossible to remain inconspicuous with such a large group. If this Crimson Queen had truly allied herself with the Betrayers, as the warlocks of Tsai Yin suspected, she would move against them as soon as they arrived in Herath. Kan Xia seemed to think they could disguise themselves as a merchant delegation, and he had convinced her brother of this plan. Cho Lin wasn't so sure, though.

"Oh!" Kan Xia exclaimed, as if just remembering something. "A servant pressed this into my hand outside in the street. She said it was for you." He withdrew a small roll of parchment from the folds of his robes and held it out for her to take.

Puzzled, Cho Lin accepted the scroll. A message from her brother? Or from Red Fang? Who else knew she had left the mountain? She studied the characters pressed into the wax seal. *Bai Hua*. She had known someone by the name, many years ago. But certainly it couldn't be her.

Cho Lin broke the seal and opened the scroll. The writing was firm and graceful, with a playful edge. She had seen it before. How could this be? Her thoughts whirled as she read.

Long-Legged Lin, I can't believe you have come to my dreary little town. My old servant recognized you yesterday as you passed her coming through the city gates. Do you remember Aunty Cao? She insisted she had seen you, but of course I laughed away her words, for why would you ever visit this awful place? Yet now I am told the lanterns have been raised outside the Cho house, so you must really be here! Visit me tonight! I want to hear all about your adventures and what is going on in the capital. My manse is the last and the largest on the Street of Orchids. I will wait for you! Don't you dare leave without a visit!

Bai Hua,
first wife of Dao Lis,
head magistrate of Ras Ami.

Cho Lin let the scroll fall to the table, more than a little shaken. This was not what she'd been expecting at all. An echo from a time long vanished.

"Who is it from?" Kan Xia asked, concern in his voice as he studied her.

Cho Lin rolled a small piece of wax between her fingers. "Kan Xia, you were with my father when he brought my brother and me to live with him at the Jade Court, weren't you?"

"I was. Your father had the old emperor's ear in those days."

"Do you recall the children I used to play with?"

Kan Xia nodded. "Yes. The sons and daughters of the Thousand Voices, and also a few of the boys who were being groomed for the Phoenix Throne."

Cho Lin picked up the scroll again. "This is from one of my old playmates. We were close, almost like sisters. I'd heard she married an official in a city outside of Tsai Yin, but I had no idea she lived in Ras Ami."

"And so this is an invitation?"

"Yes. She wants me to come tonight."

Kan Xia waved his hand, as if to dismiss the very idea as preposterous. "Of course, you will politely refuse. We know someone hired assassins to kill you, and I very much doubt they will have given up after one failed attempt. Here within these walls you are safe."

"I can protect myself, Kan Xia."

"But, Mistress –"

Her voice hardened. "You forget yourself. Only the emperor and my brother can command me."

Kan Xia lowered his eyes, his face reddening. "Yes, Mistress."

Cho Lin stood suddenly. "The Street of Orchids is only a short walk away. This is likely to be my last night in Shan for many months, and I mean to enjoy it."

Kan Xia swallowed. "As you wish, Mistress. But the sword –"

"Comes with me." She strode across the courtyard and picked up the slender black bag she had left leaning against one of the red pillars. It looked like a carrying case for a keppa, the long stringed instrument that was becoming popular among the noblewomen of Shan. Anyone who saw her on the street would assume she was a musician on her way to a performance, or a lady returning from her evening lesson. They couldn't suspect that inside the bag was the most legendary weapon in the Empire of Swords and Flowers.

"A few warriors of Cho should –"

Cho Lin made a cutting gesture with her hand. "What better way to attract attention than with an armed escort? I will go alone."

Kan Xia ducked his head in acquiescence as she shouldered the bag. "As you wish, Mistress."

His lowered eyes looked hurt. Cho Lin sighed. "I will be fine. You know I appreciate your care, Xia. Grant me this last night to savor a civilized life. Tomorrow, our journey into the north begins."

He said nothing, but she thought she saw his expression soften. Good. They would have to traverse a thousand leagues together, and it would be best if they weren't annoyed with each other before they had even set off.

Cho Lin slipped between the forest of red pillars, nodding at the pair of grim-faced Cho warriors guarding the compound's entrance, and stepped out into the streets of Ras Ami. This was a quiet district, broad avenues hemmed by soaring walls, behind which towered the multi-story houses of the port's richest families. Paper lanterns dangled from the ornate metal posts arching over the road, drenching the slate tiles in shades of red and green. Cho Lin breathed deep of the evening air, enjoying the scent of the pear trees lining the road. There was another flavor layered underneath this sweet smell: the distant aroma of meat grilling. Her stomach rumbled, reminding her that she'd barely touched her supper. Hopefully Bai Hua was having some delicious snacks prepared.

The Street of Orchids was quite close by, barely more than a stone's throw from her family's compound. She followed it to its twisting end, and soon arrived at a soaring manse ablaze with dozens of hanging lanterns. Bai Hua must have expected her to accept the invitation.

And how could she refuse? They had been close during those golden summers, when the very air had seemed to shimmer with the wonder and magic of the Jade Court. Cho Lin remembered the celestial courtiers, tall and straight-backed in their rich black vestments, proceeding in stately columns into the soaring hall where they would then prostrate themselves before the Phoenix Throne. And she remembered that shiver of excitement she'd felt every morning when the great doors clanged shut, the sound signifying that until nightfall the imperial grounds belonged to her and her coterie: Jai Po, dashing and cunning, with a smile that would have charmed an immortal; Bai Hua, a plump little girl who danced and sang as well as a courtesan trained by the Swallows; and the three boys who were studying to succeed the elderly emperor: Tan Ho, Rei Xin, and Dai Feng. Feng – sweet, doting Feng – had eventually ascended to the throne, though Cho Lin had not spoken to him in many years.

There were no guards outside the manse, which surprised Cho Lin slightly, but of course in a civilized city like Ras Ami there would be little need for such overt displays of security. It would take a thief of uncommon brashness to rob from this district – the full might and ingenuity of the judiciary would be brought to bear if such a crime occurred. Far better if those blackguards contented themselves with the sparser but safer pickings in the merchant and tradesmen districts.

A silken cord dangled beside the arched wooden moon door, which had been beautifully carved with a serpentine dragon.

One of the servants of the Four Winds, she suspected, and this suggested that the honorable Dao Lis must have mercantile as well as administrative interests. The dragons of the Four Winds were usually venerated by those who dared venture across the trackless waters.

She pulled the cord, and from within the manse she could faintly hear a musical chime. Moments later the door was opened by an elderly woman in a servant's simple green hanfu dress, the deep lines in her face suggesting she had spent many years toiling in the fields before coming to work for this house.

"Aunty Cao?" Cho Lin guessed, and the hint of a smile touched the old woman's creased face.

"Welcome, Mistress Lin." Her accent was rough, flavored by the eastern hills. "The lady of the house will be very pleased to see you. Follow me, please."

Cho Lin fell in behind Aunty Cao. The manse was grand, especially for the home of a provincial official. The lintels above each doorway they passed through were carved with elaborate landscape scenes, intricate friezes of rolling hills scattered with tiny pagodas. Glazed white vases only a little smaller than Aunty Cao lined the walls, decorated by herons and fish drawn in jagged blue brushstrokes. These looked like artifacts that might have predated the destruction of the ancestral lands of Shan, and only a great family could possibly have retained such treasures. Bai Hua hadn't married very far below her station, it would appear.

To Cho Lin's surprise, they did not enter the courtyard in the center of the manse but skirted its edge as they moved to another wing of the great house. Aunty Cao paused outside an open doorway and gestured for Cho Lin to enter.

She stepped over the threshold and found herself in a small parlor, its walls decorated by long tapestries. Cho Lin tensed as a tall beautiful woman rose from a couch where she had been reclining.

"Older sister!" cried the woman, her eyes bright and her smile radiant as she rushed towards Cho Lin in almost girlish excitement. She wore a dark green cheongsam patterned with blooming flowers, and her long, glossy black hair glistened like the water of a lake at night. With obvious joy, she clasped Cho Lin's hands and gave an affectionate squeeze.

Cho Lin gaped. Bai Hua? Her last memory of her was of a chubby girl, her face a mask of concentration as she performed a slow and stately dance in front of a gathering of court ladies. But yes, there were the dimples she remembered, and the laughing eyes were the same . . .

"Younger sister," Cho Lin said, still amazed by the transformation. "It's been too long."

"How long?" Bai Hua asked, dragging Cho Lin towards a pair of cushioned chairs positioned beside a low wooden table. "Ten years? Twelve?"

"At least. I was trying to remember myself, to be honest."

"Well, now that I see you again I feel like we've never parted!" Bai Hua exclaimed happily, gathering up her long dress as she sank onto one of the chairs. "Put down your bag and sit. Is that a keppa? Have you brought it to play?"

"No, no," Cho Lin said quickly, a little flustered. "It's . . . it's . . . uh, a wall hanging I bought earlier today."

Bai Hua's laughter was high and free. "Ah, Long-Legged Lin. Still a terrible liar, I see. But I won't press you, if that's Cho family business."

Cho Lin smiled gratefully and sat, leaning the long bag against her chair. She suddenly felt a little self-conscious, as she was dressed in her simple traveling clothes, while Bai Hua shimmered in her radiant silken dress. A beautiful butterfly to Cho Lin's drab moth. A true lady of Shan, even though they were both daughters of Jade Court mandarins.

The old pain briefly surfaced, but Cho Lin tamped it down, forcing a polite smile for her old friend. It wasn't Bai Hua's fault that she had lost her childhood . . . and the life she should have had.

"Come, have a cup of wine with me," Bai Hua said, leaning forward to fill two cups from a silver pitcher on the table. She glanced at Cho Lin with a mischievous glint in her eye, as if daring her to refuse.

"Wine? I have to travel tomorrow, Little Hua, and I don't want to set out with a heavy head."

Bai Hua waved her words away. "This is firewine, from the barbarian lands. Very rare! My husband will be aghast if we drink some, so I do hope he's punctilious in keeping records of his stores. He's adorable when he's angry."

Cho Lin shook her head ruefully and picked up her wine. Same old Little Hua. How many times had that impish smile led their little band into trouble?

"To old friends," Bai Hua said, and drank deeply.

"Old friends," Cho Lin murmured, sipping from her cup. The wine's spicy tartness surprised her, as it was far different than the sweet yellow and green wines from Shan. But it was delicious – perhaps she *could* find something to replace her nightly tea while traveling in the north.

"So, you must tell me what brings you to Ras Ami. You said you were traveling?"

Cho Lin licked her tingling lips. "Yes. I'm setting sail tomorrow for the barbarian city of Herath, in the desolate northlands."

Bai Hua raised her painted eyes. "Whatever would compel you to undertake such a terrible journey?"

"It's my father," Cho Lin began, swirling her wine. She had spent the walk over to Bai Hua's house carefully crafting her story. "I'm not sure if it's common knowledge yet, but he was killed while on a trading expedition in the north. My brother received word only a few weeks ago and sent a message to me while I was studying with the monks on Red Fang."

Bai Hua opened her mouth, as if she wanted to ask more about that, but bit back whatever she was going to say by taking another quick swig.

Cho Lin continued, knowing she would have to answer many questions later about Gold Leaf Temple – no doubt her time atop the mountain had been gossiped about among the nobles of Shan. "A few of his personal effects were returned to us, but there were a few priceless heirlooms – a moonstone ring from before the Raveling, a jade pin that had once belonged to the Empress Bin Mei – that are still missing. I am to see if they can be found."

Bai Hua set her cup down. "An adventure," she said, with a possibly-affected hint of envy. "How romantic."

"If you think sleeping in a cramped ship's cabin with only moldy rice to eat and stale water to drink sounds like an adventure, perhaps you could accompany me. We could share a room."

Bai Hua cocked her head, as if actually considering this offer. Then she sighed in mock sadness. "I have too many duties here, unfortunately. Though the thought of the two of us striking out together is rather tempting. A vagabond swordswoman and her trusted companion, earning our way in the world with the edge of your blade and my indefatigable charm." Bai Hua laughed again. She took another sip of wine, and when she set down the cup her face had grown serious. "Ah, Lin. How did you slip the bonds that bind us? How did you avoid all this?" Bai Hua gestured around the richly-appointed room, with its rosewood furnishings and long, flowing landscape paintings. "You should be married to some boring mandarin of the Court, and yet instead you are a disciple of Red Fang, on a quest that will take you into the barbarian lands."

A warmth had stolen into Cho Lin as Bai Hua talked. It pooled inside her belly, sending out tingling waves that made her hands feel numb and her head spin. How long had it been since she had drunk wine? This firewine from Gryx must be incredibly potent for a single cup to make her so unsteady.

Cho Lin rose, bumping the low table with her leg and knocking over the wine decanter and her empty cup. "I'm sorry," she said, holding tight to the back of her chair to keep herself from falling.

Bai Hua watched her calmly as Cho Lin stood there swaying. She took another unhurried sip.

The room tilted, and Cho Lin's breath rasped in her throat. She couldn't feel her arms or legs. "What –" she managed to whisper hoarsely, and then the hanging lights blurred as she toppled backwards. Her head struck the floor, but the pain was far away, like a bell ringing from a great distance.

She was falling within herself, and she became aware of a slow thudding, a sluggish pulsing that was gradually slackening.

Her heart. Her heart was stopping.

Cho Lin stared up at the ceiling, willing herself to live.

She was being moved. Someone had grabbed her ankles and was pulling her along the floor. Then the whisper of a panel being drawn back. Darkness. Her head struck the edges of stone steps again and again as she was pulled down a set of stairs. She couldn't feel anything, though. Cho Lin tried to twist her body and break free of whoever had a hold of her, but she was weaker than a babe.

The steps ended. Light flared in the blackness, a flickering torchlight. Above her there was an ancient picture painted on the ceiling. It filled her vision. She concentrated, trying to make out what it was, panic washing through her in waves.

A hill, with a great stone door set in its side. A procession of Shan nobles was approaching this entrance, men and women attired in clothing that had been popular long ago. And at the back of this column walked an old man in the robes of a warlock, his back bent by age and the terribleness of his task. In one hand he held the hand of a small black-haired child. In the other he held a curved knife.

Cho Lin tried to scream, but she only managed a thin rattling.

Hands grabbed her shoulders and pulled her into a sitting position, her back against a wall. Her head lolled as she struggled to keep it up. She was in a small room with earthen walls, empty of furnishings except for a slab of cracked black rock. Bai Hua crouched in front of her, studying Cho Lin as if deep in thought. She was tangling her fingers in her long, black hair, just like she had done when they were children together. *Bai Hua!* Cho Lin tried to scream. *What are you doing?*

Cho Lin heard the faint scrape of footsteps descending the stairs. Moments later Aunty Cao entered the room carrying the bag Cho Lin had brought to the house. The old woman untied its end and withdrew the sheathed Sword of Cho, then held it out for her mistress to take. Bai Hua rose and crossed the small chamber, gripping the proffered hilt with two hands. She carried it gingerly, as if it were a snake, and turned back to Cho Lin.

"It looks like any other sword," she said, slashing the air clumsily. "And yet gods have fallen before it."

Not gods! Cho Lin wanted to cry. *Demons! Monsters!* Anger and fear filled her. She was going to die.

Bai Hua approached her again, struggling to keep the tip of the heavy sword from dragging on the floor.

Cho Lin's pulse thundered in her ears, each beat slower than the last. Her heart was faltering, her blood congealing in her veins.

"The venom of the black silk spider," Bai Hua murmured, studying the spiraling lines of poetry that wrapped around the sword's dragon-bone hilt. "The same poison, actually, that turned your brother into a ruined husk."

Cho Lin would have gasped in surprise, if she could.

Bai Hua must have seen the slight widening of her eyes, and she smiled. "Yes. It was a servant of the Chosen who poisoned your brother, all those years ago. Her, in fact." She nodded towards Aunty Cao. The old woman stared at Cho Lin with coal-black eyes, her face expressionless. "Cao was a high priestess of the Raveling long before she became my nursemaid. She was the one who gave the poison to our servant in your house. What I slipped you was a far weaker dose, because I want you aware of everything I say, and of everything I do to you." She ran her finger along the edge of the sword, leaving a dark smear of blood.

The veil of terror that covered Cho Lin's racing mind lifted slightly. She drew a deep, shuddering breath. Wait. This was not how she was going to die. It couldn't be.

"I hated you," Bai Hua said throatily, twisting and turning the sword as the trickle of blood traveled down its length. "You acted nothing like a mandarin's daughter. You climbed trees and played with servants and challenged the boys to archery contests, and yet instead of being disciplined, everyone loved and praised you. If I had so much as fallen and skinned my knee my mother would have beaten me for conduct unbecoming of a Shan lady. You were always so *special*."

Cho Lin willed herself to ignore Bai Hua. She closed her eyes, focusing inward, on the Nothing within the Self. She struggled to pull herself deeper into the darkness.

"And Jai Po adored you, the fool. Followed you around like a puppy. I think he loved you up until the day I cut out his heart and fed it to his dogs."

Cho Lin concentrated on her pulse. The old masters, the ones who had attained Enlightenment, had claimed such perfect mastery over their bodies that they could slow their heart when they needed to stop poison from spreading. But this venom was different: the paralysis was coming about because her heart was grinding to a halt. Could she . . . could she quicken it again?

Far away, the words of Bai Hua floated on a bitter wind, but she paid them no heed.

"They were innocent. The last innocents of Shan, for after what happened to them we were all stained with a terrible guilt. And that can only be washed away when the Raveling covers this land. We escaped once, when we should not have."

Cho Lin pushed deeper within herself. Down here, in the depths, the shuddering of her heart consumed her, drowning out the rantings of her childhood friend. *Doom. Doom. Doom.*

She focused on the emptiness, embracing it. She became a part of that slowing drumbeat, letting it mingle with her inner Self. An absolute calmness filled her. Then, as easily and as thoughtlessly as if she was lifting her arm, she made her heart quicken. Cho Lin felt her blood begin to flow faster in her veins, and a tingling warmth spread along her limbs.

Her finger twitched.

"So fitting, that the very sword that banished the Chosen will cut off the head of the last descendant of Cho Xin."

Cho Lin opened her eyes. Bai Hua loomed over her, the Sword of Cho upraised, her face contorted by hate and madness.

The dam inside her buckled and burst, and suddenly she could move again. With a strangled cry of triumph Cho Lin surged to her feet, pulling one of her butterfly swords from where it had been hidden within the folds of her robes. She buried the short blade hilt-deep in Bai Hua's stomach, reaching up with her free hand to catch her childhood friend's arm as she tried to bring the sword down upon her head.

For a moment they were locked together, their faces nearly touching. Bai Hua's eyes were rounded by shock, and blood trickled from the corner of her mouth.

"That's for poisoning my brother, you bitch," Cho Lin snarled, then ripped her butterfly sword free. Bai Hua stumbled backwards and collapsed, the Sword of Cho slipping from her fingers to clatter on the floor.

Cho Lin turned just as Aunty Cao flew at her, screeching, long black nails reaching for her neck. She twisted away from the old woman, letting her rush past her, then slashed out with her sword. Aunty Cao's shrieking abruptly ceased as her head separated from her shoulders.

Silence.

Cho Lin sank to her knees and drew in a shuddering sob.

Time passed. How long, Cho Lin wasn't sure, but when she finally surfaced from her shock she thought it was deep into the night. She had calmed her breathing, but there was a new sound in the room: a swarm of bloodbelly flies had descended upon the bodies of Bai Hua and Aunty Cao, and their droning filled the small chamber.

Slowly, Cho Lin stood, still a bit unsteady from the lingering effects of the poison, and returned the Sword of Cho to its bag. She forced herself to stare at her old friend. Bai Hua's eyes were wide and glassy, and her lips were parted in open-mouthed surprise. Her delicate hands clutched at the wound in her belly; her beautiful cheongsam dress had been shredded and stained with blood.

The impossibility of this situation made Cho Lin dizzy. Behind concealing hands, there had been whisperings about how members of the Jade Court and their families still pledged loyalty to the Raveling. Titillating gossip, but very few truly believed such things actually existed, including Cho Lin. Her father had, though, and had made it his task while advising the emperor to try and uproot the last twisted remnants of that terrible faith. But he had found little evidence, despite much effort.

And yet here was proof the cult had survived. This earthen chamber was old, and from the look of the chipped black altar it had been used for many years. How many others had spilled out their life here? Bloodbelly flies nested where there was death and laid their eggs in necrotic flesh. This unholy sanctum had seen sacrifices before.

Cho Lin stumbled up the rough-hewn stone steps and emerged again into the empty parlor. Nothing had changed – the silver decanter was still on its side, the wine cups knocked to the floor from when Cho Lin had upset the table as she'd fallen. Were there no other servants in the house? Perhaps they had been dismissed for the night, so they could not witness what their mistress had planned.

The door to the underground chamber was an ingenuously wrought panel that blended perfectly with the walls, and Cho Lin carefully slid it closed. If the servants in this house were not aware of the evil deeds done beneath this roof, then the bodies of Bai Hua and Aunty Cao might remain hidden for days. By the time they were discovered, Cho Lin would be on a ship to Herath, and beyond the reach of any judicar who might want to ask her questions.

Cho Lin glanced down at her bloodstained robes. She would have to return to the Cho compound by way of the back alleys – she looked like she had been the victim of a robbery. Then she would gather her things and head down to the docks, hopefully before the sky began to lighten. She would find the *Loyal Gull* and convince her captain that they should sail immediately, without the rest of her companions.

Tonight had proven one thing to Cho Lin – she could trust no one.

9: KEILAN

EARLY THE NEXT morning they were ushered by a troop of guardsmen through the awakening city. Keilan hardly recognized Lyr after the storm: the brooding edifices of dark stone now gleamed in the light of a new day, and the twisted stone creatures crouching on the roofs had in turn become the perches of countless dark-winged birds. Their challenges to the dawn could be heard above the clangor of the streets below, where merchants and tradespeople pulled tarps from over their stalls and took down storm shutters, sloshing through puddles as they prepared for their first customers of the day.

As they approached one of the city's smaller southern gates, Keilan saw the same ornate carriage the Lady Numil had ridden inside during the pilgrimage to the Oracle's temple the day before. This must have been one of the less trafficked entrances to the city, as no other travelers looked to be preparing to leave through its low stone archway. Perhaps it was a night gate, as usually they were only kept open after the sun had set. Three horses laden with saddlebags cropped at a patch of grass near the gate, their reins held by one of the demon-helmed guardsmen. The other warriors of Lyr moved a respectful distance away so they could not hear what was being said, and spread out across the road to keep the curious away.

The Crone's servant Telion was astride his own mount, a garron with a dappled gray coat that matched the color of the bald warrior's leather armor.

"They've come," he said loudly, leaning forward in his saddle when he caught sight of Keilan and Nel. Another servant in the livery of Lyr swung open the carriage's door, and then helped the Lady Numil climb down. She emerged blinking from the darkened interior, wrapped in so many layers of shawls to ward away the dawn chill that Keilan doubted he would have recognized her if they had passed her on the streets.

"It's good to see you both this morning," she said, her black eyes twinkling above the scarf wound around her face. "I'd half feared you would change your mind after a night's rest."

Keilan glanced at Nel, but she did not meet his gaze, continuing to stare straight ahead with her jaw clenched. They'd argued long into the night, in fact, with Nel trying to convince him that the Crone's plan was a dangerous gamble, and that they should return immediately to Herath. But just as the storm had passed, leaving behind a reborn city, so Keilan had felt the same after waking this morning. This was what he had to do – for the Oracle who had sacrificed herself to give this warning, for everyone he loved who would suffer if the dark future he had glimpsed came to pass, and also, it was true, for himself. These were the mysteries that had defined him his entire life. Who was he? Where had his mother come from?

"We've arrived at something of an agreement, Lady Numil," said Nel. "We'll go east to try and find this sorceress . . . but there's something we need from you, as well."

The old woman folded her arms and arched a brow, and Nel stumbled over her words, as if suddenly realizing she was making a demand of one of the most powerful women in Lyr. For someone who had grown up in the tangled alleyways of the Warrens that would certainly be more than a little disconcerting.

"You must tell Queen d'Kara what happened here. What we saw. And why we're not returning to Herath. The threat of these demons hangs over everyone, and with her power and the magic of the Scholia she might truly be the world's best hope, instead of this mysterious sorceress. I don't know . . . I don't know if she'll agree with what we are doing, but I hope she'll understand why Keilan believes we must."

The old woman bowed her head slightly. "Of course. This matter passes beyond the petty rivalries of cities and kingdoms. I had already planned to send back the rangers – once, of course, you've put enough distance between yourselves and Lyr that the trail has gone cold – and I will send a letter or accompany them myself. I will try and convince her that your decision to seek out this sorceress was wise."

"Please do that," Nel said quickly, and for the first time Keilan saw how nervous she truly was. "The queen has a legendary temper, and if she feels we betrayed her we'll find ourselves in a cell beneath Saltstone soon after returning to Herath. She does not forgive quickly."

"I know the queen. She is passionate and strong-willed, and sometimes impetuous. However, she is also no fool. She may rage at first, I'll grant, but by the time she sees you again I believe she will have come to understand why you have done what you did. There is also some respect between us, and my words will carry weight."

A note of resignation crept into Nel's voice. "Then that's it, I suppose." She turned to the gate. "We should be off."

"Wait," the old woman said, holding up a small silver bell. "Keilan, I have a gift for you." She rang the bell, and behind her the liveried servant drew forth from the shadowed confines of the carriage a long object wrapped in dark cloth. With quick steps he approached Keilan and held it out for him to take.

"Careful, it's sharp," the old woman said as Keilan accepted the object.

He unwound the cloth, revealing a sword in a black scabbard. The silver guard was finely wrought to look like a pair of outstretched wings, and the pommel was carved into the head of a raptor, perhaps a falcon, with two glittering red stones for eyes. The grip was ebonwood, smooth and dark. Keilan touched the hilt lightly, his breath stolen by the beauty of the sword.

"I can't accept this, Lady Numil. It's too fine a weapon for me."

The old woman snorted. "Too late, you've already taken it. My house is filled with such rubbish, and most of it stays on the wall covered with dust. My worthless nephews have no use for a blade like this – they just want to swagger around with the long dueling swords that are so popular nowadays, pretending to be bravos."

"Any gifts for me?" Nel asked, leaning closer to inspect the sword. The shadow she'd been laboring under seemed to lift slightly as she studied the old woman's gift. "Something also jeweled, perhaps?"

"How about this, little thief: I will pardon your past transgressions in our city. There are a few rich merchants and even an archon or two who remember you."

Nel sighed. "I suppose it would be nice to visit the city without fear of being clapped in chains." She pointed at the grazing horses. "Those are for us, yes?"

The old woman nodded. "You've enough gold and silver in those saddle bags to stay at the finest inns from here to Theris, although I would caution against flaunting your wealth on the road."

"Well, now Keilan has a sword and I have my daggers, but will that be enough to deter thieves? We don't make the most imposing pair." Nel nodded towards the old woman's servant astride his garron. "Is he coming with us? He looks like he can handle those swords."

Lady Numil shook her head. "You wouldn't want Telion as your companion. Handy enough with those swords, but take him away from his soft bed and mince pies and he gets quite irritable."

The mounted warrior spread his arms wide. "I am a – how did you say it, Lady Numil? An . . ."

"Epicurean."

"Yes, very epicurious. I've come to enjoy the best things in life after working in your house."

Keilan frowned in confusion. He'd thought Telion was meant to accompany them as well, since he'd arrived on horseback. "Then who?" He paused when he saw Nel's face had paled as she stared past him, back the way they had come.

"No," she whispered, and then again more forcefully. "No!"

Keilan twisted around, following where she was looking, and he felt a stone settle in his stomach. Striding towards them, trailed by a laughing throng of dirty-faced children, was the Pure.

He had again donned his white-scale armor, and his eyes flashed with Ama's holy radiance. His hand rested on the copper hilt of his white-metal sword, and his unsullied cloak rippled behind him in the breeze.

When the pack of urchins saw the line of guardsmen up ahead blocking the road they turned and fled, shrieking in exaggerated fear. The paladin did not seem to notice that he'd lost his entourage as he passed through the guardsmen and came to stand before them. He bowed to Lady Numil, his face impassive. As he straightened, his burning gaze found Keilan, and he nodded slightly.

"What is he doing here?" Nel demanded. Keilan felt a twinge of unease when he noticed one of her daggers had appeared in her hand.

"He will be your protection," the old woman replied calmly.

"Protection?" Nel cried. "He's tried to kidnap Keilan twice! He wants to drag him back to Menekar, then cut him open and see if he bleeds golden light!"

The paladin turned to fully face Keilan. "I'm sorry, Keilan. It is my order's sacred duty to protect the world from the dangers of sorcery. I've never held any malice towards you . . . and, to be truthful, I fervently hoped you would find salvation in the light of Ama. Surely on your travels – and in the terrible future we saw together in the cavern – you have witnessed what horror sorcery can bring down."

"Then you still wish to take him back to your temple in Menekar?" Nel asked. "Sacrifice him to your god?"

The Pure matched the knife's angry glare with his own burning gaze. "I want the world to be safe. It was my city, my home we saw utterly destroyed. A million people live in Menekar – how many escaped that devastation?" He nodded towards the old woman. "Lady Numil has convinced me. She has told me you will try to find that sorceress who can slay those demon children. I do not care to ally myself with a sorceress such as her, but if she can avert the destruction of Menekar, I must."

"There is no safer way to travel," the old woman said quickly, interjecting before Nel could respond. "I could send a host of guardsmen with you flying the colors of Lyr, but that will not stop the bandit princes of Kesh's red desert. They've been bold in recent months, even raiding well-protected caravans along the Iron Road. But no robber would be foolish enough to attack a paladin of Ama returning west with a boy and a young woman. If word trickled out the response from Menekar would be swift and brutal. Even the padarasha might send out his celijan riders, as he still adheres to the old treaties his forebears signed. The Pure are not to be disturbed when they are hunting those with the taint of sorcery."

What she said made sense, and Keilan saw that Nel realized this as well. But the blazing fury in her eyes had not subsided.

"What if you want us to lead you to this sorceress so that you can lop off her head? Would the leaders in your faith also agree to making common cause with those they have dedicated their lives to destroying?"

Keilan was surprised to see Senacus flinch at Nel's words. Something she had said had struck him.

The paladin turned again to Keilan, and for the first time the raw emotion Senacus felt could be heard, even though his calm expression still did not waver. "I descended beneath Uthmala to save you from dark sorcery."

It was true. Keilan remembered the horde of monstrous spiders surging against the white crescent of the paladin's blade – he and Nel would have died if Senacus had not come to their rescue.

"When I returned to Menekar, my order's High Seneschal told me that because I rescued you and the Dymorian magister I should open my veins across the Radiant Altar. It was only because I could now sense you and they wished to bring you back to Menekar that I was spared. They told me I should not have compromised, that you should not ally with a lesser evil to destroy a greater."

The paladin drew in a deep breath. He glanced at Lady Numil, hesitating for a moment before continuing. "But I know now that corruption has taken root in the highest ranks of the faith. The shadowblade who traveled with me was a sorcerer, and someone in the temple must have been familiar with his true nature. I cannot trust the mendicants of the temple – and so I must rely on Ama's guidance. I prayed last night for an understanding of what I should do." The paladin took a step towards Keilan, his voice almost pleading. "And Ama's answer was revealed. I must be your guardian on this quest."

Keilan swallowed, his gaze flickering between the paladin and Nel. He did not hate Senacus. Even on the road to Chale, after he had been taken from his village, the paladin had spoken kindly to him and tried to reassure him about what was to come. Then Senacus had saved their lives under Uthmala, risking his own. And even though the paladin had traveled across Araen months later to steal him away from Saltstone, in the end he had abandoned Keilan at the gates of Herath, betraying the mission given to him by his masters in Menekar.

Still, Senacus had been an ally and guide to the man who killed Xin. Nel had not forgiven him, that was evident. She had chased him all the way to Lyr with bloody revenge in her thoughts, and now she was being asked to accept him as a companion. Could she? Or would she stick a dagger in him the first time he turned his back to her?

Keilan felt the weight of many eyes on him. Everyone seemed to be waiting for what he had to say. A wash of cold fear went through him – was he the leader here? Would they all truly defer to him and accept what he decided?

Calming the nervous fluttering in his stomach, Keilan stepped towards Senacus and held out his arm. "We need your help."

10: SENACUS

THE IRON ROAD. Stretching from the Gilded City of Lyr on the Derravin Ocean to Gryx on the coast of the Broken Sea, it was the artery upon which the wealth of kingdoms flowed. Merchants carrying spices from the Sunset Lands, ebonwood from Dymoria, and intricate bone carvings from the artisans of Seri all traveled south from the Cities, skirting the fringes of the red desert and passing through the bazaar tent-towns that traded in the riches of ancient Kesh. Then, laden with new treasures – richly embroidered carpets, strings of shimmering pearls, and fragrant myrrh and sandalwood – the caravans would continue on to the slave-city of Gryx, where the goods would be sold and the wagons filled again with Shan silks and celadon, silver jewelry from the Shattered Kingdoms, and iron from the black mines where the Fettered of Gryx endlessly toiled.

Despite the Lady Numil's dire warnings of Keshian bandit princes, Senacus knew the road was the safest route across Araen. Storms like the one that had just lashed Lyr were common in the Derravin during the winter months, and therefore traveling by ship this time of year would carry some risk. Along the Iron Road every city and kingdom benefited from the stream of merchants and travelers, so a great effort was made to keep it maintained and free of thieves. It was far safer than the Wending Way, the northern road binding east and west that Senacus had traveled with Demian on his way from Menekar to Herath. But still, on their own Nel and Keilan likely would have encountered some dangers. Not now, though, in the company of a paladin of Ama.

Senacus twisted around in his saddle, half-expecting to find himself alone on the road. But a few horse-lengths behind him rode Keilan, slumped a little as if struggling with the weight of his new responsibility, and even farther back was Nel. She hadn't sheathed the dagger she'd drawn at the city gates and was using it to cut slices from a golden pear she must have found in her saddlebags. Beyond her, barely visible over the forest through which they'd just ridden, were the crenellated tops of Lyr's tallest towers. He returned his gaze to Nel and found her scowling at him. Sighing, he looked away.

His life's path had taken a dramatic new direction over the last few days. During his frantic flight down the coast he'd thought it almost certain the rangers of Dymoria would catch him before he could find sanctuary in Lyr. The decision he'd been faced with then was whether to die with his sword in his hand or allow himself to be returned to Saltstone in chains. But, to his surprise, the old mare he'd traded for after he'd exhausted his own horse had proven far hardier than he could have hoped, and suddenly it had seemed possible that he could reach the Gilded City before his pursuers. For a moment, he'd allowed himself to consider what he should do then – return to Menekar and try to unmask the sorcerers who had insinuated themselves in the highest corridors of power, or bring his suspicions to one of the abbots of the larger temples outside of the holy city.

Then had come the confrontation outside the gates of Lyr, his brief imprisonment in the archon palace, and his interrogation by the Lady Numil and the Council of Black and White. Senacus had been confident the archons would not wish to antagonize Menekar, and that soon he'd be released, but then the summons from the Oracle had arrived. Such a request could not be ignored – there was more than a little doctrinal confusion in the Tractate regarding the nature of Lyr's Oracle, but all the sources agreed she had strange powers that must be respected. Even High Mendicants and emperors had made the pilgrimage to beg for her insights into the future. He'd been expecting some vague pronouncement he'd have to carry to men wiser than him for interpretation, but there, in that forsaken cavern, he'd actually suffered the horror that was hurtling towards the world.

It had left him shattered. Menekar would be destroyed, its temples and palaces and soaring walls reduced to dust. A chalk-white sky that mirrored the plains below would be flensed open, bleeding strange colors, while the sun, Ama's eternal throne, had vanished. And those blackened corpses, twisted together to make that unholy temple . . . Senacus hadn't told the others, but he'd recognized one of those unfortunate souls. It had been the High Seneschal, the old paladin who had entrusted him with the task of bringing Keilan back to Menekar. He'd been suspended over the arched entrance where the demon children had emerged, his outstretched arms and legs brushing a ring of severed arms that had been twisted to form some monstrous parody of the thorned wheels on which heretics of Ama were left to die.

Only sorcery could have produced this devastation. A thousand years ago the wizards of old had broken the world, killing millions as empires vanished in an instant. Now the Oracle had gifted him with the knowledge that a new doom was coming, and this time Menekar would not be spared. Forestalling this cataclysm was the highest goal of the Pure. It was the reason they had ranged the lands for centuries, seeking out those tainted by sorcery and bringing them back to Menekar to be Cleansed.

Keilan had some connection to all this. He was uncommonly strong, a sorcerer unlike any Senacus had sensed before. The Crimson Queen wanted him. Demian and the mysterious, powerful sorcerers the shadowblade had been allied with wanted him. And the Oracle had shown Keilan the vision for a reason – the Lady Numil had told Senacus the boy knew the silver-haired sorceress who had opposed the demon children, and that he was going to try and find her in the hope of enlisting her aid before the doom came down. Lady Numil had then asked Senacus if he would accompany Keilan on this quest. He had spent much of last night praying over what he should do.

And now here he was, guardian to a boy who must still be wary of him and a young woman who looked like she wanted to put a dagger in his heart.

"Senacus."

He returned from his musings to find that Keilan had ridden up beside him. "Yes?"

"Do you know why I followed you to Lyr?"

Senacus shook his head. He'd wondered about that and had been planning on asking the boy after they stopped for their evening meal.

"I told you that night in Herath that I'd seen Demian in the memories of another sorcerer. That they'd participated in some ceremony that caused the cataclysms a thousand years ago."

"Aye. I remember."

"There were others in that ancient memory, including that sorceress we saw in the Oracle's vision. She . . . she looked like my mother. It's why I came after you. I hoped you'd know something about Demian that would give me some clue about that sorceress."

Senacus glanced sidelong at Keilan. "So you did not come for revenge?"

"No. I don't hate you like . . ." His words trailed away, but Senacus knew of whom he was speaking.

"I never learned anything about Demian. I had my suspicions, but I wasn't certain he was a sorcerer until your words convinced me after I took you from Saltstone."

"I know that. I think I knew that before I joined the rangers hunting you. I just had to do *something*."

"I don't even know if the shadowblade survived. He was supposed to meet us before we reached the gates of Herath, but he never did."

"Xin stabbed him. He fled, but Nel thinks the wound was fatal."

"Xin?"

"He was my friend." Keilan's words were heavy with sadness. "The warrior who was with Nel when she found you standing over me in Saltstone. Demian killed him. He was . . . he was special to Nel. That's why she hates you."

Senacus twisted the reins he held, chiding himself for being so blind. So that was it. He'd thought her distrust and hatred were because she was a companion to a magister of the Scholia, and he had led the assassins inside Saltstone. No, it was more personal than that. Her lover was dead because of him. Silence stretched as Senacus considered this.

"The Iron Road . . . does it pass near Ver Anath?"

He nodded at Keilan's question. "Aye. Cuts through the heart of the city. We'll be there in a few days. I would suggest we spend the night inside enjoying the luxuries of city living. It can be hard to find a comfortable bed and a bath on the road."

"There's someone I want to meet in Ver Anath. A seeker of the Reliquary. He's a wise man, and he might know something that can help us."

Senacus nodded. "Very well."

"Good. I'll go tell Nel."

Before Keilan turned his horse around he reached out and laid his hand on Senacus's arm. "Thank you for coming with us."

Even through his armor the boy's touch burned him, and Senacus had to restrain himself from flinching. Such raw, festering power. Was it a strength that could be used to inflict a new cataclysm upon the world? The thought chilled him. He truly did not want to have to kill the boy.

The weather worsened as they pressed east along the Iron Road. A succession of brief, intense showers – perhaps shreds of the storm that had so recently battered Lyr – left them soaked and turned the hard-packed dirt road to churned mud. Luckily, there were no shortages of inns and eating houses between the Gilded Cities, and every evening they found a roaring hearth and a hot bowl of stew to banish the day's chill. Yet even as their clothes dried and their hands warmed, the cold hostility coming from Nel did not lessen. She refused to sit at the same table as him, and since Keilan always joined her that meant Senacus ate alone, as when other travelers noticed his eyes and the armor beneath his cloak they quickly moved away as well. He was used to this: the paladins of Ama always walked a solitary path. The holy radiance of Ama made most men uncomfortable, for even in the souls of the faithful there were dark corners they did not want to be illuminated.

Still, Senacus wished for Keilan's company. There was much he wanted to ask the boy . . . and if this continued all the way to the Shattered Kingdoms it would be a long and lonely journey.

In the late morning of the third day, cracks began to appear in the stone-gray sky. By the afternoon the clouds had cleared completely, and not long after that Senacus caught his first glimpse of the Scholar's City. It was a brief flash on the horizon, like steel catching sunlight at just the right angle.

"Ver Anath," Senacus cried to the pair well behind him on the road.

A moment later Keilan cantered up alongside, shielding his eyes against the brightness of the day.

"Truly? I can't see anything yet."

"Look," Senacus said, pointing into the distance. "Can you see that glint over those hills?"

"That's the city?"

"Aye. The greatest building of the Reliquary is crowned by a mighty dome sheathed with gleaming red tiles. When the sun rises and sets it can look like a flame burning over the city."

"We are candles in the dark," Keilan said softly.

"What's that?"

Keilan ran a hand through his hair, still peering intently at where he had seen the flash. "Seeker Garmond told me that was written over the entrance to the largest library in the Reliquary."

"This is the seeker you wish to speak with?"

"Yes. He's a wise man. And . . . I have to tell him about Xin."

Senacus glanced at Keilan, and then at Nel behind them. "You were all companions?"

"Not just companions. Friends. Xin and I . . . we spent many evenings in Seeker Garmond's wagon. I was teaching him how to read – he was a slave, a Fist warrior, and learning was forbidden in Gryx."

"Speaking of forbidden things," Senacus said, "I won't be welcome in the Reliquary."

Keilan turned to him in surprise. "Oh? Why's that? What did you do?"

Senacus chuckled when he saw Keilan's face. "It's nothing to do with me personally. The faithful of Ama and the seekers of the Reliquary have a somewhat fraught relationship. The seekers wish to explore all the world's mysteries . . . and that includes sorcery. The Pure, however, demand all sorcerous tracts be destroyed, to stop others from pursuing the arcane.

A thousand years ago, soon after the cataclysms, the armies of Menekar marched over the Spine to restore order and cleanse the land of the sorcery that had fractured the world. They forced every city and kingdom still standing to give over any sorcerers that survived to the Pure, and also to sign treaties promising that they would allow the paladins of Ama to search their lands for the remnants of magic. The treaty signed with the seekers states that once every three years a delegation of the Pure will have unfettered access to all the libraries of the Reliquary, to make sure they have not resumed their investigations into sorcery. I was once a part of such an embassy. But at any other time, the paladins of Ama are not welcome within."

"Will you wait for us outside?"

"I'm not a dog, Keilan. I'll find us some rooms in the city. There's an inn where the Pure usually stay, The White Hart. The owner is devout, and we can be assured safety and privacy there."

They rode on, and soon Ver Anath resolved from the midday haze. Behind the city walls soared a forest of white spires, and looming over everything was a great edifice of dark gray stone that would have dwarfed the fortress of Saltstone. It looked to be several huge buildings grafted together from different eras, though the construction at its heart – to Senacus's eyes – resembled the great temple of Ama in Menekar. Mostly that was because of the massive dome that bulged into the sky, though the red tiles here made the Reliquary look like it contained a great flame. The temple of Ama was covered in gold leaf that in the sun was supposed to transform it into a physical incarnation of the Radiant Father's holy light.

Beyond the city the Dreaming Sea spread like a sheet of beaten silver, speckled with the sails of ships swirling around Ver Anath's green-stone harbor. Senacus remembered the wild, white-capped fury of the Derravin, and it was a stark contrast to these tranquil waters. It was easy to imagine how the Dreaming Sea had been named.

Guardsmen in meticulously polished armor holding kite shields emblazoned with a thorned rose watched them as they passed through the city gates. Within, the buildings were constructed of either white wood or gray stone, and most were veined with creepers and vines. When Senacus had last been in the city it had been during the summer months, and these walls had been a riot of colors, the air filled with the heady scent of countless blooming flowers. Now, only a few pale blue winter roses dotted the vines, and Senacus thought it lent the city a kind of stark beauty.

He slid from his horse and waited for Nel and Keilan. "I'll meet you later at The White Hart," he said when they finally reached him and dismounted. "It's easy enough to find. One of the largest inns in the merchants' district." He gestured at the mountain of gray stone rising over the city. "I don't think you'll have much trouble finding your way to the Reliquary."

"No . . . no," Keilan replied, staring up in evident awe. Nel seemed more interested in the delicate flowers clinging to the wall near her, and as he watched she leaned closer, reaching out as if she was about to pluck one.

"Don't do that," Senacus said, more harshly than he intended. Nel jerked her hand back as if he'd told her poisonous spiders nested among the vines. "They're very protective of the flowers here," he explained, softening his tone. "You'll be whipped and spend a day in the stocks if they catch you pulling one from the walls."

She arched an eyebrow. "Truly? Over a flower?"

"So I was told," Senacus replied.

"A sensitive people," she said tersely, brushing past him as she led her horse down the city's main thoroughfare. The avenue was lined with merchants' stalls, and judging by the crowds they must have arrived at one of the busiest times of day. "Come on, Keilan."

As the boy moved to follow her Senacus caught his arm, and the tingling puissance he felt through Keilan's tunic made him shiver. "Be careful. This is not usually a dangerous place, but there may be others out there still looking for you."

"I will be," Keilan said, and then he hurried to catch up with Nel before she vanished within the loud bargaining throng of Ver Anathans.

Senacus watched them until they disappeared, trying to ignore his twinge of worry, and then started down a different street. He remembered the way only vaguely, but luck was with him this day and eventually the road emptied into a large square dominated by a marble building of a familiar style. A circular window of stained glass was above the entrance, a golden disc at its center. Several of the faithful were prostrating themselves on reed mats in the shadow of the building, mumbling the prayers of redemption and forgiveness written down long ago in the Tractate. As Senacus passed between them a few noticed him and gasped in surprise, then redoubled their chanting.

At the doorway to the temple a young mendicant met him, the awe in his face evident. "Holy brother," he breathed, sketching the eternal sun in the air between them. "Welcome to the house of Ama."

Senacus returned the gesture. "Brother. I need to write and send an urgent missive to the High Seneschal."

The mendicant ushered him inside, bobbing his head. "Of course. Come in, come in. The abbot's chambers have ink and parchment, and I'll bring you the temple's seal. We can dispatch a courier . . . "

The mendicant's eyes suddenly widened as he caught sight of something. He pointed, his face pale. Curious, Senacus followed his gaze to his own belt, from which hung a slightly wilted blue rose.

11: KEILAN

"WAIT HERE," SAID the hook-nosed scholar, frowning in obvious disapproval as he studied Keilan and Nel from behind his desk. He gestured for the young boy hovering beside him to lean in closer, and then whispered something into the child's ear. The boy listened, gave a quick nod, and then dashed across the vast hall towards a massive archway that hinted at an even greater space beyond, his sandals slapping on the marble floor.

Nel seemed oblivious to the scholar's disdain. She rocked back on her heels and started whistling, hooking her thumbs into her belt. Suddenly, she sneezed violently, the sound echoing in the Reliquary's antechamber and making the scholar jump – coincidentally just as he bent again over the ancient book he was reading.

"Sorry," Nel said, sniffling as she wiped her nose. "It's chilly outside. I seem to have caught something."

The scholar closed the grimoire loudly and returned his attention to the intruders. When they'd first entered this antechamber to the Reliquary proper he'd kept them waiting for nearly a full watch, and when he'd finally deigned to notice them he'd been dismissive, telling them in no uncertain terms that they should leave and not disturb the seekers. Whatever they wanted paled in comparison to the importance of the work being done within. When Nel had shown him Vhelan's seal and claimed to be a representative from the magisters of the Scholia his eyes had widened slightly, but it wasn't until Keilan asked after Seeker Garmond by name that he had grudgingly agreed to send a message to the scholar.

Nel gestured at the huge statue looming over the scholar's desk. It dominated the great room, an older man in flowing robes with his cowl pushed back to reveal a face with an expression of intense concentration, his stone brow furrowed and his lips pursed. "Is that one of the Aspects of Ama?" asked Nel. "Kind of looks like it."

"No," the seeker said, his tone suggesting he felt like he was speaking to a particularly stupid child. "That is Valichen II, a king of Ver Anath, who founded the Reliquary thousands of years ago. His earnest wish was to protect the knowledge of the world from ignorant barbarians." Keilan noticed the scholar put great stress on these last few words.

"A little under dressed for a king, isn't he? And where's his crown?"

"King Valichen cared little for the empty trappings of wealth and power. This statue is said to be a perfect likeness of the king, as he often dressed like a seeker himself to demonstrate his dedication to the search for truth."

"A perfect likeness?" Nel continued blandly, staring up at the statue. "So he was a giant, is what you're saying."

The scholar blinked in surprise, as if having trouble understanding what she'd just said, and then his face colored. Keilan wiped his mouth to hide the smile he couldn't hold back. The seeker muttered something under his breath and opened his book once more, pointedly ignoring them. Nel turned slightly towards Keilan and winked.

Keilan's heart lightened to see the improvement in Nel's mood. Ever since they'd parted ways with Senacus near the gates of Ver Anath it had been as if the old Nel had returned. It seemed the black clouds that had been following her since Xin's death had cleared a little.

The sound of sandals on stone approaching again pulled Keilan from his thoughts. Through the great archway an old man was hurrying towards them, his smile broad and his eyes bright, the boy who had been sent to fetch him struggling to keep up.

"Garmond!" Keilan cried, joy at seeing the scholar again swelling in his chest.

"My boy!" the seeker exclaimed, rushing to Keilan and gathering him into an embrace. "My Kalyuni scholar! So good to see you."

Garmond's gray robes smelled of dreamsmoke, and the heady scent brought back memories of the many evenings Keilan had spent with the scholar in his wagon along the Wending Way.

Garmond drew back a pace and looked him up and down. "You're getting bigger, I think, and it's only been a few months since last I saw you. Eating well in the Scholia, it looks like." His brow crinkled. "But what brings you here? Has the queen finally swallowed her pride and come to ask for our help in unraveling the mysteries of those old books you brought out of the Barrow?"

"No . . . much has happened. There was an attack –"

Nel cleared her throat loudly. "Seeker, is there somewhere we can talk that's more private?"

Garmond glanced at the scholar behind his desk and then the small boy, both of whom were watching this exchange with wide-eyed interest. "Yes, of course. We'll go up to my study. I have some interesting things to share with you, as well, investigations about that creature we encountered along the Way. Follow me."

"Wait," said the scholar, finding his voice again. "Seeker, I must insist that the girl stays here . . ." He trailed off as Garmond turned to him, bushy gray eyebrows raised.

"She is my personal guest, novice."

"Yes, but decorum insists . . ."

Garmond's face darkened, and he took a step closer to the scholar, who shrank back into his chair as the old man loomed over him. "Are you suggesting," the seeker said, his voice low and menacing, "that I am . . . *indecorous*?"

The younger scholar blanched. "No, no. Of course not, seeker. What a ridiculous thought."

Garmond's expression brightened again. "Good. I would hate for my old friend the Light of the Lore to hear any such whisperings."

"Yes, seeker." The scholar's face had paled, and he swallowed.

Garmond crooked a finger, inviting Keilan and Nel to follow. They fell in behind the scholar as he passed beneath the archway. "Come, boy. I know you must be excited – allow me to welcome you to the Reliquary of Ver Anath, the greatest repository of knowledge in the known world. And allow me to welcome you as well," he added quickly, briefly turning to bow to Nel. "Please excuse the rather rude welcome. For some reason, it was decided long ago that the most disagreeable seekers would be placed as doormen. Keeps us from being bothered by every fellow who wants his lineage traced or family heirloom appraised."

They passed through a labyrinth of twisting stone corridors, up and then down spiraling staircases, and through more vast, echoing halls populated by stern-looking stone men brandishing books and scrolls like they were weapons. Garmond continued talking the entire way, recounting in exhaustive detail the history of everything they encountered.

"That chamber was where Seeker Juniath researched and wrote his seminal treatise on the ethicists of ancient Menekar . . .

This cheerful fellow was known as Malakan the Dour, and they say the only time he smiled was when he saw the expression the masons had carved into this statue . . . That great chunk of stone is a shard of the Winding Stair, dragged all the way from Nes Vaneth many centuries ago, well before that city was claimed by the Skein . . . "

Suddenly he paused, as if just remembering something, and turned back to Keilan. "I knew I was being forgetful. Tell me, where is Xin? Did he stay behind in Herath? I miss his agreeable stoicism more than I thought I would."

Keilan felt a sharp pang in his chest.

Garmond's smile vanished when he saw Keilan's expression. "What's wrong?"

"Xin . . . " Keilan began, and then had to take a moment to gather himself. "He died."

Surprise shivered the old man's face, and he reached out to steady himself on Keilan's arm. "By the Lore. He was a good man. Did he . . . did he choose in the end to follow his brothers into the darkness?"

"No," Keilan said softly. "No. He died saving us."

"He saved me," said Nel, stepping forward. "He fought a shadowblade . . . a shadowblade who was also a sorcerer. The assassin escaped, but grievously wounded. He might have died, we don't know. He killed Xin with some black sorcery."

Garmond was silent for a long moment, his lips pursed, all traces of his good humor gone. "I sense much has happened since I left Herath. And I do not think you came here on a social visit. Something terrible is afoot. Quickly, no more dawdling."

Soon after, he stopped outside a nondescript wooden door, similar to the countless others they'd seen as they passed down the winding corridors. "And here we are. My study," the seeker said, fumbling with a key that was attached to his belt with a frayed bit of string.

"Come in, come in," he said, ushering them inside. "Find some seats."

"There are seats in here?" Nel asked incredulously, stepping carefully over a contraption of metal and glass tubes that had been inconveniently placed just at the entrance to the chamber. Keilan found himself wondering the same thing. Garmond's study looked to have been buried under an avalanche of books: grimoires with cracked leather bindings were stacked into unstable-looking towers, shelves were bursting with more volumes, and in the center of the room, which looked like it had once been a clear space, the stone floor was covered with open folios showing intricate drawings and sketches of strange-looking machines.

Garmond moved with practiced grace through the clutter and slipped behind a mound that could have been a desk hiding beneath the detritus. Keilan noticed several artifacts he had first glimpsed in the seeker's wagon those many months ago: the jeweled skull of some large rodent, a crystal sphere wedged atop an ebony stand, and an unstoppered bottle of scholar's milk, the deadly libation which had nearly blinded Vhelan when the wizard had tried to match Garmond drink for drink one night along the Wending.

The seeker gestured at several stools that were currently serving as perches for a number of long, coiled snakes that looked to have been preserved sometime in the previous century. "You can move my collection of Keshian asps. Be careful. I had their poison glands removed quite a while ago, but there's still some residual venom that leaks up through the scales. It might make your fingers numb."

Nel shuddered, staring at the colorful serpents in obvious revulsion. "I hate snakes," she muttered, and dutifully Keilan stepped forward to push the snakes off the stools. They slid to the floor with a hollow thump. A tingling spread up his fingers where he had touched the scales, and he dispatched a silent prayer to the Deep Ones that Garmond hadn't accidentally skipped one of the snakes while arranging their de-venoming.

The seeker found a chair beneath the clutter and sat, steepling his hands in front of his face. "Now, tell me what has happened."

"Assassins attacked Saltstone," Nel said after a quick glance at Keilan. "Dozens of shadowblades swarmed the fortress, hunting for magisters. At least a score of sorcerers were killed, including several of the queen's senior advisors."

"By the Lore," Garmond whispered, pulling at his beard.

"And the kith'ketan were not alone. There was a paladin as well, one of the Pure. He tried to steal Keilan away with the help of a strange shadowblade, different than the others. One who used magic."

"A paladin and a sorcerer, working together?" Garmond murmured. "How could that be?"

"Yes, it seems impossible," Nel said pointedly, and Keilan knew she was directing this at him.

"The man wasn't just a shadowblade or a sorcerer," Keilan said, refusing to look at her. "He was a thousand years old, an immortal from before the great cataclysms. I saw him in a vision."

The seeker blinked his watery blue eyes and shook his head, as if trying to make sense of this. "What are you speaking about, boy? You'll have to start from the beginning."

And so he did. Keilan explained about the arrival of the Min-Ceruthan sorcerer Jan in the court, his revelations that there were other powerful immortals interested in the rise of Cein d'Kara and her Scholia, and the queen's efforts to exhume his buried memories. He spoke of what he and the queen had witnessed inside Jan's mind, the terrible sorcery that had used the devastation of the cataclysms to fuel the spell that rendered a cabal of powerful sorcerers immortal. When Keilan had finished, ending with him stumbling down from Ravenroost and collapsing in Saltstone, Nel picked up the tale, describing Keilan's kidnapping and the fight between the mysterious shadowblade-sorcerer and Xin.

"Some version of this tale will arrive in this city shortly," Nel finished. "I'd say within a day or two there will be rumors swirling in the streets. Likely the Light of the Lore has already received a bird about what happened."

The surprise was plain in the seeker's face. "I'm so sorry to have left you both and Xin. I thought . . . I thought I should return to the Reliquary and find out something about the creature that ambushed us along the Way. I never thought you'd still be in danger."

Nel waved away Garmond's words. "You couldn't have done anything, seeker. You're not a warrior or a wizard."

"Did you discover anything?" Keilan asked, leaning forward.

"I did," Garmond said, his hand drifting to a haphazard stack of ancient books. "Not much, and most of it is written in High Kalyuni. But enough for the rough history of these creatures to emerge. Fascinating reading, actually." The shadow was lifting from the seeker's face as he spoke, the edge of excitement Keilan remembered from whenever something had piqued his curiosity returning.

Garmond rummaged among the mess and finally pulled out a crisp sheet of vellum that didn't look nearly as old as the other yellowing fragments of paper and ragged tomes covering his desk. "The translation from High Kalyuni is taxing, as I know you are aware, Keilan. And I have had to beg and cajole my colleagues just to do this much. But there are some fascinating insights about that monster we encountered. This is from the personal diary of one of the blue wizards of Kalyuni, written perhaps a decade before the cataclysms." Seeker Garmond cleared his throat and began to read aloud:

"We found another one this morning. Cherise has some special talent for ferreting out the creatures; she says they smell different, almost stale, like a wash of air escaping from a tomb that has been sealed up for ages. I do not notice anything. Their mannerisms, the way they move . . . the illusion is so perfect because they appear so mundane. The one today was a butcher, a plump little man with a cheerful smile. We came across it during a routine sweep of the Shards. It was out in front of its shop, hacking away at a slab of goat, carrying on trivial conversations with the people in its neighborhood. Cherise stiffened beside me, and then without hesitating she unleashed Javinka's Holocaust.

"The people of the Shards are not accustomed to wizard duels in their markets. Everyone screamed and fled, terrified beyond reason. Which was good, because only we hunters saw the transformation. Within that pillar of silver fire the genthyaki's shadowy outline unfolded, swelling twice as large as it had been before. It screeched like a wounded animal, covered in rippling flames. We joined our power to Cherise, creating a swirling maelstrom that utterly obliterated everything.

"The creature was destroyed. I know the Greater Gendern wants one of these monsters brought before him to study, but I've heard of what they are capable of doing when they are not taken unawares. Zinoch said they tried to bind the genthyaki they found outside of Kashkana, but it slipped out of their restraining spells like a man shrugging out of a shirt and killed four green adepts before escaping.

"No, better to destroy these things. There is nothing complex about what they are. They are predators, and we are prey.

"After the creature had finally been consumed, we sifted through the rubble of its shop and found a wooden hatch buried in the ground, sealed with powerful spells. Belop has some skill in untangling such wards, and he managed to open the door. In retrospect, I wish he hadn't.

"Beyond it we found a great underground chamber – though perhaps 'chamber' is the wrong word, since that implies a space hollowed out by a man. No, this was some kind of burrow, as an insect might make. And the smell that came billowing up . . . the butchery above must have hidden the odor from the rest of the neighborhood, because it was unspeakably foul. Within, there were dozens of bodies encased in some gray, threadlike substance, hanging from the low ceiling like monstrous fruit. They were gaunt, desiccated, drained, though there was still blood inside them, as Cherise found out when she tried to cut one down. No, they had been emptied of some other vital essence . . . I know not what. The genthyaki had sucked them dry, like slurping marrow from a bone, leaving only a hollowed shell."

A tingling had crept up Keilan's spine as Garmond read. "The way he describes the monster 'unfolding' – that's exactly what we witnessed during the ambush along the Wending Way."

The seeker nodded. "Yes. These monsters – whatever they are – have been feeding on mankind for a thousand years, at least. The ancients knew of their existence and were hunting them down."

Keilan shuddered. "The book I was translating after the attack, the one given to me by the spirit of the Barrow . . . it implied that the knowledge of these creatures had been forgotten or repressed. Which would suggest that –"

"– They were thought to have been hunted to extinction," Garmond finished. "I wonder if the one you struck down was the last of its kind, or if there are others out there."

Nel leaned forward. "We have to assume the monster was allied with the shadowblades and ancient sorcerers who tried to steal Keilan away from Saltstone. And that it was not the only one. Which means – if these creatures can truly mimic humans so perfectly – we must be suspicious of everyone we meet."

They were all silent for a long moment, lost in their own thoughts. Keilan was remembering the horrible night of the ambush, Xin striking down the wraith as it flowed towards them in the long grass . . . the bloody glow of the Shan's lanterns in the small clearing . . . how the shape-changing monster had lifted Cho Yuan like he was a child and the sound his neck had made when it snapped, like a branch breaking.

The Shan.

"Master Garmond," Keilan said, and the seeker surfaced from his own thoughts, blinking. "We came to you because we need the Reliquary's help."

"Something new? Unrelated to the monster or the attack on Saltstone?"

Keilan and Nel shared a glance. "We don't truly know," he said slowly. "It would seem very different, but perhaps there are some connections of which we are unaware."

Master Garmond settled back in his chair, and Keilan explained what had happened since the failed attempt to kidnap him. He recounted the frantic pursuit of the Pure as he fled south from Dymoria, how they had caught up with the paladin outside the gates of Lyr, the archon council and the summons by the Oracle. He told Garmond of what she had said, and of the vision she had shared with them. And how this doom and the dark children they had seen had come from Shan.

When he had finished, Garmond leaned back, tugging on his white beard. "Fascinating. You realize, of course, that Oracles are never infallible. Sometimes they can misinterpret what they see, or conjure their visions out of whole cloth, if the madness has finally seeped into their souls."

"Lady Numil believes this Oracle is still sane," Nel said. "She thought enough of this prophecy to send us on this ridiculous hare chase."

"And what would this threat be, exactly?" Garmond muttered. "Perhaps we should consult an expert in the matter of the Shan."

Keilan's heart leapt: this was exactly why he had wanted to visit the Reliquary. If there was any place in the world that might be able to shed some light on the mysteries they were fumbling towards, this was it. "An expert?"

"I have a colleague who owes me a favor. He's a bit prickly, but he is also recognized as one of the foremost authorities on that strange southern people. Let me send him a summons."

Garmond heaved himself from his chair and threaded his way between the piles of books and apparatus littering his office. He took down a small tarnished bell from a hook and held it in front of the flared opening of a silver tube that snaked up the stone and vanished into a chink in the chamber's wall. Garmond rang the bell in front of the tube's mouth and a few moments later came a tentative knock on the door.

"Come in," the seeker said, and a small boy slipped into the room. He might have been the twin of the apprentice who had first gone to fetch Garmond.

"Halin."

"Galin, sir."

"Yes, yes. Halin-Galin, dash over to d'Verin's quarters and implore him to come meet us here. If he hesitates, remind him of the small debt he owes me for giving him the Blightwood mooncap mushrooms he needed to overcome his . . . personal problems."

As the boy scurried out the door, Garmond turned back to his guests. "Powerful aphrodisiac," he said simply.

Nel coughed to hide her smile.

"The Shan . . . the Shan . . . " Garmond murmured as he returned to his chair. "An interesting people. A mysterious people."

"What do you know about them?" Keilan asked.

"More than most and less than some. They arrived in our lands a thousand years ago, shortly after the cataclysms obliterated the Mosaic Cities and the holdfasts, refugees from some mysterious disaster in their own homeland. A fleet of ships unlike any had seen before, boats as large as castles, accompanied by turtles the size of dragons. They settled south of the newly-formed Broken Sea, in the ruins of the Imperium, and quickly forged an empire that rivaled Menekar in size and strength."

"What happened to their old homeland?" Nel asked.

Garmond shrugged. "I don't know. I believe even the scholars who study the Shan are uncertain. Some say it was a great sorcery that slipped the control of Shan's warlocks – they have a proud magical tradition as well, I've heard, like the ancients of our own histories – while others suggest something more natural: a volcanic eruption, a terrible drought, an invasion by yet another migrating people."

Nel's brow crinkled. "Surely it's easy enough to ask a Shan what happened. Merchants and emissaries from the Empire of Swords and Flowers are constantly traveling to and from the Gilded Cities."

The seeker held up his hand to show that he agreed with her. "Of course, of course. But the truth of what happened a thousand years ago seems to have been suppressed among the common people. Most have only a vague knowledge of the doom that pushed them into the sea. And the scholars and mandarins who have been exposed to the actual histories are remarkably tight-lipped – the Shan are a private and secretive people."

Keilan started as the door to Garmond's chamber suddenly slammed open. He twisted around as a young, gaunt scholar burst into the room. Colors swirled and settled around him: unlike most of the other seekers, who dressed in drab vestments of gray or black, this scholar wore a shimmering silken robe that flashed red and green and yellow. It reminded Keilan of the clothes he had seen Cho Yuan wearing while the Shan had traveled with their caravan along the Wending Way.

"Garmond!" exclaimed the seeker, his face dark. "I have explicitly stated that I am never to be disturbed during the third watch."

"D'Verin," Garmond replied mildly, gesturing at another stool half-submerged in his room's clutter. "Please, have a seat and greet my guests."

The scholar of the Shan spared a cursory glance at Keilan and Nel, then returned his attention to Garmond. "I was making real progress in my meditations today! I felt the Nothing within my Self –"

Garmond waved away his words. "You felt nothing? What are you complaining about, then?"

D'Verin's face flushed a deep red. "No, I felt *the* Nothing, the emptiness that fills our deepest –"

"Yes, yes, congratulations on feeling your nothing. I'm sure you'll touch it again in good time."

Keilan imagined he could hear d'Verin's teeth grinding. Suddenly a tremor passed across the scholar's face, and his anger seemed to melt away, the lines in his brow vanishing and his jaw unclenching. He breathed out, slowly and deeply.

"I am releasing my emotions. I am mastering myself in this moment."

"Excellent," Garmond said. "Too much anger curdles the blood. Unbalances the humors."

Keilan thought he saw d'Verin's eye twitch, but the scholar's expression remained tranquil.

"Why am I here, Garmond?"

The elderly seeker gestured at Keilan and Nel. "Old friends are visiting me: this is Nel, an assistant to a senior magister in Herath, and Keilan, a student in the Scholia. They need answers about the Shan. You are the most learned among us in these matters."

The compliment mollified the scholar somewhat, and he offered a curt bow. "Greetings. I am Naskal d'Verin, the Khamorian scholar here at the Reliquary, specializing in the history, culture, and language of the Shan people." He glanced at Nel and Keilan, and then twisted around, as if he must be missing someone more important. "Emissaries from the Scholia arrive with questions about our southern neighbors? How intriguing. What has happened?"

Nel cleared her throat and sat forward. "The Oracle of Lyr. She gave an odd prophecy and we need to know if what she said has any relevance to someone well-versed in the history of Shan."

D'Verin cocked his head to one side, his curiosity evident.

"The Oracle warned of a terrible threat coming from Shan."

The scholar waved his hands, as if to dismiss her words. "Unlikely. The Shan people are not conquerors. They are quite content with the knowledge that their empire is the most brilliant and refined in the world, and that everything worth owning already exists within its borders. The few times the Empire of Swords and Flowers has been drawn into battle, the aggressor was clearly the emperor of Menekar."

"It wasn't an invading army the Oracle saw in her visions. It was . . . children."

"Children?"

"Yes, they . . . they looked like street urchins, ragged and starving. Perhaps they were –"

The scholar's mouth fell open. "Gods . . . " he whispered, and he reached out to steady himself on a teetering pillar of books. The pile collapsed, nearly taking d'Verin to the ground as well, and Keilan leapt up to catch him before he could fall.

"The Betrayers," the scholar muttered, clutching at Keilan's arms.

"What are the Betrayers?" Garmond asked, leaning forward, his eyes bright with interest.

D'Verin pulled himself from Keilan and collapsed onto the chair he had just vacated. His gaze was distant and empty.

"Demons . . . or something else. The harbingers of the Raveling."

"What is the Raveling?"

D'Verin glanced at Keilan, his face pale. "The Raveling was what destroyed the ancestral homeland of Shan. The Betrayers summoned it or woke it. The texts are vague as to what exactly it was: one account speaks of a darkness in the sky that reached down to scour the lands of life. Another describes endless coils that moved like living hills, crushing cities and squeezing mountains to dust. But whatever the Raveling was, all the sources agree that these demonic children brought about that destruction."

"What happened to them?"

D'Verin acknowledged Garmond's question with a slight nod. "That, at least, the scrolls are clear about. A hero of Shan, the wielder of a demon-slaying sword, hunted down the Betrayers and slew them. But their essence could not be destroyed fully, and their souls – or whatever passes for souls among creatures like them – were trapped inside a chest constructed by the greatest warlocks of Shan. They were imprisoned, but this did not stop the Raveling from continuing to destroy all it touched, until the tattered remnants of the Shan people were forced to launch their great fleet from the last port still standing on their shores. They abandoned their lands forever. What happened to the chest containing the Betrayers was never revealed, though I suspect the warlocks kept it in Tsai Yin, within the towers they built from the bones of the great turtles that accompanied their ships across the ocean."

"So if the Oracle has seen these children in her visions of the coming doom . . . "

"Then they must have escaped their prison," Nel finished for Keilan.

A moment of silence passed in the room. Finally, d'Verin ran a hand through his wild shock of red hair. "If this prophecy has any truth to it, I must inform the Light of the Lore."

Seeker Garmond turned to Nel. "Will you return to Herath and tell the queen of this?"

She glanced at Keilan and shook her head. "The Oracle . . . she claimed that a woman has the knowledge of how to avert what is coming. A woman who could destroy these children. A woman who Keilan has seen before."

Garmond's brows lifted in surprise as he shifted his attention to Keilan. "Truly? Who?"

Keilan squirmed uncomfortably under the scrutiny of everyone in the room. "A sorceress from the distant past. I saw her in a vision I shared with Queen d'Kara – she looked almost exactly like my mother. The Oracle's vision suggested there was some connection between them, and that if I find out where my mother came from I might find this sorceress as well. So we're travelling back to my village to search for clues."

Garmond tugged on his long beard thoughtfully. "You told me once about your mother, I remember. A terrible tragedy."

Keilan nodded. "Yes." His last memory of his mother swam up from the depths where he kept it hidden. Her head had been bowed as she walked unsteadily towards the door of their hut, his uncle Davin gripping her arm roughly. The eyes of the rest of the men in the small room were vacant, almost as if they expected to wake up the next day and discover that this had all been a dream.

But it hadn't been.

She had turned back to Keilan before they'd dragged her outside, her pale face partially hidden behind her long hair. "I love you," she'd said, and then she had disappeared into the night. His father had held him back from running after her into the darkness.

Why had that happened?

Where had his mother come from?

And what was the thread connecting her to the Oracle's prophecy?

Keilan's hand slipped to the hilt of the sword the Lady Numil had given him. He would find what answers there were in his village – and he had a few questions of his own to ask the ones who had taken his mother.

12: CHO LIN

THERE WAS A purity to the emptiness, Cho Lin decided, as she stood upon the raised forecastle of the junk and stared out at the dark swells rippling into the horizon. She could lose herself easily out here, in the middle of the trackless ocean, much like how she had lost herself in meditation beneath Gold Leaf Temple. The Nothing within the Self yearned to be surrounded by such a featureless waste, for it reflected the depths within.

Not that there weren't still some distractions, at least during the day. Sailors scurried over the deck, pulling on ropes or climbing the masts like frantic monkeys, conversing and cursing in a tumbling pidgin variant of proper Shan, a sea language so different that Cho Lin understood barely half the words.

It was because of this that she had begun staying up almost until the dawn and sleeping well past midday. At night, the sea was an endless black desert stretching out to the edge of existence. And the silence. She could close her eyes and sit with her legs crossed and, save for the gentle rolling of the deck and the sharp tang of the sea air, it was like she was again in her monk's cell, willing herself to fall towards the Nothing.

She had seen a few wonders at night, when most of the others were asleep. Once, she had opened her eyes from her meditation and found the sea around the boat ablaze with shimmering blue light. Countless small shapes had writhed together, strands gleaming in the darkness like ghostly serpents. After a while the boat had passed out of this strangeness, and gradually it had dwindled behind them before finally fading into blackness. Another time when the moon had been bright in the sky, gilding the ocean with silver light, she had seen something vast and dark break the surface less than half a *li* from the boat. It made no sound, but a spume of water had risen from its back, glittering in the moonlight. A whale, she suspected, though she had never imagined they could grow so large.

Cho Lin knew she made the sailors nervous. The captain had told her of the ancient superstitions about having women on board, and her presence upon the deck at night had deepened their concerns. Most of them avoided even looking in her direction, and only the captain had spoken to her since they had departed the port of Ras Ami.

This did not bother her; Cho Lin had been an outsider ever since her father pulled her from her childhood games and set her on this path. Right now, she honestly didn't mind having more time to herself, so she could consider carefully all that had happened recently. The release of the Betrayers. The death of her father. Her brother entrusting her with the Sword of Cho and imploring her to find and once again bind the demons before they could work their malice on the world. Bai Hua's betrayal, and how this suggested the Raveling had sunk their corruption deep among the great families of Shan.

After some contemplation, Cho Lin had realized that the enormity of what was happening had blinded her to details that were right in front of her face. It was a mistake the monks of Red Fang Mountain would have chided her for making.

As Ras Ami had dwindled into the distance, she'd realized it had been her brother who sent the assassins to kill her on the road from Gold Leaf Temple.

The thought had struck her so hard she'd staggered and had to lean heavily against the boat's railing. The captain had rushed over to her, begging her to go below deck and rest until she had gotten her sea legs, but she'd waved him away with the cold disdain expected of a Jade Court mandarin's daughter.

Of course. The ambush had been a test. If she'd been killed, she would have been proven unworthy of being given the Sword of Cho. There was some merit to this reasoning: if she could not overcome four assassins, even though one was a Tainted Sword, then her pursuit of the Betrayers could only end in disaster and death. It was just like something her father would have done – her brother had his mind, if not his body. Cho Lin's childhood had been an endless series of such tests, and she had passed all of them . . . except, of course, for her first test, which her father had never forgiven her for.

She had not been born a boy.

"Lady Cho."

The captain's soft voice pulled her away from her thoughts. He stood a few paces from her, his craggy, nut-brown face lowered respectfully.

"Yes?"

"If it pleases you to see the Watcher, I invite you to look towards the north. We will be close enough soon that even this fog won't be able to keep it hidden away."

Cho Lin nodded very slightly, an almost unimaginably generous gesture. He gaped at her for a moment, then recovered and ducked his head again to show his great thanks for her kindness.

She peered where he had indicated, but the murk that had covered the ocean since the dawn was impenetrable.

"On a clear day, we would be able to see the edge of the barbarian lands. That coast is claimed by the terrible empire of Kesh. Do you know of it, Lady Cho?"

"I have heard stories. I cannot believe them to hold much truth."

"Oh! But you should, my lady! I have only spent a few days in their cities of white clay, but I can assure you that the most incredible tales you have heard are indeed true. All men and women must go veiled, to show their subservience before their Lonely God. They have creatures that look like horses, but with two great humps upon their backs. And their emperor, the padarasha, ascends to the throne after proving himself the best in all Kesh at playing tzalik, a game which I'm sure you've seen the youth of Shan enjoying in their shameful indolence. I have even heard," the captain lowered his voice, leaning closer, "that if the first-born child is a girl, a family will bring her to one of their dark temples and –"

Cho Lin slipped her hand from her long sleeve and held it up slightly, and the captain instantly ceased his babbling. "I am not interested in the barbarism of Kesh."

The captain's ruddy cheeks flushed, and he bowed in apology. Before he could withdraw, however, Cho Lin spoke again.

"Tell me about the Watcher. Do you truly think we will see it today?"

The captain bobbed his head. "Indeed, Mistress Cho, this fog cannot hide – look!" He pointed off the starboard side of the junk, forgetting his manners in his excitement. By uttering a command to one of her station she would have been expected in Tsai Yin to demand his topknot cut off as punishment, or at least have had him beaten.

But that was not who she was. She played the part of the Shan noble only because it was expected of her here.

Ignoring his impropriety, she peered into the murk, hoping to glimpse the legendary Watcher. How many poems and songs had described that moment when the Ten Thousand Sails had emerged from the fog – on a day probably much like today, she realized, though coming from the other direction – and seen their new homeland for the first time?

Wisps of silk pulled apart
By the gentle hands of Heaven
We pass out of the coddling mist
Of our long cocoon.
We are reborn
Moths straining towards the trembling light
Of a new world

A shadow loomed deep within the fog. Cho Lin felt a little trickle of apprehension, as if this vague shape was a great wave building in the distance, or a creature rising from the depths. On the deck below her the sailors shouted and pointed.

As they approached the shape the mists swirled and parted, revealing a giant warrior half-sunk in the water, waves lapping against the swirling designs carved into his cuirass. Slung over one arm was a shield that would have dwarfed the imperial palace in Tsai Yin, a great lidless eye sunk into the verdigrised metal. His other arm was extended out, but whatever it had once held was a mystery, as it ended before the elbow in a jagged, hollow stump. The warrior's face was hidden behind a crested helm so spotted with guano it appeared white, while the rest of the towering bronze statue had long ago acquired a green and black patina that almost matched the color of the water in which it waded.

"There must have been a great city here once," Cho Lin said quietly.

The captain did not reply. A respectful silence had fallen among the crew as their boat drifted closer. Cho Lin imagined a sprawling city of black stone, pillars and amphitheaters and avenues, with this great bronze warrior standing guard on a hill above the city. She had seen Kalyuni ruins before, of course. They were scattered throughout the Empire of Swords and Flowers, though the lands of the Shan would have been a distant southern frontier for the Imperium. The greatest of their cities were drowned beneath this very sea. The Sea of Solace, the first Shan to arrive had called it, for it had offered sanctuary after decades of drifting upon the oceans. But the northern barbarians had another name for the sea, a name she assumed came from the devastation that had been wrought when the ocean had surged over the mountains and engulfed these lands – the Broken Sea.

"Captain," Cho Lin said, remembering something she had wanted to discuss with him.

He blinked, shaking his head slightly as if waking from a dream, and turned away from the great statue. "Yes, Lady Cho?"

"I want to arrive in Herath as quickly as possible. I know you planned on stopping in Lyr first, but you will press on to Dymoria. You may unload your goods in Lyr on the return journey."

The captain's face paled. "Lady Cho . . . I implore you to reconsider your request. Our hold is filled with silken streamers and porcelain for the wedding of an archon's daughter, and we will miss the celebration if we bring you directly to Herath."

Cho Lin ground her teeth in frustration. She did not wish to ruin this captain or whoever had backed this trading venture, but she also did not want to waste time in Lyr while the Betrayers were loose in the world.

Would the demons even be in Herath, though? Her brother believed they were, and he had said the warlocks suspected the same. The evidence was circumstantial, but compelling. Powerful magics had been used to steal away the chest that bound the Betrayers, while at the same time, after two thousand years, a kingdom ruled by a sorceress queen was rising again in the north. The queen or one of her servants must have been the thief – but she could not possibly suspect the danger she had unleashed upon the world. Or did she? What kind of a woman was Cein d'Kara?

But what if they were wrong? What if she found nothing in Dymoria? She would be alone, in the savage barbarian lands, with no idea how to continue her search. The thought made her chest feel hollow.

She frowned at the captain. "Very well. A single day in Lyr to unload the goods. But I don't want any of the sailors going ashore. As soon as you have finished, we sail north. No delays, or my brother will hear of it."

The captain bobbed his head gratefully. "A thousand thanks, Lady Cho. Our gratitude is as deep as the ocean – I promise, on my children, we will bring you with great haste to the city of the Crimson Queen."

13: DEMIAN

DEMIAN AWOKE.

He lay in a circle of flattened white grass, his head pillowed on his saddlebag, and stared up at a sky stained red by a bloody dawn. Many years ago, some fool had told him that such a morning meant a great murder had been committed during the night: cold steel had pierced a king's back, or an emperor pushed from a tower's window. A superstition, of course. The kind of scaffolding the weak-minded employed to keep their realities from collapsing. The world had an abundance of mysteries, certainly, but a rising sun did not possess some mystical connection with the intrigues of a royal palace. The sky was simply red.

Demian rolled to his feet, wincing at the pain in his side. He had been traveling for more than a month, yet still he felt a twinge every morning when he woke. It had been worse along the Wending Way, deep in the Mire, as the coldness of the marshes had slithered beneath his bandages and plucked at the festering edges of his wound. Some mornings it had been a struggle just to haul himself up into his horse's saddle. Yet he had persisted, crossing the north for the second time in as many months. The Spine had been the worst, treacherous paths winding through narrow defiles and along vertiginous cliffs, and once, when his horse had stumbled on some loose rocks and thrown him, the cut in his side had split open. He had stitched himself back up again as best he could with needle and thread, cursing his horse's clumsiness . . . while also thanking all the gods that the beast hadn't been lamed in the fall.

The journey across the white plains had been much easier. Winter had gripped the lands west of the Spine, but here the days were still warm. Many nights he had barely felt a chill. And while most travelers who dared to brave the plains feared lions or strangling serpents lurking in the long grass, those creatures were wise enough to avoid him.

Demian gave his horse a handful of oats while he chewed on a strip of salted mutton. He studied the horizon, where the endless sea of white rippled into the crimson sky. There was something out there, at the edge of his vision, a distant shape that flashed red in the dawn light. He squinted, but he couldn't quite tell if it was a mirage or not. Was it possible he had arrived at Menekar already? He knew he had cut quite a few days of travel by not going south to find the great road, instead blazing his own way through the grasslands, but he'd thought the imperial city was still a few days to the east. The longer he stared at that shimmering lump in the distance, however, the more certain he was that his long journey was finally over.

Would Alyanna be surprised to see him? She would assume he had survived the disastrous assault on Saltstone, surely, but he suspected she also must be aware that he and the paladin had not retrieved the boy. An embarrassment, though Demian knew Alyanna had also failed – as incredible as it seemed, the young queen had bested her in a sorcerous duel, and she had been forced to flee like a dog with its tail tucked between its legs. Following his own fight with the slave warrior, Demian had dragged himself to the courtyard where he had first activated the riftstone . . . but the portal linking Saltstone with the emperor's pleasure garden had been severed. Alyanna must have survived and fled back to Menekar.

A single step to cross the distance that had just taken him a month on horseback to traverse. Frustrating – if he had recovered just a little faster from being stabbed by that slave he could have arrived in the courtyard before Alyanna. Who knew what trouble she had gotten herself into while he hurried to rejoin her? He hoped she had abandoned her schemes to destroy Cein d'Kara – clearly, she had underestimated the Crimson Queen. But he suspected she had not. It was not in her nature to admit defeat.

The pale grass whispered against his horse's belly as he rode towards the shape on the horizon. Gradually it resolved into a great ivory palace perched atop a stony plateau – to Demian it resembled a white lion of the plains lounging upon a rock, surveying its kingdom with casual arrogance. Beneath the sprawling palace, most of the great city was hidden behind walls larger than any he had encountered, save for the iron that girdled Vis. The only building that could be seen was the golden dome of Ama's temple, which blazed in the harsh sun.

A few leagues from the city, Demian joined the great western road he had avoided when he had first come down out of the Spine. He fell in among a stream of pilgrims and travelers, some in wagons or on horses, and many others on foot. Menekar was the oldest and greatest city in the known world – at least since the cataclysms had swallowed Min-Ceruth and the Mosaic Cities – and the hub of an empire nearly as vast as the fractured lands to the west. All roads led to her, the Mother of Cities. Dirty children peered warily at Demian from the back of a rickety cart filled with vegetables, while farther ahead a more prosperous merchant rode escorted by a pair of men-at-arms in conical steel helmets. The wagon beside them was filled with dusky-skinned men and women, their eyes empty and wrists bound. Slaves.

The droning of a repeated mantra, punctuated by groans and shrieks, made Demian turn in his saddle. Behind him a line of filthy men shuffled on bare and bleeding feet, while mendicants in the pristine white robes of Ama paced behind them, lashing their backs with leather flails. Demian frowned. This was the Scourging, the holiest of pilgrimages for the faithful of Ama. It was a procession from the holy site in the shadow of the Spine where the first of the Pure, Tethys, had been transformed into an instrument of divine retribution against the Warlock King, to the great temple of Ama. A ten-day forced march, whipped along constantly by the clerics of the Radiant Father. More than a few pilgrims had died in the dust before reaching the holy city. Fools.

No one paid Demian any mind. Just another traveler on his way to the marble heart of the world.

The walls swelled larger and larger, until their soaring crenellations blotted out the midday sun, and their approach was plunged into shadow. Without narrowing at all, the great western road passed into the city through the vast Malachen Gate, which was so high that thirty men could have stood on each other's shoulders and still not been able to touch the stone above. Demian squinted, staring up at the ancient, mottled patch of the wall above the gate. This was where criminals and traitors were hung by their wrists until they died of exposure or eagles tore open their bellies. When Demian had last come through these gates more than a dozen had been hanging, most still alive, and the travelers below had skirted the space below them. Afraid, he suspected, of passing beneath the condemned when death finally claimed the unfortunates and their bowels unclenched.

But today the rows of iron manacles were empty, save for one. A large crowd was gathered beneath, watching silently. There was no jeering or taunting, as Demian had witnessed before. They almost seemed respectful.

When he neared the crowd, an older matron turned away and stumped closer to him, shaking her head and leaning on a cane.

"Who is that?" he asked when he was sure she'd seen him watching her.

The old woman narrowed her eyes. "That's Torrinis. Been white vizier for near fifty years."

Demian blinked in surprise. He knew that name. Perhaps the second most powerful man in Menekar, after the emperor. "Truly? What was his crime?"

The old woman studied him, as if unsure she should answer. "He was a traitor, or so they say." From her tone Demian doubted very much that she believed that. "Now there's only the black vizier to counsel the emperor. May Ama preserve us." She sketched a quick circle in the air, glancing around as if afraid someone had overheard her, and then pushed her way into the stream of travelers passing through the gate and into the city.

With a last look at the hanging white vizier Demian followed her, jostled by the crowds. An awed sound rose from those around him as the newcomers to the city spilled from beneath the gate and onto the Aveline Way, the broad avenue that sliced through the heart of the city. On either side of the great road rose towering white buildings, carved of marble and basalt and inlaid with veins of quartz that flashed in the brightness. Images were incised into the stone: lions stalking buffalo across the plains, legionaries brandishing swords, graceful women clad in jokkas balancing water jugs on their heads. Some of those carvings had come to life, as long-necked beauties watched the crowds from balconies draped with vegetation, their eyes heavy-lidded and ringed with khol, lips quirked in secret smiles.

Sirens paid to lure travelers to inns . . . and their effectiveness was obvious, as Demian noticed the rich slaver leading his entourage towards one of these guesthouses, his eyes fixed on the pale-faced maiden leaning against the balustrade above. For a moment Demian was also tempted to take a room – though not because of the company on offer. No, the thought of sinking into a copper tub filled with steaming water and washing away the grime of his travels was making his skin itch in anticipation.

He snorted and shook his head. For centuries he had dwelled among the kith'ketan, in a tiny chamber carved from the mountain's flesh. His will had been hardened, turned to diamond by the tremendous pressure of the stone pressing down from above. And yet after only a few months away he was already afflicted by weakness.

He had to see Alyanna.

The one weakness he had never overcome.

The imperial pleasure gardens had faded with the changing seasons. When last Demian had passed along these ceramic paths, jewel-bright flowers had hemmed his way; now, the first breath of winter had withered many of those blooms, though the gardeners had evidently been hard at work pruning and replacing them with delicate replicas fashioned from gold wire and colored glass. The imperial grounds were supposed to be immune to time's ravages, reflecting the eternal glory of their god, but the sight of this gleaming metal sprouting from the browning grass left Demian feeling cold. Ama was not the one who could bestow eternal life.

That would be the Weaver.

He found her pavilion empty. Demian slipped inside the hanging silken flaps, his hand on the hilt of his sword. The great wide bed was made up and looked not to have been slept in for a long while. He ran his hand along the sheets, and his palm came away stained slightly yellow by a thin layer of pollen. A sweet-smelling breeze wafted inside, rippling the hanging silks and tinkling a set of musical chimes suspended above the bed.

There was a small metallic bird with wings of colored glass set on a low side-table, staring at him with jeweled eyes.

Where was she?

Everything was just as he remembered from when he had visited her before . . . except that the rosewood chest with its Shan symbols was no longer here. Demian felt a trickle of unease. Alyanna and the demon children were missing.

He stilled himself, receding into the pavilion's shadows, and reached out with all his senses. Silence, except for the wind rustling the branches outside and the faint chirping of a songbird. He turned inward, feeling the thunder of his heart, hearing only his slow and steady breathing. Grasping his power tightly he extended questing filaments, searching the gardens and the Selthari Palace for any traces of sorcery. The Pure were there in the palace: searing, blinding, empty. Husks of men overflowing with the terrible burning light, yet unaware of his presence; Demian was like a snake in the long grass around their feet, invisible. Faint traces of Alyanna surrounded him. He tasted the heady residue of her magic here, in the pavilion – but it was old and stale. She had been gone for many days, like the demon children and their rosewood prison.

Demian stepped into the thin shadow cast by the candelabra. The darkness embraced him. So cold, so terrible. It clotted in his mouth, caressing his skin with long bony fingers. He pushed through the emptiness, walking the stone path that floated in the blackness, ignoring the faint chittering sounds that seemed to be calling him further into this place. Following those noises meant certain death – that was one of the first lessons he had learned under the mountain, at the feet of the daymo.

A wavering glow to his left. Not a witchlight – those could be just as dangerous as the distant voices, and had led careless kith'ketan too deep into the shadows – but a portal from this place. He moved in that direction and thrust himself back into the living world. Demian emerged in the shadow of a gnarled banyan tree, sending an iridescent bird with a glimmering tail crashing through a bed of velvet nightblossoms, shrieking in aggrieved surprise.

He needed information. What had happened here?

Demian glimpsed a slice of pastel fabric through the tangled branches. Low voices, the chime of a young girl's laughter. He glanced down at his travel-stained clothes and the jutting hilt of his long sword. Could he risk showing himself? Surely the concubines in these gardens would report him. Demian gritted his teeth. What weakness. Let them tell the Pure or the emperor. There was no way they could know who he was, or what he was capable of.

Demian pulled aside the pavilion's flap and stepped inside. Dreamsmoke hazed the room, the spent lamp perched on a mound of folded silks, its flame long having guttered out. The rest of the space was filled with piled cushions and pillows, and three beautiful women, who turned to regard him curiously with heavy-lidded eyes. They were deep in the clutches of the drug – likely they imagined him to be some apparition summoned forth from the smoke.

"Hello," one of the concubines murmured, stretching out like a cat and giving him a sleepy smile. "Welcome to paradise."

Another woman, a raven-haired beauty with the dusky skin of an Eversummer Islander, laughed at this and buried her face in a pillow.

But the last concubine blinked uncertainly at him, a flicker of recognition in her eyes. She was from Dymoria, he guessed, with fiery red curls and skin white as milk. He knew her.

"I am searching for one of the emperor's courtesans," he said, addressing the red-haired girl.

"Well, you've found three," said the dark-skinned concubine, giggling. "Luck turns towards you today, stranger."

The Dymorian girl's face had turned even paler, if that was possible.

"Where is Alyanna?" he asked her, holding her frightened gaze.

The mirth in the pavilion instantly vanished. Demian could see that the concubines were trying to surface from the dream-smoke, very aware that something important was happening.

"I don't know any Alyanna," the red-headed girl whispered.

Demian stepped closer to the concubines and sat, settling himself cross-legged on a cushion with his hands resting on his knees. The lingering remnants of the dreamsmoke were making his head swim.

All three of the girls were now staring at him fearfully, and he forced an empty smile. "Come, I remember you," he said, addressing the red-haired concubine. "You were in Alyanna's pavilion the last time I visited these gardens. I have just returned from a long journey, and I find her vanished. Where is she?"

The girl swallowed hard, her fingers kneading the silken cushions. She shook her head slightly.

Demian sighed. She knew something, that was obvious. But how best to draw it out of her? He could threaten. Hurt her until she talked.

Cut her! Kill her!

With a slight grimace, Demian pushed aside those thoughts. They were not his own. It had been too long since Malazinischel had fed, and the sword thirsted.

There was a better tact, one where she could be convinced to keep his presence in these gardens secret.

"If she is in trouble, I can help her."

The dusky concubine glanced at the red-head, who was still staring at Demian like he was some predator that would leap at her if she looked away. "Bex," she said softly. "Perhaps we should . . ."

"No," said the other girl. "What can he do? He's just one man."

"He's not," whispered Bex. "He's . . . like her. Special. I remember him."

"Is she alive?" pressed Demian, leaning forward. The other two concubines drew back, but the red-haired girl didn't flinch.

"I don't know."

"What happened to her?"

"She was . . . taken."

"By whom? The paladins of Ama?"

The girl shook her head curtly. "No. It was dark, very late at night. I was woken by sounds outside in the garden. I pulled aside the flaps to see if it was Alyanna returning – she had been gone since the early evening. Sometimes she did this, vanished for days at a time, and who else could it have been, at that hour?"

"Bex," murmured one of the other concubines urgently, shaking her arm. "Don't say any more. If he hears you told this stranger these things, we will all be strangled."

The red-haired girl twisted her arm free. "He won't say anything. He is Alyanna's friend."

"The birds have ears," the girl insisted. "They'll fly back and tell him whatever you say."

"Him?"

"The black vizier," said the Dymorian concubine. "He took her. When I looked outside the pavilion, I saw him striding through the gardens with Alyanna slung over his shoulder like a sack of grain. She looked dead." The girl couldn't hold back a sob, and she rubbed quickly at her eyes. "I don't think she was, though. She couldn't be. She was too strong."

Demian watched her face closely, searching for any hint of falseness. Nothing. And no wonder she had been so hesitant to tell him what she'd seen – informing on the empire's spymaster was certainly taking a huge risk. She must have truly loved Alyanna. The Weaver did have that effect on others.

Demian rose from the cushion. "Then you haven't seen her since? And you have no idea where he could have taken her?"

The girl shook her head again. "I don't know. Do you think she's alive?" Her voice cracked on these last words, her face twisted in fear and sorrow.

Demian attempted a comforting smile. "Alyanna is alive, and I will find her."

He slipped from the gardens as easily as he had arrived, by way of the shadowy paths only a kith'ketan could walk. Briefly, he was tempted to explore the halls of the Selthari Palace, perhaps even to hunt down this black vizier who had kidnapped Alyanna from these grounds, but in the end he decided he should not be so rash. This was a dangerous place, even for Demian. The Pure were immune to his sorcery, and he had crossed blades with enough of the paladins of Ama to hold a wary respect for their skill and strength. A few even had the ability to summon a blazing radiance that would banish the shadows that were his greatest advantage in any fight. No, better to find a refuge where he could contemplate his next move.

And he knew where he should be able to find the perfect place.

Demian stepped from the darkness, into the shadow of the palace's soaring marmoreal walls. Drawing his cowl up he walked the tiled streets of the imperial district, ignoring the petty bureaucrats with their tonsured scalps and flowing robes. His travel-worn clothes attracted a few curious stares, but since no soldiers were summoned or questions asked Demian assumed they had decided he was a messenger on official business.

He followed the roads that sloped downward. It was his experience that in every city built on a hill, the powerful perched themselves at the peak while the poor clustered at the base. Sure enough, the mansions with their ornamented porticos and balconies gradually shrunk in size, then gave way to buildings of baked mud several stories high. Women in jokkas clustered at the entrances to these soaring structures, chatting as they washed vegetables in the large communal basins fed by stone channels from the great aqueduct that carried water from lake Asterppa throughout the city. These were the homes of tradespeople and merchants and the families of the soldiers and bureaucrats who served higher up the hill.

Demian continued on, until at last the ground leveled off and he walked among the slums of Menekar. The clay bricks of the apartments here were crumbling, and a few of the structures had even partially collapsed, spilling debris into the streets that no one had bothered to clean. Lurid images were drawn in colored chalk and charcoal on the walls, white figures that looked suspiciously like the Pure having their glowing members attended to by naked women. Wolves with the heads of men – the details so pronounced Demian could only assume that they were actual leaders in the city – were tearing apart a young woman, the word 'the Empire' arching over her halo of golden hair. One of the wolves had a plump face and the uptilted eyes of a Shan – wasn't the black vizier a refugee from the Empire of Swords and Flowers? Apparently, he was not popular down here in the city's depths.

The streets here were far more crowded than in the wealthier districts higher up the hill. Costermongers leaned against ancient carts filled with vegetables, and butchers had laid out strips of unrecognizable meat on ragged blankets, constantly lashing the air above their wares with leather flails to keep the flies from settling. A ragman draped in layers of colorful cloth called out the virtues of his wares, while a crowd of children had gathered around a seller of skewered locusts glazed with honey. Other urchins dashed about in tattered clothes, laughing as they tried to send their friends tumbling into those passing by. One little girl was shoved hard and collided with Demian, her thin arms flailing as she tried to catch herself. His hand flashed out and grabbed her wrist as she tried to slip her fingers inside his cloak to get to his coin pouch. She glanced up, startled, and he shook his head. When he released her, she vanished into the crowds without looking back, quick as a mouse darting into a chink in a wall. The children scattered, abandoning their game, a few pausing to shout curses quite inappropriate for their ages.

Finally, Demian found what he was looking for: a black crescent burned into a wall beside an alley's mouth, barely larger than a splayed hand. It looked like it could have been a natural blemish, some remnant of a long-ago fire, but Demian knew better. He turned down the alley, stepping over the sprawled corpse of a dog, its face a festering mass of maggots.

Deeper in the alley, shadows shuffled away from him as he strode into the darkness. He paid them no heed. They would not be so foolish as to assault him, and if they were then Malazinischel would feast. At the thought a tingle of anticipation crept from the sword at his side. *Patience,* Demian urged. He suspected blood would be shed soon enough.

There. Another crescent daubed in black paint above a small wooden door. Demian pushed at the rotten wood and the door swung open on rusty hinges, revealing a set of chipped stone stairs descending into blackness. Sour air billowed up from the depths as he started on the steps – apparently other denizens of the slums had used this space for refuge also. He smelled urine and blood and dead moldering flesh.

When he reached the bottom of the stairs he summoned a silver ball of wizardlight, and the darkness fled before him. He stood in a cellar that must have stretched under much of the large tenement building above him, the wan light flitting among a forest of structural pillars. He saw a blackened space where someone had recently set a fire, and hunched across the far wall was the slumped shape of a man. Demian's hand strayed to his sword's hilt but then he realized the body was missing its head.

His boots scraped upon the stone floor as he explored the deeper reaches of the cellar, looking for another sign. He found the final black crescent painted on the far wall, above a rent in the plaster and brick that would be barely large enough for a small child to squeeze through. Demian extinguished his wizardlight, and the darkness rushed in to embrace him.

But it was not complete. Through the crack in the wall he could faintly see a ghostly glow. Good.

Demian conjured up his wizardlight again and moved the shimmering sphere behind one of the cellar's pillars. Then he strode forward, into the puddle of shadow his light had formed on the floor.

The dark place again. He turned around, back towards where he knew the other light to be. There it was, hovering a dozen paces from him. This radiance was different than a normal flame: a smear of light danced above it, vaguely man-shaped. It watched him as he approached, and Demian nodded. The soul did not acknowledge his greeting. Demian stepped into the light and reappeared on the other side of the wall, in a new chamber. The fetid stench was fainter here, replaced by a staleness that suggested dust and ages long past. He stood over a corpsetallow candle set in a stand of twisted black metal, its pale flame writhing as if there was a strong wind gusting through the cellar. Which of course there was not. These candles were used by the kith'ketan to create permanent doorways from the shadow paths, since the bound spirits would never consume the tallow upon which they were trapped.

This chamber was older and grander. The pale light played upon an elaborate mosaic set into the ceiling, and several arched exits led from the room. Demian pulled his wizardlight through the crack in the wall and sent it floating down one of the passageways. He followed it, trying to move quietly. He didn't want to alarm anyone who might be here.

Demian explored the ruins, moving through several rooms of what looked like an abandoned villa. He had been beneath a few of the world's oldest cities, and they were all much the same, built over the bones of the past. If he dug deeper, he was sure he'd find the homes of an earlier people, all the way back until Menekar was just a sprawl of stone huts.

Rubble and collapsed stone blocked off many of the passageways, and he followed the ones that remained clear until finally he found himself in a large room dominated by a great stone altar – this would have been the house's center, where sacrifices were made in the name of Ama. Statues representing the various Aspects of the god lined the walls, casting strange shadows as his wizardlight came to hover over the altar.

He was not alone.

"Come out," he spoke into the stillness, his voice echoing.

Something uncoiled within the darkness, emerging from behind the Aspect of Grief. Demian's wizardlight played upon shimmering black cloth but could not penetrate the penumbra that swaddled the sword at the figure's side. Large blue eyes watched him from above a silken veil; the smoothness of his skin suggested to Demian that this kith'ketan was very young to carry a shadowblade.

"Welcome, brother," said the assassin softly. "The Paths are dark and cold. Rest here for a while, before the shadow calls again."

Demian inclined his head at the ritual greeting. "You know who I am?"

A long pause. When the kith'ketan finally spoke again, there was an edge to his voice. Good, he felt fear. "Yes. You are the Undying One. In the mountain, stories are whispered."

Demian wondered what those stories could be. The rest of the world spoke in hushed tones about the assassins under the mountain, and they in turn told tales about him. Even legends had legends, it appeared.

"Are you alone?"

The kith'ketan nodded. "We traveled here from many places when we received the summons and gathered in these catacombs to wait for the sorceress's signal. I was left behind for any stragglers who arrived late."

"And none came?"

"Several did. I told them the rest had already left, and so they departed, back to where they had come from. But the last arrived more than a fortnight ago. Until you. Did you also come because of the daymo's message? Or do you know what happened to those who went with the sorceress?"

"Most are dead."

The kith'ketan shifted nervously. He really was very young – no wonder he had been the one left behind. He must have been given his shadowblade less than a year ago. "Dead? More than twenty brothers had gathered here. Some of the older ones . . . they told us such a number had never come together before. That this was no normal pilgrimage. They said we must have been doing the will of our lord directly."

Demian shrugged. "I suspect you were. I was there when the bargain was struck between the sorceress and your master. But the daymo underestimated the Crimson Queen and her school of wizards."

The blue eyes blinked rapidly above the veil. He looked shaken, Demian thought. *It is always unsettling when illusions are stripped away and the truth revealed.* No doubt the boy had been raised on stories of his order's holy mission, and how through their master's will they would remake this world in his image. Finding out the kith'ketan were just one great power among many would certainly be jarring.

"You saw them die?"

"I saw their bodies. Perhaps some escaped, but we failed in the task we were given."

Composure was creeping back into the assassin's voice again. "And the sorceress?"

"That is why I have returned."

The kith'ketan's eyes narrowed. "She survived?"

"She did, and she fled back to Menekar. But she was taken prisoner. I do not know how they discovered she was not a simple concubine, but apparently they did."

"If that is the case, they must have killed her."

"Perhaps, or perhaps not."

"You mean to try and find her?"

"Yes. And you are going to help me."

14: KEILAN

A HARSH WIND tumbled down from the red hills rearing to the west, stinging Keilan's skin and filling his mouth with grit. He spat out sand and lifted the cloth around his neck to cover the lower half of his face, thankful that Senacus had suggested they buy the desert veils before departing the last trading post. They weren't in the desert proper–the red waste of Kesh lapped the other side of those hills–but the low bulwark of ragged stone could not completely hold back the sand and searing wind.

"I'd prefer not to sleep out in this," Nel said, shielding her eyes from the swirling grit.

Keilan glanced up at the darkening sky. "We may not have a choice. That rock might have cost us a comfortable bed and a hot meal."

Nel rubbed her horse's neck affectionately. "At least she's walking all right now. I was afraid she wouldn't be able to continue on."

Keilan nodded his agreement. A sharp stone had become wedged in a hoof earlier, and it had taken all the trust that had developed between Nel and her horse – and her skill with a dagger – to extricate it without further injury to anyone. Still, they had lost a good part of the day, and this segment of the Iron Road was the last place Keilan wanted to be caught between rest houses. There was little refuge from the winds blowing off the waste, and the merchants at the last market town had warned them of bandits that laired in the red hills.

"It looks like Senacus has seen something," Keilan said, squinting into the haze. Up ahead the paladin had stopped and was waiting for them.

Keilan kicked his horse into a canter. As if to show how well she had recovered, Nel's horse soon passed him, plumes of red dust rising in her wake. Senacus hunched in his saddle as he watched them approach, his white cloak and armor smeared with grime.

"What is it?" Keilan asked. Senacus pointed further ahead, where a rocky spur from the nearby hills encroached upon the road.

"There's shelter there from the dust," Senacus said, raising his voice to be heard over the wind. "But others have realized this as well."

Keilan peered into the shadows gathered in the lee of the stony outcropping. There might have been shapes there, but he couldn't make them out clearly. "Are those wagons?"

Senacus nodded. "Aye. But they're not merchants. I see a firebird painted on the side of one wagon, a two-headed snake on another."

"Kindred," Nel muttered. "They're not likely to share their camp."

"They might," Keilan said. "I know a girl in the Scholia, an apprentice like me, whose mother was Kindred. She taught me something about her people. They're wary folk, but for good reason." The Kindred were a wandering people, traders and tinkers, grudgingly welcomed in most towns for the goods and news they brought, but also watched with suspicion. Common stories had the Kindred stealing away babes and beautiful maids and practicing dark and wild magics deep in the forests, far outside the boundaries of civilized lands. Tamryl had insisted to Keilan that these tales had less than a shred of truth to them, and if any young women had run away to join a Kindred caravan they had done so of their own free will and were most often fleeing an abusive father or husband.

"The Kindred do not welcome the Pure," Senacus said, wiping at the red dust coating his white-scale cuirass. "Ancient disagreements. They dislike outsiders invading their privacy, and the faithful of Ama must seek out sorcery everywhere."

"So you'll camp here while Keilan and I enjoy some Kindred hospitality?" Nel asked.

Senacus shrugged. "I do not fear the night. Do as you will."

"No," Keilan said, patting the flank of his horse as it whickered uneasily, spooked by a sudden gust of stinging wind. "You still have that amulet that hides your light. Take off your armor and join us."

The wind strengthened even further, shrieking like a banshee as it whipped the paladin's cloak out behind him. Keilan hunkered lower on his horse until it had abated, fervently hoping the Kindred would allow them to share their fire.

"There's wisdom in your words," the paladin said with a sigh, and swung down from his horse.

By the time Senacus had stowed away his scale armor and the distinctive white-metal blade of the Pure, the sun had nearly completed its descent behind the western hills, casting the Iron

Road into shadow. Up ahead Keilan could see the glimmer of light from within the circled wagons, and the campfire throwing twisting shapes upon the rocky cliff face rising up beside the Kindred encampment.

Nel and Keilan also slid from their saddles, and together they approached on foot, leading their horses. In a stark land known to be a home for bandits, Nel had said it was best to present themselves as unthreatening as possible, and Keilan agreed. He would prefer not to see arrows come flying out of the gathering dark.

To his surprise, they had nearly made it to the camp before a man moved out from behind the edge of a wagon, his hands resting on the hilts of a pair of scimitars. He was young, and wore a vest cinched by a sash that left his upper chest bare, despite the evening's chill.

"Hold, and come no further," he commanded in the common tongue, his words thickened by a strange accent. "Who goes there?"

"Travelers," Nel said. They had decided she should be the one to speak. "We were caught out on the road as night began to fall. May we share your fire?"

The Kindred guard stroked the hilts of his swords and studied them carefully, his gaze lingering on Senacus. "No. I suggest you continue on your way. These are dangerous lands we pass through."

Keilan took a step forward and the man tensed, half-drawing one of his scimitars. "Wait," Keilan said, holding up his hands to show that they were empty. He cleared his throat. "*Rhevis gan,*" he said, hoping he'd gotten the intonation correct.

The man hesitated, and then released his sword. "You . . . you know our tongue."

"Just a little. I have a friend among the Kindred. She taught me those words, in case I ever needed your people's help."

"And who is she?"

"Tamryl Devangine, daughter of Melika the healer."

The man crossed his arms across his bare chest, bowing low to them. "That name is known to us. I am Feren, son of Haveril. Enter our camp and be welcome."

They followed the man as he threaded his way between the brightly painted Kindred wagons. Scenes from epic stories unfurled along their sides, some tales Keilan knew, others he did not. In one, a blazing firebird lifted from the remnants of a shattered sun while a white dragon, coiled into the shape of a moon, watched from above. The next showed a giant with tree-trunk legs stooping to accept a bouquet of wildflowers from a small girl with blossoms in her hair. The Kindred were renowned as master storytellers, able to craft pictures with their retellings that were just as vivid as illustrations in a book.

Within the circled wagons a few dozen men and women were gathered around the fire, holding out skewers threaded with meat. The men were garbed in some variation of the open vest and billowy pants Feren was wearing, and the women wore long, loose, flowing dresses. Colorful ribbons were twined in the hair of many of the younger women – Keilan remembered Tamryl had said this meant they were unmarried, but old enough to wed.

Every face turned towards them as they emerged from between the wagons.

"*Bej anak ven anak, Feren*?" asked a seated older man, his curiosity evident in his voice and face.

"*Mahal, Therin. Chasol yishan ven teris. Tamen gerdao Melika du tressen Tamryl.*"

The older man shrugged and stood, wiping his hands on his pants. He also crossed his arms and bowed towards them, as Feren had done. "Greetings, travelers, and be welcome. Share our fire and meat. I am Therin, and this is my family. Any friend of Tamryl, daughter of Melika, is a friend of mine."

A few of the Kindred shifted to make space for them around the fire, and Feren gestured for them to sit. No sooner had Keilan settled himself than a pretty girl with bright blue ribbons in her dark hair handed him a skewer, smiling shyly. Keilan ducked his head in thanks, feeling his cheeks start to burn, and the girls seated beside the one who had given him the skewer elbowed their friend and burst out in giggles.

To hide his embarrassment, Keilan bit down on the steaming meat. His mouth flooded with the taste of spiced lamb, perfectly cooked, and he had to restrain himself from going back for another taste before he'd swallowed what he was chewing.

"Thank you," Nel said, accepting her own skewer. "We will remember this kindness."

Therin waved her words away. "It's good you've come. I was just thinking the mood this evening is too dour. We needed a reason to celebrate something." He cleared his throat. "*Nevis gala ven mok terath fir mes atuan,*" he said loudly, and at once all conversation stopped and attention turned to Therin.

"*Nevis gala ven mok terath fir mes atuan,*" the shouted response came from the rest of the Kindred.

"What does that mean?" Keilan asked Feren, who had crouched beside him.

"When the night is long and cold, burn bright to scare the darkness," he replied around his own mouthful of lamb. "Unfortunately, I have to scare the darkness in another way." He clapped Keilan on the shoulder. "Enjoy the song and dance. I must return to my post."

"Thank you," Keilan said as Feren tossed his empty skewer on the ground and stood.

"My pleasure," he said, then smiled, gesturing with his chin towards the Kindred girls. "It seems you have some admirers."

Keilan swallowed and risked a glance across the fire. The girl who had given him the skewer was staring at him through the flames, twining the blue ribbon in her hair around her finger as her friends whispered in her ears.

Perhaps Feren needed some help guarding the camp.

Keilan was just about to slink away from the fire and the attention of the Kindred girls when he noticed a fiddle had appeared in the hands of Therin. A small cheer went up as he started in on a skittering melody that began slow but soon was dashing like a rabbit running for cover, faster and faster and faster . . . until it stopped abruptly.

"Tella tella tella, mock mock mock!" yelled all the Kindred as one, then they clapped three times loudly in unison, and a moment later the fiddle resumed its frenzied racing.

A woman with curly black hair bereft of ribbons bounced to her feet and took a step back from the fire. Laughter and more cheers followed as she stamped her boots and spun, her long frilled dress flaring. She raised her hands to the sky and shook her arms and bells sewn into her sleeves rang in time to her kicking feet. Another woman with streaks of gray in her hair joined the first, and they twirled around each other, the hems of their dresses nearly touching. When the fiddle player lifted his bow they stopped instantly, and the cry came again from the other Kindred:

"Tella tella tella, mock mock mock!"

The dancing continued, different women rising to their feet to replace the ones who grew tired. Keilan soon found himself clapping along with the others and chanting every time Therin paused his playing. He lost himself as the night swirled and the music carried him away from this desolate road beside the red wastes.

He wasn't sure how long he sat there, enjoying the spectacle and the fresh skewers pressed into his hands every time he finished the one he held, when he noticed an odd tingling had begun in the back of his head. Surprised, Keilan pushed himself back from the fire, wondering if what he felt could be true. He knew this feeling. But here? Now? He climbed to his feet, glancing at the shadowy wagons and the darkness beyond them. Somewhere out there . . .

He saw movement, and a flicker of light. Many small shapes. Keilan slipped around the edge of the wagons, the prickling in his skull growing stronger. A circle of children – perhaps seven or eight – were crouched around an old man who was sitting cross-legged. His face was lined, with only a few wispy strands of hair still clinging to his head, but his eyes were bright and lively as he coaxed a small fire to life from a few twigs and clumps of dried grass. The children – none of whom seemed older than ten – shrieked in excitement as the old man began to move his fingers and mumble under his breath. Keilan couldn't hear what he was saying, but to his astonishment he could *see* what the old man was doing. Around his fluttering fingers strands of something were gathering, twisting with the rise and fall of his muttered incantations.

The old man was doing sorcery, and Keilan could see it!

A trembling tongue of flame reached from the tiny fire, as if pushed by a wind Keilan could not feel. It did not flicker, but kept its shape, and what looked like fingers unclenched from a small hand – then, with visible effort, a man no more than a span high made of rippling flame stepped from the fire. It turned its empty head to regard the giants looming above, then danced a quick jig in time to Therin's skirling fiddle. The children laughed and clapped their hands, and the old man smiled. Beneath the dancing fire-creature the scrub was blackening, sending up thin tendrils of smoke. With a last wave at the Kindred children the sorcerer's creation leapt back into the diminished fire and then vanished as the flames rose higher again.

Keilan's heart was beating wildly. He had seen how the old man had done that, how he had lashed the sorcery together to animate the flames. He wanted to try . . . could he do the same thing? He . . .

Keilan glimpsed movement out of the corner of his eye, and he turned to see Senacus vanishing into the night.

Oh, no.

He caught up with the paladin where they had tied their horses to a post near one of the wagons at the edge of the encampment. His hand was grasping something wedged inside his bedroll, and as Keilan moved closer he saw that it was the hilt of his white metal sword.

"Senacus," he said, stepping out of the shadows.

The Pure did not turn around. "Keilan. You felt it as well."

"Yes. What are you doing?"

The paladin pulled his sword half-free, the faint moonlight running like quicksilver along the naked blade. "What must be done."

Keilan stepped forward and grasped Senacus's arm. "What do you mean?"

The paladin shook himself free. "That man is a sorcerer. I have pledged my life to protect the world from his kind."

"He is performing for children!"

"You said you saw what sorcerers had done in the past," Senacus snapped back. "They brought down a doom that nearly consumed everything. If we choose to spare one sorcerer, we risk it happening again. You think that man is innocent, but I have seen other men who were thought to be innocent, and what they were capable of doing would chill your blood. The lure of using power against those who do not have it is too strong for anyone to resist."

Keilan grabbed the paladin again, more roughly this time. He pulled hard, and Senacus stumbled slightly, finally turning to face him. "I am a sorcerer! Are you going to kill me?"

Senacus flinched as if struck. He released his sword's hilt and his hand fell on Keilan's arm. "You are a boy. You can still be Cleansed, and Ama can decide if you should be spared to rise again."

"And if I resist you? If I refuse to come to Menekar after all this is finished? Will you strike me down?"

Senacus's jaw clenched, and his grip on Keilan's arm tightened.

Keilan ignored the pain and stared fiercely back at the paladin. "If that is what you plan on doing, kill me now. I will never be Cleansed. Never."

Something shivered in the paladin's face. He was silent for a long moment. "I won't kill you, Keilan," he finally said softly. "Even if the High Seneschal commands it."

"Then let the old man live," Keilan pressed. "He is just a grandfather entertaining his family. Will you murder all the Kindred here? They will surely fight to protect him. They have shared their fire and their food."

The paladin's shoulders slumped. Moving slowly, he unlooped his horse's reins from the wooden post where it had been tied up. Without turning back to Keilan he started leading his horse away, into the darkness.

"Where are you going?" Keilan cried after him.

"I will meet you on the road tomorrow. Sleep well," he said over his shoulder, then continued on, and was quickly swallowed by the night.

15: THE CRONE

LADY WILLA RI Numil grimaced as her carriage trundled along the broken streets, pain shivering up her spine with every jarring bounce. She shifted, trying to find a slightly more comfortable spot among the mound of plush cushions, but it was hopeless. Was the driver making a game of hitting every hole in the street?

She leaned forward, rapping with her ebonwood cane on the panel across from where she sat, and a moment later it slid open.

"Yes, Lady Numil?" Her driver's voice sounded strained, like he was expecting her complaints.

"Are you trying to shake me to pieces in here, Havrid?"

"No, my lady. My deepest apologies. The roads in this part of the Salt are nearly as bad as in the Warrens. I don't think they've been repaired in a hundred years."

With an annoyed sigh she sank back into the cushions . . . and then was thrown forward again as the carriage lurched like one of its wheels had nearly fallen off.

Agony erupted in her lower back, and she hissed in pain, her grip on her cane white-knuckled. Why had the gods made aging so terrible? You'd think after putting up with this mess of a world they'd created for seven decades they'd allow her to live out her twilight years in comfort. But no. Every day was a constant litany of aches and chills and cramps, punctuated by the occasional bout of intense pain.

Finally, her carriage shuddered to a halt. The door swung open, and she was poised to leap out of the carriage, surprising the constable standing outside. What was his name? Ah, Benwise. Handsome boy, if a bit simple.

"Lady Numil!" he exclaimed, hurrying to take hold of her arm.

"Constable," she replied, letting him help her down. Gods, it felt good to have the ground beneath her feet.

The smell was worse out here, though. This section of the Salt was mostly uninhabited, just rows of huge warehouses where the merchants and trading houses stored their goods. Because of the lack of people, it made a perfect area to dispose of various unsavory things, such as the offal from the nearby fish market that wasn't even wanted as bait, or refuse that was too rank for more populated neighborhoods.

Not that there weren't a few denizens who called this district home. In the fading light Willa saw a shadow recede deeper into one of the alleys between the warehouses. They were probably confused about what a gilded carriage from the Bright was doing down here, on the insalubrious side of the docks.

She was a bit confused herself. "Constable," she said, continuing to steady herself on his arm as he guided her towards one of the looming warehouses, "why exactly did you call me down here so late? Your message was a bit cryptic."

Benwise cleared his throat nervously. "My lady, you asked to be informed if we discovered anything odd while fulfilling your orders regarding the Shan."

Interesting. Willa had dispatched her eyes and ears to observe the few Shan who resided here permanently – but it was devilishly hard to glean any information from them, since they spoke their strange, tumbling language to each other, and rarely ventured outside their walled compound in the Bright that served as both a diplomatic station and a home for the merchants who lived in Lyr year-round. She had instructed her constables to detain the Shan traveling through the city, before they could vanish behind those high red walls. Since they were in the Salt, she assumed it was sailors who had been detained.

"So you've found something on one of the Shan ships in port?"

Benwise shook his head. "No. One of our cutters happened upon a Shan trading junk some ways off shore, sailing north to Herath. As per your instructions, the captain diverted the ship to Lyr so the sailors could be questioned. One of them is inside the warehouse."

The Oracle had claimed that the looming threat she'd seen would originate from Shan. With so little to go on, Willa had cast her net wide, trying to extract information from every Shan she could find. She'd also consulted with several scholars who had studied the history of that mysterious people and asked about these dark children they'd glimpsed in the vision. The answers she'd gotten had been largely incoherent – one scholar had read somewhere about children being sacrificed to placate the gods in old Shan, another thought the children could be the demons worshipped by some sort of death cult in the Empire of Swords and Flowers. The few Shan she had managed to question were tight-lipped on the matter, though Willa had watched several times while her constables questioned them, and she thought a few had known more than they were sharing.

They crossed the empty street and Benwise pushed open the door of one of the ancient, listing warehouses, holding it open as she hobbled inside. The room was small, an antechamber for the proper storage space beyond, and was dominated by a scarred table where a half-dozen watchmen in the blue and purple of the archon council lounged in rickety chairs, intent on a game of chalice. Telion was there as well, leaning against a wall – damn, how had the man beaten her here? One of the guardsmen glanced over as she entered, then his mouth fell open and he leapt to his feet.

"Lady Numil!" he cried, and at this his compatriots quickly stood, knuckling their brows.

"I'm sorry, my lady," Benwise apologized, glaring at the watchmen. "This lot must have arrived while I was outside waiting for your carriage."

Willa waved his words away. "Never mind. Constable, I want to know more about what you've discovered."

"It wasn't me," Benwise said, pulling out one of the chairs so she could sit. "Lady Philias noticed something was strange first."

Willa chuckled. "A word of warning. I wouldn't call her 'lady' where she can hear you."

"Ah, well, then, Goodwoman Philias –"

"Probably even less accurate."

"Yes, ah, she was the one who said to send for you."

Most interesting. Had there been a sorcerer among the sailors?

"And where is Philias now?"

Benwise gestured towards the entrance leading deeper into the warehouse. "In there. With the Shan."

Willa heaved herself to her feet again. "Well, then, let's see what was so important that I had to suffer through that horrid carriage ride."

The warehouse was huge, and empty of any goods except for a collection of shattered crates pushed up against one wall. This building was actually owned by the Numil family and had long ago been re-purposed as a space to get answers from the recalcitrant. Birds or some particularly large breed of bat fluttered among the high rafters, which were gilded bronze by the light falling through the large holes cut just below the roof. Dust glittered in the spears of light that reached the ground, and Willa could feel a sneeze starting to build. She slipped her handkerchief from her pocket in anticipation.

There were more watchmen here, another four or five, all holding crossbows in a manner that suggested they did not expect any trouble. They were arrayed casually around a man seated in a chair in the center of the room. Willa could see his hands were bound behind the chair and that, surprisingly, he wasn't Shan. Philias was perched on the edge of another chair, facing him. Willa couldn't see her face, but from her posture it looked like she was staring intently at the bound man, who in turn seemed to be trying his best to avoid meeting Philias's burning gaze.

Willa brought her cane down loudly as she approached Philias and the man. The former nun of Ama stood, turning to her.

"You took your time," she said.

Willa sniffed. "Those rich in years know that by dashing about, one misses important details. Better to be slow and thoughtful, rather than hurried."

If Philias had pupils, Willa thought she would be rolling them. "Well, I'm not sure if the time I spent with this fellow waiting for you revealed any important details."

Willa glanced over at the man, who was staring at them with eyes rounded by fear. Poor little duckling. Interrogated by Lyrish guardsmen and a woman with the eyes of the Pure. He must think he had been accused of something terrible.

From a cursory inspection there was nothing noteworthy about the sailor. He was old enough to have a few strands of gray in his brown hair, but his skin was still smooth and unblemished. If Willa was to guess, she'd have thought he hailed from somewhere in the Shattered Kingdoms, or perhaps the middlelands.

Philias motioned for Willa and Benwise to follow her a little ways from the man, outside of his hearing. Telion had wandered in from the front of the warehouse and was flipping a dagger to himself a few paces away. "Do you notice anything odd?" Philias asked.

Willa shook her head. "Should I? He seems to be just a sailor. We could go down to the taverns on the docks and drag out dozens who look just like him."

Philias frowned, a flicker of frustration passing across her face. "I hoped you might see what I'm missing."

"And what is that?"

"Why he's strange! There's something different about him, but I just can't place it."

"He's not gifted?"

Philias gave her an exasperated look. "I know what sorcery smells like."

Willa adjusted her grip on the ebony ball topping her cane, trying to keep the annoyance out of her voice. "Tell me why he's here."

Philias crossed her arms and indicated Benwise with her chin. "He sent for me when the Shan ship was brought to the docks. Like you asked, I've been accompanying the constables and the watch when they've been questioning the Shan in Lyr." The exact nature of the threat from the Empire of Swords and Flowers hadn't been made clear in the Oracle's vision, but Willa had a suspicion sorcery might be involved. After all, the last world-ending cataclysm had come about from the machinations of wizards. It had made sense to Willa that Philias and her Pure senses should be present when the Shan were brought in.

"So you went aboard the ship?"

"Yes. Stern to galley – I've never been on a boat so large. It was like a floating city! But I didn't notice anything strange. The hold was stuffed with trade goods bound for Herath, silks and ceramics and the like. Nothing made my senses tingle in the crew's quarters, though the captain had a few interesting items infused with some minor enchantments. But there was this . . . sensation I had while traipsing through the ship. I felt almost dirty, like there was some oily residue coating everything. Again, not sorcerous in nature.

"So then we went above deck and lined up the crew. This one stuck out immediately, of course –" Philias pointed at the bound man. "– simply because he wasn't Shan. But even beyond that, the . . . taint . . . seemed to be coming from him. Like he was secreting it. Even now I can taste it in my mouth."

"And what does it taste like?"

"Blood and ashes."

Blood and ashes. Willa turned back to the sailor, who was looking around the warehouse like he could divine a way out of his predicament if he searched hard enough.

"Something you've had in your mouth often?"

"I'm just trying to describe it. That's the best I can do."

Philias sometimes had a tenuous grasp on both her powers and her sanity, this was true, but there *was* something troubling about this situation. What was it?

Then it struck her. *The man hadn't said anything since she entered the warehouse*. That was odd. No protestations of innocence. No pleading for mercy. Surely he must have noticed how deferential the Lyrish watchmen were to her, and that his fate was in her hands. And yet he hadn't spoken a word.

Willa stumped over to the bound sailor and stared hard into his eyes. They were wide, yes, and darting about like he was terrified . . . but he wasn't perspiring. And his breathing hadn't quickened at all. Slow and steady.

He was pretending to be afraid.

"Who are you?"

The man remained silent. "He's a mute," Philias said, coming to stand beside Willa. "The captain told me so. Made clear he wanted to join the ship's crew in Ras Ami using only gestures.

Kept to himself on the journey. Good with ropes and could climb the rigging like a monkey. That was about all he could tell me about him."

Cold unease was starting to creep up Willa's spine. The longer she stared at the man, past the false fear, the greater the sense that something was watching her from behind those eyes.

Sometimes she was such a foolish old woman.

"Philias, come here."

"Yes?"

"I want you to touch his arm."

Willa could see the disgust in Philias's face even without turning to look at her. Those who had suffered through the Cleansing disliked coming into contact with the skin of others – as Philias had explained it, everyone who was not filled with the burning light of Ama felt cold and waxy. Like a corpse.

"Philias?"

"Fine," she said with a sigh. Willa stepped back a pace to give her room.

Philias crouched down, bringing her face close to the bound sailor. "I want this even less than you do," she said, and then reached out for his arm.

"No," said the man, and Philias paused, glancing uncertainly back at Willa. His voice was iron dragged across stone.

"Why not?" Philias asked, turning again to the sailor.

"Because," he grated. "Your eyes. They burn."

The light from above seemed to darken, as if a cloud had passed across the sun.

Suddenly Philias was reeling backwards, clutching at her face. Flesh fell away in tatters. Blood. Screams.

The man was standing, the leather straps that had bound his arms broken effortlessly. Philias stumbled and fell; much of her cheek had been torn away, revealing glistening red.

His hands. They had changed – his fingers now were tapering claws, long and black, and a squirming darkness seemed to be leaking from the points of those talons. Something moved beneath the man's skin, near his throat, a shape sinuous and monstrous, his face bulging oddly as it wriggled past his jaw.

The thrum of crossbows. A bolt took the creature in the shoulder, the force making it stumble back a step. It hissed and charged the watchmen, bounding towards them on all fours like an animal. Then it was among them as they dropped their crossbows and struggled to draw their short swords. More screams and arcing blood as the creature lashed out with its claws.

"Behind me!" Telion cried, pushing Willa back as he drew his swords.

The watchmen who had been in the entrance charged into the warehouse brandishing pikes. They halted for a moment, shocked at the sight of what was happening. The creature turned, moving faster than Willa thought possible, sidestepping a thrust pike and jabbing its now sword-length fingers into a watchman's belly. The dark claws slid in effortlessly, emerging from his back.

Willa rushed over to Philias and knelt down. Her face was a bloody ruin, strips of skin hanging from her shredded cheek and scalp. Willa glimpsed part of her jawbone. Blood was everywhere, though by some miracle both her eyes were unharmed. She still breathed, bubbles of blood appearing from between her lips. Willa pressed her handkerchief to where she saw the most blood escaping, a jagged wound in her neck, trying to put some pressure there and staunch the flow.

Silence. No more screams. She glanced up from Philias.

The creature was stalking towards them like a beast, drenched in the blood of the slain guardsmen. Bodies were piled behind it, some torn apart, their limbs scattered.

Telion positioned himself between them and the creature. His swords did not waver, brave man that he was.

Its face. There was no expression. No hate. No joy. Just calm purpose. The creature's talons had grown so long their tips now dragged on the wooden floor of the warehouse.

Willa took up her cane and with a twist pulled off the ebony ball topping the shaft. "What are you?" she screamed as it approached. "Are you like the children?"

The creature cocked its head. "How do you know the Chosen?" it hissed in a cracked and broken voice.

Willa swallowed away her fear. She was far too old to be afraid of dying. "The Chosen, eh? Silly name." Steeling herself, she stepped towards the creature.

"Lady Numil, flee!" cried Telion, trying to block her.

She ignored him. "I always said I'd stare death in the eye when he came for me."

The creature lunged. Telion swung his swords.

Lady Numil threw the ebony sphere she had taken from the top of her cane. It struck the creature's chest and shattered, splattering liquid that hissed and smoked. The monster shrieked, clutching at its bubbling face with rending talons. Telion's sword bit into its shoulder and the creature stumbled backwards, shaking its head as its melting flesh began to smoke. Telion cursed and shook his head as some of the droplets struck him.

The creature leapt away, crossing the room in two great bounds. With preternatural quickness it scuttled up one of the walls like a monstrous spider, its claws gouging great chunks from the wood. A moment later it was gone, vanishing through one of the high windows.

"God's blood, what was *that*?" yelled Telion, sheathing his sword and clapping his hand to his still-smoking cheek, his eyes wide from the pain.

"A gift from the artificer lords of Seri. A weapon even an old woman can use. I'm afraid your face might be permanently scarred, Telion. Lucky you were never handsome."

"What? No, I mean that thing!"

"I do not know. Now help me with Philias. We need to bring her to a chirurgeon quickly."

Telion seemed to emerge from his daze. "I know of one in the Salt. More used to treating sailors and whores, perhaps, but he's a learned man."

Willa clapped her hands. "Excellent. Pick her up and let's be off. I'll try and keep her from bleeding herself dry."

Gently, Telion scooped up Philias, averting his eyes from her mangled face. She moaned and muttered something unintelligible.

"What will we do about that thing?" he asked, his voice thick with pain. "It's loose now in the city."

Willa found herself staring at the dead watchmen scattered about. "The ship it was on was headed north, to Herath. I believe it's finally time I went to see the queen."

16: CHO LIN

BARBARIANS.

Alone in her room at The Cormorant, the inn where she had found lodging upon arriving in Herath, Cho Lin sat at a small table and regarded her supper with grim resignation. The servant girl who had delivered the plate had muttered something, probably the name of what animal it had been hacked from, but between her shyness and Cho Lin's struggles with the northern tongue the origin of the bloody slab in front of her remained mysterious. She prodded it with the pronged utensil the girl had also delivered with the meal, and red juice spilled out onto the table. Had it even been cooked? Where were the spices and peppers? This was what wild beasts ate in the forest – was it any wonder the men of these lands were covered in hair and smelled so terrible?

As if in response to her musings, laughter and incoherent bellowing floated up from the common room below. Yesterday, when Cho Lin had pushed through the door to The Cormorant, she thought she'd happened upon a brawl – the clamor had washed over her like a wave, burly men and women stumbling together and shrieking, the heat of the hearth and all the bodies pressing together so overwhelming she had nearly swooned. Instead, her hands had gone to the hilts of her butterfly swords, ready to defend herself if necessary. But then she'd noticed the musician up on the raised stage, playing some small, stringed instrument.

Dancing. The graceless revelry had been a dance.

She had much to learn.

As a girl, her tutors had instructed her about the northern barbarians: their customs and history, the names of their kingdoms and empires, the teachings of their philosophers and ethicists. Cho Lin had nearly been reduced to tears on several occasions by strict Teacher Chen, who had forced her to memorize the convoluted grammar structure and characters of the northerners' language – those strange squirming symbols that represented sounds rather than things. Endless afternoons spent living in terror that she would err while reading *A History of Menekar* or *The Anagogics* and feel the crack of the bamboo switch on the back of her wrist, all the while just wishing she could be outside dashing through the gardens with her lost friends.

But the lessons had served her well. She could understand most of what the northerners were saying, and she had successfully navigated several transactions, including securing this room and buying a few changes of the local garb. Warm woolen breeches and tunics, necessary in this cold city, along with a dark, cowled cloak, should allow her to move about without drawing attention to her foreignness.

Listening to the clamor swirling up through the floorboards, Cho Lin was surprised to feel a pang of such loneliness that she let her eating instrument fall to the table with a clatter. She was alone in this room. Alone in Herath, a stranger in this strange city. Alone in the kingdoms and the satrapies and the suzerainties of these uncivilized lands, a thousand leagues from anyone she knew. She had felt loneliness before – oh, yes, she had – but at least she had always shared a common language and culture with those around her.

Cho Lin pushed her plate away. She was being foolish. She had been on her own for a long, long time. It had begun after the poisoning ten years ago, when her father had set her on this solitary path – a path that should have been walked by her brother. No more afternoons in the gardens with her friends. Instead, an endless succession of teachers and tutors had molded her into an instrument to fulfill her family's destiny. Teacher Chen. Tall, beautiful Lady Ping, who had taught her the social intricacies she had no interest in. And Wan Min, the disgraced Tainted Sword who had introduced Cho Lin to the martial secrets of Gold Leaf Temple. On Red Fang she had made friendships, of a sort, but the very nature of the monk's philosophy was that Enlightenment could only be attained by turning inward and forsaking the outside world.

She had always been alone. It was her fate. And all that training, all the blood and tears, had been preparing her for this task, for this moment. More than a thousand years had passed since her ancestor struck down the Betrayers, and her family had been readying themselves for their return ever since. The ghosts of her ancestors were watching her, she knew, from beyond the veil. Including her father.

With a shake of her head Cho Lin took up the eating utensil again. She needed her strength. Ignoring the juices seeping from the meat she stabbed a glistening chunk and shoved it into her mouth.

Soft. Salty. There was a hint of some herb or spice that had been rubbed into the meat. She chewed and swallowed. It wasn't disgusting. Maybe even . . . delicious?

Cho Lin suddenly became acutely aware of just how ravenous she was. She took another bite.

When she had finished eating, she donned her cloak and slipped the keppa case containing the Sword of Cho across her back, then left her room and descended the stairs to the inn's first floor. She drew up her cowl and skirted the edge of the common room, which although still crowded had quieted to listen to a hunch-backed old man standing alone upon the stage. He was singing in a trembling but beautiful voice, and though Cho Lin couldn't understand much of the song, from how the words hung heavy in the smoky air and the solemn faces of the listeners she could tell she wasn't the only one who appreciated his singing.

Perhaps there was more to these people than she first thought.

Cho Lin waited until the last tremulous note faded, and then left the inn as the common room behind her erupted into cheers. The evening air had a biting chill, and she pulled her cloak tighter, thanking the seven mothers that she had had the wisdom to trade her thin silk and cotton robes for hardier Dymorian garments.

The Huntress gleamed in the night sky, the Arrow she had loosed arcing towards the swollen moon. Cho Lin wondered what the barbarians saw in the jeweled darkness. Did their gods also cavort across the heavens? Did they see the same things in the stars?

She murmured a small prayer to the Huntress, asking for her help this night. There was no guarantee that the Betrayers were here, and even if they were, she wasn't sure how she would recognize their spoor. She hoped the sword strapped across her back would give her some sign – her family's legends claimed it would alert her to the demon's presence.

Her eyes wandered to the vast fortress looming over the city, bulked against the night. That would be the place to start.

The streets were mostly empty at this hour. In the great cities of Shan, lamp-lighters kept the roads well-illuminated, and as much commerce was conducted during the evening as the day. But in Herath most of the light actually came from the buildings themselves, spilling from the open doorways of taverns and brothels or puddling beneath windows where lanterns hung or candles had been placed. The few folk who shared the street with Cho Lin seemed to be either hurried or furtive, walking briskly or skulking in the shadows, their faces, like hers, lost in the recesses of hoods or cowls. A few seemed to be taking more than a cursory interest in her, so Cho Lin ducked into one of the narrow alleys pressed between the crumbling buildings.

Before she had taken more than a few steps, though, something shifted in the darkness. She tensed, her hand going to the hilts of her butterfly swords, as a large shape moved to block her way. She turned to leave the alley, and found its mouth was now filled by two of the men who had been watching her on the street – one was large and hulking, his face covered with tattoos, the other smaller and ratty.

"I'm sorry," she said, trying to find a way around the pair, who shifted to stop her.

The smaller man chuckled. "No need to be sorry, little lady. We're happy you decided to come into our alley."

Cho Lin didn't know the word *alley,* but she could infer what they meant. "This alley is yours?"

The smaller man's head bobbed. "It is, it is. Well, not *mine,* really. Belongs to Choll."

Cho Lin glanced over her shoulder. The third man had crept closer, though he didn't seem to be preparing to leap at her. She suspected he was waiting for the smaller man's command.

"Choll is who?"

Even in the gloom she could see the look of exaggerated incredulity on his face. "You don't know Choll? He's the boss, the big –"

"Are you going to move?" Cho Lin said, cutting him off. "I want to leave."

The small man scratched at his cheek. "We can move. But you have to pay a –"

"You are robbing me?"

The man guffawed. "Robbing is a dirty word. We're business people –"

Cho Lin had heard enough. "You are robbing me," she said, and stepped towards the alley mouth.

The larger man put his arm out to stop her and she caught his wrist and broke it. He screamed at the snapping sound and fell to his knees. She whirled around at the scrape of the larger thief's feet as he charged her, jabbing her hand into his neck. She took just enough off the blow that she didn't crush his throat, and he collapsed like a sack of meal.

The smaller man hadn't moved. He gaped at her like a caught fish, and she kicked him in the head, sending him sprawling. That made him finally stop talking, though the other two, who hadn't said anything before, were now making noises: the one with the broken wrist was still on his knees, mewling in pain as he rocked back and forth. The other was emitting a tortured wheezing sound as he struggled to breathe.

No city guards or passersby seemed inclined to investigate what had just happened, but Cho Lin didn't want to risk drawing too much attention to herself. The streets here were evidently not as safe as in the cities of the Empire of Swords and Flowers. She should take another route.

Cho Lin brushed her hand against the stone rising up around her. Ill-fitting, with plenty of handholds. To someone who had scaled the cliffs of Red Fang, this would prove no challenge.

Leaving the three would-be thieves behind her, Cho Lin pulled herself up the wall, her fingers finding the crevices.

The building was only three stories, and the gently sloping roof was tiled in slate. She crouched on the eaves, gazing out over the shadowed cityscape. It looked like the rolling sea at night. Here and there towers pierced the sky, deeper black against the velvet sky. In the distance Saltstone brooded, speckled with lights. The queen would be there. And so would the Betrayers, if they were indeed in Herath.

Cho Lin's slippered feet whispered across the tiles. When she was sure she had found her balance she increased her speed, until she was running down the canted roof. The edge hurtled closer. The Nothing unfolded within her and she embraced it, strength flooding her legs.

Cho Lin gathered herself and leapt, an alley flashing past below her, gone in a heartbeat. She landed smoothly, barely breaking her gait. This roof had a squat brick chimney, and she dodged around it, disturbing birds that had nested within. They rose into the air, shrieking, but in moments their cries were fading behind her. She jumped again – the next roof was a full story above her, and she caught the edge and swung herself up in one fluid motion. Her heart was thundering with the sheer joy of giving herself over to the Nothing. She hadn't run like this for many months, since before she had gone into seclusion in the cells beneath Gold Leaf Temple. But it reminded her of the training she had done with the monks, dashing across the jagged karst formations that ringed Red Fang, all her cares and troubles fading as she embraced the hard strength nested deep within her Self. In the Nothing.

Finally she paused, panting, on the roof of a building that nearly pressed up against the outer fortifications of Saltstone. The walls looked to be smooth stone, the great blocks mortared together so seamlessly Cho Lin doubted even she could climb it.

She needed to find another way inside. Leaping from roof to roof she skirted the curtain wall, until she noticed some movement below her. A covered wagon pulled by a pair of shaggy ponies was trundling towards a small door set in the side of the fortress. From its lack of ornamentation, Cho Lin suspected this entrance was used to ferry food and goods inside; without hesitating, she swung herself over the edge of the canted roof and dropped into the alley below.

As the wagon passed by the alley's mouth, Cho Lin dashed out and pulled herself up into its bed . . . and nearly gagged from the smell. The wagon's shadowed contents looked like large, circular rocks, but that certainly wasn't what they actually were. Her eyes watering, Cho Lin squeezed herself into the back of the wagon behind a stacked pile of these pungent objects. She prodded one of them, and it gave slightly, as if beneath the hardened crust there was a softer middle. It couldn't be food, could it?

The clop of the pony's hooves slowed, and a moment later the wagon shuddered to a stop.

"Nagrin! What do you have today? Anything worth taking a little slice of?"

There was the sound of a throat clearing and an impressive amount of phlegm being hawked. "Baern. I've got enough Visani cheese to catch the Queen of Mice herself. But it's not for the likes of you. Magisters and nobles, not ugly scum born at the bottom of the Slopes."

Harsh laughter. "Gods, I can smell it. Hurry on inside and get that filth out of here. Wouldn't want to eat it anyway – I'll keep to my mutton and ale, thank you very much."

Cho Lin heard the creak of a large door opening, and with the sound of a whip cracking they lurched forward again. There were thin gaps in the side of the wagon where the wooden slats came together, and Cho Lin lowered herself to the floor so she could see what was happening outside. They'd entered a courtyard that must be used for delivering goods, as crates and chests were piled beside a few empty wagons. Servants in livery displaying a serpentine red dragon uncoiling across a wash of white sky were attempting to tip a great iron-banded ale barrel on to its side so it could be rolled. It was so large, though, that if they were not careful it would certainly smash on the flagstones. The drama seemed to have captured the attention of everyone in the courtyard, as a handful of guardsmen in tabards displaying the same dragon were watching the servants' struggles with obvious amusement.

Cho Lin crept to the front of the wagon and risked a quick glance outside. No one was watching, so just as the wagon shuddered to a stop she leapt down and strode quickly across the flagstones towards an open doorway. Her heart jumped like a rabbit, and she was sure someone would cry out an alarm, but the Immortals favored her and she slipped inside without being noticed.

Cho Lin paused inside the doorway, willing herself calm. She started when a loud crack sounded from outside, followed by harsh laughter. Apparently, some noble would go without their favorite ale tonight.

Adjusting the keppa case slung across her back, she started down the passage that led deeper into Saltstone. If questioned, she would claim she was a musician summoned to perform for the evening feast, though she suspected no one would bother interrogating her. She was a young woman in a fortress teeming with sorcerers and warriors, and she –

Cho Lin gasped and went reeling against a wall, her thoughts scattering. She'd felt something. Like she was an instrument and the sword upon her back one of its strings, vibrating from being plucked. Again it came, a trembling that made her whole body quiver.

The Sword of Cho had scented the Betrayers. Her pulse quickened again. The warlocks had been right – it was the Crimson Queen of Dymoria who had unleashed them again upon the world.

She moved through the corridors of Saltstone as the watches passed and the night deepened. As she'd hoped, the hurrying servants paid her little mind, and she might have been invisible to the guards on patrol, given how their gazes seemed to slide over her. Apparently, young women in simple garb carrying musical instruments were not considered much of a threat in the fortress of the Crimson Queen.

Gradually, Cho Lin learned how to let the sword lead her. If she moved too far in the wrong direction she'd feel the blade growing warm through her tunic, until the heat was almost painful. When she was back on the path the sword thought she should follow, the quivering would begin, as if the blade itself was excited.

After much wandering she found herself at the base of one of Saltstone's many towers. It was different than the others, which were crowned by rounded cupolas: this tower's summit had been reduced to a jagged ruin. The stones around its base were cracked and shattered, as if something heavy had fallen from above. Cho Lin chewed her lip, wondering what could have sheared the top of this tower off and sent it crashing down. No lights were visible in the narrow windows – it looked to have been abandoned.

But the sword was insisting that what she sought was within.

A pair of grim-faced warriors wearing cloaks of deep scarlet flanked the tower's doorway. They seemed a different breed than the other soldiers she'd seen as she explored the fortress: the make of their arms and armor seemed finer, and they did not speak to each other as they kept watch. There was something valuable within.

Lowering her head meekly, Cho Lin skirted the tower's base. She felt the eyes of the guards following her, but apparently she was not a strange enough sight to warrant raising an alarm. The back of the tower nearly pressed against one of the fortress's soaring walls; here, far from any torches, Cho Lin stepped into the pooled shadows and ran her hands along the tower's rough stone. Glancing up, she saw a deeper blackness high above, and without hesitating she began to climb.

The ascent was far easier than ones she had made on the cliffs of Red Fang, and soon her fingers curled around a window ledge. She lifted herself high enough that she could glance inside the darkened room, but saw nothing. The sword on her back was thrumming so hard she had to bite her lip to keep her teeth from chattering.

Silently, she pulled herself over the ledge and dropped to the chamber's floor. She paused, listening intently.

They were close. The demons that had driven the Shan from their ancient lands. For over a thousand years her family had been preparing for this moment . . . but it was never supposed to be her.

She let out a long, shuddering breath and moved towards the deeper blackness. She passed through it into a larger space – her eyes were adjusting quickly to the dark, and she could tell she stood upon a landing in a great staircase that spiraled upward. Below her she could see a faint puddle of light spilling from the tower's entrance.

Cho Lin started climbing the stairs, and the sword rejoiced. What if the demons flew at her out of the darkness? She reached over her shoulder and untied the knot securing the end of the keppa case, then reached within and drew out the Sword of Cho. The leather-wrapped dragon bone handle was warm in her grip, and a tingling had begun to spread from her hand into her arm. The legends of her family said that when the blade's metal passed through the corrupted flesh of the Betrayers their spirits would be banished back to the chest. Whoever had loosed them the first time could do so again; she had to find the chest and secure it. She would have to convince the queen of the danger the demons posed . . . or kill her.

When she reached the next landing, she felt the sword pull her towards an iron-banded door. Cho Lin pressed her ear to the dark wood. Nothing. She gave the door a tentative push, but it was locked. Could the chest be inside? Is that what the sword was leading her to?

She noticed a key hanging from a metal peg driven into the wall and felt a little flutter of unease – the door was locked to keep something inside from escaping. But surely the Betrayers would not be deterred by wood or stone.

Cho Lin breathed out slowly, preparing herself for whatever she might find within. She was unwilling to slide her sword back into its case, so she was forced to take up the key with her left hand and fumble it into the lock, wincing at the sound of scraping metal. For a moment she feared it would not fully turn, but then came a hollow thunk and the door cracked open. Adjusting her sweat-slick grip on her sword, she raised it into a stance that would let her lunge or defend, depending on what she found within, and pushed the door open.

No demons came boiling towards her, but she did not let down her guard as she shuffled inside. Moonlight poured through a barred window, striping the room in silver and black. There was a low table near the door, and a cabinet or closet of some kind. Her boots sank into a thick carpet. Despite the open window there was a smell to the room: not rancid, but as if someone had been kept inside for far too long.

Something shifted in the darkness underneath the window, where the moonlight could not reach. Cho Lin tensed.

"Who are you?"

It was a man's voice, rough and cracked. The shape leaned forward, brushing the edge of the light, and Cho Lin glimpsed pale hair. "Have you come to kill me? That's a very big sword for a small girl."

Cho Lin's eyes darted around the room. Were the demons there, crouched in the shadows? Was this a trap? The sword in her hand was thrumming only slightly, as if satisfied that it had brought her to this room. But *why* was she here? Did the sword want her to kill this man? Was she endangering herself and her mission by not striking him down now?

"Who are you?" she hissed softly, still not lowering her blade.

A low chuckle. "Since you are the one entering my room at night brandishing a sword, I believe you should answer first."

She ignored this. "I will not play games."

The man moved again, coming further into the light. He still had not risen to his feet, and now Cho Lin could see why: manacles wrapped his wrist, chains trailing into the darkness behind him. "My name is Jan."

"You are a prisoner?"

The man raised his arms. "Yes."

"What did you do?"

"Something I did not intend."

Cho Lin's thoughts whirled. The sword had brought her here, so this man must have some connection with the Betrayers. But she did not think the demons or the chest were here now. "I am searching for something."

"What?"

"They look like children. They –"

"I know them."

Cho Lin swallowed away the dryness in her throat. "How?"

The man ignored her question. "You're from Shan, aren't you? I can hear it in your voice. And I've seen swords like that before. I remember . . . there were symbols carved into the wood, Shan symbols."

"What wood?"

"Those things . . . they killed someone I knew. I tracked them for a thousand leagues, and at the end of my hunt I came to a rosewood chest. They were inside."

This man had found the Betrayers' prison. That must be why the sword had brought her here – it could sense their taint on him. "I must find that chest," she said.

"Why?"

"Those demons . . . they are dangerous."

"I can lead you to the chest. I know where it is."

Cho Lin studied him skeptically. Why was this man here, rather than some cell underground? What had he done? He said he'd tracked the Betrayers. What was he? Not a sorcerer, otherwise a prison like this would never have held him.

"Why should I trust you?"

The man shrugged. "I have nothing to offer you except my word. But you should know that the queen or her servants will turn their attention here soon enough, and then you'll join me as her prisoner."

He was right, she knew. If the queen was a sorceress then she might already be aware that Cho Lin had entered this room. There was no time to waste.

Pushing aside her doubts, Cho Lin stepped forward. "Hold out your arms."

The man did as she commanded, and with a single clean strike Cho Lin sliced through the chains as easily as if they were silk bindings. The man gave a startled gasp when the metal links clattered to the floor.

"Your sword . . . "

"It is special. It cuts metal as easily as flesh."

She struck off the other chain just as smoothly, then braced herself, half expecting the man to leap at her. But he merely stood, his fingers touching the ends of the sheared metal. He was a good head and a half taller than her, with broad shoulders. Yet if he did attack her Cho Lin had no doubt that she could overpower him. There were no warriors in the barbarian lands like the disciples of Red Fang.

"Later, a . . ." she searched for the word " . . . a blacksmith can strike that iron still on your hands. Dangerous to do with my sword."

The man nodded. His hand went to a metal collar about his neck.

"And that as well."

He shook his head. "No blacksmith can remove this."

Cho Lin slipped her sword back into its keppa case. "Then you wear it. Now, quickly – as you said, we must leave."

17: DEMIAN

RECESSED IN THE shadows, Demian leaned against the alley's brick wall and watched the white building. It was nondescript, several stories of mottled stucco, nearly identical to the rows of prosperous townhouses that lined the streets of this neighborhood. The avenue here lacked the raucous tumult of the poorer districts, but it was not empty: slaves in the spotless robes of rich households hurried by carrying baskets full of fruits and vegetables, and rich merchants lounged on gilded palanquins carried by the hairless men of the Whispering Isles. A pair of legionaries sauntered past, the sunbursts of Ama engraved into their cuirasses flashing in the sun.

None of the passersby even glanced at the white building. It almost seemed like they were intentionally ignoring it . . . and the men who occasionally arrived at its door.

They were mendicants, all of them, dressed in robes of purest white hemmed with gold. Each of Ama's holy men approached and knocked twice, and the door slid open just wide enough for them to enter. After a few hours they would reappear again, returning to their sacred duties with a bit more spring in their step.

When they donned the white robes, the mendicants of Ama swore vows of celibacy. But the leaders of the church wisely turned a blind eye to establishments like this. Better to have a place reserved for the inevitable indiscretions, rather than forcing the priests to find their needs among the flock. Demian had learned that zealots were necessary for the establishment of a faith, but afterwards, without a bit of pragmatism concerning the weaknesses of the flesh, a religion would not last long.

Demian pushed himself from the alley's wall as his quarry finally appeared, briskly approaching the white building's entrance. He wore the white robes of a mendicant, but instead of gold his vestments were banded with black.

An inquisitor.

The door cracked open and the man slipped inside. Demian unslung the bag on his shoulder and pulled out a wad of white cloth. Quickly, he donned the robes he had brought – the weave was not as fine as that which a true mendicant wore, but he didn't anticipate any careful inspections. The priests inside had their minds on other things.

Demian stepped into the deeper shadows, slipping into the other place. He stood upon one of the ancient stone paths hanging in the emptiness. Not far from him the path split, then split again, branching out to reach dozens of points of radiance floating in the darkness. These were doorways formed by shadows. Demian had often wondered who had built these paths, and what agency rearranged them as the light in the other world changed. The answer to that mystery had never been revealed to him.

Long experience of navigating these paths had given him an intuitive knowledge of which of these doorways would lead inside the white building. He moved quickly, ignoring the yawning abyss below. A scene resolved on the other side of the portal as he drew closer: mendicants relaxing on couches and comfortable chairs, some sipping on wine as they conversed, others intent on games of tzalik or chalice. Servants circulated among the clerics of Ama, refilling their cups from ornate decanters or fanning them with shimmering feathers as long as a man's arm. Every one of these servants, male and female, were young and lithesome, draped in robes cinched to accentuate their narrow hips and long limbs.

If he stepped through this doorway Demian would emerge near where several mendicants were deep in conversation, and though he would enjoy the looks on their faces, he would have no chance of accomplishing his task. So he moved on from this portal, searching for a more isolated spot. As luck would have it, the next doorway seemed to be behind something large enough to cast the opposite wall in shadow. A shrouded Aspect of Ama was recessed in a niche in front of him, arms outstretched as if beckoning him forward. Demian thought this Aspect was Compassion, which was an odd choice for a house such as this.

Warmth and noise washed over him as he left the other place behind. When viewed from the shadow world the colors had seemed muted, washed out, and he hadn't noticed the cut flowers scattered about the Aspect's bare feet. He breathed out slowly, his skin prickling as the coldness faded away. Then, with the confident stride of someone who was exactly where he belonged, he came around the pillar and surveyed the room. It took him only a moment to find his quarry: the inquisitor he had seen entering the building was speaking with a fat mendicant, gesturing with a long-stemmed wine glass as he made some point. Demian plucked a cup from the tray of a passing servant and slid onto a velvet couch, watching the priest out of the corner of his eye.

The wine was a good vintage: tart, with hints of fruit and spice. As Demian's gaze wandered around the room, his thoughts returned to the poor pilgrims suffering under the lash as they made the long journey to the holy city. Blood mixing with dirt on that long and dusty road, while these mendicants enjoyed wine and sweetmeats delivered by beautiful youths. When Demian was younger, such hypocrisy would have made his anger burn hot; long ago, though, he had come to accept that this was not a perversion of a just society – rather, this was exactly why society had developed. The entire edifice had been built so that the powerful could extract what they wanted from the weak.

Demian pulled back from his musings as the inquisitor clapped the fat man on the shoulder and moved towards the back of the room, where a wide set of pink-marble steps ascended to a second-story landing. Draining the last of his wine, Demian stood from the couch and followed. None of the mendicants or servants spared him a glance as he started on the stairs. Ahead of him, the inquisitor had reached the top.

Demian's hand slid along the twisted copper bannister, and at the touch of the cool metal a long-forgotten memory rose up . . .

With one hand he steadied himself on the gilded railing, while with the other he held tight to his brother, their fingers laced together. Behind them, a tall man in yellow robes ushered them along, prodding Demian whenever he paused to catch his breath. The stairs seemed to go on and on, the cold stone seeping through his thin slippers, numbing his toes . . . Though the climb was uncomfortable, he wished it would continue forever, for he knew what waited for him in the dark room above . . .

He shoved down the memory. This was not the time to be distracted.

As Demian arrived on the landing he turned, glimpsing a flash of white robes as the inquisitor vanished inside a room. The hallway here was carpeted in a fine Keshian weave, and the wall sconces were decorated with elaborate carvings that shimmered with crystals and other precious stones. A servant turned the corner ahead, coming towards him carrying a pile of linens.

His movements were a bit unsteady, and when their eyes met the boy flinched and ducked his head, as if afraid.

Demian paused outside the chamber the inquisitor had entered, listening. From within he heard a man's voice. His cadence was odd, as if he was speaking to a simpleton.

Or a child.

Demian cracked open the door and slipped inside, quickly closing it behind him. The room was small but richly appointed, dominated by a large gilt mirror and a wide, low bed mounded with cushions. A beautiful young boy with dark eyes lay upon the silken sheets, a horse carved from red wood clutched protectively to his chest. The inquisitor was standing beside the bed, and as the door clicked shut he turned to Demian angrily.

"What is this, mendicant?"

Demian put his finger to his lips.

"How dare you –"

"Be quiet," Demian said calmly, and the inquisitor's mouth snapped shut, his eyes bulging in outrage. "If you cry out, I will remove your tongue."

Demian's fingers slammed into the man's throat just as his lips started to part. The inquisitor made a strangled sound, the anger in his eyes melting to fear. His hands flew up, scrabbling at Demian's grip, but the shadowblade batted them away.

"I have questions for you. If you answer them truthfully, I will let you live. Nod if you understand."

The inquisitor jerked his head once in agreement.

"Good. I am going to release you." Demian let go of the man's neck and he reeled away, gasping, steadying himself with a hand on the bed. The boy scooted farther from him, cowering among the cushions. Demian paid him no mind.

"Now. You are an inquisitor of Ama. Do you serve in the temple, or in the catacombs below the palace?"

The man eyed Demian warily, rubbing at his neck. "The catacombs," he finally rasped.

Demian nodded. Good. Most inquisitors fulfilled their duties in the catacombs, but there were a few who served at the pleasure of the High Mendicant and Seneschal directly.

"I am looking for someone. A sorceress who might have been brought to the catacombs a few months ago. Perhaps delivered to you by servants of the black vizier."

It was only a flicker in the man's face, but it was enough.

"Does she still live?" Children could be Cleansed and reborn as the Pure, but adults never survived the ceremony.

The inquisitor licked his lips. "Yes."

"Where is she?"

The man swallowed, his hands twisting the silken sheets. "Deep. The faithful stay in the first few levels of the catacombs, but the passages spiral down much farther. She's the personal prisoner of the vizier, and his servants are the ones who bring her food and water."

"Is she collared?"

"Ama would never allow sorcery beneath his holy palace –"

Demian cut him off with a sharp gesture.

"She was bound hand and foot, so she could not form her magic."

"That would not matter. There is something else." Demian withdrew a curved dagger from beneath his robes.

The man paled, his eyes widening. "It is a secret of the faith . . . sorcery is suppressed in the catacombs. The remains of thousands of the Pure are interred there, and Ama's gift lingers in their bones."

Interesting. Demian knew that the sorcery-inhibiting collars designed by the wizards of the Kalyuni Imperium had been infused with the ashes of cremated paladins, but he had not known the power of the Pure would persist for so long.

So Alyanna was alive. Had she been tortured? Were her mind and body whole?

The inquisitor watched him carefully. "My lord –" he began, but Demian stopped him again with a raised hand.

"Boy," Demian said, turning to the child, who had watched this exchange with wide, uncomprehending eyes. "Has this one ever hurt you?"

The boy glanced from the inquisitor to the shadowblade.

"Does he hurt you?" Demian repeated, his tone softening. The boy nodded slightly.

"Go," Demian told the child. "Leave this room."

Quick as a rabbit the boy slid from the bed, dashing for the door. Demian heard it creak open behind him.

The inquisitor's face was now a sickly gray. "But you said . . . "

"And you said in your vows that you would shepherd the children of men into the Light. It seems we are both liars."

Demian lashed out with his dagger, leaving a gash across the inquisitor's neck. Clutching at the wound, the man thrashed in the bed, blood bubbling from between his fingers.

Demian bent and wiped the dagger clean on the sheets, then turned away from the dying priest. The door was still slightly open, and he glimpsed the child watching solemn-faced through the crack.

"Hold on to your hate," Demian told the boy as the inquisitor gave a last gurgling cry. "It is the only thing they can never take away."

Then he stepped into the shadows, and the coldness closed about him once more.

The undercity beneath the imperial capital was a vast and sprawling labyrinth. Demian had spent centuries below the mountain, in the narrow passages that threaded the home of the kith'ketan, but that place had been carved from the rock by hands that did not belong to men. There had been an otherworldliness, a sense compounded by the presence that had made its lair in the mountain's bowels. The undercity, by contrast, was an amalgamation of sewers and catacombs and tunnels that had grown together to honeycomb the space beneath Menekar. There were even entire streets and buildings that looked to have been sunk below the ground, remnants of a vanished age.

The young shadowblade had explored the winding passages of the undercity in the months since he had been tasked with waiting for more of his dark brothers to arrive. Demian thought of him as Whisper, because of his soft voice, though the kith'ketan forsook their old names when they were gifted their swords. Whisper told Demian of some of the wonders he had seen: a great head of smooth dark stone jutting from a tiled wall, water black as pitch dripping from its empty eye sockets; a ruined temple to some nameless god or demon, its nave filled with headless skeletons; an albino lizard several times the length of a man that had swum past him as he had been mapping the sewers that flowed beneath the streets. And when Demian had told him they would need to penetrate the catacombs beneath the Selthari Palace, where the inquisitors of Ama labored to purify the souls of sorcerers and heretics, Whisper had claimed he was certain some tendril of the undercity extended that far.

So they had spent days delving farther than the young shadowblade had gone before, sometimes in darkness and sometimes following a ball of Demian's wizardlight. The first extended foray they made had lasted a full day, and they had been forced to finally turn back when they finished the last of their food and water. Further explorations met dead ends, impassable ruins, and in one instance a chasm that plunged down into oblivion. Demian had nearly given up hope of finding what they sought, and had begun to contemplate other means of ingress, when, quite unexpectedly, he realized they had passed beneath the palace.

It began as a creeping sense of wrongness that swelled larger as they paced a crumbling passageway inlaid with grimy mosaics. The wizardlight he had sent farther ahead sputtered and vanished, as if it were a flame that had suddenly been placed under glass.

"What is it?" Whisper said, his shadowblade leaving its sheath with a hiss.

"I'm not sure," Demian replied, pausing to unpack the lantern he had brought. "But I have my suspicions."

The walls of the corridor were pocked with holes, dark niches the lantern's light revealed to contain skeletons. Most appeared to have been undisturbed since they had been laid to rest, their bony hands laced across their chests and their jaws shut, as if they had died while sleeping. But as his light skittered over the bones Demian noticed that on more than a few skeletons were the signs of violent ends. Here a skull had clearly been staved in, and here the ribs had been shattered. Light glinted among the yellowing bones: a tarnished copper disc inscribed with the sunburst of Ama hung around the neck of one skeleton. As Demian slowly walked down the passage, he noticed the same amulet in every niche.

"These were the Pure," Demian said. A tingling puissance radiated from the bones, making his skin crawl. He tried to grasp his sorcery but felt it slither away, smoke between his fingers. It was like death had concentrated the power wielded by the paladins in life, and Demian shivered. He had been collared once before, an age ago, and it had felt the same. Like he had suddenly been rendered deaf and blind.

Surprisingly, he felt a thin trickle of fear. Foolish – he was not only a sorcerer, but a shadowblade and a swordsinger. No warrior had trained for as long and with the same discipline as he had.

Even still, he should be careful. Demian crouched in the middle of the passage and drew forth a slim object.

"What's that?" Whisper murmured, turning from the bones he was examining.

"A precaution," Demian said, standing the corpsetallow candle and its cold flame in a metal holder.

"You took that from the meeting place?"

"Yes."

"But that is the beacon. What if more of our brothers arrive in the city?"

Demian set the candle down on the stone and stood. "How many have arrived in the last fortnight?"

There was a pause. "Just you."

"And likely no more will come before we return."

They left the sallow light of the corpsetallow candle flickering behind them, and the faint silver and blue glow was quickly swallowed by the blackness. Demian kept the lantern lit as they passed through the winding corridors of the catacombs – one of the powers bestowed on shadowblades was the ability to see in darkness, but the gift was not total. The lantern illuminated far more, even though Demian could tell Whisper was becoming agitated. Those who grew up under the mountain preferred the darkness.

"What if someone sees the light?"

Demian smiled faintly. "I pity any poor soul that stumbles across us."

They continued through the twisting labyrinth, choosing corridors at random when they diverged. Despite Whisper's concerns, they did not meet any guards or inquisitors – the catacombs seemed abandoned, just a sprawling crypt. Demian tried to keep a rough count of the number of skeletons they passed, but quickly gave up. There were thousands, at least, and while most had been placed in the wall niches, a few were laid down on stone biers in small antechambers off the main passages. Some of these paladins still clutched their white blades, that unnatural metal untarnished despite so many centuries.

Several times they found themselves where Demian was certain they'd been before – there was little to distinguish the corridors, but he was sure he had seen a skull canted the same way, or an identical bit of fallen masonry littering the ground. He was considering laying down some kind of trail so they'd know if they were walking in circles, but then Whisper drew in his breath sharply.

It was a larger entrance than they'd seen, the ceiling slanting upward to accommodate thick stone columns, and as they approached Demian could see what was engraved upon the broad lintel: the sunburst of Ama above a message in archaic Menekarian: '*The Light Will Reveal*'. And there was indeed light within; it puddled in front of the entrance, burnishing the stone a rich gold. It did not flicker or dance like the light thrown off by flame – it looked, unbelievably enough, like daylight.

Demian set down his lantern and crept closer. He pressed himself against one of the columns and peered into the chamber. It was vast, soaring more than a hundred span high and extending perhaps a thousand across, empty save for a few tiered steps that climbed to a platform in the middle of the room. Light pierced the wall high up near the ceiling and lanced down to illuminate the top of the dais and the woman who hung there motionless. Chains extended from her slim arms, vanishing into the blackness, and her bare feet dangled above the platform. The robe she wore was in tatters; dark lash marks laced her back, and rivulets of dried blood reached down her legs. Her long black hair was matted and tangled.

Alyanna.

Demian rushed into the chamber, ignoring Whisper's startled cry to wait. He didn't care – he hoped there was someone here for him to kill. He would tear down the palace if she was dead.

He bounded up the steps three at a time, dreading that he would put his hand on her and find her flesh cold. Relief flooded him when he gently touched her leg and it twitched in response.

"Weaver," he said softly, coming around in front of her. "Can you hear me?"

His heart quickened as she stirred, lifting her head slightly. Demian sucked in his breath when he saw that her face was a mess of purple and black; her lips were split, and around her eyes was so swollen and bruised he doubted she could open them.

"Demian . . . " she rasped, before a shudder passed through her and her head fell again.

"I'll get you down," he said, drawing forth Malazinischel. He sliced through the chains and caught Alyanna as she collapsed into his arms.

"Be careful . . . " she murmured into his ear " . . . my slave . . . "

"Undying One!" hissed Whisper from where he crouched at the base of the steps, pointing towards the entrance they had come through. A fat man stood in the doorway, the light from the lantern Demian had left outside the chamber shadowing his features.

"Greetings! Please excuse my surprise – I had no idea guests would be stopping by today."

The accent was Shan, so this must be the black vizier of Menekar. Demian's grip tightened on his sword's hilt. *Cut! Bleed!* Malazinischel shrieked in his mind, and Demian did not try to dissuade the blade. This was the one who had taken Alyanna – almost certainly it was on his orders that she had been tortured. Demian kept expecting for a regiment of guards or the Pure to rush into the chamber, yet no one else came as the vizier strolled a few steps closer and crossed his arms over his chest, slipping his hands into his long sleeves. He did not seem worried.

"I know that sword. How many of my kin did you slay, swordsinger?"

Coldness filled Demian. The genthyaki. Alyanna's pet had somehow survived and slipped its leash. He had hunted them down long ago, before the cataclysms, but always with other sorcerers at his side. They were the most dangerous enemies he had ever faced – faster and stronger than any warrior, capable of drawing as much sorcery from the Void as the greatest of Talents.

He might die here today.

The long shadow cast by Demian and Alyanna stretched down the steps, and Whisper moved closer to it. Demian knew what he was thinking and almost bade him stop – perhaps if they waited for the genthyaki here they could try and attack it from two sides. Then again, a shadowblade in the back would also kill the creature.

Whisper vanished as he touched the edge of the shadow. Now the beast had to be distracted.

"I killed many of your kind, monster. Malazinischel remembers the taste, and hungers for it again."

The genthyaki sighed. "Ah. A thousand years, and still you prattle and boast. Age does not make your race wiser, it seems."

"Yet for all your power, your race has always skulked in the shadows."

The genthyaki chuckled. "Skulking in shadows, you say . . . " He withdrew his hands from his sleeves. Then he moved, faster than Demian thought possible, whirling and reaching *into* the darkness beside him. Whisper came stumbling out, wrenched forward by the genthyaki's grip on his arm.

How was this possible? Even from this distance Demian could see the shock in the shadowblade's eyes, visible above his veil. He tried to pull away, but he might have been straining against iron.

"We built the paths in the darkness, manling," the creature hissed, shaking Whisper like he weighed nothing. "And you think you can hide from me in them?"

The genthyaki clamped his other hand on the shadowblade's collarbone. Then, as if he was pulling a fly's wing from its back, he casually ripped Whisper's arm from his shoulder. The sound of cracking bones and tearing meat was terrible, but Whisper's screams were worse. Blood gouted from the gaping hole, soaking the genthyaki's dark robes. With a contemptuous snarl he tossed the severed arm aside, then scooped the shadowblade's throat from his neck.

"Weaver . . . Alyanna . . . " Demian said numbly.

He felt her small hands tighten on his back. "Kill me," she whispered.

The genthyaki was stalking towards them, the shape of the black vizier molting away to reveal the monster beneath. Gray flesh erupted from its dark robes, studded with curling thorns, as the nubs of leathery wings pushed from its back. The creature swelled huge and lean and terrible, its face twisting into something that resembled a horse's skull. One side of the genthyaki's face had been scarred by fire, the burned flesh pink and glistening.

He could not fight this thing. Perhaps if he could call upon his sorcery . . . but not here, with the bones of the Pure dampening his power.

There was only one chance.

"Alyanna, you must be strong. I can take us away, but there will be pain. Can you stand it?"

She said nothing, but he felt her shift against him. He took that for acceptance. "Brace yourself," he said, and stepped into the shadow cast by the hanging chains.

He stood upon the stones hovering in the emptiness. Alyanna gasped as the coldness washed over her – the first time in this place, he knew, was like being thrown into an ice-cold lake. The shadowblades spent years hardening their bodies against the chill so that they could withstand it for a few hundred heartbeats. Alyanna had far less time than that before she slipped into shock and died.

Hoisting her over his shoulder, Demian began to run. He watched where every one of his steps fell upon the narrow path; a single mistake, and they would plunge into the abyss below. He desperately hoped she would not start thrashing when the cold became too much to bear.

He stumbled and nearly fell as a shriek erupted from behind them. *God's blood, the genthyaki has followed us here*! Alyanna moaned, and Demian gritted his teeth and plunged on.

After passing the light that represented the lantern he had set outside the chamber the path did not diverge; no other glowing doorways hung in the emptiness, as there were no other shadows in the endless blackness of the catacombs. Except for one.

In the distance he glimpsed a hazy point of silver light. He was surprised it was so close – the straight path to where they had entered the catacombs was not actually very far. He willed himself on faster, until his legs ached and his breath burned ragged in his throat. At any moment Demian expected to feel the genthyaki's claws at his back, tearing Alyanna away and shredding his flesh. But it did not come, and for a brief moment he allowed himself to hope the genthyaki had vanished . . . but then the shriek came again, closer than before. Alyanna gave a strangled sob.

The light swelled closer, and he could see the vaguely man-shaped soul writhing in the dark. While the corridors in the catacombs had twisted and turned, the path in the blackness ran straight and true, through walls and solid rock. It had been less than a hundred heartbeats, but already Alyanna must be feeling the toll of this place.

Eighty paces.

Fifty.

Demian heard the rasp of talons scraping against stone.

Thirty.

Ten.

Another piercing scream, so close he imagined he felt the monster's hot breath on his neck.

He threw himself forward, into the light, and landed hard on the stone floor of the catacombs. Screaming in triumph, he scrambled to smother the corpsetallow candle, willing the soul into oblivion.

Darkness rushed in. Demian collapsed on his side, gasping. After a moment, he squirmed closer to where Alyanna lay unmoving and turned her over.

"Weaver . . . speak to me. Please."

He saw with the twilight eyesight of the kith'ketan her throat working to form words.

"Kill me," she croaked again, and a tear trickled from her swollen eyes.

"Weaver, we escaped. But it will come after us once it finds a way out of there. We need to flee. I can carry you, I just need a moment to gather my strength."

She shook her head weakly. "No . . . Demian. Kill me."

"Why?"

With a great effort, she forced her eyes open. A brilliant golden light flooded the passage, and Demian recoiled in horror.

Alyanna had been Cleansed. She was one of the Pure.

18: KEILAN

THEY SKIRTED THE edge of the great southern city of Gryx, where the Iron Road ended, staying outside its tall red walls in one of the trading towns where caravans made camp. The next morning, they were awoken by the prayer horns of the Lonely God winding in the city, and they emerged blinking from their guesthouse to find a hundred believers of the Keshian faith prostrating themselves before a great tongue of flame dancing within a copper brazier. A passing merchant informed them that in the great square of Gryx there was a flame as tall as a palace's tower, a ladder of fire into the sky begging for the Lonely God to abandon his solitude and climb down to join his followers once again.

Keilan also saw one of the pens where slaves were stabled. Nel told him that this muddy encampment ringed by guards was but a shadow of the massive markets within the city where the Fettered were bought and sold. Most of the people Keilan saw milling about in the camp didn't seem angry or scared – more resigned than anything else. When he told this to Nel, she had nodded, and said most of the slaves had been sold into servitude by their own families to pay off some debt or escape famine. Slavery, in some ways, was safer than being poor – you would likely be bought by someone with wealth, so you would always have food on your plate and a place to sleep. And while Keilan saw a few sullen, angry-looking men, Nel told him that usually they did not end up in these markets. They would be sent to the fighting pits, and their lifeblood would mingle with the red sands in front of a roaring crowd.

Listening to the stories of the harsh lives of slaves brought back memories of the nights along the Wending Way, teaching Xin how to read. The Fist brother had been willing to trade his life for the knowledge his masters had denied him. Keilan suspected that some of these slaves he now saw, with their carefully blank expressions, secretly harbored similar thoughts.

After Gryx, they followed a road that climbed into the Blackmonts, heading towards the Kingdoms. These were the largest mountains Keilan had ever passed through, though they paled in comparison to the vast peaks he had seen towering to the north as they'd ridden along the Wending Way. He grew a little dizzy as they went higher, but the feeling vanished the next day when they descended into a valley filled with familiar-looking trees.

As they crested one of the last foothills of the Blackmonts and saw the red forests of the Shattered Kingdoms sweeping out into the distance Keilan had felt something in his chest, a mix of excitement and panic. Somewhere ahead of them, over the rolling sea of leaves, was his village. Sella. Mam Ru. His father.

He had been born there and lived his whole life among the mud huts and fields and forests. He had fished with the other villagers, eaten with them, helped them rebuild their homes after storms. And in the end, they had turned their back on him and let a paladin of Ama take him to what they certainly must have assumed would be his death.

And they had murdered his mother.

"Are you all right?" Nel asked soon after they left the last of the hills, matching his pace as they rode beneath arching branches, some of which were bare, some still speckled with color.

"Yes. I'm just . . . " He struggled to put what he was feeling into words.

"Nervous? Scared?"

"No . . . "

"Angry?"

Keilan glanced at her, and Nel nodded.

"You have a right to everything you feel. They hurt you. And they hurt your mother. I think . . . I think you have a lot buried deep down inside you. It will need to come out, eventually, or it will fester and become something worse."

"You told me your mother was murdered," Keilan said. "Did you forgive?"

Nel looked away. "No," she finally admitted. "I never did. For years I hated, and it poisoned something inside me. I couldn't . . . love others. Except for Vhelan, and he became my family. He kept me alive during those years in the Warrens. Otherwise I would have turned into something else and ended up dead in a gutter. It wasn't . . . it wasn't until I met Xin that I felt like I could open myself to another person."

Keilan's hands tightened on the reins. "What about the men who took my mother? Can I forgive that? Can I forgive . . . my father for not stopping them?"

Nel was silent for a long moment. "I know it will be difficult. Perhaps forgiveness is the wrong word. Maybe you can try and understand why they did what they did. Your village . . . what is it like?"

"It's small. Poor. We never had much. My mother's books might have been the only ones in the village."

"Did you feel that way when you lived there?"

"No."

"Why?"

Keilan swallowed, suddenly understanding. "Because . . . I didn't know any better. All I knew was the village."

"And now?"

"Now I've seen great cities and kingdoms. I've met queens and princes and sorcerers."

Nel nodded again. "Perhaps they murdered your mother and let the paladin take you away because they were ignorant and afraid of what they did not understand."

"That doesn't make it better," Keilan said sharply.

"No? My mother was killed by a rich man. The life of a whore meant nothing to him – she was a thing to be used and thrown away. But he knew what he did. Your villagers . . . they acted out of fear. Their whole lives they'd probably been told that sorcery was evil. That it would bring down disaster and death upon their families. They were trying to protect themselves. And I think your father . . . when he did nothing to save your mother, he was trying to protect you."

That struck Keilan so hard he rocked in his saddle. "Me?" he said softly.

Nel stared at him intently. "Keilan . . . what would have happened if your father had fought the men who came for your mother? Could he have stopped them?"

"No," Keilan whispered, his thoughts wandering back to that terrible night, the shapes in the darkness outside his hut demanding for the door to open.

"They would have beaten him. Maybe killed him, if he fought hard enough. It was probably only because he had been born in the village that he was not immediately guilty himself. If he had fought for your mother and died, what would have happened to you? Would one of your relatives have taken in a cursed child?"

Would Uncle Davin have cared for him? Keilan found he couldn't speak and had to shake his head.

"So your father gave up the woman he loved to save you."

Tears prickled Keilan's eyes, and he bowed his head. He felt something within him shift. It was like a tight knot he had been carrying around for years finally unraveling. He took a deep, shuddering breath.

"Some people do terrible things because of malice. But not all. Most people simply don't know what they're doing is wrong."

Keilan's thoughts were churning. After a moment he glanced up, and his gaze was drawn to the white cloak of the paladin riding a hundred paces ahead.

"Senacus," Keilan murmured. "It's the same. He doesn't know."

Surprise flitted across Nel's face, and then she grimaced. "Well," she said. "He has to learn."

The journey from Gryx to the Kingdoms boasted far fewer inns and eating houses than the Iron Road, and as the day began to fade Nel decided they should find a suitable place to spread their bedrolls. Keilan knew she felt uncomfortable hemmed in by the forest, so he wasn't surprised when she suggested they camp at the edge of a meadow speckled with golden flowers. Earlier that day, in a stroke of great good fortune, they'd encountered a hunter on the road who had sold them a brace of coneys. So as Nel began to awkwardly clean the animals, Keilan gathered kindling from the edge of the nearby forest. By the time he'd returned and built a fire Nel still hadn't finished, as she seemed surprisingly squeamish when it came to removing the fur and guts. When Keilan offered to help, she scowled and turned away so he couldn't see what she was doing. He shrugged and sighed and stretched out in the grass, enjoying the pleasant feeling of not being in his saddle.

A ways removed from their campfire Senacus had also found a spot to rest, his back to a fire-blackened stump and his eyes closed. Keilan watched him, turning over what Nel had said earlier.

What had happened to the paladin? What was it like to be Cleansed? What horrors had he seen as he hunted sorcerers across Araen? If Keilan knew, would he understand why Senacus was so uncompromising he would consider executing a grandfather in front of his grandchildren? That seemed impossible. And yet . . . he didn't think the Pure was evil. Senacus was doing what he thought was right.

Coming to a decision, Keilan stood and went over to where their horses had been tied up. He pulled the jeweled sword Lady Numil had given him from among his bags, and with almost reverential care also lifted the paladin's still-scabbarded white metal blade. Carrying both swords, he walked towards Senacus, who opened his glowing eyes as he approached. Keilan hoped the expression he saw was mild curiosity rather than outrage that Keilan had dared touch his sacred weapon – it was always difficult to read the paladin.

Keilan held out the Pure's sheathed sword. "Senacus. I've heard the paladins of Ama are some of the world's greatest warriors. Will you teach me something?"

Senacus cocked his head to one side and studied Keilan, his lips pursed. Then he also seemed to decide something, and pushed himself to his feet, brushing the dirt from his white armor and vestments. He held out his hand for his scabbard, and Keilan passed it to him. With a last, measuring look he turned and walked into the meadow.

"Come on."

Keilan hurried to catch up with the paladin's long strides. Indignant insects rose from the golden flowers as they passed, buzzing angrily, but luckily they were not the stinging sort. Near one of the few trees in the meadow, a gnarled old oak, the paladin stopped and squinted towards the setting sun.

"We can practice until the sun dips below those treetops. Sword-training is dangerous in the dark." The paladin unsheathed his sword and let the scabbard fall in the long grass. Keilan had never seen one of the famed white metal blades this close before, and he studied it with interest. The sword didn't look like steel, or even metal – it looked fragile, as if it had been shaped from ceramic, yet there were absolutely no blemishes on the blade.

"Where do they come from?" Keilan asked, and Senacus shook his head.

"I don't know. We are given them after we finish our time as neophytes in the temple, and the mendicants say the swords are forged with Ama's blessing." Senacus slashed the air with his sword. "They are light, and do not rust or break easily."

"Do the swords make the Pure great warriors?"

Senacus smiled slightly as he continued carving the air. "Certainly having a sword that does not weigh much is a great advantage. But it is only one of several. When the light of Ama fills us, we become faster and stronger than other men."

"So the Pure truly are the world's best warriors?"

Senacus hesitated. "There are some out there who could match the Pure in battle, great champions of their peoples. But as an order of warriors, there is only one other that approaches ours in strength."

"The Fists?"

"No. They are great fighters, but they are only men."

Keilan thought back to the carnage he had glimpsed in Saltstone. "Shadowblades?"

Senacus snorted. "I've never crossed swords with one of those assassins, but I'd wager their deadliness relies on cunning and trickery. No, I am speaking of the monks of Red Fang Mountain, in the Empire of Swords and Flowers. The Pure are strong because the divine light inside us gives us power beyond what should be possible, but somehow the warriors of Red Fang draw upon something similar. I've seen them fight. They can leap through the air like cats, and strike with unnatural speed and strength."

"What gives them their power?" Keilan asked, and Senacus shrugged.

"I do not know. Their secrets are closely guarded." He held out his sword so that its tapering length pointed towards Keilan's chest. "Now, you wanted to practice?"

"Yes!" Keilan said, drawing his own sword. The red stone eyes of the falcon carved into the hilt glittered in the dying light of day. He took a few practice swings, testing the sword's weight and grip. The last time he'd trained was over a month ago, atop Saltstone as Xin had instructed the apprentice magisters, and he could already tell that he was out of practice and that tomorrow his wrist would be sore.

He adopted the first form of The One Who Waits, his blade held high.

Senacus's eyes widened slightly. "You've been instructed by a Fist warrior?"

Keilan slashed downward, the third form of The One Who Strikes, and then as quickly as he could returned to the previous form. "Xin was a Fist warrior."

"He would have been killed if the masters of Gryx knew he'd taught you even a small fraction of the forms."

Keilan lunged forward again, a different variant of The One Who Strikes. "I taught him how to read, and they would have killed him for that, too. I don't think he cared much."

Senacus nodded. "It is still dangerous. Even if he did not value his own life, any punishment would have also fallen on his brothers."

"He cared so much for his brothers," Keilan said, and the paladin seemed to hear the edge of anger in his voice, as he ended the conversation by lifting his own sword.

"Come, Keilan. Try to strike me. Remember your forms, and don't hold back."

Keilan lowered his sword slightly. "Are you sure? I don't want to hurt you."

Senacus gave a small, confident smile. "You won't."

They practiced as the last shreds of daylight fled across the meadow. At first Keilan was worried he would accidentally strike the paladin, but he soon discovered that Senacus was a warrior unlike any he had tried himself against before. No matter how fast he thrust or slashed, the white metal blade was always there to turn his sword away with ringing precision. When the paladin attacked he was notably slower than when defending, allowing Keilan to parry each strike. Finally, when it grew too dark to see clearly, Senacus stepped back, sheathing his sword. He seemed barely winded – unlike Keilan, who was gasping for air.

"Good," Senacus said, real approval in his voice. "You have strong fundamentals. Your footwork is sound, and the forms you've been taught give you a grounding that will serve you well, if you can find another Fist warrior to teach you more."

"We both know . . . that's not likely," Keilan said, panting.

A thoughtful look passed over the paladin's face. "Hmm. I can't build upon your foundation in the forms, but I can teach you another style of sword fighting. Not as elegant, perhaps, but as effective in its own way."

Keilan stood and slid his sword away. "Thank you. I would be grateful."

Senacus nodded like he considered the matter settled and began walking towards the flickering light at the meadow's edge. Nel must have finally managed to clean the coneys – the delicious smell of roasting meat greeted them as they approached the campfire, and Keilan's stomach responded. He felt a pang of sympathy for Senacus, as Nel never shared any of the food she prepared with the paladin . . . but to Keilan's surprise he saw her crouched beside the fire holding three sticks threaded with chunks of crisped meat.

"Took you long enough," she said, rising. "I wouldn't have started roasting them if I'd known you'd be gone so long." She held out a stick for Keilan, and then offered another to Senacus. The paladin accepted it gently, ducking his head in thanks. She turned away as if this peace offering was nothing to be noted and returned to her spot beside the fire. Keilan found his own seat and motioned for Senacus to join them.

Later, Keilan listened to Nel's gentle snoring as he lay and watched the fire's last dying flames. He could also see Senacus, who had pulled his bedroll closer after they had finished their supper, and the paladin's side was rising and falling in the steady rhythm of sleep.

He returned his concentration to that tiny flame, reaching out to it, attempting to recreate what he had witnessed in the camp of the Kindred. Inside his mind an image formed of him out on his fishing boat, floating in a great, empty expanse. He leaned over the side, hesitating only for a moment as he stared into that dark abyss, and then plunged his arm into the water. He shuddered as *something* searingly cold flooded him.

A tiny hand extended from the flames of the campfire and curled towards where he lay, almost as if beckoning him on.

19: CHO LIN

THEY RODE THROUGH the night after passing through the eastern gate of Herath. Jan sat a horse well, Cho Lin thought, for a man who had been chained to a wall for quite some time – she guessed a few weeks, at least, given the lesions scarring his wrists that had been revealed when they'd finally gotten his manacles cut away. His hair and nails were not overlong, though, nor were his clothes reduced to rags. His dress was fine enough that he had ridden straight past the guards flanking the night gate without drawing a second look. She'd followed behind with her cowl drawn up to hide her features, afraid that the sight of a Shan on horseback would prove memorable.

Jan did not speak, and Cho Lin suspected that if she could see his features in the darkness, he would look deep in thought. He had barely spoken while they escaped from the fortress of the Crimson Queen, clinging to her silently as she climbed down the wall of the tower in which he'd been imprisoned. No words, but there had been wary respect in his face when they'd finally stood in the courtyard below. Then they'd slipped out through of the larger gates, hidden in a stream of servants returning to their homes in the city proper. After Cho Lin stopped by her room at The Cormorant to gather a few things – Jan had stayed outside in the shadows, claiming he was known inside – they had made their way to a stable and purchased a pair of nags that looked to her to have a future in the cook pot rather than outrunning the queen's hunters. The horse trader had tried to press two sleek stallions on them instead, but after inspecting all the man's stock Jan had been insistent they take the nags. The stable master's resigned expression after Jan had made his choice suggested to Cho Lin that her new companion knew horseflesh.

For most of the night they rode silently along the Wending Way, listening to the night birds warble to each other. Finally, as a pink dawn started to creep over the horizon, Cho Lin kicked her horse into a canter and came up alongside Jan.

"Why were you a prisoner? What did you do?"

The man's face – his expression lost to the darkness – turned towards her. "I was a guest of the queen, and I betrayed her. Through me another struck at her and killed many."

Ah. So that was it. "You were a part of the attack on Saltstone?" Rumors of the attempt to murder the queen had been on everyone's lips in Herath – even the man who had sold her fruit in the morning had wanted to gossip about the explosion that had destroyed the queen's tower. And the ones behind the carnage – they had been shadowblades, if the whispered words of a fruit seller were to be believed. Even in the land of Shan the legends of the kith'ketan were known.

"I did not intend to be. I was tricked."

She could hear his anger. "Who was behind the attack? Do you know?"

A long pause, as if the man was weighing how much to tell her. "I do. The sorceress who used me is the same one who commands the child demons you are searching for."

More pieces fell into place. If the Betrayers had been a part of the attack, then that would explain why her sword had sensed their presence inside Saltstone. And that would also suggest that the Crimson Queen was in fact in opposition to the demons . . . or whoever they were allied with.

Something shrieked in the forest, an almost human sound, and Cho Lin's hand found the handle of her butterfly sword.

"Just a rabbit," Jan said. "Caught by a fox or owl. When they cry out in pain they sound like children."

Cho Lin relaxed. "And this sorceress, are we heading towards her now? You said the chest was in Menekar."

"It is. In the imperial gardens of the Selthari Palace. We have a long ride ahead of us."

The midday sun had nearly crested when they reached the first rest stop along the Way. It was just a few buildings clustered off the road: a ramshackle inn and tavern, an open-air smithy, and a few wood and mud huts with barren vegetable fields spread behind them. Jan nudged his horse towards the little village, leaving the road, and Cho Lin turned her horse to follow him.

"Where are you going?" she asked when she'd caught up.

He slid from his horse. "I need a bath."

Cho Lin glanced down the road in the direction they had come. "A bath? There will be hunters. We need to go. Quickly."

Jan looped his reins around a hitching post, then looked up at her, squinting into the sun. "If the rangers of Dymoria have our trail – and I assume they do – then we are already caught. It is just a matter of when."

"Then we find a good place to do a . . . how to say it . . . secret attack."

Jan gave a crooked smile. "An ambush, you're talking about. They will come in force, Cho Lin. How many of Dymoria's elite soldiers can you kill?"

She twisted the reins in her hands. "If we ambush? Ten?"

He blinked in surprise, his expression of calm resignation briefly replaced by one of incredulity. "Ten?"

Cho Lin shrugged. "Fifteen, maybe."

He shook his head, sighing. "That's . . . unbelievable, but even if it was true it wouldn't matter. I expect fifty rangers, at least, with sorcerers accompanying them."

Now it was Cho Lin's turn to eye him skeptically. "So many? For you?"

Jan touched the metal collar around his neck. "They will assume, I think, that I know of a way to remove this."

"And why is that important?"

Jan ran his hand through his sandy hair. "Because I am a sorcerer." He watched her reaction, and then continued when she only raised an eyebrow. "This collar keeps me from using my power."

Cho Lin gestured at the empty smithy. "Someone here can cut it off."

Jan frowned. "No. There are only two ways it can be removed – with its key, which is probably somewhere back in Saltstone, or if a sorcerer stronger than the one who placed it on me attempts to unclasp it. And since that sorcerer was Cein d'Kara, I'll likely be wearing it for quite a while. Now," Jan said, holding out his hand, "some coins, please. When the rangers arrive, I'd like to meet them freshly washed."

Cho Lin pursed her lips, but she passed Jan a few Dymorian copper pieces. He smiled and nodded his thanks, then headed for the door of the inn. Cho Lin watched him until he'd vanished inside, stunned by his insouciance. How could he be thinking of a bath at this time? Had she rescued a madman?

A sword. She needed to get him a weapon before they encountered their pursuers. Cho Lin approached the smithy, which was just a forge under a patchwork roof festooned with hanging horseshoes. A shape was curled up beside the anvil, snoring loudly. Cho Lin cleared her throat and an older man with a bristly gray beard jerked awake.

"Eh? Customers?" he slurred, stumbling to his feet. Even from a dozen paces away Cho Lin could smell the sour alcohol, and she wrinkled her nose.

"Smith," she said, "I need a sword."

The old man blinked at her with rheumy, bloodshot eyes. "A Shan? God's blood, I must be dreaming."

Cho Lin gave him her most imperious stare. "No dream. Do you have a sword?"

The old man swallowed. "Mostly I just have horseshoes and a bit of tack . . ." His gaze traveled around his smithy and the random bits of metal stacked in haphazard piles. "Wait," he said, and reached down to pull an old sword out from among the mess. He held it up, studying it critically. "Yeah, that's a sword. Looks like it even has a bit of an edge to it. Now I remember; some fella had to sell it to me a while back to settle some debt over there." He nodded in the direction of the tavern. "You can have it for a silver."

Cho Lin sensed that the price was extortionate, but it seemed foolish to haggle. She dug in her pouch for a silver and held it out for the smith. He snatched it from her with filthy fingers, his eyes wide. "I hope this ain't a dream!" he chortled, biting down on the coin before slipping it into a stained pocket. He passed her the sword and she received it gingerly, careful to avoid touching his hand.

Cho Lin returned to the inn and found a seat at a rough-hewn table outside. She leaned the unbalanced hunk of iron the smith had claimed was a sword against a chair, wrapping her cloak tighter around herself to ward away the chill. What madness. Was she truly willing to fight a regiment of soldiers for this man? Even if he knew where the Betrayers could be found? She loosened her butterfly swords in their sheaths, her fingers tracing the ivory carvings set in their handles. What if she leapt on her horse and started riding east on her own? What did she owe Jan?

Cho Lin sighed, knowing she would stay. Staring down the empty road they had traveled, concentrating on that hazy point where it vanished among the distant trees, she felt herself falling towards the Nothing. Her surroundings faded, the cool strength flowering inside her, waiting to be seized when she needed it.

Cho Lin gradually returned to herself when she felt a presence beside her. Jan came over to the table and sat, pointing at the sword she'd just bought. His hair was wet, and it seemed a layer of grime had been removed, though his clothes were still filthy. He smelled noticeably better.

"Is that for me?"

She nodded.

He picked it up, testing its balance and then laying it down on the table. "I suppose it will do. Should we be off?"

Cho Lin nodded in the direction of the road, and Jan twisted around. A lone rider was approaching the inn dressed in rich scarlet robes, which seemed to be an odd choice of garment for a solitary traveler. Beneath her cloak her hand tightened on her sword's hilt.

When he grew closer she saw that the rider was young, with an almost boyish face, though his black hair was marred by a streak of gray. A twisting silver hunting horn hung around his neck. He caught them staring and waved jauntily.

"Who?" Cho Lin asked, glancing at Jan.

He shook his head slightly. "I've never seen him before, that I can remember. But those are magister robes. He's one of the queen's sorcerers."

A sorcerer. Cho Lin felt a little shiver of uncertainty. Those trained by Red Fang feared no other warriors in the world – but the Nothing offered no protection against sorcery. She would have to strike quickly and ruthlessly.

Jan must have felt her tense because he held up his hand, as if to ask for patience. "Wait. Let's see what he says."

The magister awkwardly dismounted when he reached the inn and spent a moment brushing the travel dust from his robes. Then he rubbed his hands together and blew on them. "Winter is here, eh? Excuse me. I'll return in a moment."

He pushed through the door to the tavern, calling out for the innkeep. Cho Lin and Jan glanced at each other. He certainly didn't seem threatening, but Cho Lin also didn't take her hand from her sword.

The magister returned a moment later carrying a bottle of wine in one hand and three wooden cups in the other. He looked almost giddy as he set down the cups, brandishing the bottle in front of them.

"Firewine from Gryx, and nearly a decade old! See that mark, the boar's head? That's a very good winery. Fortune turns her face to us today, it seems."

The magister slipped into a chair across from Cho Lin as he worked to open the bottle. After straining fruitlessly for a moment, he frowned and placed his finger on the cork, whispering under his breath. With a hiss the cork popped out, and he beamed.

"A handy trick," he said, winking at them as he stood again to pour a measure of the dark wine into each of the cups.

"Who are you?" Cho Lin asked in bewilderment.

The magister stood and gave a quick bow before sitting again. "My apologies. My name is Vhelan ri Vhalus, a magister in the court of Cein d'Kara. And you are?"

"You know who I am," Jan said, crossing his arms.

"I do," said Vhelan, taking a quick sip of his wine. "Ah, delicious. Yes, indeed I do. I'm sure you've realized I'm here to return you to Herath." He turned to Cho Lin. "But I have to admit my curiosity about your liberator and companion. *Nel soon*, my lady."

Cho Lin arched an eyebrow. "You speak my language?"

The magister waved her question away. "Oh, no. That's the extent of it, I'm afraid. I once knew how to tell a girl that she is beautiful, but I've forgotten. Unfortunately." Vhelan flashed what Cho Lin assumed he thought was a charming smile, and then took another swallow of wine.

Cho Lin left her own cup untouched, remembering her evening with Bai Hua, and she noticed Jan had done the same. "My name is Cho Lin. I am the first daughter of Cho Yuan, and sister to Cho Jun, both mandarins of the Jade Court."

Vhelan's fingers tapped out a quick pattern on the table, and from his expression it seemed like he was trying to understand something.

"A Shan noblewoman!" he said, spreading his arms to indicate the dilapidated buildings. "My apologies that we meet in such a rustic environment. The queen would have welcomed you to Saltstone with a feast, if she had known you were in the city."

"I did not wish to call upon your queen."

Vhelan chuckled. "Apparently! Instead, you abducted her guest –"

"Prisoner," Jan interjected.

"Unwilling guest, let us say, and fled the city."

The young magister's face held no hint of guile. It was as if he was enjoying a carefree afternoon at a winehouse with his friends.

Cho Lin didn't trust him.

"Something was stolen from Shan. Something very dangerous. This man knows where it is and has promised to take me to it."

"May I know what?"

"No."

Vhelan sighed, pinching the bridge of his nose like he was sorry for the conversation's sudden turn. "Well, then I must insist you both return with me to Saltstone."

Cho Lin held his gaze without blinking. "No."

Vhelan's expression became pained. "Ah. Are you sure? I have only to blow this," he touched the horn around his neck, "and dozens of rangers will be here in the time it takes to gallop over that rise." He turned to Jan. "Her Majesty is still angry with you, though I think she was softening. She has a fiery temper, yes, but it tends to burn fierce for a short time and then vanish – well, perhaps it smolders for a while still, but I do think the chains would have come off soon, at least."

"I'm not going back to that chamber. You will have to kill me first."

"And you, Lady Cho? Would you also die for his freedom?"

Cho Lin reached down to pluck at the Nothing inside her, feeling the coiling strength ready to flood her body. "I am a warrior of Red Fang Mountain. If you try and take my companion many of your soldiers will find their deaths. As will you. I could kill you before you put down your wine."

The magister's calm demeanor wavered. There was a trickle of unease in his eyes as he carefully set his cup on the table. "You trained at Red Fang?"

Cho Lin nodded. "And I am no Tainted Sword. I came here to fulfill the wishes of my brother and the warlocks of Tsai Yin. To hinder me would anger many of Shan's great people. This man and his knowledge are more important than you realize."

"Then come back with me and explain your mission to the queen."

"No. I cannot take that risk."

The friendliness was gone from the magister's face now. "You risk death by refusing to return to Saltstone."

"You have already decided not to stop us by force," Cho Lin said with calm authority. "If you cannot convince us to follow you to Saltstone, you will allow us to leave."

"So certain?" Vhelan said sharply, his hand going to the silver horn.

Cho Lin prepared herself to lunge across the table and bury her butterfly sword in his neck.

Then Vhelan sighed, his hand drifting from the horn to his wine cup, and she relaxed. He stroked its wooden stem, seeming to stare at something far away. "She will be wroth," he finally said softly.

Jan's eyes widened as he realized Cho Lin had been correct. "You would let us go?" he asked incredulously.

Something of his old attitude returned, and the magister crooked a smile. "The queen commanded I return with you in chains or on a bier. But I've known her for many years, and she would come to regret ending your story like this, cut down outside a nameless little town. Also, I would not wish to risk the wrath of Shan without understanding what is truly happening here." Vhelan made a dismissive gesture. "Go. And be quick about it, as the next hunter she sends after you might not be so merciful."

Cho Lin stood, inclining her head towards the magister.

Vhelan accepted the thanks by raising his cup to her. "I hope you do meet my queen. I think she would like you."

Jan snatched his sword from the table. "Farewell, magister. Tell her I hope she can someday forgive me."

"I will, sorcerer. Truly, I do not think you two will always be at odds. A drink for that day." Vhelan drained his cup and set it loudly on the table. "Ah. Now if you will excuse me, I plan on finishing this bottle before the captain waiting in the woods gets tired of standing around and comes down to see why I haven't given the signal yet."

Jan nodded at the magister and went over to where their horses were hitched. Cho Lin followed him, her hands finally leaving the handles of her butterfly swords.

As he unlooped the reins Jan bent closer to her, still keeping his voice low. "How did you know he would let us leave?"

Cho Lin allowed herself a slight smile. "I grew up in the Jade Court and was tutored by the most clever of consorts in the art of reading others. A man like that is an open book."

Jan paused, giving her an appraising look. "And what about me?"

She said nothing as she swung herself up into her saddle.

20: DEMIAN

"**THE GRASS IS** whispering."

Demian had thought Alyanna was asleep, and those words – the first she had spoken since they left the catacombs beneath Menekar and fled the city – jerked him from his own reverie. He'd been staring out at that thin dark smudge where the white plains met the arcing blue sky, the hinge upon which the world seemed to open.

"Weaver?"

The frail shape hunched in front of him on his horse lifted its cowled head slightly.

"Listen."

So Demian did. He heard the hissing of the long white grass as it brushed against his horse's belly, intimately close. Or perhaps she meant the sound of the wind as it rippled the endless plains, making the grass sway as if a great creature undulated in its depths?

"What does it say, Weaver?" he asked gently, but Alyanna slumped forward again, ignoring his question.

Was she simply imagining something that was not there, still delirious from her ordeal?

Let her rest and recover her strength . . . whatever of her old strength could be recovered.

Some things had changed forever. The heat radiating from her made his skin prickle, though it did not affect the links of his armor or the fastenings on his horse's barding. It was a warmth that only he as a sorcerer could feel. The searing light of Ama, leaking from a woman who had once been the greatest sorceress of her age.

Such an affront made his stomach churn with anger. He wanted to murder every one of those pious fools who had dared lay hands on her. Stripping Alyanna of her sorcery was akin to cutting off the hands of the finest painter in the world or mutilating the face of the most beautiful woman. To do such a thing to one so supremely talented made the crime incalculably worse.

It had been meant to kill her, he knew. A final punishment and degradation worse than death. To feel, in her final moments, the sorcery that had infused her and defined her drain away and be replaced by this horrible light. A few children survived the ceremony to rise again as Pure – cut by the mendicants while strapped to the Radiant Altar – but Demian had never heard of an adult emerging alive from the Cleansing.

What had she become?

That night, with the moon only a faint sliver, the plains were transformed into a calm black sea. There were no hills or buildings to infringe upon the sky, so the stars spread in dazzling abundance to every horizon. Here and there patches of witch weed grew among the grass, softly glowing with a spectral radiance. Demian avoided these – he had seen eyes flashing in the dark near these oases of light, and he suspected the white lions of the plains had learned to lie in wait for those foolish enough to think the witch weed offered a refuge from the night's dangers.

He would have ridden through the darkness without stopping if he could. Alyanna was not heavy, but she was an extra burden his horse was not accustomed to carrying. He wondered if his mount thought him mad – they had gone from Menekar to Herath, across much of the known world, and then immediately turned around and retraced their journey. Now, after only a few short weeks in the city, they seemed to be doing the same thing again.

He patted his horse's flank as he swung down into the waist-high grass. She had been a good mount and had long ago overcome the skittishness all animals felt in Malazinischel's presence.

His sorcery still unsettled her, though.

"Calm, girl," he whispered, tangling his fingers in her mane to try and give her some measure of comfort. Then he concentrated, summoning a shimmering bubble that encompassed them all. He heard Alyanna stir from where she slumped and reached out with his other hand to keep her from sliding off the horse.

"What are you doing?" she murmured, shielding her face with her arms, as if the mere presence of his ward made her uncomfortable.

Which it probably did.

"Setting up a camp," Demian replied as he brought a wave of magical force crashing down from above. The sorcery broke against his ward and slid away, but the plains around them had no such protection and for a hundred paces in every direction the grass was instantly flattened. He felt his horse tremble at the sound of the invisible avalanche, and Alyanna gave a little strangled cry. Demian had no idea what that would feel like to her, but he imagined it was not pleasant.

Still, there were very good reasons for doing this, and one of them became apparent when with another flicker of sorcery he conjured forth his wizardlight. Like a second moon the light drifted above them, bathing the space he had carved from the high grasses, and in response something lifted from the devastation not far from where they stood, long and sleek and white. The serpent reared back and flared its ridged hood, as if trying to intimidate whatever had brought the sky crashing down on it. Just the segment it had lifted from the ground stood nearly as tall as a man, and Demian was glad he had not accidentally blundered into the creature as it lay coiled in the grass.

He speared it with a lance of sorcery, severing its head.

Dispersing his ward, Demian began gathering the crushed grass into a large mound, hacking at it with Malazinischel when the roots proved tenacious. Then, using his sorcery, he churned the earth in a circle around the piled grass, wide enough that no sparks could leap across the ring and ignite a larger blaze. The bulwark complete, he took a flask from his saddlebag and splashed some oil on the mound, then summoned a roiling ball of flame and tossed it into the fire pit he had just built.

At least they would be warm tonight. He held out his arms, enjoying the rolling waves of heat as the first fiery tongues licked the air, then cast a glance over his shoulder at the twisting length of the decapitated snake. He wondered what charred plains serpent tasted like.

Tough and sinewy, it turned out, and more than a little bitter. Still, eating something hot and greasy was a welcome change from the salted meat and hardtack they'd choked down for their midday meal. It was also good to supplement the provisions they had, as what was in his saddlebags would have to last them until they passed out of the plains.

Demian was thankful Alyanna was eating, picking out nuggets of flaky white snake flesh from the chunk he'd grilled for her. Her movements were slow and deliberate, but Demian sensed that she wanted to devour what was in front of her; it was wise on her part not to, as despite how ravenous she must be her stomach would surely rebel if she began to gorge. Her glowing eyes were staring into the fire as if she could see something in the burning grass.

"Weaver," he said, and she turned to him. He forced himself to hold her unnatural gaze, suppressing a shiver. "How do you feel?"

With agonizing slowness, she swallowed the snake she'd been chewing. "I have been gutted," she finally said, her voice hollow. "Everything inside me has been scooped out. There is nothing but emptiness and this . . . this light."

"Does it hurt?"

She blinked slowly. "My body hurts. They cut me. Whipped and burned me. But inside, now . . . I feel nothing. And that is far worse."

"Weaver . . . "

"The Weaver is dead," she said harshly. "Alyanna is dead. She was a sorceress." Tears streaked her face, though she did not sob or cry out. They glowed bright at first, flashing as they fell, but by the time they reached the edge of her face the light had faded. "And I am not one anymore."

Troubled, Demian stood and heaved another armful of grass on to the fire. Alyanna had the strongest will of anyone he had ever met, but could any mind withstand what she had suffered at the hands of the inquisitors and the genthyaki?

"Where are we going, Demian?"

It was the first question she'd asked of him since the rescue.

"Where he cannot reach you. Where you will be safe."

"Nowhere is safe," she countered bitterly. "His hate has been stoked by a thousand years of slavery. He will hunt me down and drag me back beneath the palace and devour what's left of my soul. I know it. He brought slaves and showed me how he feasted, how he drank the mind, sucked it like insects do blood and left them drooling idiots. He will find me."

"There is one place he cannot go."

She glanced at him sharply. Demian saw confusion and hope . . . and then a dawning realization that made her face pale. "No," she whispered, her voice now edged by fear. "Not there."

"It is a sanctuary from the outside world. Nothing can enter the mountain without the daymo's knowledge. And even a genthyaki cannot stand before the kith'ketan within their home."

Alyanna bowed her head. "I failed him. The bargain was for the boy Keilan."

"*We* failed, as did his shadowblades. But failure is not betrayal. We still have an agreement – it has just not yet been fulfilled."

She raised her face to him, the tracks left by her tears glistening in the firelight. "Why are you doing this, Demian?" she whispered. "Why not leave me to the fate I deserve?"

He stared into the flames, wondering how he could answer this. After so many centuries, how could she still not know?

"Weaver, I –"

Suddenly she gasped, twisting around to stare at the wall of grass behind her.

"What –" he began, but then he sensed it as well. Points of searing emptiness, rushing closer, burning bright in the endless dark expanse.

The Pure were coming for them.

"Behind me," Demian said, drawing Malazinischel, and the surge of excitement from his sword made him shiver.

On trembling legs Alyanna scrambled across the clearing he had made, collapsing a few paces from where he stood. As she crawled past him, he kept his eyes trained on the darkness. The paladins had slowed; they were approaching cautiously. The Pure knew their prey was trapped.

"Give me a blade," Alyanna pleaded. "Something sharp. I won't go back. I won't."

Demian slipped his dagger from its sheath at his waist and tossed it in the grass near her. "Do not kill yourself until you are certain I'm dead."

Motes of light appeared in the distance, faint and glimmering. They could have been fireflies, but they did not flicker or dance. Or perhaps candles held up above the grass, if they were not so oddly paired.

The first of the Pure emerged from the long grass. He was tall and pale, with high, aristocratic features that perfectly represented the ideal of Menekarian nobility. His white-scale cuirass and the copper hilt of the white-metal sword he held gleamed in the firelight, as did the sunburst of Ama emblazoned on his shield. Red tattoos webbed his shorn head, squirming symbols that Demian had once been told recounted the ancient history of their order. The Pure stared at Demian with burning eyes, his face impassive, as two more of the paladins pushed from the grass to stand on either side of him. Three of them. Demian's heart fell.

"Thief," the first paladin said, setting the point of his sword in the flattened grass and resting his gauntleted hands on the hilt, "who are you?"

"No one," Demian said, shifting his weight to the balls of his feet.

The leader of the three cocked his head to one side, as if Demian was some strange puzzle that must be solved. "Unlikely. You penetrated beneath the palace and stole away the recently Cleansed. And while I sense no sorcery in you, its foul odor is heavy in the air."

"He is one of the Crimson Queen's magisters," said the paladin to his left, a stocky older warrior. "So he knows how to hide his power, like the one in the audience chamber."

The first paladin seemed to consider this. "Do you belong to the queen of Dymoria?"

Demian smirked and said nothing, and the Pure sighed, raising his sword. "You are dead, but I can promise you it will be quick if you tell me who your master is."

"I have no master."

The Pure shook his head, as if amazed by this foolishness. "We all have masters, thief. Now I command you to tell me who you are." As he spoke the other paladins fanned out, their white-metal swords extended.

"Who am I?" Demian said, settling into the third movement of the blue cantata, his blade held high. "I am a green wizard of Kashkana, greatest of the lost cities. I am the last of the swordsingers of the Kalyuni Imperium. I am one who has bargained with what coils deep beneath the mountain and has returned to the light. I am Demian, brother of Demichus, and I am your death, slave."

With a thought Demian compelled the fire behind him to blaze higher, and the shadow thrown by Alyanna stretched farther. The paladins drew back a step as the flames exploded with a whoosh towards the sky, but they quickly recovered and began to close on Demian from different sides. He lunged towards Alyanna's shadow, slipping into the other place; one moment his boot crunched on flattened grass, and the next he was running on the pathway of cracked stones floating in the empty darkness. Innumerable glowing doorways spread before him, all formed by the shadows thrown by the firelight. Three were larger than the others and Demian dashed towards the nearest and leapt through it, his sword already arcing.

"– dowblade!" he heard, his ears popping as he passed from the terrible silence of the paths back into the cacophony of this world.

He expected his blade to find the paladin's unprotected neck, but to his shock a white-metal sword met Malazinischel and turned his blow aside. The paladin had twisted around and brought his sword up, assuming an attack would come from behind him. Demian's balance was thrown, and he stumbled forward; he had only a momentary glimpse of a sunburst etched into steel before the Pure's shield slammed into his face.

An explosion of light filled his vision as his nose broke. Despite a wave of dizziness, he threw himself backwards without hesitation, knowing what was coming. He felt the tip of the white-metal sword slice through his outer garments, parting the ringmail coat he wore underneath as easily as if it were cloth and leaving a burning line across his ribs. Not deep enough to wound him seriously, though. Fighting through the spots flaring in his eyes Demian brought Malazinischel up to turn aside another sweeping cut of the paladin's sword. The Pure pressed him, hammering his guard with powerful blows that made his arm go numb; it had been centuries since he'd fought one of Ama's warriors, and he'd forgotten how inhumanely strong and fast they were. He could sense the other paladins approaching, waiting for their chance to strike. Demian tried to put his back to the edge of the clearing he'd made, so that the paladins would have to wade out into the grass if they wanted to flank him. It also meant, though, that he could not retreat any further without backing up blindly, and he would prefer not to risk his footing in the long grass.

Demian tasted the blood dripping from his shattered nose, and this seemed to help clear his head. His parries and blocks became less desperate; yes, the paladin was stronger than any mortal man had any right to be, but there was no elegance to his technique, no transcendent skill.

He was no swordsinger.

Finally off his heels, Demian switched from the blue cantata – which prioritized defense – to the red. Malazinischel flickered out, scraping the paladin's shield and raising a scattering of sparks. The paladin tried to regain the initiative with a quick thrust, but Demian caught the edge of the white-metal sword on the broad part of his blade and sent it skittering wide. Before the Pure could recover Demian lashed out with his sword, slipping past the sunburst shield and scoring the paladin's side. Malazinischel sliced through the scale cuirass, and grunting in pain the Pure retreated, dropping his shield to put his hand over the wound. Usually, such a light touch would barely affect a hardened warrior – but Malazinischel was not just any sword.

The paladin did not know it, but he was already dead.

"For Ama!" cried one of the remaining paladins as he rushed in to defend his wounded captain. He fought one-handed, like Demian, choosing mobility and speed over the protection offered by a shield.

Good. This was the style of the swordsinger.

Their blades came together in a flurry of strikes and counters. This paladin was an even better swordsman than the other, and Demian was forced back into the long grass. He felt more than saw the other Pure circling to his left, and he gritted his teeth, trying to shift his stance so that both paladins remained in his field of vision. Realizing what he was trying to do the paladin he was engaged with also moved to his left, trying to force Demian to turn away from his companion. He lunged forward in an attempt to draw Demian's complete attention, but he hurried the strike and slightly overextended himself. Demian caught the white metal blade with Malazinischel, letting the paladin's sword scrape down the length of his own until it clanged against his crossguard. With a violent twist he locked the paladin's sword in place, and then thrust forward with Malazinischel, catching the paladin in his throat. The gorget he wore parted like silk, blood spraying as his head was mostly severed from his neck.

It was the cry of rage and sorrow that saved Demian's life. He twisted, ripping his sword from the ruin of the other paladin's neck, bringing it around in blind desperation to try and block what he knew was coming. He was lucky – he deflected a blow that would have gutted him so that instead of plunging into his belly it sliced open his side. He stumbled and nearly fell, feeling like a chunk of him had just been carved away – it was the same area as the wound he had taken in Saltstone, though he could already tell it was much more serious. Demian slipped to one knee, fighting back the red mist that threatened to carry him off. The paladin attacked again, all pretense of composure abandoned, hacking downward. His sword was a pale crescent in the dimness, an arc of moonlight descending to cleave Demian in half.

No.

With all his remaining strength Demian brought up Malazinischel to turn aside the sword, then thrust forward, spearing the paladin through his belly. The white armor offered no resistance, Malazinischel sliding smoothly through and emerging from the paladin's back. Burning eyes stared in confusion at the length of cracked steel disappearing into his body, and then Demian withdrew the sword with a wrenching effort that sent him tumbling face first into the grass. From somewhere far away he heard the paladin fall.

Every breath was agony, and he tasted dirt and blood. He groaned, trying to turn over, but it was like a great weight was pressing on his back, grinding him into the earth. His life was leaking away, but he couldn't stop it; it was slipping through his fingers like water . . .

Hands on his shoulders, struggling to turn him over. At first he was too heavy, but finally with a great heave he was rolled onto his back, the fresh cuts in his side burning. The blood from his crushed nose had gotten into his eyes, and with a shaking hand he tried to wipe his vision clean. Someone was yelling his name from a great distance.

"Demian!"

It was the Weaver's voice, and he followed it back.

With the twilight sight of the kith'ketan he saw Alyanna above him, her eyes glowing; she was framed by an endless profusion of stars, stars she had shown him in her dream were balls of fiery twine that would eventually unspool and drift down to this world like gleaming serpents . . .

"Demian, can you hear me?"

He swallowed away the blood in his mouth. "Yes. I'm . . . I'm cut. There are . . . *ngg* . . . there are ointments and bandages in my saddle bags."

She vanished, and the stars rushed in to fill the void. He noticed he was at the bottom of a hole – no, that was the grass, rising up around him. Why was there grass here? Where was he?

The twilit Alyanna returned, and Demian felt his shirt being cut away, then blinding pain as she struggled to remove the ring-mail he wore beneath.

With the agony came clarity. He gripped Alyanna's small hand with blood-slicked fingers. "Weaver," he gasped, "we must go to the mountain. Others will come – the Pure, the false-man. Only there will we be safe. Ride for the Spine. Ride . . . "

21: KEILAN

THE FIRST INDICATION that he was nearly home was a stone by the roadside carved with the word 'Chale' and the number twelve. It was weathered and moss-encrusted, a remnant from an earlier age before the Brothers' War had shattered the kingdoms into countless jostling baronies and dukedoms.

"That's the name of the town closest to my village," Keilan told Nel and Senacus as they paused beside the marker to eat some dried meat.

"So do we go there first?" Nel asked, spitting out a piece of gristle.

Keilan shook his head. "No. A little ways on from here will be a path that splits from the road. If we follow that southeast for a few more leagues it'll lead us to my village."

"Does your village have a name? I've never heard you mention it."

Keilan was surprised that he actually had to think for a moment. "Yes. It's Tol Fen, but we never used it. We just called it 'the village'.

"I suppose if you never go anywhere else you don't need a name," Nel admitted, wrapping what meat was left in a few dry leaves and storing it again in her saddlebags. She glanced over at Keilan when she finished. "Are you prepared?"

He nodded, hoping he truly was.

The deepening light made the forest around them burn brighter. Most of the trees here were bloodbarks, which were common in the Kingdoms. Where most leaves in other lands changed from green to orange and then molted, the foliage of the bloodbark had a final hue that lasted well into winter – a brilliant, bloody red. And Keilan and the others had happened to arrive in those waning days of the old year when the leaves were the deepest shade of crimson, just before the cold winds would strip the branches bare. It was beautiful – but the nervous fluttering in Keilan's stomach kept him from appreciating the late season splendor. His thoughts were on his village, and what he'd find there.

Soon he recognized some landmarks: an ancient tree he'd watched Sella try and climb, a mossy boulder where they had played 'lord of the mountain' with other children many years ago, a thin stream trickling over slick black stones.

Keilan was reliving some of these lost moments when the sound of something blundering through the fallen leaves came from the woods up ahead. He peered among the branches, expecting to see a deer bounding away through the trees. Instead, he caught a flash of yellow hair as a boy fled into the thicket like he had glimpsed one of the Shael's demon tricksters coming down the path. Probably he'd been out here checking on snares and hadn't expected to see three mounted strangers – and since it was a rare day when anyone visited their village, it did make sense that the boy would want to be the first to deliver the news . . .

but Keilan felt a little trickle of concern that the boy had recognized him. How would the villagers react to his return?

He had his answer not long after. They blocked the path, a dozen men from his village, brandishing axes, fishhooks and torches. His uncle Davin was among them, tall and spindly and stooped, his face twisted into a scowl. Keilan recognized many of the same faces who had come to his door looking for his mother that terrible night. Davin's fat son Malik was there as well, smiling viciously, his piggish eyes narrowed in anticipation.

"What a friendly-looking welcoming party," Nel said out of the side of her mouth. "Is it possible they think we're brigands?"

"They know who I am," Keilan said softly, holding his uncle's stare. He kicked his horse ahead a few steps and addressed the villagers.

"Davin, Soman . . . I've come back."

His uncle turned and spat. "Aye. And it's an ill thing. Turn around, boy. We want no part of your deviltry." He squinted at Senacus. "Why did you bring him back, milord?"

The Pure did not answer, waiting for Keilan to continue.

His gaze roamed the crowd; most of the faces were set hard, but he thought he saw a few that looked conflicted.

"Benj," he called out, and the big man jumped as if Keilan had jabbed him with a stick. "How are things in the village?"

Benj swallowed, glancing over to Davin, but before he could answer Keilan's uncle spoke.

"You ain't welcome here, boy."

Keilan gritted his teeth, trying to keep his anger in check. "Davin, I –"

"You come about your da?" Malik said, and there was something in his voice that chilled Keilan. "You heard about him?"

He didn't want to know. He didn't.

"What happened to my da?" he asked, a coldness pooling in his stomach.

The men shifted, glancing at each other and muttering.

"He's dead," Davin said, and Nel gasped.

Keilan's hands tangled in his horse's mane as he tried to steady himself. He swallowed, fighting back the numbness.

"How did he die?"

"Don't matter how he died. Just means there's nothing for you here so you can turn around and go."

"How did he die?" Keilan repeated, anger replacing his shock.

"Of grief for having such an evil son," Davin said harshly, and spat again.

"That's not true," Keilan said, his voice rising. The sea inside him had begun to churn, stirred by his rage. "HOW DID HE DIE?" he cried, and flung out his hand towards the villagers.

Fire geysered higher from the torch Davin held, and his uncle screamed something unintelligible, throwing it to the ground and scrambling backwards. The torch exploded when it struck the path in a shower of sparks and a rush of hot air, and from the swirling conflagration a shape took form, a creature with long, crooked limbs molded from fire, with eyes like black embers smoldering in its horned head.

The villagers broke and fled, tossing down their makeshift weapons. The flame-creature watched them go, dwindling as the fire subsided.

Keilan's head was spinning, and he might have slid from his horse if Nel hadn't appeared beside him, propping him up.

"What was that?" Senacus asked, his voice hard.

"I'm sorry . . . I didn't mean to . . . "

The paladin gave him a long look, his jaw clenched, and then snapped his reins, leaving Keilan and Nel alone on the road.

"Did you know you could do that?" Nel asked, her hand still holding his arm.

"Yes," Keilan whispered. "But it wasn't the same the last time . . . "

"We need to return you to the Scholia," she said, staring at the blackened remains of the torch. "You have to be taught to control it, or it will consume you. It has happened before, even to apprentices."

Keilan did not reply. He felt the power within him recede, the sea he drew from growing calm.

Nel sighed. "Well, it looks like we won't get a warm welcome. How many are in your village?"

"I don't know. Maybe one hundred?"

"And men who can fight?"

Nel made an exasperated face when she saw Keilan's horrified expression. "I'm not saying we're going to fight them. But it certainly seems like your uncle doesn't want you back."

"Twenty, twenty-five?"

"Two dozen fishermen armed with woodcutter's axes do not frighten me. But if they did believe they had the numbers then they might rush at us, and I don't think you want a bloodbath. Yes?"

Keilan nodded. "They're not evil," he said. "Most of them, anyway. Just scared, I suppose."

Nel reached up into her sleeves and adjusted the daggers strapped to her forearms. "It won't come to violence, Keilan. They're not warriors, and they know that. Perhaps they'd try and hurt you if it was just us . . . but they'd never dare anything with Senacus here. They'll probably stay hidden in their huts or the forest and wait for us to go. But we should still be careful."

"I hope you're right," Keilan said, noticing she had slipped one of her daggers into her hand. He hoped she wouldn't have to use it.

As Nel had predicted, when they rode into the village they found it empty, the windows shuttered and the doors closed to them. On most days there would be children chasing each other around the Speaker's Rock, and old men playing tzalik in the shade of the huts, but today the common space had been abandoned. They were not alone, though. Keilan felt eyes watching him as he rode his horse through the square. He remembered the last time he had been here, six months and a lifetime ago, when the entire village had stood in a crescent around the rock and watched fearfully as Senacus had declared him to be a sorcerer. That had ended in swirling chaos, children and women screaming, his father and Sella fighting the lightbearers from Chale as the Pure's radiance ushered him into darkness.

Keilan slid from his saddle, the crunch of his boots in the gravel the only sound in the silent village. "This way," he said softly, his breath catching in his throat as he led his horse towards the small house on the edge of the square. It looked much the same, though there weren't any bushels of herbs hanging in the window frames, and the path to the door didn't appear to have been trodden in quite some time.

They had been telling the truth. His father was gone.

Keilan swallowed away the ache in his throat and approached the door. He hesitated, his hand hovering over the knotted wood. He felt Nel come up beside him, and though she didn't say anything he drew strength from her presence.

He gripped the black iron knocker his father had scavenged from the beach and rapped once, softly, but there was no answer from within. He pushed the door open.

The hut was empty – the small table where they'd taken their meals was gone, as were the chairs and the big pot that had once been suspended over the cook pit. Their bedrolls had vanished, just a few stale rushes scattered where he and his father had slept. Even the workbench where his father had whittled toys and whistles out of driftwood was missing. No recent tracks scuffed the hard-packed dirt floor.

His heart fell when he saw the chest that his father had rescued from the sea with his mother was gone as well. But surely something as valuable as books would still be somewhere in the village? Or sold to someone in Chale? Would they burn them if they thought they were tainted by his family's sorcery?

Of course they would. Dizziness washed over Keilan, and he had to reach out to steady himself on the wall. What had they done to his father? The aching sorrow in his chest sharpened into something else. He felt the roiling sorcery inside him start to churn, stirred by his rising anger. Whoever had hurt his father and mother would suffer. He could tear apart this village with a thought. He would find those responsible and punish them.

"Keilan," Senacus said from outside the hut, his voice wary. "Someone's coming here."

Holding tight to his rage, Keilan turned and strode from his childhood home. His skin tingled as he fought to keep the sorcery from slipping out of his control, his breath coming in short, labored gasps.

He would show them something to fear. Something to hate.

A man was stumping across the Speaker's square, leaning heavily on a crutch. Keilan blinked. Could it . . . could it be?

"Keilan!" his father cried, his voice cracking.

"Da," Keilan whispered hoarsely, the tenuous grip he held on his sorcery slipping . . . but the anger stoking it vanished instantly as well.

"Da!" he yelled, stumbling towards his father. Relief flooded him, and he felt the tears finally come.

His father was alive!

They came together, and his father rocked backwards, unsteady. "Careful, careful," he said, clutching at Keilan to keep himself from falling.

"Uncle Davin said you were dead!"

His father wrapped him in an embrace, crushing him against his damp beard. "I thought you were dead. I thought you must be dead." He glanced over at the silent, watching paladin and his eyes hardened. "The Pure . . . he let you return?"

Keilan stepped back, putting his hands on his father's shoulders. There was more gray threading his da's hair and beard than he remembered, the lines creasing his face a bit deeper. But there was a brightness in his eyes that Keilan hadn't seen in years.

"I was rescued from the Pure." Keilan turned and gestured towards where Nel stood watching them, a relieved smile on her face. "By her. And others."

His father shook his head in bewilderment. "Wait – you were rescued from the paladin? But here he is? And why didn't you return until now? Or send word?"

Keilan flushed. "I'm . . . I'm sorry, Da. We had to flee, and everything moved so quickly. I should have tried to get a message back to the village . . . "

His father waved his words away. "It's nothing. Nothing. You'll have to tell me everything that's happened."

"And what happened to you?" Keilan asked, pointing to his father's splinted leg.

"There's not much to tell, but let's sit down and get a hot cup of bitter root in you."

Keilan took a step towards their house, but his father laid a hand on his arm. "Not that way, boy. That's not my home anymore."

Keilan and his companions followed his father towards the opposite edge of the village, to a hut of mottled gray mud that edged a small copse of stunted white-barked trees. A well-tended assortment of flowers and herbs fringed the stone path leading to the entrance, which was filled by a slight woman with long black hair wearing a checkered dress. When she saw Keilan approaching her eyes widened, and her hands fluttered to her mouth. Then her gaze shifted to the Pure striding behind them and her face paled, her hands falling away in astonishment.

"Mam Bellas?" Keilan said, recognizing the woman. "This is her house."

"Aye, boy. And my home now, too."

Keilan glanced at his father in surprise, but his eyes were fixed on the woman waiting for them.

"She's a good woman."

Keilan tried to remember what he could of Mam Bellas. She'd been one of the villagers quietly in the background of daily life, rarely coming to the Speaker's Rock or the festival day celebrations, tending to her gardens and foraging in the woods. Her husband had died when she was very young, before Keilan had even been born. If his recollections were true, his fishing boat had been lost during a great storm that the rest of the village still spoke about with awe and dread. A few times, Mam Ru had sent Keilan to Mam Bellas's hut to ask for an herb or spice, and he couldn't recall the woman even speaking to him before she'd handed over what had been requested.

"Hello," Keilan said, ducking his head in greeting when they reached the hut. Mam Bellas murmured something back, her face coloring.

"Come on," his father said, ushering them all inside the hut and gesturing for them to sit on stools clustered around a smoldering cookfire. A battered metal pot was suspended above the flames, and Keilan smelled the distinctive flavor of bubbling bitter root. Mam Bellas hurried over and began pouring the pot's contents into wooden cups, still avoiding looking directly at Keilan or the broad-shouldered paladin who seemed to fill the hut.

The inside of her house was as homely and well-kept as the gardens outside: sheaves of cut flowers hung on the walls, giving the hut an earthy, floral smell, and the tables and stools were well-maintained and cared for. Keilan's breath caught in his throat when he saw his mother's chest pushed up against one wall. A black and white cat was curled on its lid, basking in the sunlight slanting down through a circular window.

They settled themselves around the cookfire, Senacus's stool almost disappearing beneath him. Keilan feared the stool would buckle and send the big man sprawling, but after giving a long groan of protest, the wood held.

"You've come from far away," his father said, gesturing at Keilan's travel-stained clothes. "Was it dangerous on the road?"

"The only time we were threatened," Keilan replied, "was when we came to the village. Uncle Davin and some of the others tried to turn us away. He said you were dead."

A dark cloud passed across his father's face. "That bastard. I was here at home, resting, when Bellas came through the door talkin' about how a big crowd of the men had come stumbling into the village with faces white as ghosts. A few of them quickly took their families and ran for the northern road. Others went hiding in their homes. She heard someone say your name an' hurried back to tell me. Wish I could have seen the look on Davin's face when you came up the road, high and mighty on your horse."

His father leaned forward and squeezed Keilan's leg. "Tell me what happened after he –" His father nodded towards Senacus. " – took you from the village. Where did ya get these fine clothes?"

"I never even made it to Chale," Keilan said. It was strange speaking of that day – it felt like a lifetime ago, yet only a half a year had past. "We were ambushed on the northern road by warriors of Dymoria. Nel was commanding them." He gestured in her direction and his father turned as if seeing her for the first time.

"You rescued my son? Deep thanks, lady."

Nel shrugged. "I was just doing what the queen willed."

"The queen?" his father repeated blankly.

"Queen Cein d'Kara of Dymoria," Keilan said softly.

"Is that the red queen? The one the traders and mendicants talk about?"

"Aye," Keilan replied, watching his father carefully.

"They say . . . they say she's a sorceress."

"She is."

His father stared at the steam curling from his cup. "So that's why . . . "

"Aye."

"Then you're . . . "

"Aye."

His father's brows drew together as he sipped at his bitter root tea. Then he nodded and set down his cup, sighing. "Ah. Well, I suppose I knew it in my bones. Your mother could do things that couldn't be explained – she could smell a storm coming better than even the oldest fishermen, and there was a time I saw light just spark from nothing when she was around. And you always knew where the fish were hiding." He reached up and smoothed out some of the tangles in his beard, an old habit he had when he was thinking hard on something. "So, this queen took you in, taught you some things?"

"Yes. But we learned of something terrible, so we had to come back from the west. Senacus helped us get here safely."

His father turned to the paladin. "Thank you for bringing my son home," he said gruffly.

Senacus looked uncomfortable, Keilan thought, but he accepted his father's words with a curt nod. It must be strange to sit here beside the man whose son he had stolen away. Senacus took a quick sip of his tea, and Keilan had to hide a small smile as the bitterness surprised the paladin. It was an acquired taste.

"Ferris," Senacus said, setting his cup down. "When I took Keilan from you, I did so because my order is entrusted with guarding the world against the dangers of sorcery." His burning eyes found Keilan. "Your son is not evil. He is, in truth, a very good person. Kind, honest, and forgiving."

Keilan lowered his head, embarrassed by the paladin's praise.

"Loyal to his friends. But he does have powers within him that could cause great harm. All those with sorcery inside them do. We are here," he continued, gesturing to encompass Nel and Keilan, "because we have been given a dark vision."

"A vision?"

"From the Oracle of Lyr," Keilan added quickly. "A glimpse into what might be."

"Lyr . . . " his father said slowly, rolling the word around in his mouth like it was an exotic food he'd never thought he'd taste. "I've heard stories of the Oracle. She showed you a vision?"

Senacus nodded. "Yes. A world shattered, destroyed by dark sorcery. And we were chosen to receive this warning because she thought we have a chance to avert what's coming."

His father blinked in confusion, pulling at his beard. "Well, you're a paladin of Ama. Seems like you might be able to do something about it. But my boy?"

"Da," Keilan said, leaning closer to put his hand on his father's unsplinted leg. "In the vision . . . I saw someone . . . " He bit down on his lip, unsure how to broach the topic of his mother. "But before we talk about that, I want to know what happened to you?"

His father shook his head, as if clearing it of what they'd been talking about. He rapped on the wooden strips that splinted his leg. "Foolishness, that's what. It was . . . it was hard after you were taken, lad. I don't even really remember the first few months. I never fished. Every day I drank until blackness took me – when the coin ran out I sold what I could so I could buy more. I sold your mother's necklace, my grandfather's brooch." His eyes drifted to the chest pushed up against the far wall. "But I didn't sell your books."

His brow creased, as if he was pained by remembering those dark times. "I suppose deep inside I wanted to die, though my thoughts were too sodden at the time for me to know this. Anyway, one day I wandered away from the village, down to the rocks. I remember tryin' to find my footing on the slickness, hearing the ocean, thinking I could hear your voice . . .

"Then I woke up in here, my leg hurting more than my head. I'd slipped and fallen, and my leg had snapped. Lucky I hadn't ended up in the water or I'd have gone to meet your mother right then and there."

Mam Bellas had moved beside his father while he was talking, and he reached out to touch her hand, lacing their fingers together. "She saved me. She had been gathering out in the forest and she'd seen me tumble on the rocks. Somehow managed to drag me back here and set my leg." He grinned affectionately at Mam Bellas, and she blushed. "She's stronger than she looks. Anyway, she cared for me, helped me get my strength back. Wouldn't bring me drink no matter how much I asked. And then one day I woke up with my head clear for the first time in months. Knew I didn't want any rum, and knew I loved her and didn't want to live alone no more." He glanced at Keilan and then away, as if afraid of what he might see.

He wants my permission, Keilan realized, and something caught in his throat. In the years since his mother's death he'd watched his father wither away until all that remained was a husk of the man he'd been before. But there was a change now, and the way he touched Mam Bellas's fingers so tenderly . . .

"I'm happy for you, Da," he said, laying his hand on his father's knee.

"Thank you, lad," his father murmured. Was that a glimmer in his eye? Surely not.

"So how long will you stay?" his father asked gruffly after clearing his throat. "You're welcome to our old house, for as long as you need it. Or you could sleep here," his father said quickly, gesturing wide with his arms, "though we don't have enough space for your friends as well."

"Like we said, I've come back for a reason." Keilan paused, still hesitant to bring up what they needed to speak about. "I need to know more about my mother."

His father rocked back in his chair, surprised. "Your mother?"

"Yes. Where she came from. Her family."

Keilan's father slowly shook his head. "I'm sorry, lad. Your mother never spoke of her life before I rescued her from the sea. I pushed her a few times, of course. Tried to get her to talk. Once or twice I think she even came close to telling me something. But then she'd get this look, almost like she was scared, and she'd go quiet as a rabbit. I'd say you know just as much as me."

Keilan ran a hand through his hair, trying to keep the frustration out of his voice. "Truly? You were wed for more than ten years. There were no secrets told . . . "

His father shrugged helplessly. "Nothing. It was like she'd been a gift from the Deep Ones. She used to joke with me that she was just sent here to bring you into the world."

Silence fell in the hut. Had this whole journey been for nothing? Was there nothing here that could give them a direction?

"I . . . " Mam Bellas began softly, before her voice faded away. Then she swallowed hard and stood up straighter. "I know something."

22: KEILAN

ALL EYES TURNED to Mam Bellas in surprise, and she seemed to wilt under the attention. She blushed furiously, twisting a handful of her dress until her knuckles whitened.

His father's surprise was plain. "You do?"

She nodded quickly. "I think so. I might. Or perhaps it's nothing. I don't want to raise your hopes . . . "

"Please tell us," Keilan said gently.

A strand of her long hair had fallen across her face, and she tucked it behind her ear. "You know I'm not much of a gossip," she began, speaking to Ferris in an almost apologetic tone, "but your wife –" She glanced at Keilan. "– your mother, Vera, was always a topic in the village. I thought it mostly jealousy – the women wanted her pale skin and beautiful hair, and I'd wager the men secretly wished they'd been the one to pull her from the sea. Not that they'd ever admit to that," she added quickly, showing a small rueful smile. "Anyway, you were probably too young to remember," she said to Keilan, "but your mother caught a terrible sickness one summer. She went white and cold, yet the sweat was just dripping from her."

His father made a face that showed he remembered. "There were a few deaths that year from that sickness, and I thought she was going to be another."

"You took her to Mam Ru," Mam Bellas said, and his father nodded.

"Aye. She's good with herbs and treatments, and she never showed any hate towards Vera."

"Well, Mam Ru called on me to bring over some elderleaf and ginseng. When I got to her house, your mother looked like she was just about to swim down to meet the Deep Ones. Her shining hair was just sticking to her, all limp and faded. And her skin was as white as the midwinter sky. But her eyes were open, and she was talking. Not to anyone there in the room, though. She kept saying a name, over and over again. Apologizing, asking for help."

"What was the name?" Keilan asked, leaning forward.

Mam Bellas scrunched her face, trying to dredge up the distant past. "I . . . I don't remember. It was something foreign. Not anyone in the village, I'm certain."

Keilan slumped back, disappointed. "Well, did anyone else hear what she was saying?"

Mam Bellas smiled. "Oh, yes. Mam Ru told me she'd been listening to your mother going on for days. And that canny old cat has a memory like the sea itself. She'll know it, I'm sure."

They downed the last of the bitter root tea and hurriedly departed Mam Bellas's hut, making for the listing hovel of mud and moss where Mam Ru had resided for as far back as anyone in the village could remember. Before Keilan's mother had come, she'd been the one whispered about as being a witch, and Keilan had always thought that perhaps her kindly disposition towards Vera was a way of expressing gratefulness that she no longer had to suffer sly looks and dark mutterings. Outside of his family's own home, Keilan had probably spent the most time with Mam Ru, listening to her stories about the sea and forests, helping her to gather herbs and flowers, and devouring whatever delicious stew she had bubbling in her cookpot. The thought that she knew something about his mother – but had never confided in him – did bother him, a little. But perhaps by not sharing these secrets she'd been trying to protect him.

As they skirted the edge of the Speaker's Square, Keilan caught a glimpse of movement from the road leading north to Chale. His breath caught in his throat. Had it been? He stopped, peering through the blood-red foliage veiling the road, hoping he was right.

"What is it, Keilan?" asked Nel, craning her head to try and see what it was he was looking for.

"I thought I saw . . . "

A pair of tired-looking nags crested a small rise, and seated behind them on a rickety old wagon was an old man in a patched broad-brimmed hat.

"Pelos!" Keilan cried and started running towards the wagon waving. The old fishmonger gaped when he saw Keilan, the stalk of straw he'd been chewing on falling from his open mouth.

"Pelos, I'm back!"

The fishmonger couldn't even muster a reply – the astonishment in his face made Keilan want to laugh, and his wagon had lurched to a halt because the reins had fallen from his slack fingers.

Then he was climbing down from the wagon with surprising spryness and wrapping Keilan in a crushing hug, tears streaking his face. "Oh, lad! You're alive!" He pushed Keilan away, looking him up and down. "Grown a bit and wearing such fancy clothes. And that sword! The eyes of that bird – are those gems real? Must be worth a fortune!"

"It was given to me by a woman who makes the archons of Lyr tremble," Keilan said, feeling like his smile might split his face.

The old man wiped at his face with a sleeve. "Lad, lad. Archons? Lyr? I knew it, I knew it. Remember I told you once you didn't belong here? I was right. Oh, if only your mother could see you. She'd be so proud, I know that as well."

Pelos looked past Keilan, and surprise shivered his face again. "Lad," he said, swallowing. "That's the Pure who took you, isn't it?"

Keilan turned towards where his companions and his father had gathered a respectful distance away. "It is, Pelos. But he's a . . . he's a friend now. We are on a quest together."

"A quest?" the old man said, shaking his head in disbelief. "On what sort of quest does a paladin ally himself with . . . " He glanced at Keilan, a hint of embarrassment appearing in his eyes.

"A sorcerer," Keilan finished for him. "Yes, that's what I am. Or I could learn to be one." He paused for a moment, searching for the right words. "There is something terrible coming. To an old fisherman like yourself, I'd say the horizon has gone black and the sea's starting to get choppy. However dangerous Senacus thinks I am, it's nothing compared to the storm that's about to break."

Pelos took off his broad-brimmed hat and scratched his balding scalp. "Lad, I think I get the bones of it. You've come back here because you need something."

"I do. It's important I find out where my mother came from. Do you know anything? Did she ever confide in you?"

"Your mother?" Pelos sucked on his teeth, shaking his head. "She was closed up tight as a clam about her past. Never let slip anything, that I could remember. And I would – I was mighty intrigued about where she'd come from. In my youth I sailed all over the Broken Sea, even ventured up the coast to the Cities once, and I never saw anyone with her hair. Damned beautiful it was."

Keilan set aside this small disappointment. "No matter. Mam Ru might know something. We were on our way to see her just now."

"I'll join you," Pelos said, flashing a gap-toothed grin and clapping Keilan on the shoulder. "Maybe the old buzzard has some fresh cockles to share . . . and lad, I'm not letting you out of my sight."

The old fishmonger slipped his nags from their halters and led them over to a grassy patch off the road to graze.

"You don't need to tie them up?" Keilan asked, stroking the blotchy flank of one of the old horses.

Pelos chuckled. "They know where their oats come from," he said, and the nag closest to him snorted and cast a sidelong glance at the old fishmonger.

Pelos leaned in closer to Keilan. "They know that word. Oats. Damn clever beasts," he whispered.

"I've missed you," Keilan said as they turned away from the cropping horses and began walking back to where the others waited.

"I've missed you too, lad," Pelos replied, squeezing his shoulder. "To be honest, ever since you left I've felt an emptiness inside me. And guilt that maybe I could have done something, gotten you away before the paladin arrived. I'd hoped they never would come . . . but I had suspected they might."

Keilan patted the old man's gnarled fingers, which still clutched him as if he was afraid if he let go Keilan might blow away like smoke in the wind. "In the end, it was all for the best. I've seen incredible things, Pelos. Wonders I never could have imagined."

Finally, the old man let his hand drop. "You'll have to tell me about it, lad."

Something occurred to Keilan, and he glanced up at the darkening sky. "You're coming in late, aren't you? The fishing boats must have returned several watches ago. I saw Davin and several of the other fisherfolk earlier."

Pelos chuckled. "Would have liked to have seen their faces. No, lad, the last few months I've stopped going down to the beach. I was angry about how they treated you and making them carry their catch back to the village to sell it was just a bit of pettiness on my part. Your uncle made his fat son struggle back laboring under the weight of a long pole hung with fish. Always made me smile when I saw it."

Keilan imagined Malik arriving in the village red-faced and panting, dead fish swinging back and forth as he stumbled along. The thought made him smile as well.

Mam Ru's hut was set back from the rest of the village, teetering dangerously on the edge of a small pond encrusted with green scum. The trees grew thicker and taller here, and only a thin trickle of light filtered through the lattice of branches. The flayed remains of some unrecognizable animal had been left to dangle from beneath the ancient wooden eaves of Mam Ru's hut, and as Keilan approached the door a swarm of flies rose in buzzing indignation from their feasting.

"Mam Ru!" Keilan called, loudly because he knew her hearing was failing. "We wish to speak with you!"

A thump and a crash from inside, and a moment later the door scraped open. A tiny old woman wrapped in a gray shawl blinked up at him with eyes like chips of black ice. "Keilan Ferrisorn!" She peered past him. "And Ferris himself. Pelos, you old rascal. A girl dressed like a boy. And a paladin of Ama." She clucked her tongue. "Hm. Is this when you ask me if I want to go on an adventure?"

"Ah, no. We just –"

"Good! Because I'm too old. Hm." She spoke past Keilan, directing her words at the others. "I'd invite you all inside, but there's too many of you and you'd probably break something."

"We just wanted to ask –"

The old woman's eyes narrowed to black slits. "Wait. You left the village. Broke the heart of little Sella. She moped around for weeks." Mam Ru poked him in the chest with a black-nailed finger. "What do you have to say for yourself, hm?"

"I didn't want to go!" Keilan protested, gesturing at Senacus. "He took me away!"

"And now he's brought you back. Strange, very strange." She peered suspiciously at the paladin. "What is this all about?"

"My mother."

Mam Ru's face fell. "Hm. Terrible, that. She was a good woman. Brought me fish and salt in the bad months."

"You cared for her once when she was very sick."

"Aye. She got the Wilting. I thought she was destined for the Deep, but she was strong."

"We spoke with Mam Bellas, and she said there was a name she kept repeating in her fever dreams. Something foreign."

Mam Ru glared at him shrewdly. "Hm. Sometimes the past is best left buried, Keilan. She was running from something, something terrible enough that she never so much as stepped outside this village in all her time here, far as I know."

"It's very important. Please, Mam Ru."

The old woman gave a raspy sigh. "Chalissian. When she was down in the depths, fightin' her way back, that's who she was speaking to. Apologizing and begging and thanking."

"Chalissian?" Nel murmured thoughtfully. "I know that name, but I'm not sure from where."

"Chalissian ri Kvin," Pelos said, confusion deepening the lines on his face. "That's the only Chalissian I'm familiar with. The Bravo of the Broken Sea. Captain of the *Last Lament*."

Mam Ru tapped her cheek with a long nail. "Ri Kvin. Might be I heard her say something like that, as well."

Pelos shook his head. "But that's impossible. Chalissian was one of the pirate lords who formed the Pelioti Compact near forty years past, back when I still traded and fished. He left just before the Shan navy smashed the Compact at the Bloody Shoals, otherwise the *Lament* would be down there with your Deep Ones. I'd heard he'd retired to Ven Ibras, but that was decades ago. He'd be an old man now, and not someone your mother would have crossed paths with."

"Ven Ibras?" Senacus asked, his face showing his frustration with the avalanche of names.

"A good-sized town on an island east of the Whispering Isles. With favorable winds it's a two-day sail from Chale. Used to be somewhat of a hub for the pirates roaming the Broken Sea; now, it's likely fallen on hard times. Nothing much there except forest, rocks, guano and old pirates who were smart enough to abandon the game before they lost everything."

"Your mother was sailing from somewhere when her ship foundered," mused Nel. "Maybe it was this Ven Ibras."

"It's as good a trail as I think we could have hoped for," Keilan said. "Thank you, Mam Ru."

The old woman sniffed. "Hm. I suppose you'll be running off again now?"

Keilan glanced down the path that led to the village. "Everyone's scared. It's best if I leave soon, I think."

"Any messages to pass along to your little friend when she comes around? She's going to be mighty upset she missed you here."

"Tell her I'm sorry, Mam Ru. I wish she'd been here. Tell her I always think about our time together."

Mam Ru frowned. "Hm. You're lucky you won't have to deal with her." She made a shooing gesture with her hands. "Now go. I have frogs to catch for dinner so there's no time to stand around jawing."

After everyone had said their goodbyes they trudged back across the village to Mam Bellas's hut. The setting sun had gilded the clouds in gold and bronze, but no smoke from cookfires trickled from any of the houses around the square; it was like the village was holding its breath, waiting to see what Keilan would do. His heart grew heavier as he watched his father stump along on his splinted leg, beckoning them to follow and regaling them with the feast Mam Bellas would prepare tonight. She was probably plucking a chicken at this moment, and she made the most delicious apple tarts they'd ever tasted . . .

"Da," Keilan said as they walked up the path to Mam Bellas's hut. His father paused in his recitation of the delicacies they'd enjoy later and turned to him, the lines around his eyes crinkling in happiness. "Da, we can't sleep in the village tonight."

His father's face instantly collapsed. "Lad, if you're worried about Davin . . . "

Keilan shook his head. "I'm not."

"I'm worried he will set our hut on fire during the night," Nel ventured, but Keilan ignored her.

He gestured back towards the silent, empty village. "They're terrified. Hiding in their huts or in the woods. Most of them, I know, are good people, and their fear and hate are born of ignorance, not evil."

His father opened his mouth to say something, but Keilan forestalled him with a raised hand. "The longer we stay the more disruption we bring to their lives. If they know we're still in the village a lot of children will be unable to fall asleep, afraid of what the evil sorcerer will do to them in the night."

"Why do you care about them?" his father said softly. "They killed your mother."

"And I hate the ones who did that," he said, reaching out to take his father's calloused hand, "but that was only a few. Many of the others were kind to me." Something occurred to Keilan. "Do you want to stay here, Da?"

His father glanced away, and Keilan could see his conflict. His shoulders slumped as he let out a long sigh. "I was born in the village. Lived here my whole life. Married your mother, fished the waters, had you. After they took her, I felt like there was this poison in the air, seeping into me. Making it harder to breathe. But I had to keep going for you. And then you were taken as well. I gave up, after that. If Bellas hadn't thrown me a rope, I would have died." He tugged at his beard, watching the last shreds of the day vanish beyond the horizon. "But now I have her. And anyway, where would we go?"

Keilan pulled forth the pouch containing his share of the money given to them by Lady Numil. "Hold out your hands," he told his father, and when he did Keilan poured a stream of Lyrish coins into his cupped palms. His father's eyes widened when he saw how much of the pile glinted gold and silver.

"Pelos, is that enough to buy a house in Chale?"

The fishmonger leaned in closer. "Aye. A small but tidy one, I imagine, with something still left over." He rubbed at his nose. "Seems to me, Ferris, that the lad has given you a chance here to start your life anew. I think you should seize it."

"But what would I do in Chale?" his father asked, his brow creasing as he studied the money.

"Well, that's easy enough," Pelos said. "You know fish. I could use a trustworthy man to help run my business. You can work with me."

"But what about Bellas?" he said uncertainly.

Pelos clapped him on the shoulder, nearly spilling the coins he still held in his hands. "Well, bring her and her cat and your woodworking table. She doesn't have such strong ties here, that I know. Sell your houses and come north."

"I'll talk with her," his father said, holding out the money for Keilan to take back.

"You keep it," Keilan said, pushing his hands away. "And I'll hope you'll take Pelos up on his offer."

"Keilan, I agree that we should leave tonight," Senacus interrupted, "and the day is nearly spent."

Pelos waved the paladin's concerns away. "I've done the trip to Chale a thousand times in darkness. My horses know every rock and hole along the way."

"Good," Keilan said, "because I'm not quite ready to leave yet. There's something I need to take from Mam Bellas's house."

23: KEILAN

KEILAN WAS SURPRISED to find that the gates of Chale were still open when they finally arrived. Darkness had fallen some watches past, and a pair of burning torches flanking the open doors illuminated walls of rough-hewn logs stretching away into the night. An old watchman stood in the puddle of light cast by one of the torches, pulling on his drooping gray mustache and shaking his head as their wagon trundled closer.

"By the Ten, Pelos, you're late," the night watchman grumbled. "I was just about to close the gate and let you sleep outside on a bed of your fish." He blinked watery eyes as he caught sight of the three mounted strangers riding behind the wagon. "Found some strays, did you? God's blood – the Pure!"

Pelos chuckled at the night watchman's surprise. "No fish today, Melech, so I'm afraid you'll have to find your supper elsewhere. My thanks for keeping the gate open this late – I'll let you choose your favorite from the next catch I bring through."

The night watchman muttered something unintelligible, his eyes still fastened on Senacus as they passed him on their way through the gates.

Years ago, Keilan had come to Chale with his father to see a bard perform, and the image etched into his memory was of soaring stone buildings and wrought-iron balconies suspended over the streets. It had made a tremendous impression on him when he was young, and he'd excitedly asked his mother when he returned to his village if the great cities of Gryx and Menekar were like this. He remembered her soft laughter in reply, and it had confused him at the time. Now he understood. The night shrouded much of the town, but he could tell that it could not be compared with the vastness and splendor of Lyr or Vis. Only a few of the houses were more than a single story, and there were as many mud brick houses as there were stone. The main avenue was set with flagstones, but the smaller roads branching away were simply dirt, and the only light came from a few lanterns hung outside what must be establishments for those entering the city from the south.

The plodding pace of the wagon's horses suddenly quickened, even though Pelos had not used his whip, as if the nags wished to hurry up and end their day. "These inns are not as fine as the ones near the north gate," the fishmonger said, loud enough to be heard over the clopping of hooves, "but they'll be able to draw you a hot bath and put a tankard of ale in your hands, if that's what you want. As I said, you're welcome to stay with me, though."

"Thank you," Nel replied. "With our funds depleted –" she cast a quick glance at Keilan "– we'd appreciate your hospitality."

"Good, good," Pelos cried back, pulling on the reins to turn his wagon down one of the larger side streets. "And tomorrow we'll go down to the river and find you passage to Ven Ibras. There's often a trader or two willing to ferry passengers for a bit of coin, and if there isn't I can twist the ear of my nephew to take you. He usually plies the river from here to Theris, but he's sailing my old boat and I used to bring her as far as the Whispering Isles. I bet the old girl misses the salt and waves."

Pelos's knuckles had barely grazed wood when the door to his house was flung open by a plump, scowling woman wearing a stained apron and brandishing a large wooden ladle.

"Pelos Welumsorn! Sauntering in yet again with half the night gone by. Well, you're lucky you don't have a cold supper waiting for you, and if I find out you were drinking down at the docks with Erand again . . . " Her hands fluttered to her mouth when she saw past Pelos and noticed he was not alone.

"Amela," the old fishmonger said, "please make welcome Keilan, Nel, and Senacus. They will be staying with us tonight and gone on the morrow. My friends, this is my wife, Amela."

Keilan offered a low bow and stepped forward as Pelos ushered him inside. A fire crackled in a cook pit against the far wall, an iron pot suspended over the flames. The house felt homely and comfortable – baskets of dried flowers hung from the ceiling, and intricate carvings shaped from driftwood adorned the walls. The chopped remains of vegetables were scattered across a long table, and the rich smell of simmering fish stew filled the room. Keilan's stomach grumbled, reminding him that he hadn't eaten since morning.

Amela hurriedly wiped her free hand on her apron, her cheeks flushing apple-red. "Pelos, why didn't you say we'd have guests?" she cried, giving him a hearty thwack on his shoulder with her ladle. Her eyes widened as Senacus entered her house, ducking his head to avoid striking it on the door's lintel. "A paladin of Ama? The Ten have mercy, Pelos, what have you gotten yourself into this time?"

Pelos sighed. "Senacus is the boy's guardian. They're on a very important quest, or so I've gathered, though it's not my place to pry. Tomorrow I'll take them to the docks so they can find passage down the river."

Amela reached out and clasped Keilan's arm in a grip that made him wince. "Your name is Keilan? Not *the* Keilan?" she asked, turning back to her husband. "The boy you were so upset about? You told me the Pure . . . " She faltered, her gaze finding Senacus again. "Oh."

Pelos cleared his throat loudly. "Yes, well, it turns out events were not as tragic as I feared. It has been a day of good tidings and gladdened hearts, but also very tiring –"

"You all must be starving!" Amela interjected, bustling over to the cookpot and giving what was inside a quick stir with her ladle. "Go on, get settled and find a seat. I'll have something on the table in a moment."

Keilan set down his travel bags and bedding and slipped the heavy satchel from his shoulder. He couldn't resist glancing inside at the treasures he had taken from Mam Bellas's house, the familiar cracked bindings of the books his father had rescued from the sea with his mother so many years ago.

"Aren't those a bit heavy to take with us?" Nel asked as she found a spot beside a cupboard of red wood for her own belongings.

Keilan stroked one of the covers, tracing the script that flowed across the leather. "It's all I have left of her. Perhaps there is some clue in one of them I've never noticed before."

Nel gathered up her hair, which had grown long during their travels, and tied it back with a green ribbon. "Not all answers are found in books, Keilan."

"No," he whispered to himself, too quiet for her to hear, "but even if they don't have the answer, perhaps they can help me ask the right question."

"Supper!" Pelos cried, sliding into a chair as Amela ladled stew into the bowl in front of him. He breathed deep and smacked his lips together. "I do have to put up with a fair bit of abuse, but it's worth it for the food." He flinched as his wife raised her arm threateningly, but instead of hitting him she dipped her ladle again and filled the bowl in front of Senacus. The paladin had removed his scale cuirass and white-enameled vambraces, but still, from his stiff-backed posture, seemed to be ready for battle. Keilan suspected he would be comfortable around a campfire or a lord's banquet table; eating stew in the house of a commoner, however, was probably foreign to him.

"Thank you, madam," the paladin said formally, bowing his head slightly.

"Oh, listen to him," Amela chortled as she splashed some stew in Nel and Keilan's bowls. "I do hope one of the neighbors saw him come through that door. Elga and Rohinna will scratch their eyes out in frustration tryin' to think up why he's here."

Keilan tried a spoonful of the stew – it was as delicious as he'd hoped, potatoes, leeks and chunks of fish swimming in a butter and cream broth.

"Gods, that's good," Nel said huskily, then lifted her bowl to her mouth and began to slurp noisily. When she finally lowered it she caught Senacus staring at her, his face aghast. She smiled sweetly at him, then belched. The paladin glanced at Amela, as if expecting her to be insulted, but the fishmonger's wife clapped her hands together.

"Some of the best noises a cook can hear!" she cried. Pelos roared in laughter when he saw the stricken expression on Senacus's face, then pushed himself away from the table.

"Who wants ale? I have good black stuff from the brewery here in Chale. It'll put hair on your chest, Keilan."

Nel ripped a chunk from the loaf of bread that had appeared on the table. "I'll take some," she said, dipping the crust into her stew.

"Me as well," Keilan added, and Pelos turned to the paladin expectantly.

Senacus held up his hands. "Not me, but I thank you. The vows of Ama forbid the Pure from partaking."

"Truly, yours is a harsh faith," Pelos said, his voice thick with pity.

"Don't mind him," Nel said between noisy bites, "their initiation involves embalming. It's why they're so stiff all the time."

Chuckling, Pelos vanished through a shadowed doorway, then returned moments later with a dusky jug and three cups. He poured a generous measure into each and passed two of them to Nel and Keilan.

"One advantage of traveling without Vhelan," Nel said after taking a deep draught, "is that I get to enjoy a drink. Usually he does enough carousing for both of us, and I have to stay in sound mind to deal with any trouble that arises . . . or he causes."

Keilan tried the ale – it had an earthy taste that he couldn't decide if he liked or not. "I do miss him, though," he said after he'd wiped the foam from his mouth.

Nel smiled crookedly. "Aye, me too. He's going to be incredibly jealous that we went off without him. Might not talk to me for a month."

Keilan laughed. "I can't imagine Vhelan not talking for a month."

"It is rather far-fetched," Nel admitted, bringing her cup to her lips again.

A silence settled around the table, broken only by the sounds of eating and drinking. Watching the others, Keilan felt a deep swell of contentment. His father knew he was alive and had a chance at happiness again with Mam Bellas. And whatever challenges Keilan would face in the days to come, he would not do so alone. He couldn't imagine a more contrary pair than Nel and Senacus, but it seemed the discord between them had faded during their travels together. They would find this sorceress and convince her to help them avoid the coming cataclysm. And he would finally discover the truth about his mother.

Pelos raised his cup. "Let us drink to your success and safe journeys. My old heart soars to see you again, Keilan, and to meet your new friends."

"Hear, hear," Nel cried, banging her cup on the table and then lifting it high. "Someday, the bards will sing of the quest to find the fisherboy's mother!"

Morning brought a herd of aurochs thundering through Keilan's head. He stumbled along behind Pelos as they wove through the streets of Chale, the old fishmonger seemingly unaffected by the many cups he'd drunk the night before and the mercilessly bright sun.

Keilan kept his head down; the dizziness seemed to abate somewhat if he concentrated on the churned road. But he knew when they moved through a crowded market space, as he heard the surprised mutterings when the townspeople caught sight of Senacus. The Pure were not such an uncommon sight in the Shattered Kingdoms, but still an appearance by one of Ama's warriors was worthy of gossip.

Gradually, the sounds of cattle lowing and goodwives haggling faded behind them, and the dirt beneath his boots gave way to planks of pitted wood. Keilan finally looked up, blinking at the harsh glare reflecting off the Lenian. The river was narrow, no more than a few hundred paces wide, and so sluggish it appeared to not be flowing at all. A half-dozen boats were tied up at the docks, including a large merchant carrack that wallowed so low in the water Keilan wondered if it could make it all the way to Theris without scraping the river's bottom. Gulls that had followed the ships in from the Broken Sea turned gyres in the sky, shrieking.

Pelos made his way towards an ancient, salt-scarred fishing boat with an upswept prow that tapered into the leering, monstrous visage of Ghelu the Toothed, most fearsome of the Deep Ones. Such carvings were common enough that even a few of the smaller boats in Keilan's village had been adorned with similar ornamentation – it was an old belief that creatures from the depths would not dare to attack a vessel displaying the image of one of the vengeful sea gods.

Three young men squatted on the dock beside the boat, intent on a game of chalice. One of the players tossed down his cards, cursing, then noticed them approaching and stood.

"Losing again, Seric?" Pelos said with a shake of his head.

The young man smoothed down his black mustache, his eyes flicking uncertainly from Pelos to the three strangers accompanying him. "I'm up on the day, Uncle," he said slowly. Keilan noticed he had the red-stained teeth of a kennoc-nut chewer.

"Ah, but what about the month? The year?"

Seric cleared his throat noisily and spat over the dock. "Haven't had to pawn the *Sea Beggar* yet, if that's what you're getting at."

"Is she still sea-worthy?" Pelos asked, nodding towards the boat. "You've kept her in the river for a few seasons now."

Seric spared a glance over his shoulder. "Aye, she'll sail the waves still. I wouldn't take her to Kesh, but she could get to Gryx so long as there's no storms." He turned back, gesturing at Senacus. "What's going on? Does the paladin need to get somewhere?"

"Ven Ibras."

The young man spat again; he missed the water this time, a wad of red splattering the docks. "The *Beggar* will make it there. We'll have to spend a night out on the water, but the Shael haven't shown themselves much recently. Is the pay good?"

Nel lifted a pouch and shook it and the man's mouth broke into a red-stained smile at the sound of clinking coins. He stepped away from the chalice game, ignoring the grumblings of the other two players, and clapped his hands sharply. "Right," he said, speaking to Senacus, who he seemed to have decided was the leader of their small group. "We can cast off as soon as you're ready and the boys who usually crew the *Beggar* return. The sooner we leave, the earlier we'll arrive tomorrow. Too late and we might have to spend a second night out on the boat, and that means we should add another water barrel to my stores. We should . . . " His words trailed off as he squinted at something beyond them, towards the town proper. "Eh. Friends of yours, paladin?"

Keilan turned. A pair of mendicants were hurriedly approaching in their direction, white robes flapping. With them were warriors in leather and chain, the golden sunburst of Ama displayed prominently on their surcoats and tabards. Lightbearers, local men who had pledged their swords to the faith. Keilan wondered if any of them had been among the group that had taken him from his village those many months ago. With a start he realized that one of the mendicants – the younger of the two – was in fact the cleric who had brought Senacus to his village. Keilan's last memory of the mendicant was his face twisted in fear as the paladin had proclaimed him to be a sorcerer, and he wore a very similar expression now. The older mendicant looked more determined than afraid, and he clutched something in his hand, perhaps a small piece of parchment.

"Brother Senacus!" the elder mendicant cried. "Brother Senacus!"

Everyone turned to the Pure, who Keilan thought looked less than pleased. "Yes?"

The mendicants and their entourage halted a dozen paces away. "Thank the Radiant Father we caught up with you before you departed," said the mendicant, wiping his brow with his gold-hemmed sleeve.

"You have news for me?" Senacus asked.

The elder mendicant bobbed his tonsured head. "Yes, yes. A bird from the temple arrived last night. A *white* pigeon, from the roost of the High Mendicant himself!" He stepped forward and held out the slim cream-colored scroll he'd been carrying.

Senacus accepted the parchment and glanced at what it contained, his lips moving slightly as he read. When he had finished, he frowned.

"We'll arrange an escort, of course," the mendicant said. "I know a few of the lightbearers have always wanted to see the holy city and –"

"No."

The older mendicant blinked in confusion. "Eh?"

"I cannot return to Menekar at this time."

"But . . . But you read the message."

Senacus held out the parchment, but the mendicant made no move to take it again, his face slack with surprise. "I cannot return now."

"The High Mendicant commands it! He has sent birds to every temple west of the Spine demanding that you proceed to Menekar at once with the boy –" He glanced nervously at Keilan. "– and the artifact he entrusted to you."

"I have prayed many times to Ama about these matters, I assure you. My way is clear – I must accompany this boy on his quest. If he succeeds, he might turn aside a doom that is coming to claim these lands."

"But you cannot refuse the High Mendicant!" the older cleric said shrilly, looking around to his followers for support.

"I can, and I will. Believe me, I have very good reasons, ones I cannot share with you at this time. You must trust me."

The mendicant made a cutting motion with his hand. "No! The Tractate is clear on these matters. The Pure are the sword arm of the faith, but they are subordinate to the emperor and the High Mendicant. You will be cast out of your brotherhood if you disobey!"

Senacus's expression remained impassive, but Keilan had traveled long enough with the paladin that he could see the conflict roiling beneath the surface. "Tell the High Mendicant that what I do is for the good of all."

"I . . . I must command you to be seized, then." He turned to his lightbearers, swallowing hard. "Warriors of Ama, bind the wrists of this renegade paladin and the boy. The High Mendicant insists that they return at once to Menekar."

A few of the lightbearers shifted their feet, but none moved to apprehend the Pure. "Warriors of Ama!" the mendicant tried again, more impassioned. "The Pure has been misled, perhaps by a demon –" he shot a hard look at Nel, and she snorted and rolled her eyes. "– perhaps by the boy sorcerer's honeyed tongue!"

"He gave the boy up to a sorcerer from Dymoria!" cried the younger mendicant, trying to rally the lightbearers. "You remember, yes? His corruption must have happened long ago! We are honor-bound to execute the will of our High Mendicant and bring the Pure before him!" The mendicant took a few confident steps towards where Senacus waited, but then faltered as he noticed that none of the warriors were following. Realizing he was all alone, he quickly scurried back.

"Seric, is it?" Nel said, turning away from the followers of Ama.

"Aye, goodwoman."

"Ready your boat to sail."

"Aye."

Pelos joined his nephew in preparing the boat, bending to loosen the rope wrapped around the iron spike driven into the docks while Seric leapt aboard and started hauling on the lines that would raise the patched sail.

"Come on, lad," Pelos said, motioning for Keilan to come aboard. "Best you were away."

The older mendicant's face had flushed crimson and his jaw was opening and closing, but he seemed unable to say anything more. With a last, long look Senacus turned from the outraged cleric and stepped over onto the boat.

"Goodbye!" Nel cried cheerily to the mendicants as the wind filled the unfurled sails and began to push them farther down the river. Pelos, still crouched on the docks, waved a more somber farewell.

24: KEILAN

THE *SEA BEGGAR* drifted south, borne along by a favorable wind and the strong currents of the river Lenian. Along the banks, salt marshes speckled with great mounds of cut hay gave way to a thick tangle of bloodbarks, roots reaching like splayed fingers down into the water, branches laden with crimson leaves casting the river's edges into shadow. They passed a boat much like the *Beggar* heading upstream, a dozen rowers straining hard against the current. A man in a bright green coat who looked to be the captain gave a familiar wave.

"Rhabin," Seric muttered, then paused to spit into the river. "Must think I'm mad."

"Why's that?" Nel asked, her hands on the low railing and the strong breeze tangling in her hair as she watched the other boat recede.

Pelos's nephew gestured at the empty benches and the long oars piled in the middle of the boat. "Usually I'd take five or six strong boys with me for when the wind or current is contrary. But one of those light-blinded fools was going to do something stupid if we didn't push off back there."

"What will we do then when we reach the sea?" Keilan asked, fearing he already knew the answer.

Seric offered another red-stained grin. "This ain't a leisure cruise. If the wind ain't friendly when we get to the deep water your arms are going to be mighty sore by the time we reach Ven Ibras."

Nel glanced disdainfully at the oars. "And if we part ways there? How will you get back?"

"Hire a crew. There's good money bringing folks . . . and other things . . . from the islands to Theris."

"So this isn't your first time sailing to Ven Ibras?"

Seric chuckled at Keilan's question. "No, it ain't. My uncle may have told you I stay on the river, but that's only what he knows. Truth is, I go to Ven Ibras every few months. There's a few goods that sell for cheap in the islands and most dearly in the Kingdoms."

Nel snorted, tapping her boot on the wooden hatch at the bottom of the boat. "Sounds like your hold has seen a lot more dreamsmoke than it has fish."

Seric shot her a look of surprise. "Might be it has. The Iron Duke don't allow dreamsmoke through the city's gates no more – says it rots the soul – but the river trade is harder to stop."

With that Seric leaned back, his hand on the tiller. Nel turned away with a sigh, returning her attention to the swiftly-moving riverbank. Keilan found a comfortable spot near the prow, enjoying the feel of being on a boat again after so many months on land.

Eventually the river widened, the water becoming choppier as they neared the mouth, and soon the *Beggar* passed into the sea. They stayed close to the coastline, and Keilan recognized familiar landmarks: a ragged line of dun hills, a sweeping expanse of blood-red forest, black rocks like jagged teeth marking the entrance to the bay where his village had fished. He thought he could see tiny black specks beyond the rocks – perhaps his Uncle Davin, returning in relief to a life devoid of sorcery and strangers. But the doom that was coming would not spare his village, no matter how much they wished to ignore the outside world.

Keilan was lost in thought, the lands that had once encompassed his entire world dwindling into obscurity far behind them, when a warm prickling told him that Senacus had come to stand near him. He looked away from the horizon and found the paladin leaning with his elbows on the railing, watching the shore slide past.

"Senacus," Keilan said, and the Pure turned to face him, the light from his eyes muted in the strong midday sun, "was it hard to refuse the mendicant on the docks?"

The paladin brushed aside a stray lock of his silver hair that the wind had displaced. He'd also allowed it to grow long on their journey east. "In a way," Senacus said slowly, as if choosing his words with care. "But I've been disobeying the leaders of my faith ever since I agreed to help you on your quest. I was tasked by the High Seneschal himself with bringing you to Menekar."

"What I don't understand is how they knew we were traveling together. Do you think the Lady Numil or one of her servants informed the High Mendicant?"

Senacus shifted uncomfortably, glancing at Keilan quickly and then looking away. "I told them."

"What?" Keilan said in surprise.

"I wrote to them, when you were visiting your seeker friend in the Reliquary."

Keilan's hands tightened on the railing. Senacus had betrayed them? Had Nel been right not to trust him? "Why would you do that? You knew what they wanted."

Senacus sighed deeply, and Keilan saw in his face how much this admission pained him. "It was Menekar we saw destroyed in the Oracle's vision. I had to tell them that something terrible was coming, so that they could prepare. I sent a letter describing what we saw in the coral cave . . . and why it had been shown to you. I told them I had prayed to Ama and this was the path I strongly felt I should take."

Keilan's mouth twisted. "It seems they didn't agree."

Senacus hesitated a moment, as if unsure whether he should say something. "There's more. As I told you, I cannot trust those chosen to lead the faith. I believe there is corruption in the temple – after all, I was dispatched to capture you with a sorcerer at my side. Whoever sent Demian with me must have known what he was. That thought terrifies me. But the High Seneschal – I saw him, dead in the Oracle's vision. I thought he could be trusted. Now, though –" Senacus squinted into the sun, his jaw clenched "– the only one who can command me is Ama, and when I need his guidance I will turn within myself to ask him."

Keilan put his hand on Senacus's arm, and the paladin flinched, then smiled sadly. "Look at us," the Pure said. "Sorcerer and paladin, ancient enemies brought together."

"Perhaps that is what the world needs," Keilan mused. "For everyone to set aside their hate."

Senacus grunted his agreement, his gaze returning to the distance.

Keilan watched him. The realization that the paladin's world had changed just as much as his own jarred him. Perhaps the changes were even greater for Senacus; the rock upon which he had built his life – that his faith would always oppose sorcery and its dangers – had been split asunder.

"Senacus, I have another question for you. In my village . . . in Chale, you were so reserved. So quiet."

The paladin nodded slightly. "Yes. It was not my place to interfere."

"What do you mean?"

"It was your time. Also . . . I wanted to see what you would do. Would you lash out in anger for what they had done to you and your mother? Would you hurt your uncle for the pain he had caused you? I was worried on the road when I saw you use sorcery to frighten them."

"And now?"

Senacus picked at a loose splinter in the deck railing. "Every follower of Ama chooses an Aspect of the Radiant Father to guide their actions. Some choose anger or hate. I do not – the Aspect I try to hold in my heart is compassion. And I think you are the same."

"Land!"

Keilan squinted in the direction Seric was pointing, shielding his eyes from the sun. For a moment he saw nothing, and then he became aware of the thin dark smudge clinging to the far horizon.

"Is it Ven Ibras?" he asked, and Seric nodded.

"Aye. We've made excellent time – thank the Shael for this wind. It always has been at our backs."

Their journey had seemed to be a blessed one. After staying close to the coast for the first day they had anchored with the western forests of the Kingdom still in sight, and while they had slept on the boat's deck the seas had been so calm that Keilan dreamt of being rocked to sleep in his mother's arms. Then the next morning they had turned south, venturing into the open ocean, and luckily the wind had shifted to accommodate their new direction.

It had been comforting to be aboard a boat again, with all the familiar sounds and smells. He'd spent much of the journey leaning out over the side, listening to the hiss of the waves against the hull and watching the sun glitter on the water. Nel seemed less enamored with sailing, as any food she attempted to put down ended up soon over the side. When Keilan had approached her with a bladder of water drawn from one of the barrels on board and asked her to drink, she'd turned to him with a face so pale and haggard that he'd then suggested she should rest in the ship's hold and lie down for a while out of the sun. That had actually summoned a sickly smile and something between a laugh and a sob. Apparently, she did not find appealing the thought of trying to rest in a dark, cramped space that reeked of fish, dreamsmoke, and whatever else Seric had smuggled.

Soon they would be back on land, though, as the smudge in the distance was rapidly growing larger, and Nel could eat a meal without the deck rolling beneath her feet. When they had approached close enough that Keilan could see the outline of a sizeable town nestled at the base of a forest-cloaked hill, Seric gestured at him to catch his attention.

"Hey, boy. There's some sandbars out here, so I need to keep my hand on the tiller. Open up the hatch and pull out the orange and green cloth bundled inside. We need to fly those colors when we get into the harbor so everyone knows whose protection we're under."

Keilan nodded. "And whose protection is that?" he asked as he made his way across the deck.

"Man's name is Pak Tan. He's a trader, of sorts. Well, more like a middleman. Matches goods to captains or stores them in his warehouse."

Keilan gripped the tarnished handle and pulled, but the hatch barely budged. "What happens if we don't show his colors?"

Seric chuckled grimly. "Well, the people of Ven Ibras left piracy behind many years ago, but they're still a bunch of thieves."

Keilan continued straining until with a rusty squeal the hatch finally swung open. Foul-smelling air washed over him, and he wrinkled his nose, nearly gagging from the stench.

"You should . . ." he began, but then something white and round swam up from out of the darkness of the hold. He scrambled back, crying out as it emerged from the hatch – thin arms clawing for purchase on the deck, snarled yellow hair, and a dirty face with one green and one blue eye . . .

"Sella!" Keilan cried out as the girl hoisted herself from the depths.

"What in Garazon's black balls is *that*?" Seric yelled. "And what is it doing on my boat?"

Sella took a few big gulping breaths of the fresh sea air as everyone stared at her in open-mouthed astonishment, then she rushed over to Keilan, who was still on the deck, and threw herself at him.

Her first punch hit him in the side, the second boxed his ear and made his head spin. He raised his hands against her flailing arms, but then she was hugging him, her face on his shoulder.

"Sorry I smell so bad, Kay," she whispered into his ear. "Down there it ain't nice."

"What were you doing in the boat?" he asked numbly, still in shock. Her fingers clutched at his back like she was clinging to a rock in the middle of the ocean. With some effort Keilan managed to push her away, his hands on her knobby shoulders. "How?"

She lowered her mismatched eyes. "Hiding. Cause I knew you wouldn't let me come."

"Who are you, child?" Nel asked harshly, crouching beside them. Senacus loomed behind her, frowning, his arms crossed.

Sella glanced at Nel and the towering paladin, and Keilan saw fear in her wide eyes. Then she scowled fiercely. "I'm Sella. Banny's girl."

"Banny?" Nel asked, the confusion clear in her face.

"Her father," Keilan explained quickly. "Sella's my oldest friend. She's from my village. Well, near my village."

"So near," Sella said with venom, "yet you couldn't stop by the farms and let me know you'd come back."

"Well, I . . . you know, I just . . ."

Sella snorted and looked away. "Hmph."

"How did you get in my boat, child?" Seric asked angrily. "Tell me, or by the Ten I'll toss you over the side and let you swim back."

Sella glanced back at Keilan, and he saw the fear in her eyes again. "I won't let him do that," he said quickly. "But you need to tell us how you got here."

Sella swallowed hard, casting an uncertain glance at the red-faced Seric. "I came down to Mam Ru's in the morning an' she told me you had been there the day before. She said you were looking for news about your mama, and that you'd gone up to Chale with Pelos." Sella wiped at her eyes, and her hand came away wet. She sniffled. "I couldn't believe you'd come back and then left without seeing me. So I ran all the way to Chale. Found a little barn outside the walls an' slept in the hay. Then went inside, and what do I see but him," Sella said bitterly, pointing a grubby finger at Senacus, "walkin' through town with half of everyone staring at him like he was Ama himself. I remembered he's the one that grabbed you an' took you away," she shot another foul look at the paladin, who raised his brows in reply, "and then there you were, stumblin' along beside him. I followed you all and when the priests started making a ruckus on the docks I slipped onto the boat when no one was looking and found a place to hide. Been down here forever and a day, feels like."

"But why?"

Sella turned her angry eyes to him. "Cause I wasn't about to let you run off again!"

"What about your da and ma? Your sister?"

"Well, I'll come back," Sella said slowly, as if she was talking to a simpleton. "With you, once you find out about your ma."

"You're going back as soon as Seric puts us on the docks," Nel said firmly. "He's stuffing you once more in that hold and not letting you out until he gets to Chale."

"No, I'm not!" Sella yelled back, putting her hands on her hips.

"Oh, yes, you are," Nel replied, shaking her finger at Sella. "Our path is far too dangerous for children."

"Keilan's with you," Sella said, jerking her chin at him. "He's only three years and two months older than me."

"Keilan has been trained by a Fist swordsman and fought monsters."

Sella glanced at Keilan, her eyes round. "Really, Kay? Monsters?"

"Well, I –"

"You're helpless," Nel continued. "Just a little girl."

"I remember her fighting quite fiercely," Senacus said softly, and they all turned to him. It might have been his imagination, but Keilan thought he saw a ghost of a smile tugging at the corners of the Pure's lips.

"Be quiet, paladin," Nel said, rounding on him. "Seric is taking her back to Chale –"

"No, I'm not," said Pelos's nephew calmly, and then spat red juice over the side.

"What?" Nel and Keilan said at once.

"Ain't going back to Chale for a while," Seric said, digging something out of his ear and flicking it away. "I'm gonna keep on sailing for a while until Ama's faithful forget all about me. Maybe a month or two. I'll keep heading west; always wanted to see the Whispering Isles. Don't want to return and have some big stupid lightbearer try to beat out of me where I sent you all."

"Then what about the girl?" Nel exclaimed, gesturing at Sella.

Seric shrugged. "Don't know what you should do. All I do know is that she's your problem, not mine."

The harbor of Ven Ibras was natural, formed by a pair of sandy arms that reached out from the island. Their rocky fingers nearly touched, which left only a small gap to pass through; Keilan could see the ancient remains of a large ship that had foundered on something submerged under the waves, and he was glad

Seric knew how to navigate these waters. Beyond this treacherous barrier a half-dozen great ships lay at anchor, all of wildly varying make. Keilan recognized a Dymorian caravel like he had seen before in Herath, its upswept sterncastle lined by wooden merlons that made it resemble a floating castle tower, and there was a long sleek ship, the lidless eye of Lyr painted near its prow. Tied to all the ships, banners like the one Seric had raised up his mast snapped in the wind, though there seemed to be at least four or five different designs and colors that Keilan could see.

Rising beyond the docks, which bristled with the masts of smaller boats, was the town itself, clinging to the side of a sharply sloping hill. The forest was so thick that the buildings seemed to be either emerging from among the tangle of limbs and leaves or in the process of being swallowed by it. The base of the hill almost touched the sand of the beach, and only a thin crust of buildings did not cling to its side as it soared upward.

"Look!" Sella cried, pointing at the gleaming rocks as their boat passed through the mouth of the harbor. Keilan squinted, and with a start realized that what he had assumed to be rocks of a reddish color were in fact basking lizards the size of small horses. The creatures were so still that for a moment he entertained the notion that they were stones carved as guardians for the town, but then one slipped off its perch and splashed into the dark water, vanishing at once.

"Locals here call them gug-gug lizards 'cause of the sounds they make at night," Seric said, expertly steering their boat through the gauntlet of rocks and sandbars. "They swim in the shallow waters and lie around in the sun, but they're also out there in the forest. They keep away from where people live, for the most part, but don't go exploring beyond the edge of the town. They have a bite that'll freeze the blood in your veins, and a few of 'em have found a taste for man flesh."

Sella clutched at Keilan's arm, and he could see the excitement in her wide eyes. "They're like dragons, Kay! Like in the stories you used to tell me!"

"They're just animals," Nel said, shaking her head. "No treasure to steal away or riddles to trade for. And you're about the perfect size for a snack."

Seric guided them up to the docks and found space among the other boats, then – nimble as a cat – he leapt off to wrap a rope around a wooden pillar. A gaunt old man in ragged clothes rose from where he'd been crouching and without a word Seric passed him a coin. The old man bit down on it, then grunted in satisfaction and turned away.

"He'll watch the *Beggar* while we're ashore," Seric said, motioning for them to follow him. As Keilan stepped on to the wooden planks he noticed Senacus had donned the amulet that hid his true nature and packed away his white-scale armor. Probably a wise decision if they did not want to draw undue attention to themselves.

The docks were a riot of activity, sailors from what seemed like a hundred different lands milling about. Despite all the time Keilan had spent in crowded cities over the past months he had never been around such a swirling assortment of color and cultures. Every shade was represented among the chaos, from the ebony of the distant jungles of legendary Xi to the milk-pale skin and red hair of Dymoria. Some attended to tasks, repairing bits of broken boats or carrying boxes and rope, while others congregated around the stalls and tables that had been set up where the shadow of the forest infringed upon the sand. This seemed to be the market of the town, and the array of goods on display was dizzying. Piled high on a length of red wood were bolts of luxuriant cloth that looked to be as fine a weave as Keilan had seen the magisters of Dymoria wearing. Elsewhere, under a checkered tarp a fat man sat fanning himself with a broad leaf, urns brimming with colorful spices and peppers spread before him. The largest crowds were gathered around a charcoal pit over which several cooked chickens dangled, and a man with a cleaver who was expertly dismembering a crisped bird.

"I remember Pelos saying something about how the island was a shadow of what it had once been," Nel remarked as they parted to make way for a pair of hairless men carrying what looked to be a broken mast on their shoulders.

"It was," Seric said over his shoulder as he led them towards one of the paths leading up the hill. "Ven Ibras was founded as a way-stop for the pirate ships that preyed on the shipping lanes between the Empire of Swords and Flowers and the northern lands. Twenty years ago the Shan navy finally had enough and smashed the pirates in a great battle."

"The Bloody Shoals," Keilan said, remembering what he had heard earlier.

"Just so. From what I gather, Ven Ibras withered to almost nothing afterwards – then, perhaps a decade ago, merchants started using it as a central place to trade goods, somewhere that was beyond the watchful eyes of the Shan emperor and the other kings along the coast."

Sella squealed as she caught sight of a burly man with a bright yellow snake wrapped around his neck; it almost looked like it was nesting in his bristly black beard. The serpent lifted its head from his shoulder and swayed in her direction as if curious about the noise, its tongue flickering. Sella gave a cry and clutched at Keilan's arm, but to his surprise he found her eyes were bright with excitement.

They started to ascend the path up the hill – carefully, as it was slicked by a layer of leaves fallen from the canopy arching overheard, and also because hidden beneath those leaves was a tangled skein of roots. Shadows moved in the high branches, chittering as they passed. On either side of the trail, houses of red wood were set back among the trees and vines, all of them raised up on stilts that left a gap taller than Sella between the ground and the platforms upon which the structures had been built.

"I've been here during storms," Seric said, anticipating Keilan's question, "and the water just pours down the hill. The houses would be flooded if they were built lower."

Keilan imagined a torrent of water flowing beneath the stilt-houses as the Shael raged above and the waves crashed against the beach below. It seemed a precarious life, bounded by the dangers of this wild island and the merciless sea.

It was cooler in the shadows of the forest, but biting insects swarmed them as they struggled up the steep path, clouds of small black flies and also larger, humming things that looked like dragonflies but caused blood to flow when they jabbed with their curving stingers.

"Ow!" Sella cried, slapping at the air. She dashed ahead a ways in an attempt to escape the insects.

"We need to get inside," Nel said, wincing as she rubbed at her neck.

"Aye," Seric said, pointing up ahead at a rambling building of gleaming red wood recessed among a copse of twisted banyan trees. "That there's The Haven, the beating heart of the island. Best place for a drink and to find answers."

Keilan's first thought as they pushed through the door was that if this was the heartbeat of the island then somebody needed to go fetch a physicker. The air seemed to hang honey-thick inside, and the few shapes hunched around the rough-hewn tables ignored their entrance. Insects bumbled in the amber light filtering through the large slatted windows, their droning the only sound in the large common room.

"Hm. Gets a bit more fun at night," Seric said, ushering them towards the back, where a hugely fat Shan reclined on a chair that seemed specially built to support his bulk. Perched on two much smaller stools were a pair of boys younger than Keilan – from the cast of their smooth faces they could have been brothers, but one had straight hair black as ink, and the other an unruly mop of golden curls.

The fat Shan stirred as they approached. "Seric! Been a long time. I just got word you sailed in flying my colors. That mean you're looking for work?" He raised a massive hand to indicate Keilan and the rest. "Who are they? Your family?"

Seric forced a chuckle, as did the two boys. That must have been a joke, Keilan realized.

"No, Pak. Passengers who paid their way to get here. They have business on the island."

The Shan's uptilted eyes narrowed. "Traders, then? What goods did you bring?"

"Not traders," Nel said, stepping forward. "We're looking for someone."

The Shan gestured for them to seat themselves at his table and snapped his fingers towards the drowsing serving girl pillowing her head on her arms at another table. She jerked up at the sharp sound.

"Fenny! A bottle of Lyrish blue. And some spiced crayfish."

"We don't want to impose –" Nel began, and Pak snorted.

"Ha! That's for me, girl. If you want something, you bloody well order it yourself. Unless, of course, you have business to discuss and we reach a good deal."

Nel flashed a crooked smile. "An ale for me, then, Fenny. And for my friend here." She inclined her head towards Keilan. "Milk for the child and the big fellow."

"I don't want milk," Senacus said curtly, and he turned to the serving girl. "Water, please."

Everyone jumped as the Shan slapped his hand on the table. "Ha! Milk and water. Are you sure you lot have come to the right island?"

"That depends," Nel said, leaning forward with her hands clasped together. "We're looking for Chalissian ri Kvin."

The serving girl placed a dusty green-glass bottle in front of the Shan, but he ignored it. "The Bravo? Well, he's here in Ven Ibras, but he's not the most friendly of sorts. I doubt he'd agree to see you."

"Can you send him a message?"

Pak rubbed one of his chins at Nel's question, as if considering. "Might be I could. My boys here could run up to his manse, pass a message to him through his steward Gen. Say . . . for a copper drake?"

"I have Lyrish copper, but the same weight. And that's fine."

The fat Shan grimaced, as if wishing he'd asked for more. "Done, then. Alax, Erix, scurry on over to the Bravo's place and tell him . . . " He looked at Nel expectantly.

"Tell him we've come asking about someone he once knew," Keilan interrupted. "A girl with silver hair. Tell him it's very important we speak to him about her."

The two boys glanced at each other, and then as if by some unspoken agreement they slid from their stools at the same time and dashed for the door, nearly knocking over the serving girl who was returning to their table with a greasy basket overflowing with bright red crayfish.

"Oy! Watch it, you monkeys!" she yelled at their retreating backs, then slid the steaming basket onto the table and turned away, muttering.

"Eat," Pak said, gesturing at the crayfish, suddenly more generous. "It's good to seal a bargain with food."

They had cracked the last of the shells and Keilan was sucking the delicious juices off his fingers when the door to The Haven banged open and the two boys burst through. Seric and Pak paused their rather dry conversation about the price of various fruits in different cities at this time of year as the boys ran up to the table.

"Pak! Pak!" they cried in one voice between great gulping breaths. "Gen said to send them up at once! He said he's been expecting them!"

25: ALYANNA

THEY WOULD DIE in these mountains.

It was only a matter of time before the genthyaki or the Pure found them, she was certain, but at the first glimpse of their pursuers she had resolved to slit Demian's throat with the dagger he had given her, then plunge the blade into her own heart. She would not go back. And for Demian, it would be a mercy. The pain she had endured under the palace . . . the loss . . . Better to die a quick death here than suffer like she had. Like she still did.

A harsh screech made her look to the sky, her heart in her throat, but it was only one of the carrion birds turning slow gyres high overhead, its raptor gaze no doubt fixed on Demian. Alyanna glanced back at the shadowblade – he was slumped forward with his head down, the only indication he was still alive the fact that he had not yet slid from his saddle.

She had been dreading that sound as she led the horse through the narrow valleys and along the rocky slopes of the Spine. The creak of leather and the slither of cloth as he toppled over, and then a final thud as he hit the ground. It was only a matter of time, she knew. His wounds were too severe; she had done what she could with her limited skill, cleaning and binding where the paladin's sword had scored his side, but his end was fast approaching. The thought left her hollow. Demian had been her steadfast ally for over a thousand years . . . he had always come when she needed him, and though she had never admitted it to him, she had relied on his calm strength in those dark moments when her own convictions had wavered. Without him, the other sorcerers would never have joined the ancient compact that had resulted in their immortality. He had always been a rock for her to cling to, no matter what storms were raging.

He was her friend. And when he died, she would truly be alone.

Alyanna paused, her breath ghosting the chilly air, and squinted up at the jagged peaks rising around them. It was as if they were inside the maw of a monstrous creature, its teeth gnawing the sky. So high. How would they find their way to the other side of the Spine? It had been a miracle they had not ended up at the bottom of some rocky gorge, a feast for the birds that had followed them so patiently since they had left the plains.

The narrow defile they had recently descended into was choked with stunted trees and rocks tumbled from higher up the slopes. The horse was having trouble picking its way through the detritus, but at least the way was not impassable. That would change eventually, though. And when it did, Alyanna would be faced with the decision of what to do with Demian. Could she leave him behind, after he had descended into the catacombs to rescue her? It was a choice she did not want to have to make . . . but she knew it would not be her who faltered first. She was getting stronger, somehow, despite the arduous journey. It was this light inside her, this terrible, blazing light. The Cleansing had burned away her sorcery, leaving nothing behind, not even the ashes of her power, yet it was somehow strengthening her body – her legs barely ached after a day of hard climbing, and the pain from the inquisitor's tortures had faded to a distant memory.

What had they done to her?

"Demian," she said softly, touching him lightly on the leg. He stirred, raising his head, and tried to focus blearily on her. Around his broken nose the flesh was mottled purple, but the rest of his face was even paler than usual.

She gestured at the mountains ahead of them. "Are we still going in the right direction?"

He licked his cracked lips, obviously struggling to see into the distance. "I think so."

Alyanna sighed, hoping his head wasn't addled. The mountains certainly all looked the same to her.

"No," he said, more firmly. "I know so."

She glanced at him sharply. "How?"

Demian raised a wavering hand, pointing at something up ahead. Alyanna turned, then gasped, her hand scrabbling for the dagger in her sash.

A man crouched on a lichen-stained rock, watching them. He was dressed in a simple tunic and leggings of black cloth, and a silken veil covered the lower half of his face. A penumbra of shimmering darkness sheathed the sword at his side.

He hadn't been there a moment ago, she was sure of it.

She mastered herself. "Greetings," Alyanna cried, her voice echoing in the gorge. "We seek sanctuary with the kith'ketan. We beg the daymo for his assistance in our time of desperate need."

The shadowblade said nothing, but below him, from the darkness cast by the rock, stepped another of the assassins. Above his veil his eyes were a vivid green, and they narrowed as he studied Alyanna.

She gestured behind her, at Demian slumped in his saddle. "I bring with me the man you call the Undying One. He lived for centuries among you, I know this. We were ambushed by paladins of Ama, and they wounded him badly. He needs aid."

The shadowblade on the rock leapt lightly to the ground. He approached Alyanna, his hand on the twisted ebony hilt of his unnatural sword. "Your eyes," he said, his voice cracking slightly, as if this was the first time he'd spoken in a long time. "You have been filled with the light of Menekar's god."

"Not by my choice," Alyanna said, more harshly than she intended. "They Cleansed me . . ."

"Are you the sorceress the Undying One brought into the presence of the daymo, and with whom a bargain was struck?"

Alyanna swallowed – the assassin had not let go of his sword's hilt. "Yes." She winced, half expecting him to lash out with that shard of darkness.

But he did not. The shadowblade nodded and turned away from her. "Follow me," he said simply, then began to pick his way through the stone-strewn gorge.

Alyanna let out a shuddering breath. She jerked the reins she held, and the horse clattered forward over the rocky ground. "You might have said something . . ." she said, but then she saw that Demian's head had lowered again, and he was swaying unsteadily in his saddle.

"God's blood," she muttered, going to him and laying a hand on his leg so he wouldn't fall. He jerked awake again at her touch, then groaned and clutched weakly at his side.

"The kith'ketan . . ." he began, and she gave his leg a gentle squeeze.

"They are taking us back to the mountain."

He slumped even further, though in relief or exhaustion she couldn't say. "I hope . . . I hope they do not kill you."

Alyanna pursed her lips, watching the shadowblade up ahead as he slipped among the tumbled boulders.

She hoped so, too.

The kith'ketan led them along narrow trails seemingly cut from the mountains, some barely wide enough for their horse, the walls of stone rising so high around them that only a thin slice of the sky could be seen overhead. Alyanna thought she could still make out tiny black specks marring the blue – they were nothing if not tenacious, those birds.

She wished she could still pluck them from the sky with her sorcery.

The path twisted and turned, and several times she thought they'd arrived at a dead end, only to have the kith'ketan draw back some hanging vines to reveal a passage or to find a hidden way recessed behind a seemingly random rock piling. They passed a deep pool so clear it was like a pane of glass, fed by a hissing waterfall that tumbled from a hidden alcove far above. Staring at the veil of falling water, Alyanna felt a strange tingling begin to crawl along her skin. She rubbed at her arms, dismissing the sensation. No, that was impossible. But when they crossed a natural bridge over a chasm, a slab of rock that had tumbled just perfectly to span the abyss, the tingling returned, insistent. She found her breath coming in short, almost panicked gasps, and when they rounded a spot where a gnarled mountain tree thrust onto the path she already knew what they would find: a great bronze door set into the mountain's flesh, veins of glimmering quartz radiating from it like streaks of lightning frozen in the white stone.

"No," she whispered, the reins falling from her slack fingers.

It was the entrance to Tivana, the mountain fortress where a thousand years ago she had conspired to end the old world.

"Yes, Weaver," Demian rasped behind her, his voice heavy with pain. "Welcome home."

The door clanged shut behind them with a sound like rolling thunder. The reverberations trembled the air in the great hall in which they stood, echoing among the square stone pillars and disturbing a nest of creatures lairing in the crevices above. Leathery wings flapped as the things soared higher into the gloom, chittering.

It was familiar, though not exactly as she remembered.

The pillars had once been twined with colored silk and affixed with shining mistglobes. Sofas wrought of copper strands and mounded with cushions had been scattered about, and marble water basins had been set just inside the entrance for the refreshment of those arriving or leaving the mountain. Now the hall was barren, as if it had been abandoned long ago.

Which it had. And yet . . .

A pair of cowled youths stepped from beside the pillars. Both held wooden rods, from which dangled translucent spheres she would have guessed were blown from glass, though their surfaces had a strange shimmering sheen. Clinging to the inside of each of these spheres were dozens of small, wriggling worms that glowed with a faint blue luminescence and gave the solemn faces of the youths an unearthly pallor.

"We did not know you would be bringing your own light," said one of the shadowblades softly, striding forward. Despite the silence of the hall, a quiet so deep she could hear Demian's labored breathing, the assassin made no sound when he moved. It was as if he was as insubstantial as a ghost. Alyanna did hear the shuffling steps of the child acolytes as they turned to follow him, and after a few moments she was outside the wavering circle of blue light cast by their strange lanterns. The radiance spilling from her eyes illuminated a little, but the light was quickly swallowed by the suffocating darkness. She shivered – it truly felt like something was watching her, out there beyond the limits of what she could see.

"Come," said the other shadowblade as he passed her, carrying the unconscious Demian in his arms as easily as if he were a child. "We must bring the Undying One to those who can help him."

They exited the great entrance hall through a doorway shaped like a tiered triangle – this was one of the strange architectural flourishes of the wraiths, the creatures that had first carved this place from the stone. The wraiths had once lived almost as men in their mountain redoubts, tunneling labyrinthine dens that spiraled deep underground. Now the creatures persisted only in the wilds of the Frostlands and had long ago fallen into barbarism. They were little more than animals, but once they had been a mighty people, well before the first empires of man had arisen in these lands. Mighty wars had been fought between the emerging holdfasts of Min-Ceruth and the ancient, deteriorating wraith kingdoms.

They descended a wide staircase clearly hewn from the stone for human legs – a legacy of her own efforts, as when she had chosen this mountain she had imported hundreds of skilled slaves from the Imperium to transform this wraith nest into a comfortable sanctuary. And in the end, it turned out the final beneficiaries of her efforts were the kith'ketan. She shook her head, still reeling from this revelation. When had they occupied the mountain? And why?

The two youths turned from the passage, entering a small chamber, and the shadowblade carrying Demian followed. Inside was a raised slab of dark stone covered in a thin layer of something that might have been moss, a tall, crooked figure looming beside it. The man – if it was a man, as its features were recessed inside a cowl, and its shape was hidden beneath heavy robes – gestured for the shadowblade to lay Demian down upon the slab. Alyanna gasped when from the figure's dagged sleeve emerged a twisted hand, withered and blackened like a limb that had been held inside a great flame.

The figure jerked its head in her direction at the sound. "The Pure," it said, in surprisingly smooth and cultured Menekarian. It reached up with its monstrous limbs – both were the same, she saw – and touched the hem of its hood. Alyanna feared what horror would be revealed, her breath quickening, but when the cowl was drawn back the face of a handsome young man emerged into the room's soft blue light.

"I was changed against my will," Alyanna said, trying not to stare at the man's arms.

"Interesting," the man murmured. "Perhaps I will study you later. I've always been curious about how the Cleansing alters the body." Then he turned from her, staring down at Demian.

"I know him," he said simply, brushing a gnarled finger along Demian's cheek.

"It is the Undying One," one of the shadowblades said.

"And yet he is dying," replied the strange young man. "How unexpected."

"Yes," continued the shadowblade. "And the daymo wishes him saved. Can you do it?"

The twisted man studied Demian for a long moment, his gaze traveling the length of the sorcerer's limp body. Then with startling quickness he slashed with his hand, Demian's already tattered shirt parting before the hooked talon at the end of his finger. He prodded the flesh beneath, frowning. "The wound is deep and layered over an older injury. Some corruption has set in, but it seems like there is no internal bleeding. I believe I can bring him back from the Paths."

The shadowblade who had carried Demian into the room nodded curtly. "Do so," he said, and strode towards the door, the other assassin and the two youths turning to follow him.

"Wait," Alyanna cried, almost grabbing the shadowblade as he passed, before stopping herself. "What about me?"

The eyes above the assassin's veil revealed nothing. "Hope that he survives," he said without emotion.

Then she was alone with the twisted physicker and Demian, the only light in the smaller chamber that which spilled from her eyes. There was a narrow bench against one of the walls, and as the man circled the sorcerer, prodding and muttering, Alyanna sat, suddenly acutely aware that she had not slept in days.

The thought of falling asleep in this place, with this creature hovering over her, was too terrible to contemplate. So she forced herself to concentrate on what was happening. To her surprise and revulsion, it looked to Alyanna that the shadowblade physicker actually pressed his finger into Demian's now-exposed wound, black blood trickling across his belly. The sorcerer moaned, squirming, and after a moment of watching him intently the physicker withdrew his finger and brought it to his lips. His tongue – strangely thin and long, Alyanna thought – flickered out to taste Demian's blood.

"What are you?" she asked, her stomach turning at the sight.

"A man who was too curious," the physicker said distractedly as he tore a clump of what she had thought was moss from the bed Demian lay upon, kneading the substance in his withered hands, "and wished to see the face of God." He pressed the moss onto Demian's wound, covering it completely, and the sorcerer's pained murmurings subsided.

Watching him minister to Demian, Alyanna remembered another time, and another grievously wounded man that had been brought into this mountain. Savaged by wyverns, she'd thought Jan would die when they found him – one of the beast's barbed stingers had plunged into his belly, and his skin had been turning black from the poison flooding his body. But the Visani fallowmancer Querimanica had shown his unparalleled skill in restorative sorcery, somehow knitting Jan's broken body together and purging the poison from his veins in the span of only a few days. It had been an awesome display. Healing magic was one of the most difficult branches of sorcery to master – life was exceedingly complex, and to regrow flesh and mend bones took an incredible knowledge that could only be gained from deep study and an exacting attention to the smallest detail.

With sorcery, it was always easier to destroy than to create.

"Weaver."

Alyanna came groggily awake. She had been dreaming that she'd returned to the mountain where she'd broken the world and found it full of living shadows . . . She raised her head, rubbing her sore neck.

Jan was sitting up, watching her; the torn remnants of his shirt had been removed, and in the chamber's dim light his pale skin seemed to glow. Except for where he'd been wounded, as a smear of black covered most of his side. No . . . not Jan.

It was no dream.

"Demian," she said, rising from the bench and approaching the sorcerer. "How do you feel?"

He gingerly touched the blackness encrusting his torso. "Well enough, I suppose. This is the work of the kith'ketan. Did they . . . did they put anything in my ear?"

"I didn't see, but I fell asleep while the physicker was attending to you. Your ear? What could they put there?"

Demian grimaced. "A worm. It burrows within the skull and lairs in the brain. The daymo breeds them . . . after a while the host is nothing more than a husk and cannot help but answer without hesitation any question." His hand went to the side of his head, as if he could tell by touch whether one was squirming inside him right now. "I hope he still considers us allies."

Alyanna laid her hand on Demian's arm. "They seemed to still respect you. And their physiker brought you back from the brink."

The sorcerer nodded. "I lived in this place for a long, long time. All of them have heard tales of the Undying One."

Alyanna shuddered. The darkness . . . the emptiness . . . the weight of the mountain pressing down from above . . . and of course, lest she not forget, the deranged murder cult. "How could you live here? And why?"

Demian ran a hand through his sweat-damp black curls. "I returned a few centuries after the ceremony. I was searching for answers, at that time – I'm not sure why I looked for them here, but I had exhausted nearly everywhere else. I wanted solitude, I think, and I thought no other place would be as empty." He stared into the gloom, quiet for a moment. "But instead I found the kith'ketan. There were fewer of them then, and their legend had not yet begun to spread. A prophet had brought them here, a man they called the daymo. He spoke of a god beneath the mountain, a god who would flense the world and expose its secrets for them in exchange for their devotion."

"But there's nothing here," Alyanna said. "No god. We would have sensed it long ago."

Demian glanced at her, his face solemn. "There was nothing then. Now there is."

Alyanna swallowed, remembering the sense of being watched from the darkness. "What is it?"

The sorcerer shook his head. "I have my suspicions. But perhaps this is not the time or the place to share them."

Alyanna peered into the darkness. It had seemed to thicken as they spoke, but surely that was her imagination . . .

"You said you were meditating here?"

Demian winced as he explored the edges of the mossy bandage with his fingers. "Aye."

"Why?"

"As I said, I was also . . . *ng* . . . searching for answers when I came back. For a long time after the ceremony that . . . made us . . . I wandered, trying to unravel the riddles of existence. Where does the world come from? What is our purpose here? What will be our fate? I thought the answers would be out there, somewhere, and with my immortality in hand I now had the time and patience to discover them. A secret hidden in some ancient ruin, perhaps, or in the ramblings of a mad desert mystic. Always I was disappointed." He raised his sword arm above his shoulder, testing its range of motion. "But I did find something. South of the Broken Sea, in the Empire of Swords and Flowers, I came across a temple clinging to the side of a mountain. The monks there could do the impossible – leap incredibly high, and break stone with their bare hands. And yet I felt no sorcery to explain these powers."

"You're speaking of Red Fang."

"Aye. The daisun monks were the inheritors of a tradition that stretched back to the ancestral lands of Shan, far across the ocean. Through intense meditation and discipline they could perform incredible feats."

"And you discovered how they did it?"

Demian nodded curtly. "In a sense. I never achieved their level of mastery, even after centuries of meditating. But perhaps that was because of what I already was."

Alyanna leaned closer, intrigued. "What you were?"

Demian raised his hand, and a sphere of wizardlight flared into existence. The radiance filling Alyanna made her shiver as he summoned forth his sorcery. It was so strange, to feel the magic welling in another, when for an age it had been twined with her very soul.

"A sorcerer. Within us there is a thread to elsewhere, a place of limitless power."

Alyanna nodded. The Void. The realm of gods and demons and other creatures beyond the ken of mortals.

"You know this, of course. But the revelation of the monks is that this passage to the beyond is not restricted merely to those born with the gift. Everyone in the world, not only sorcerers, is connected to the Void. We are unique because this power bubbles within sorcerers like a spring, and after training we can shape it with our will – and what we are capable of doing is only limited by our ingenuity and the size of the reservoirs within us. But the daisun monks, through their intense meditation, have also discovered this pathway to the Void. They call it the Nothing within the Self. And the greatest of them have learned how to plumb these depths to strengthen their bodies far beyond what is natural. The difference is that they reach *into* the Void and draw forth something, while we merely make use of the sorcerous dribblings that collect within us."

Alyanna felt like she had to sit down. The idea that those who lacked the gift of sorcery could also access the Void was stunning. Such a heretical belief would have had Demian sanctioned or even executed in the days of the Imperium. Was it possible? If anyone could reach into the Void . . . did that mean she could learn how to do this as well? Had her path to sorcery truly been closed forever, even though the spring inside her had dried up? A tiny flame of hope kindled within her for the first time since she had been strapped screaming to the Radiant Altar.

"So all the time you spent under the mountain you were trying to find this Nothing within the Self?"

Demian let his wizardlight sputter and fade. "Yes. And I never did. Perhaps it is because, as I said, I am already a sorcerer – or maybe I am missing secret knowledge the monks somehow kept from me, despite my . . . strident questioning."

"Centuries in this place . . . a long time for a fruitless search."

"It did not feel so long," Demian mused. "Time flows differently here, especially deeper, down where my chamber was situated." He hesitated, as if uncertain how to express himself. "Do you remember when you dreamsent to me, how strange the feeling was to be aware within our dreams? Like you were watching yourself from a distance. The air was honey-thick, unreal . . . that is what it was like for me under this mountain. I would emerge from my meditations to find a decade had passed, and even though the kith'ketan left food and water in my cell, and I must have consumed it, I have no memory of doing so. When you dreamsent to me here, I almost did not realize what you were doing because it was already so similar to my life beneath the mountain." He paused again, and when he spoke once more his voice was distant. "It was a waking dream, truly."

"What do we do now, Demian?"

Her question seemed to shake him from his reverie. "We rest, Weaver. We both need to recover, I think. I'm certain the daymo will call on us before long, and we will discover then whether we are still within his good graces."

Alyanna clenched her fists. "What use would I be to him now? What use am I to you?" she said harshly, trying to keep the bleak hopelessness from rising up. If she let it consume her – if she faced what she had become – she wasn't sure how long she could keep on living. "I should kill myself and free you from whatever obligation you think you have –"

She started as Demian's hand closed around her wrist. His grip was like an iron manacle, and he leaned closer to her, staring without flinching into her blazing eyes. "You are Alyanna ne Verell. It was with your brilliance that you bent the world to your will, not your sorcery. Remember that. You are still the Weaver."

She turned away so he would not see her tears.

26: THE CRONE

THE GUARD IN his flowing scarlet cloak set his hand on the head of the dragon beautifully carved into the wood and pushed. The great red door swung slowly open, and then he stepped into the royal audience chamber, holding it wide. He nodded at her to enter and struck the stone floor twice with the haft of his halberd, announcing her presence.

Willa swept inside, her head held high and her face a careful mask that betrayed nothing. Her jeweled slippers sank into a thick Keshian carpet patterned with red and white diamonds, which stretched the length of the long chamber to where a throne of burnished golden wood rose atop a three-tiered dais. The woman seated on the throne seemed older than Willa remembered, even though it had only been a few years since she had attended the queen's coronation – Cein d'Kara had always cultivated an aura of strength and certitude, but before there had been an edge of youthful innocence that hadn't been entirely obscured by the white cosmetic she layered on her skin and the imperious mien with which she held court.

Ruling had hardened her, Willa realized, as it did most who bore the heavy burden of a crown.

"The Lady Willa ri Numil, envoy of the archons of Lyr," a liveried servant cried, and the Crimson Queen raised her slim white hand, beckoning for her to approach.

Trying to hide how much her hip was paining her, Willa stepped forward. The space between the door and the dais was filled with a fractured panoply of colored light from the great stained-glass windows high up on the walls. Stern-looking stone men brandishing swords in heroic poses watched her pass – Willa had known several of those kings when they had ruled here, hard men who had held these proud and fractious lands together through will and steel. Cein d'Kara was both very different from the harsh kings who had come before her, and very much the same.

Willa was surprised at the emptiness of the audience chamber. There were no nobles milling about, no courtiers or sycophants desperately trying to be noticed. Just a few more of the scarlet-cloaked guardsmen spaced throughout the hall, several servants wearing white tunics emblazoned with the serpentine dragon of Dymoria, and two men standing on the second-highest step of the dais, flanking the throne. Willa's eyes flickered between them as she drew closer. One was a Shan, tall and straight-backed, wearing the same red cloak as the other warriors here, though this one was clasped by a golden brooch shaped like a coiling dragon. She knew him: Kwan Lo-Ren, the captain of the queen's Scarlet Guard. His left arm hung in a sling, and much of the skin on the left side of his face had been scraped away, but he still looked more than capable of defending the throne. He had been wounded during the assassination attempt on the queen, she had heard, and some of the rumors that had reached Willa's ears had even claimed he'd died. She had suspected, though, that he'd survived – he had always seemed like a hard man to kill.

The other man was dressed in the wine-colored robes of a senior magister. He looked young to be standing at the queen's side, but a streak of white did blemish his black hair.

"Welcome to Herath, Lady Numil," said the queen when Willa had nearly reached the base of the dais.

Willa bowed, gritting her teeth as pain shivered through her. "Queen d'Kara. It is an honor to come into your presence again. I wish to extend the warm regards of the Council of Black and White."

The queen studied her for a long moment, her face impassive. Willa prepared herself for an exchange of flowery rhetoric, perhaps some subtle verbal swordplay that would establish the boundaries for this audience. That was the way of the Gilded Cities, even between the bitterest of enemies. There were rules to these kinds of exchanges. Traditions that must be observed.

The queen evidently did not care. She leaned forward, her fingers curling around the end of the throne's upswept armrests. "Where are my rangers, Crone?" she asked, and though her voice was calm her eyes flashed with anger.

Willa fought back the urge to swallow, trying her best to keep her expression unruffled. "They are all safe, Your Majesty. They are being treated as honored guests in the archon's palace."

"You mean in the cells beneath the palace. You are holding them captive."

Willa crushed her small trickle of apprehension, as the queen would surely sense any weakness. "It was necessary."

Cein d'Kara leaned back in her throne; from her clenched jaw and the whiteness of her knuckles she was not even attempting to hide the signs of her anger now. "Has Lyr sided with my enemies? Do the archons dance at the end of strings held by Emperor Gerixes?"

"No, Your Majesty," Willa said quickly. "We would not be so foolish as to align ourselves with Menekar against you."

"Then where is the paladin they were pursuing, which they did by my command? Is he also a guest of the archons?"

This was quickly deteriorating. "No, he –"

"And there was a boy among the rangers, a student from my Scholia. If he has come to any harm in your city my wrath will be terrible, I promise you."

"He was not harmed when in our city."

The queen's eyes widened. God's blood, she'd caught that qualification.

"You mean he is no longer in Lyr? Where is he?"

Traveling east with the Pure who tried to kidnap him from Saltstone. Willa bit back on this admission, though. Perhaps it was not the time quite yet – Cein's grandfather had been famous for personally wielding the greatsword that had cut off the heads of those who delivered bad news to him, and while the queen certainly seemed more enlightened than her predecessors, Willa still did not want to provoke the infamous d'Kara temper.

"Keilan is safe." *I hope,* she added silently. "Please, Your Majesty, much of great import has happened that I believe you have not yet been informed about. Give me a moment to explain."

Willa interpreted the queen's stony silence as an invitation to proceed. "Thank you, Your Majesty. As I am sure you know, the rangers you dispatched south to capture the paladin finally caught up with him just outside Lyr, in sight of our own soldiers. The captain of the gate realized that the wisest decision would be to have the archons pass judgment on who should be favored in this situation, and so all were brought before the Council of Black and White."

"And the Council's session was interrupted," the queen said. "By an emissary from the Oracle."

"Yes." For once, Willa was pleased for the existence of the Dymorian informants in the archon's palace. "She summoned Keilan and the paladin Senacus to the House of Many Streams. I accompanied them as well."

The young magister turned and whispered something to the queen. Cein d'Kara pursed her lips at his words, as if in annoyance, but then she nodded curtly.

"What about Keilan's companion? A young woman once from Lyr?"

The ruffian girl. "She also came to the Oracle's temple and shared in the vision we were given. She is still at his side, to my knowledge. She left the city with him."

"Tell me about this vision."

Willa twisted one of her jeweled rings, a nervous uncertainty rising up in her. She must convince the queen of the threat foreseen by the Oracle. If she failed, she would have made an enemy of the most powerful ruler in the west. Her city would suffer if she could not make Cein d'Kara understand.

"It was shared with all of us in the coral chamber. You've been there, I know."

"Twice," the queen said quietly. "Once when I was very young, only a girl. And then again of course when I visited Lyr soon after my ascension to the throne."

Willa did her best to hide her surprise. Cein had come before the Oracle when she was still a princess? How did she not know this? Something to investigate later, she told herself. "This was no ordinary audience with the Oracle, Your Majesty. She did not make some vague pronouncement and send us on our way. No, she actually *showed* us her vision. We were in fact drawn into the future she had seen."

The queen steepled her hands, her expression thoughtful. "Interesting. I have read about that happening before, many centuries ago. The Oracle died from the strain of doing this, I believe."

Willa remembered the pale corpse dangling from the coral, and the young girl swimming across the pool to take up the sacred mantle. "It has not yet been widely shared, but when we returned from where she sent us we found that the Oracle had perished."

"And what did she show you?"

"Doom. Destruction. We stood in the remnants of the Selthari Palace and saw Menekar spread below us in ruins. The sky had been torn open and was weeping blood. Some terrible sorcery had been unleashed on the world."

"You saw only Menekar destroyed?"

"Yes, but the Oracle said all the lands were the same. And the ones who had brought about this tragedy were there. We saw them."

The queen was silent, watching her intently.

"They came from Shan, the Oracle said. Twisted, monstrous children. They had summoned forth whatever had broken the sky and sundered the earth."

Surprise shivered the faces of the two men standing below the queen, and they glanced back quickly at her. They each knew something about this. The Crimson Queen ignored them, though, her face guarded.

"As we watched, a sorceress arrived from the sky to challenge them. She brought the severed head of one of these child-demons and tossed it at their feet. They struck at her with sorcery and she responded in kind, but before we saw who the victor would be we found ourselves back in the Oracle's temple."

"This sorceress," the queen said, her voice sword-sharp, "did she have dusky skin and raven hair?"

"No. She was pale and had shimmering silver hair unlike any I've seen before."

The queen blinked, as if this was not what she was expecting. She laid a long finger to her lips, her gaze growing distant. "Silver hair . . ." Her eyes suddenly snapped back to Willa, and they were not friendly. "You sent the boy to find her."

How did she piece it all together so quickly? "Y-yes. It must be why the Oracle wanted to show Keilan her vision. She knew he had seen the sorceress before. And that he might be able to find her before this doom came down on us all."

"You dispatched an untrained sorcerer, barely more than a boy, along with a young woman who was once a thief, on a quest to find an immortal sorceress who was one of the wizards responsible for the cataclysms that destroyed the old world."

And here was the admission that would get her drawn and quartered. "And the Pure."

"What?"

"The paladin of Ama is with them as well. He saw the same vision we did, and he pledged to protect them on their journey."

The queen shook her head in disbelief. "And how long ago did they depart Lyr?"

"More than a month. They must be in the Shattered Kingdoms by now." *If nothing has happened to them.*

"Well, this explains why my messengers to your council were not received. And why my rangers were not released."

"I was waiting to discover what I could about this threat from Shan. I thought you would be . . . understanding of what I had done if I could present a more complete picture of what was happening."

Willa waited with growing dread for the queen to order her guardsmen to drag her down to the dungeons. What else could she expect, after such a strange and mad story?

The silence stretched as the queen appeared to consider what she had said. Then Cein suddenly rose, startling the two men standing below her.

"Come with me, Lady Numil," she commanded as she started to descend the dais. "There are things you must know as well."

The queen led her to a chamber deeper within the fortress, a small windowless room dominated by a great golden basin filled to the brim with water. No tapestries or sconces adorned the walls, and since there was no furniture other than the gilded basin Willa found herself unsure where she should stand. One of the legendary mistglobes that had been common before the breaking of the world hung from the ceiling on a delicate silver strand, the brightness coiling within its depths bathing the room in a pale light. Cein paced the edge of the basin, trailing her fingers in the water as Kwan Lo-Ren shut the door behind them.

"You're ready to try it, then?" the young magister asked, his eyes fixed on the golden basin.

"I am," the queen said, lifting her fingers from the water and flicking them dry. "But first, let us – how do chalice players say it? – flip all the cards we have on the table." She turned to face Willa. "Lady Numil, beneath the surface of the world, great forces are moving. A month past, an alliance of ancient sorcerers and shadowblades tried to kill me and kidnap the boy Keilan. And their assault on Saltstone did not seem like the culmination of a long war, but rather the opening skirmish. That is why your description of what the Oracle showed you does not surprise me – there is much more to come, I am certain."

"My queen, there is something you must know," Kwan Lo-Ren said.

Cein looked at the captain of her Scarlet Guard in mild surprise. "You know something?"

Kwan Lo-Ren's face was troubled. "I do, Your Majesty, though it is with a heavy heart that I must share my knowledge."

With a gesture, the queen bade him continue.

"I have heard many things in your presence recently," Kwan Lo-Ren began. "First, that it was a Shan who slipped into the fortress and freed the sorcerer –"

"A Shan did what?" Willa blurted, forgetting for a moment that she was in the company of a queen.

Cein held up her hand to show her indulgence with the interruption. "Yes. One of the ancient sorcerers involved in the attack – though I suspect, unless I am being naïve, he did so unwittingly – was captured and imprisoned here in Saltstone. Someone snuck inside and freed him and fled east; I sent hunters after them, but in the end the one in command allowed them to escape." Willa could not miss the pointed glance she cast in the direction of the young magister.

"What was the name of the Shan girl?" Kwan Lo-Ren asked the magister, who had wilted under the queen's glare.

"She said her name was Cho Lin," replied the magister.

"Cho Lin," Kwan Lo-Ren repeated softly.

"I don't understand," Willa said. "Why didn't you capture him again?"

"Because it would have been bloody," the magister said quickly, and from his tone it sounded like this was not the first time he'd had to defend his decision. "The girl claimed to be both a disciple of Red Fang and the daughter of a Shan lord, and the sorcerer said he would die before returning. I truly believed, Your Majesty," he continued, his voice almost pleading, "that you would not have wanted either of them dead, which is what would have been risked if we had tried to take them by force."

"As I said before," Willa said, "the Oracle stated that the threat would come from Shan. And then a Red Fang monk penetrates Saltstone and frees one of these ancient sorcerers who attacked you? They must be allied together with the demon children."

"I do not believe so," Kwan Lo-Ren said slowly. "These twisted children you saw – what did they look like?"

Willa thought back to the vision, of those creatures emerging from their house of blackened corpses. "Skin so white they appeared to have been drowned. Tangled black hair and tattered clothes."

The captain of the Scarlet Guard nodded, his face grim. "The Betrayers."

Cein d'Kara's eyes narrowed. "You know them?"

"I do. The true story of them has largely been effaced from my people's histories, but every child of Shan is told of how they are responsible for the loss of our ancient homeland."

"They ushered in the Raveling?" Cein asked.

Kwan Lo-Ren nodded. "Yes, my queen. And the thought that they will return to the world chills my blood. They are creatures of hate and vengeance."

Willa plucked at the hem of her sleeve, a coldness growing inside her at the Shan's words. "How will they bring about the destruction I saw in the Oracle's vision? What was the Raveling?"

"A scouring," Kwan Lo-Ren said. "But more I do not know. Perhaps no one outside of the bone-shard towers in Tsai Yin has this knowledge." His brow knitted, as if he was considering deeply what this all meant. He looked shaken, and to see that from such a formidable man worried Willa.

"Why did you want to know what the Shan girl's name was?" asked the queen, and this seemed to return Kwan Lo-Ren to the chamber.

"Magister Vhelan said it was Cho Lin. The Cho are one of the great families of Shan, with a history that stretches back for thousands of years, well before the Thousand Sails fled the old lands. They are rich and powerful . . . but above all else, they are known as the foremost demon hunters of Shan. Cho Xin was the man who defeated the Betrayers in the final days of the Raveling. He slew their physical bodies and bound their spirits to a rosewood chest the warlocks had constructed. This Shan girl told Vhelan she was searching for something. I would wager she is searching for the Betrayers."

"She said Jan knew where the thing she was searching for was," the magister said.

"So these sorcerers are allied with the Betrayers," the queen said with cold disdain. "They already brought down one cataclysm, and now they plot to do so again." She stared into the basin's water. "The threat has begun to emerge from the gloom. But what can we do?"

"There is something else, Your Majesty," Willa said softly. "And it was the reason I came north. You see, after the Oracle pronounced that the doom she saw would come from Shan,

I commanded the defenders of Lyr to investigate any travelers from the Empire of Swords and Flowers. A wild attempt to discover more about what was coming, but it bore fruit." The creature that had haunted her nightmares rose up again, long black talons dripping blood as it stalked across the warehouse towards her . . .

"It was a sailor on a Shan ship sailing to Herath, though it looked like a man from the north. When it was questioned, it . . . changed. It was monstrous, and it slew seven guardsmen before escaping. It . . . it claimed to know about these demon children, the ones you believe are the Betrayers."

"It was coming to Herath?" asked the magister, glancing at the door as if he expected the creature to burst through it.

"More enemies," the queen said bitterly. "And this only reinforces that we need to be allies in this, Lady Numil. Lyr and Dymoria must stand together."

Willa bowed her head. "I agree, Your Majesty. Petty rivalries must be put aside."

"And we must find others we can trust," the queen said, drawing something from the folds of her dress. It looked to be a small stoppered vial of some dark liquid.

The magister's eyes widened. "You are going to attempt it, my queen?"

Cein stepped closer to the golden basin. "Yes. We must be certain of the intentions of Jan and this Cho Lin."

"What is that?" Willa asked as the queen held up the vial so that the light from the mistglobe illuminated its contents.

"Blood," she said matter-of-factly. "Taken from the immortal sorcerer while he was in Saltstone."

Blood magic! Willa breathed out slowly. Only necromancy was considered a darker shade of sorcery – what was the queen doing?

The queen seemed to notice her expression. "There is great power in blood, and it can be a useful tool. It is only evil if the exsanguination results in death or undue suffering. This time, it did not."

"What will you do with it?" Willa asked, her mouth dry.

"Spy," the queen said simply, and tilted the vial so that a few drops fell into the basin. Willa stepped closer, fearful of what she might see, but nothing seemed strange. The blood was – as to be expected – slowly unspooling in the water, like smoke drifting across a winter sky.

A look of intense concentration passed over Cein's face. Her cheeks flushed, her lips pulling back in a grimace to show her gritted teeth. The mistglobe hanging above them flickered, as if whatever the queen was doing threatened to destroy it.

The water shimmered, colors seeping into it. They swirled, coming together to form shapes . . . trees . . . mountains. Willa's heart quickened. It was like they were staring through a window into another place.

Sorcery. Willa did not have the same compunctions about magic as most others – she had, in fact, even employed a few sorcerers when it benefited her city – but still it made her feel uneasy. Such power in the hands of a young woman who was already the queen of a great kingdom. There might come a time when Cein's ambitions would put her in opposition to the Council of Black and White. Willa dreaded that day.

The image in the basin finally finished resolving. There was a horse on an ancient, rutted road, and its rider from behind looked to be a woman. The hood of her cloak was drawn back, and her black hair was bound in a long pony-tail that reached nearly to her saddle. To the left of this woman, in the far distance, a line of mountains reared stark and imposing. The lands she currently rode through looked to be moors, a rolling gray waste pocked by tall clumps of ragged grass.

"They are almost to the Mire," said the magister softly.

"They?" Willa asked, peering into the basin, looking for the second traveler.

"The Shan girl and the sorcerer," the queen answered her. "We are seeing through his eyes."

Willa drew in her breath. She had never heard of any sorcery like this before.

The queen touched the water lightly, and the scene dissolved in the ripples. "We must keep watching. I want to know more about this Shan girl . . . and what she is hunting."

27: CHO LIN

THE PALE FIELDS. It was the place where the forgotten dead roamed – the unloved, the lost, the spirits with no ancestors to burn incense and paper wealth in their honor. Her tutors had told her that the fields were not a real, physical location that could be visited, but rather a state of existence for ghosts unlucky enough to pass beyond the veil with no family left behind. But Cho Lin had always imagined it, even in those childhood sessions, as a spectral wasteland stretching into eternity, rolling gray hills pierced by skeletal trees, with a murky sun hidden behind dark clouds.

And now, deep in the barbarian lands, she had found a place that perfectly matched her imaginings.

A fell wind moaned, sweeping over the moors and making the barren branches of the few trees near the road clack together. She shuddered, pulling her cloak tighter. Herath had been cold compared to the warmer lands of Shan, but out here, without walls and buildings to shelter behind, she felt as if she might lose feeling in her limbs. Already her fingers and toes had gone numb.

"We'll stop at the next inn we come across for the night," Jan said loudly over the gusting wind. "We don't have enough blankets, and we could freeze out here if we make camp and can't get a fire to catch."

Cho Lin glanced at the frozen ground and the dry, dead-looking grass and nodded her agreement. "This place is terrible," she said bitterly, and Jan chuckled.

"The moorlands are bleak, I'll grant you that. But when we truly enter the Mire tomorrow you'll look back at this part of the journey with fondness."

"The Mire?"

Jan gestured with his arm to encompass the gray wastes. "At least here it's dry. The Mire is a swamp teeming with snakes that will crawl right into your bedroll and swarmed by insects waiting to feast on your flesh. League upon league of desolation. When last I traveled through it I could use my sorcery to keep me warm and safe. This time we won't have that luxury."

Cho Lin's heart fell. She had fervently hoped that what was ahead of them would be an improvement over this. Clutching tight to the thought of a fire and a hot drink, she hunkered down in her saddle and silently cursed these forsaken lands, trying by force of will to make an inn materialize farther up the road.

"We can stay there," Jan said, nodding in the direction of a dilapidated collection of clay bricks and scarred wooden beams.

Cho Lin blinked in surprise. She'd thought the building was just another abandoned farm like the many they'd passed along the Way, but Jan had already slid from his horse and was leading it towards a listing barn beside the larger structure. Now that she peered closer she could see smoke rising from the roof, almost obscured by the fog, and light trickling from around the edges of the shuttered windows.

A roadside inn in Shan – even a small way-stop deep in the wilds – would be bedecked with colorful lanterns welcoming travelers and inviting them inside. This place, by contrast, looked more like a robbers' hideout than a place to find a comfortable bed and a good meal. Cho Lin glanced once more at the moorlands, and the cold wind chose that moment to rise again, stinging her face and whipping a few stray strands of hair across her eyes. Sighing in grim resignation she slipped from her horse and moved to follow Jan.

Inside the small stable were a few other horses that looked to have recently been ridden; evidently, the inn was indeed in use. Cho Lin hitched her mount beside Jan's and then spent a moment gathering hay for the horses from a large pile in the corner. When she was finished she shouldered her travel bag and the long case containing the Sword of Cho, and when she turned again to the entrance she found Jan watching her.

"For a noble-woman of Shan, you seem comfortable in the stables."

Cho Lin pushed past him, heading for the inn's entrance. "I've spent most of my life outside the Jade Court," she said to him as he followed her. "The other daughters of the mandarins would not recognize me, I think."

She lifted the iron knocker and rapped loudly, and a few moments later a heavy thud sounded as something barricading the door was set aside. A woman's plump face, her cheeks apple red, filled the crack as the door opened slightly. Her eyes brightened when she saw them, and she swung the door wide, smiling.

"Welcome, you weary souls! Come, come!"

Warmth washed over Cho Lin as she stumbled inside. She had envisioned that what was within the inn would match the dreariness outside, but to her great surprise the common room was homely and inviting. A fire crackled merrily in a hearth of black stone, making the air hazy with the sweet smell of burning wood, and trestle tables filled most of the space. Several travelers in mist-damp cloaks were hunched over steaming bowls or mugs of dark ale, and a few of them turned to stare with interest at the new arrivals.

"You look like a couple of bog-men, you do," the matronly woman nattered as she led them to one end of a table and motioned for them to sit. She squinted at Cho Lin, patting her arm after she had slid onto the bench. The familiarity was galling, but Cho Lin restrained herself from jerking back from the touch. "A Shan, the Silver Lady save us. Haven't had one of you folk come through here in near three years, I would say. And you're so beautiful! You'll tell me if any of these louts bother you." She waved in the direction of the very harmless-looking travelers who had continued gawking at them: a handful of scrawny, pock-faced youths and a fat man with a cleft lip.

"Thank you," Cho Lin murmured, surprised by the solicitousness. Perhaps it was the custom here.

"Some food and drink?" the woman asked cheerily.

"Anything to eat that's hot, with a cup of your strongest ale," Jan said, running his hand through his sandy hair.

"We've a nice chicken soup on the fire and a fine Leskan stout. But perhaps you'd like to try a bit of marsh juice? That'll fill your belly with fire and get your blood hot for other things too." She winked at Jan and then glanced at her; when Cho Lin realized what the woman was alluding to she had to fight back a startled gasp at the impropriety of the suggestion.

"The stout will be fine," Jan said, unable to restrain a slight smile when he saw Cho Lin's horrified expression.

"And you?" she said, turning to Cho Lin.

Ignoring the flush she felt in her cheeks, Cho Lin held her head high and met the woman's eyes with cool composure. "Soup. And a hot drink. You have tea?" she asked hopefully.

"Tea?" the woman repeated, chuckling. "No tea in these parts. How about some mulled mead?"

Cho Lin glanced at Jan. "Mead?"

"Northern tea," Jan said quickly.

"If the drink is hot, yes, I want."

"Be back soon," the woman promised, and then vanished in a swirl of her tent-like dress. Cho Lin felt dizzy from the exchange, but that might have been the heat from the fire after so long riding in the freezing wind.

"Relax and enjoy this," Jan said, unclasping his cloak and setting it beside him. "We have a few hard days of travel ahead of us. There are no inns like this in the depths of the Mire."

"You said we might freeze if we camp outside."

Jan nodded, rubbing at his wrists, which were still chafed red from the manacles he'd been wearing when she had found him. "More than a few travelers must need supplies before attempting the Mire. They'll sell some heavy travel blankets and furs here, I'm sure."

She caught one of the pocked youths staring at the metal collar around Jan's neck, which was visible now he had removed his cloak. "You should be careful," she whispered, leaning closer. "Maybe they think you are an escaped slave."

Jan's fingers found the iron torc, and he gave it a little tug, as if in some vain hope that it might spring open. "They won't. There's no slavery in the north. They are more likely to assume that this is some strange city-folk fashion. Ah, here we are."

The bustling serving woman returned with a tray laden with two bowls of steaming soup and a pair of tall wooden mugs. She set everything on the trestle table and waited as Cho Lin dug out a few coins from her pouch. "Will you two be needing a cove for the night?"

Cho Lin looked at Jan blankly. "A cove?"

"An alcove." Jan pointed along the far wall, which was divided into a half-dozen small spaces, each separated from the common room by their own curtains. "For sleeping. It's common in these smaller inns."

"Two coves," Cho Lin said quickly, pulling out a few more coins.

The woman plucked a silver from her outstretched hand, grinning at Cho Lin's obvious discomfort. "Enjoy the meal, then. Holler if you need anything else."

After the woman had flounced away again, Cho Lin frowned at Jan. "No rooms? We sleep just in there?"

"You'll be safe," Jan said after taking a long swig from his ale and wiping the froth from his lips.

"Of course I'll be safe," Cho Lin hissed. "I will break the neck of anyone who comes through my curtain at the night time. But men and women sleeping almost side by side, in the same big room, just a cloth between us . . ." She shook her head. "*Weiguan*."

"What's that?"

Cho Lin thought for a moment, trying to summon forth the correct Menekarian word. "Barbarians. You are all barbarians." She dipped her ladle in the soup and slurped the hot broth: it was rich and hearty, with chunks of carrots and potatoes mixed in with the shredded chicken. It was the most delicious thing she had ever tasted. She felt the chill leave her bones as the soup settled in her stomach.

Jan chuckled, watching her reaction. "Try the mead. You'll like it."

She gripped the battered tin handle and brought the cup to her lips, though she did not yet taste the amber liquid inside. Cho Lin breathed deep, enjoying the feel of the steam on her face. "Something sweet?"

"That's honey."

Honey. She liked honey in her tea. Cho Lin took a tentative sip; she tasted sweetness, yes, but also something spicy, and cutting through it all the sharp tang of rice wine. For a moment she considered spitting out what was in her mouth . . . but she did not want to look like a barbarian in front of these barbarians. She swallowed.

"It is like hot wine," she said reproachfully. "You did not tell me."

Jan shrugged and held out his cup to her. "Let us share a drink, yes? A few days ago, I was in chains in a tower. You freed me, and I thank you."

Cho Lin tapped his cup with hers and then took another quick drink. It really was quite good. "I freed you for a reason."

"To find the demon children."

"Yes."

He set down his drink carefully, the curiosity clear in his face. "Tell me – why are you the hunter who was sent? Why not one of the warlocks? Or a soldier? Why not –"

"A man?" she finished for him.

Jan offered her a rueful smile. "That's a bit blunt . . . but yes. And I mean no disrespect. You said you trained at Red Fang, so clearly you can fight. But you're not more than twenty years old. Surely there was someone older . . . someone more experienced for a task such as this."

With her fingernail Cho Lin traced a whorl in the grain of the table's wood. "I am from the Cho family. We are legendary in Shan as demon hunters."

"But you have no brothers? No father?"

"My father died only a few months ago," Cho Lin said, fingering the edges of this still-fresh sadness. "He died in these lands – in the north, even – hunting the Betrayers. The demons of the chest. My brother . . . he was poisoned when I was a young girl. He lived, but his body was broken. He can no longer lift a sword or ride a horse." She glanced away, remembering the Cho estate during those terrible months when her brother had hovered on the border between life and death. Her father had been beside himself. Lord Cho's presence had always loomed over her life, as distant and immutable as the mountains, even though his attention had been focused on the machinations of the Court and the training of her brother. She had been an afterthought to him during her own childhood, valuable only when she would grow older and could be used as a tool to forge an alliance with another of the great houses. But then . . .

"After it was clear that my brother could never become what my father wanted, he turned to me. He could have recruited one of his nephews, perhaps, but there was an old hate between him and his brothers. And I was his blood, even if that blood flowed through a girl's weak body.

"So he came, one day, to the garden as I played with my friends. I was nine years old. He led me away from the game we were playing and brought me down twisting paths to a dark glade where a man waited with two training swords in his hands. My father told me my childhood was finished. That I must now carry the family's honor."

"A heavy burden," Jan said quietly.

"Yes. But I was strong. The man who taught me, he was a Tainted Sword. Once of Red Fang, but he had left the temple in disgrace. I learned much from him. And when I had reached the limit of his skill, I left for Gold Leaf Temple to continue my training. I passed the abbot's tests. I joined the order. Even my father had never done that."

"He must have been very proud."

Cho Lin allowed herself a small smile. "Perhaps. He never said such things. I was always a tool for the family, ever since I was born. Only my purpose changed."

She brought her drink to her lips and was surprised to find it empty. Jan saw this and motioned for the serving woman to bring them another round.

During her long months in seclusion at Red Fang, Cho Lin had tried her best to maintain her focus on pushing deeper and deeper into the Nothing. But unwanted thoughts had inevitably encroached while she was alone in the darkness. Some had sprung from what her brother had told her on her last night in the family's estates, just before she had departed for the temple. He had informed her that their father – still a fairly young man – had taken a third wife in the hopes of siring another son. His first wife – their mother – had killed herself when Cho Lin was an infant. His second wife had turned out to be barren. But this new wife was not much older than Cho Lin herself, and the woman's sister had already given birth to five healthy boys. Perhaps, her brother had said with a sly smile, she would never need to take up their father's mantle.

She had turned this over and over in her cell beneath Gold Leaf Temple. Her father could carry the Sword of Cho for another twenty years, at least. If a male child was born in the next few years, then there would be plenty of time to groom him to take up the ancient responsibilities of the Cho family. And she would be passed over, an insurance against a misfortune that in the end had never happened.

But she had given up her life for her family. No mandarin of the Jade Court would marry a woman who had trained with the daisun monks. She would have no manse, no estate, no life among the noble ladies of Tsai Yin.

No children.

No purpose.

And so, in the blackness of her cell, she had felt an anger growing inside her. She suspected it was what had kept her from reaching the farthest depths of the Nothing. But she had been unable to set this resentment aside.

And then the shocking news had come of her father's death and the escape of the Betrayers. After a thousand years, the Sword of Cho was needed again.

Fate certainly had a sense of irony.

"Deep thoughts," Jan commented, watching her closely.

Cho Lin took another swallow of mead. Her head was pleasantly light now. "I am wading through the River Memory," she said quietly, quoting one of the old poets, "and trying not to be swept away."

"Sometimes that is difficult," Jan replied, also softly.

The odd edge to his voice made her glance at him sharply. "What about you? How did you end up in that tower, truly?"

Jan was silent for a moment, his fingers drumming the side of his cup in a quick pattern. It almost looked to Cho Lin like he was plucking the strings of an instrument.

"You speak of memories. Of swimming in them and trying not to drown." Jan paused, gathering himself. "Until very recently I had only a few scattered memories. The rest were behind a haze I could not see through."

"You were struck on the head?"

"No. They were . . . taken away. And the one who did that to me offered to restore them if I did something for her. I had to travel to Dymoria and present myself to its sorcerous queen. I was to hide my own power and take the measure of hers."

"The one who stole your memories gave you this task? You should have forced her to return what she had taken."

Jan smiled sadly, shaking his head. "I did not know she was the one who had done it. And she did not steal them . . . I remember everything now, and I know that it was I who begged her to make me forget."

"Why?"

"Because I had done terrible things. I could not live with myself if I could remember."

Cho Lin found a fresh cup of mead before her, and she took another deep draught, watching Jan carefully over the rim. "And now?"

He looked up from the table, and the pain evident in his eyes surprised her. "There is a memory I am clinging to. It is something I learned long after my mind was first purged . . . and after I had discovered this great secret, the sorceress did her magic and made me forget again, with the hope that this truth would remain hidden forever. But I remember now. And I will not forget this time."

Cho Lin awoke on a bed of stale rushes, her head throbbing. She groaned and struggled to her feet, steadying herself with a handful of the frayed curtain that blocked the entrance to her tiny alcove. Her throat was parched and her lips dry. What was the appeal of drinking rice wine? She resolved to never do so again.

Pulling aside the curtain, she shuffled into the inn's common room. The tables were empty, but the plump serving woman was there carrying two buckets sloshing with water towards the kitchen. When she caught sight of Cho Lin she smiled, but it didn't seem to touch her eyes.

"Afternoon!" she said loudly, setting down the buckets. Cho Lin watched the water enviously.

"Good afternoon. May I have some water?"

"Of course! Let me find a cup." She turned to go, but before she did Cho Lin noticed that her gaze flickered somewhere else.

Cho Lin followed the direction of that quick glance . . . to the curtain of the alcove Jan had slept in last night. It was drawn back, and Jan and his bags were gone.

"Where is my friend?" she asked before the woman could vanish through the door to the kitchen.

"I – I don't rightfully know –"

Jan was gone.

The woman gasped as Cho Lin appeared beside her. It must have seemed like sorcery, because her face paled and her eyes went round with fear.

"Where is my friend?" Cho Lin repeated, her hand closing around the woman's wrist.

"He left last night," the woman said, her words tumbling out in a rush. "After you went to bed."

"Where did he go?"

The woman swallowed. "I don't –" She squeaked in pain, and Cho Lin relaxed her grip slightly.

"I must know."

"I'm not certain which way he rode, but Old Jansen's son was in here this morning, and he said he was out trying to catch frogs last night and he saw a rider going hard on the road. Might have been him."

"East or west?"

"Well, that's why he thought it was worth mentioning. Wasn't riding along the Way. He was going north, and that's not a direction most folk go."

North? "To the mountains?"

"To what's beyond the mountains. The Frostlands." The woman sketched a circle in the air in front of her, some warding sign. "Where the Skein dwell."

28: KEILAN

"KAY, LOOK AT this!"

Sella's excited voice came from the balcony, floating through the gauzy curtains on a sweet-smelling breeze. Keilan glanced up from the strange carving he'd been examining on a shelf cluttered with artifacts – it was a block of ancient scrimshaw shaped to resemble some tentacled creature with a single staring eye, and it looked unnervingly familiar.

"Kay! Quickly!"

Seated at the room's round table, Nel sighed and rolled her eyes, then brought the hilt of her dagger down on a large brown nut. The shell split with a crack, and in a single smooth motion she reversed her dagger and pried loose the innards.

"Go see what she wants," she said, tossing the seed into her mouth and brushing the remains of the shell to the side.

Keilan stepped through the rippling curtains, blinking in the bright sunlight, and onto the balcony of red wood. Sella was perched on the edge of the balustrade, leaning out over the tangle of vegetation that looked poised to engulf the mansion.

She was pointing at a tree knotted with vines and speckled with small yellow flowers.

"Look!" she cried. "Can you see?"

Keilan moved to the edge of the balcony, savoring the day's warmth. They'd been waiting for a long time in the shadowy coolness of the sitting room, for a full watch at least. He tried to see what Sella was so excited about, but she appeared just to be pointing at a knobby bump growing from the tree's gray bole.

"What is it?" he asked, searching for what had excited her.

"Watch this," she said, showing him a nut in her hand. Then she hurled it at the vine-wrapped tree. The nut bounced off the trunk . . . only it wasn't the trunk, as what he'd thought was a knot on the tree suddenly lifted and scuttled away. The crab's mottled gray shell would be large enough to sit upon, and it perfectly blended with the bark and vines.

Sella laughed happily, clapping her hands. Keilan couldn't hold back his own smile. He had seen this reaction from her countless times when they'd been exploring the beach or the woods – unalloyed joy at the simple wonders of the world. He'd missed her so much . . . after all, in the years since his mother's death she had been his only friend in the village.

It saddened him that he would have to send her away.

"Sella," he began, unsure of how to say what he must. "You shouldn't have come."

She turned to him, the happiness in her face vanishing.

"You don't belong here," he continued, pressing on before she could say anything. "You should be back on your farm, helping your da."

One of her hands tightened on the railing as she tucked a strand of her yellow hair behind her ear with the other. "My da doesn't want me there."

"Yeah, he does."

"No, he don't," she said, and Keilan could hear the edge of bitterness in her voice. "He thinks just like the rest of them. That I'm unlucky."

Keilan pursed his lips. She was speaking of her mismatched eyes, one blue and the other green, and he knew that she was right. In his village, only Mam Ru would even speak with her, and Sella had confided in him before that it was the same in the farms to the north.

"You know what it's like, Kay," she said, tears welling in her eyes. "I know you do. The way everyone looks at you when a calf dies or there's an early frost. Like it's because you did it."

"But it's too dangerous for you here," he persisted. "You don't know what I've seen. Monsters and spirits and spiders big as dogs. You're not safe."

"Well, what about you?" she retorted, jutting her chin out. "I know you well enough. You didn't turn into some great warrior or wizard in the last half-year."

"I *have* to do this, Sella."

"You don't," she said, turning away. "There's a hundred hundred folk older and stronger and smarter than you. Almost everyone in the wide world, in fact. You *want* to do this."

She was right, he grudgingly admitted. The lure of finding out the secrets of where his mother had come from was powerfully strong. It was the great mystery of his life, and the answer now seemed tantalizingly close.

"I do, yeah. But I have Nel and Senacus to help and protect me."

"They can protect me, too."

Keilan raised his eyebrows. "Well, Nel might not. She seems quite annoyed with you."

Sella gave him a fierce look. "I don't care. She's mean. I'm not going back until you do. And since Seric said he's not returning to Chale, I don't think there's anyone to take me home."

Keilan sighed and rubbed his face. What was he going to do with her? She was right. He couldn't simply put her on a boat headed to the Shattered Kingdoms – he'd never forgive himself if anything happened to her.

"We can find –"

A door scraped open inside the manse. Sella and Keilan shared a quick glance, and then they hurriedly pushed away from the balustrade and slipped back through the curtain.

The same tall man who had led them to this room had returned, and now stood in the doorway with his arms crossed. He was one of the hairless men of the Whispering Isles, his smooth teak-colored skin gleaming like he had rubbed himself with oil. Keilan could not tell if he was thirty years old or fifty. The hairless man pursed his thin lips, his gaze traveling from Nel seated at the table to Senacus standing beside a faded oil painting of a ship in a storm to Sella and Keilan framed by the billowing curtain.

"The captain will see one of you," he said, the cadence of his speech almost musical. "The boy who knew the girl Vera, who lived in this house for a time."

The hairless man brought Keilan to another room in a different wing of the manse. It was paneled in more of the gleaming red wood, though here the moldings were of finer make, and bookshelves stretching from the floor to the ceiling had been built into the walls. His breath caught in his throat as his gaze traveled along the sweep of dark leather bindings – there must be a hundred books, perhaps even more. And they were not the only wonders; like in the previous chamber, strange artifacts were displayed on low tables: a barbed harpoon of some dark metal, a cracked curving tooth the length of Keilan's forearm, and a skull that looked vaguely human . . . but only a single large eye socket was in the center of its forehead.

Seated behind one of these long tables in a high-backed chair was an old man. He rose as they entered, and Keilan was taken aback by the breadth of his shoulders and his imposing height. He filled the room like a storm cloud; his forked black beard was streaked with gray and bound by iron rings, and his craggy face seemed hewn from stone. He must be nearly seven span tall, Keilan marveled, and was dressed in faded finery that looked like it had been fashionable sometime in the last century. The collar and sleeves of his shirt were fringed with lace, and his vest was done up with tarnished golden buttons. Behind the old pirate a yellowed and stained map of the Broken Sea spread across the wall.

He tugged on one of his beard-forks with fingers that glittered with silver rings and studied Keilan, frowning.

"Captain," the hairless man said smoothly. "This is Keilan Ferrisorn. He claims to be the son of the girl Vera." Then he retreated, drawing shut the chamber's door behind him.

The pirate lord's face seemed to grow even darker at his mother's name, and Keilan felt a rising apprehension. Could there have been some trouble between them long ago?

"My lord," he said, taking a tentative step closer to where Chalissian loomed. "I am sorry to disturb you. I heard you knew my mother."

The old man reached for a dusky bottle on the table in front of him and, with a flick of his huge thumb, removed its cork. He poured a measure of dark liquid into a cup of green glass and then sank back into his chair.

"Vera," he rumbled, lifting the glass to study its contents. In his massive hand the cup looked like a tumbler. Then he tossed back the drink and grimaced.

"Sit," he said, and Keilan slid into a cushioned chair on the opposite side of the table.

Chalissian filled his glass again without offering any to Keilan. "So you are her son."

"I am. She died a few years ago."

"How did she die?"

"She drowned."

The old man nodded slightly, as if he had expected this. "A good way to die. I've seen a lot of men get taken by the sea. The water fills them up, pushing out their life, and the spirit wriggles free and swims away. Sometimes you can glimpse those ghosts at night, in the moonlight, staring up from under the waves."

Keilan swallowed, unsure what to say to this.

"So you've come here," Chalissian said, his black eyes glittering, "to Ven Ibras and my home. Why?"

"I need to know about her life."

"'A man must first know where he came from, in order to discover where he must go.' Do you know who said that?"

"The . . . the carpenter on the road to Verayne. In Jesaphon's book of tales."

The old man set down his glass so hard Keilan feared it had cracked.

"You are right. And you are like her – learned. Can you believe I caught her here –" Chalissian gestured to encompass the rows of bookshelves. "– late at night, hunched over this very table? Reading." He chuckled. "A servant! The gall of it, to sneak into her master's study and burn down his candles when she needed to be up for her morning chores only hours later. And she showed no fear when she saw me standing in the doorway. I knew then that she was different."

"Please, my lord. How did she come to work in your house?"

The old pirate sipped his drink. "She appeared during a storm," he said, his voice growing more distant, as if dredging up these memories was returning him to the past. "Wet and shivering outside my door. She begged for a place to sleep and food to eat, promised to work hard. I don't rightly know why I said yes – my heart is usually black iron, but there was something about her. Maybe it was her hair, like a stream of silver. Never seen anything like that before or since, and I have sailed all over the world."

"Did she say where she had come from?"

The old man shook his head, the forks of his beard swinging. "Never spoke of it. But I can respect those who want to leave something behind."

A sinking sensation was spreading in Keilan's stomach. Was this where the trail ended? Had this entire journey been for nothing? "Did she bring anything with her?" he asked, hearing the edge of desperation in his voice.

"She was wearing a dress. It was old, I remember, but rich. Like a noblewoman might wear who has fallen on hard times. She was carrying a bag, but the only things inside were books. That was a strange thing, as those books were written in the old Kalyuni script. She could've sold them to a merchant in town for enough coin to buy her own house, but she never would have done that. They were her treasures."

"How long did she work here?"

"A few months. I was good to her, kinder than any master should be." His face darkened, his bushy brows drawing down. "And then one morning she didn't appear when I rang the bell. Had slipped out during the night without so much as a farewell. Stole some food before she left, and I heard later that she had gone on a boat headed towards the Kingdoms."

"I'm . . . I'm sorry. I'm sure she had a good reason."

The old pirate grabbed the dusky bottle and upended it into his glass, spilling some of the drink onto the table. "I raged back then. I am still a captain, and there is nothing that angers me more than mutiny. Your mother, she didn't show me loyalty when I'd done her a kindness." The old man stood suddenly and turned away from Keilan, staring at the tattered map of the Broken Sea that covered the wall.

The sound of the door opening made Keilan glance behind him. The hairless man who had led him to Chalissian's study filled the doorway, motioning for him to come. With a final look at the old pirate, his back still to him, Keilan hurried across the room and slipped into the hallway. The hairless man gently closed the door, his face impassive.

"The captain, he has a black temper. It will pass like a squall, but for the time it is best to let him be."

"I didn't mean to anger him. I just had to ask about my mother."

The hairless man held up his hands, as if to show that he understood. "Yes. And I remember your mother as well. I was working in this house when she first came here." He glanced at the closed door, his lips set in a thin line. "He loved her, I think. Not as a man does his wife, but as a father does his daughter. She would read to him for hours – the captain, he never learned how, but he loves his books."

"Do you know why she left?"

The hairless man shook his smooth head. "I do not. But there were rumors . . . whisperings at the time all over the island about strangers appearing at night at many doors to ask questions about a girl. I was there when Vera heard about these things, and I remember her face. She was frightened."

"Strangers? What did they look like?"

He shrugged. "I could not tell you. I never saw them. But others who did said they wore cloaks and went cowled, never showing their faces. And they vanished when she did, and were never seen again."

"Perhaps . . . perhaps someone else on the island will remember something about my mother, or these strangers who might have been searching for her."

The hairless man nodded. "Perhaps. And you may stay here, in this house, while you ask these questions."

That surprised Keilan. "Truly? I thought your captain was angry with me?"

"He is more sad than angry, I think. It is an old sorrow he never truly set aside. He will want you here, and when he calms down he will have questions about your mother's life after she fled the island. She was a great mystery to him, one he has never forgotten."

29: ALYANNA

DEMIAN HAD BEEN right about the dream-like quality of life beneath the mountain. Sometimes when Alyanna awoke on her bed of moss in her tiny grotto she could only lay there, unable to move, her limbs heavy as stone, unsure whether she was still asleep or not. Above her, pale blue worms would crawl inside the crystal sphere hanging from the ceiling, their movements sketching patterns that would mean something to her if only she could concentrate a little harder . . . if only the tingling in her head would abate for a while and she could think clearly again.

Darkness. Silence. Meals were piles of insects that looked to have been ground by mortar and pestle, but not so fine that she couldn't find the odd antennae or mandible still whole within the mash, all served on broad flat mushrooms that smelled like spoiled meat. Young acolytes emerged from the blackness at what seemed like irregular intervals, set down her supper or breakfast, and retreated again without saying a word. Some would keep their eyes closed, as if they did not wish to see her; others would squint or blink against the radiance that spilled from her. Alyanna wondered if these children had ever encountered a woman before – there were no girls among their number, that she had seen, and she could remember no women when she had previously dealt with the kith'ketan in the imperial gardens, before the assault on Saltstone.

What would compel these people to live beneath the mountain, and to devote their lives to darkness and murder?

She spent some of her waking time with Demian as he recovered. The swordsinger drifted in and out of consciousness, and even when he was awake he often seemed unaware of where he was or what had happened. On several occasions he spoke to her as if they were still students at the Arcanum, where she had first met him over a thousand years ago. He had been damaged back then, an orphan boy raised with his twin in the pleasure houses of Kashkana, desperate to develop his power so he could earn the influence to set his brother free. Alyanna had come from an equally humble background, the daughter of a violent and poor sharecropper on the hardscrabble plains outside Mahlbion. Their tremendous natural Talent could not be denied, though, and it had brought them to the foremost of the creches, where they had been surrounded by the children of the Imperium's elite. During those early years they had remained outsiders, reviled for how their abilities had allowed them to rise up into a higher caste and claim positions above their peers. Over time they had become both allies and rivals, two of the greatest Talents the Mosaic Cities had produced in generations. Eventually, though, they had drifted apart after finally earning their colored robes, but when Alyanna had gone searching for others who might share her dreams of immortality, Demian had been the first to answer and pledge himself to her cause.

Despite their long history and, at times, close partnership, they had never been lovers. Alyanna had never known Demian to take a partner of any sort, in fact, and she had come to think of him as lacking that most basic of passions – perhaps it had been excised by whatever horrors he had experienced as a child. But now she wasn't so sure. Watching him sleep, his untroubled face and the gentle rise and fall of his chest, she began to wonder . . . He had come for her, into the place most dangerous to sorcerers in the entire world, when he must have known he would likely find her broken or dead. Could friendship be enough to justify these actions? Was it possible that the last swordsinger of the Imperium *loved* her?

These thoughts and more consumed Alyanna as she wandered the mountain's halls. Twisting passageways that seemed so familiar and yet so different, spilling into chambers where the remnants of the sanctuary she had constructed here could still be found, if she looked carefully enough. Scraps of copper that once had formed the twisting frames of the furniture she had imported from the cities of the Imperium a thousand years ago; shards of glass from shattered mistglobes, still slightly infused with the glow of sorcery; bits of metal and ceramic. A large swathe of the fastness seemed to have been abandoned, but the majority of what she had renovated long ago was simply closed off to her – including her old quarters. Those sections were guarded by solemn-faced acolytes slightly older than the ones who brought her meals, and they shook their heads and moved to bar her way when she tried to walk past them.

Alyanna was surprised to discover, however, that one area was outside of the inner sanctum claimed by the kith'ketan. She stumbled upon it quite by accident as she explored deeper and deeper into the corridors open to her. It began as a crawling sensation that made her shiver, and as she pushed on further the feeling strengthened, until her heart was beating fast and her breathing became labored.

When she finally entered the chamber, she nearly retched; the miasma of sorcery still clung to the walls and the table that filled the space a thousand years on. The soul jewel she had forged in the black kiln was gone, and she wondered to where it had been moved. At the culmination of the ceremony that had rendered Alyanna and the others immortal, its core had cracked, so it could never be used again for such a purpose, but still vestiges of the sorcery had lingered in its facets. It was why they had fled these halls with such haste afterwards – the scraps of souls still adhering to the jewel had been leaking some fell poison into the air, and a few members of her cabal had even sickened before they'd managed to escape.

But now the jewel was missing, and only faint traces of it lingered. Still, those sorcerous reverberations were enough to make her nauseous, and so she hurriedly left the room where she had claimed immortality all those years ago.

She returned to Demian's chamber and found him awake and lucid, being attended to by the strange kith'ketan physicker.

"I've been in the ceremony room," she told Demian as the man with the withered arms changed the moss encrusting his wounds. He was healing well, Alyanna noticed, the flesh underneath pink and glistening, with no hint of corruption that she could see.

Demian grimaced as the physicker used his gnarled fingers to pack the moss tight. "And so you're wondering where the jewel has gone."

"Yes."

"I've seen it," he said, swinging his legs over the edge of the dais as the physicker stepped away. "It's still here, under the mountain. Or what's left of it."

"The kith'ketan have claimed it?"

Demian shook his head, then paused, as if considering her question further. "They may have been the ones who moved it," he said slowly. "I'm not sure."

"If not them, who?"

He prodded the moss bandage on his side, then sucked in his breath, wincing. "Not who," he gasped, his face pale from the pain. "What."

30: CHO LIN

ANGER DROVE HER those first few days as she chased Jan north, an indignant rage that he would betray her trust. She had rescued him, shown herself willing to die for his freedom, and this was how he repaid her? By sneaking away while she slept, like a thief in the night? Surely he must have some understanding of the importance of her task. He had told her he had seen what the Betrayers were capable of doing, that he had tracked them down after they murdered someone he knew.

So as the barren moorland gradually gave way to frozen tundra and she began the treacherous ascent into the ice-sheathed Bones of the World, she considered all this. Cho Lin did not think he was simply trying to be free of her and the promise he had made. After all, why would he head north, into the Frostlands, which the Shan knew to be the wild and forsaken edge of the world? There must be a reason he had ridden this way – some justification for his betrayal. In the shadow of the white-hot flame of her anger a small ember of curiosity began to smolder.

It took her four days to pass through the mountains. The path she followed was not a road in the traditional sense – there were no distance markers that she could see, or furrows to suggest that wagons or horses had regularly churned the earth. But there did seem to be a route that wended between the stony skirts of the Bones, clear of any impassable rivers or cliffs that might have forced her to try and climb higher into the range. Even in these lower reaches, though, as she passed through the valleys and the frozen river beds, the cold was almost unbearable. She had bought as many furs as the innkeeper back in the moors would sell to her, but no matter how many layers she huddled beneath every night she still woke with ice in her hair and numb fingers and toes.

At least she knew she was going in the right direction. Almost as soon as she had started after Jan, along the way the innkeep had claimed he was seen riding, the Sword of Cho had begun to quiver again. Just as it had when it first led her to Jan's prison in the fortress of the Crimson Queen, and so she at least could be certain that he had not doubled back or tried to mislead her. He truly was journeying into the Frostlands, as mad as that seemed.

Cho Lin emerged from the Bones onto a wide snowy plain bounded far to the east and west by dark forests. The sky here seemed to be a deeper shade of blue than in the south, and though the sun did little to warm her, it was so bright she had trouble staring into the distance, the glare reflecting upon the snow making her eyes water. If she squinted, though, she could see mountains far ahead, soaring and ice-capped, even more formidable than what she had just passed through, their peaks draped with ragged streamers of clouds like silken prayer flags.

The landscape was so monotonous that at first she thought the corpses were a mirage. She glimpsed them as she crested a small rise, a speckling of dark shapes sprawled in the snow below. From this distance she couldn't see exactly how many, but as she approached, her horse carefully picking its way down the broken scree of the slope, the scale of the slaughter became apparent. There were dozens of bodies, perhaps as many as fifty, and it looked to her from where they had fallen that they had been cut down while trying to flee. A few had made it some distance from where most of the others had been killed, and Cho Lin's eyes were drawn to a young woman lying face down in the snow. Her long yellow hair was matted with blood, and she clutched the hand of a small boy who was half-buried in the snow.

Cho Lin slid from her saddle and approached the dead woman and the child. A cold wind gusted, rippling the furs that swaddled the bodies. She crouched beside the corpses, noticing the ragged cut in the woman's cloak – someone had stabbed her from behind before bashing in her head. Cho Lin didn't want to examine the boy to see how he had died – the mere fact that someone had murdered a helpless child was sickening enough. In Shan, conflicts between the great houses were settled by armies of professional soldiers, and retribution was never taken upon commoners, even if their village or town had supported a rival lord. A massacre of innocents like this would certainly incur the displeasure of Heaven.

The wind gradually faded as she knelt there, the feel of it prickling her exposed skin subsiding . . . but to her surprise, its mournful cry persisted. It even seemed to strengthen. She glanced up in confusion – that sound was not the wind. As she did this, she saw a shape that had been hunched among the corpses rise, turning towards her. Cho Lin cried out, scrambling to her feet. Her horse seemed to notice her alarm, or perhaps it suddenly scented something strange, as it whickered uneasily and stamped its feet in the snow.

For a brief moment Cho Lin thought the scavenger was a man clad in some strange pebbled hides, but she quickly realized her error as the thing began to lope in her direction. It moved with the fluid grace of a predator despite its stunted legs, its arms so long and knobby that its taloned hands nearly brushed the snow. Its skin was scabrous, a mottled gray that was almost lizard-like, and stretched so taut over its bones that she could see its ribs clearly.

She had heard of these creatures, though like most in Shan she'd thought them to be myth. *Gaitunpan* – ghost apes of the snow. Cho Lin shrugged out of her heavy furs so that she could move more easily and drew her butterfly swords. She cut the air in a quick pattern, trying to warm her stiff arms and wrists, and breathed deep, reaching towards the Nothing.

The creature rushing at her made a harsh keening sound, and behind it, among the scattered corpses, another half-dozen monstrous heads suddenly rose. *By the Four Winds,* Cho Lin thought, her jaw clenching, trying to calm the flutter of her heart and stay focused on the Nothing. Of course it couldn't only be the one.

The ghost ape flowed across the tundra towards her, barely breaking the surface of the snow despite its height – it would have towered over any man, she realized, yet it was so gaunt it almost seemed to bend inward, its sunken chest devoid of muscle. From the quickness with which it moved and the length of its blue talons Cho Lin was certain it could still tear her apart if it caught her.

She lifted her swords and waited as it rushed closer.

It keened again, its breath ghosting the frigid air. She glimpsed jagged fangs jutting at odd angles and red slitted eyes.

Then it struck. Talons curved like raptor claws lashed out, seeking her throat. It was fast, but time itself seemed to congeal around her as Cho Lin grasped tight to the Nothing. She snapped her head back and twisted away, the talons carving the air less than a span from her neck. With one of her swords she slashed the ghost ape's side, leaving a line of black ichor across its ribs, and with the other she cut at the creature's extended arm. Flesh and bone parted, split, and the monster reeled away clutching a stump that ended just above where its hand had been.

Black blood spurted; Cho Lin felt it speckle her face in hot droplets as the ghost ape stumbled back. The taste was bitter on her lips. She followed the creature, swords flickering, opening up more wounds. It fell to one knee in the snow, cradling the ruin of its arm, and managed to raise its face to the sky and begin a miserable crooning just before she severed its head.

As it toppled to the side, six more of the monsters were revealed behind it, rushing across the snow, only moments from reaching her.

She gave in to instinct. This was not a swordfight, so much of her training was useless. She could not parry or block or use the momentum of her enemies to her advantage. Despite long sessions learning how to fight multiple foes, nothing she had done had prepared her for this.

They came at her from several angles, claws flashing. Cho Lin whirled closer to one of the creatures and slashed its throat, then slipped behind it in one quick motion as it sank to its knees. She tried to use the dying creature as a shield, keeping it between her and the rest of the pack, and the ghost apes hesitated, hissing in confusion. Two of the monsters apparently decided they wanted no part of her and instead swarmed her horse. Why hadn't it bolted? The poor thing must have been frozen with fright. Her horse's death cry was high and piercing and mercifully ended quickly as they tore into its flesh.

The remaining three edged closer, trying to circle around the dying ghost ape, which was clutching its ravaged neck as blood leaked from between its talons to stain the snow. Then, as if an unspoken agreement had passed between them, the ghost apes rushed at her screeching with talons outstretched. Cho Lin back-pedaled furiously, her boot slipping on the snow, and she had to drop one of her swords and throw her hand out to catch herself so she wouldn't land on her back.

Blue death arced towards her. Cho Lin rolled to the side and back to her feet as the talons gouged the snow where she had been a moment before. The ghost ape followed her and she lashed out wildly, trying to keep it from coming so close that she couldn't dodge when next it tried to grab her with its claws. Her sword caught its hand and several of the curving raptor claws were sliced away; the monster reeled back, shrieking in pain, more black blood jetting from the wounds.

She sensed movement behind her and a weight slammed into her, sending her sprawling forward, lines of fire opening up across her back. Her remaining sword was jarred from her hand and as she fell she focused on the carvings in the tumbling handle, straining for them, trying to pluck it out of the air as time moved honey-slow around her . . . Her fingers brushed ivory and then the sword was beyond her reach and the monsters were closing on her, incensed, a shifting mass of gray hide and blue talons and red tongues lolling between yellowed fangs.

Cho Lin struck the ground and rolled, throwing out her arms in a desperate bid to ward off the creatures. She screamed, not in fear but in rage that this was how the end would come, reduced to food for these monstrous things. Distended slavering jaws would close around her outstretched hand in moments; she would thrust her fingers so far down its throat it would either choke or she'd grab its heart and squeeze until it burst . . .

No teeth or talons ripped into her. The closest ghost ape stood over her swaying, staring at a tapering black point that had emerged from its chest. Its slitted red eyes blinked in confusion, and then another arrow took it in the neck in a spray of black blood. The monster fell over.

More arrows rained from the sky and the ghost apes crooned in dismay and turned to run, holding up their knobby arms as if that could protect them from the falling death. Another fell, three black-fletched arrows sprouting from its back, and then a third collapsed as a shaft embedded itself in its calf.

The ground was shaking. Cho Lin twisted around to see a line of horsemen charging the panicking ghost apes. Behind them she glimpsed a dozen archers lowering their bows.

Hooves thundered around her, tossing up snow and clumps of frozen earth. Long spears flickered down from the riders, impaling the ghost apes as they cowered or fled. Keening death-cries trailed into gurgling silence. Cho Lin could only watch in shock, her elbows in the snow propping her up, as the mounted warriors dispatched the ghost apes with practiced efficiency.

Then it was over. One of the warriors slid from his saddle, long yellow braids swinging, and with a flourish of his great ax cut off the head of the last of the whimpering monsters. More of the riders leapt down, their boots crunching heavily in the snow. They laughed, loud and boisterous. Cho Lin felt blood trickling from the stinging cuts across her back.

The first warrior to dismount loomed over her, his hands still gripping the long haft of his double-headed ax. He was young, not much older than her, and his eyes were the same blue as the northern sky.

"Who are you?" he asked in stilted Menekarian, crouching beside her to scoop up a handful of snow and rub away the ghost ape's black blood from the curving head of his ax. She heard no challenge in his voice; just curiosity.

"I am Cho Lin," she replied as more of the blond-braided warriors came to stand around the ax bearer. "From the Empire of Swords and Flowers."

The warrior's brows lifted. "Shan. Far-away place. You are spider-eater?"

That old foolishness. A few street food vendors sold barbecued spiders on skewers in trading ports and for some reason all the northern barbarians thought they were eaten at every meal.

Cho Lin climbed unsteadily to her feet, and the warrior rose with her. She tensed, but the man made no move towards her.

"I don't eat spiders," she said, bending over to retrieve one of her butterfly swords from where it had fallen in the snow.

Another of the warriors said something in a guttural tongue and the ax-man nodded sagely. "Ah. He says I am wrong. Not spiders. Shan eat worms."

"Worms?" Cho Lin said, shaking her head as she also cleaned her blade. "We don't eat worms."

His face crinkled in confusion. "What you eat, then?"

"The same as all people," she said as she found her other sword lying beside the headless body of one of the ghost apes. She paused for a moment as she caught sight of her eviscerated horse – the ghost apes had only swarmed it for a few moments, but still they had managed to slice open its belly, and now most of its innards were spread steaming across the snow.

"Hope you eat horse," the warrior said, and a few of the others chuckled. So he wasn't the only one who understood Menekarian.

"You are Skein?" she asked, turning back to the blond ax-man.

"Aye. Clan of the Stag. I am Verrigan, *Gundeschkal* of these men."

It felt like the blood had stopped trickling down her back – the cuts must have been very shallow – but the burning sensation was getting stronger. She concentrated on the Nothing to keep the pain from showing in her face.

"Thank you for killing the ghost apes."

"Ghost apes? Ah, the wraiths." He nudged one of the corpses with his boot. "So bold to come out and eat the dead in the day. It is good we do this. Hroi hates wraiths. He will give good reward for so many . . . how you say . . ." He touched his scalp with his fingers.

"Hroi?"

"The thane of the White Worm. Now king of Nes Vaneth." The warrior glanced around, as if suddenly realizing the strangeness of her traveling alone in the middle of this vast white wasteland. "Where you going?"

"I was chasing someone who has come through the Bones."

"Thief?"

"No. He made me a promise and then broke it."

The warrior's gaze lingered on the dead woman and her child and the sprawled corpses of the ghost apes, then drifted to the jagged peaks of the mountains rearing behind her.

"Broke a promise, eh? You Shan are strange people. Promise is not worth your life."

"I have to find him. He is a man from the south. His hair is darker than yours and he has a metal circle around his neck."

The warrior nodded. "We met him yesterday. The skald."

"Skald?"

"Singer. He said he can sing some of the old songs, wants to learn more. So he goes to Nes Vaneth."

Cho Lin's heart leapt in her chest. She knew where Jan was going now. "Then I have to go there, too."

The warrior slung his ax across his back, slipping the haft through a leather strap so that the blades stuck out over his shoulder. "We go back now. You can come with us. My thane Kjarl want to meet you, I think."

Another of the Skein pushed through the gathered warriors and barked something in his harsh tongue. He was the largest man Cho Lin had ever seen, almost as tall as the ghost apes had been, but while those creatures had been gaunt and thin this man was as thick around as a temple's pillar, and muscles corded his bare arms and neck. He was holding an arrow in his huge hand, gesturing with the black-iron tip in her direction.

The blond ax-man listened for a moment and then turned to her. "Kelissan, he say it was his arrow that saved your life. Killed the wraith about to kill you. He say by the old law you are his now, you have –" his face scrunched up, as if he was straining to summon forth the right words. "– you have blood debt."

"Tell him he has my thanks, but my life is my own."

With a slightly pained expression Verrigan relayed this message. The giant warrior's face clouded, and for a moment Cho Lin thought he was going to take a step towards her.

"Kelissan has the right," the blond ax-man told her, putting his hand out to restrain the warrior. "But first we bring you to Kjarl. Then I think you are Kelissan's thrall."

"His thrall?"

Verrigan concentrated again for a moment. "Slave! You will be his slave. Or . . . maybe wife," he said, his face brightening. "You are not ugly. Small and thin, but not ugly."

"Take me to Nes Vaneth," she said through gritted teeth. The pain crawling along her back was quickly eroding her patience.

Verrigan nodded, and then said something loudly in his grating language. A few moments later another of the warriors approached leading one of the Skeins' stout, long-maned horses.

"You can ride Belishank's horse. He is dead. But be careful, this horse throw Belishank in a fight. Not good horse."

Cho Lin drew one of her butterfly swords and bent to slice through the straps that secured her travel bags to the corpse of her own unfortunate mount. She hefted the bag and went over to the Skein horse, taking the reins from the warrior.

She paused before she swung herself up into the saddle, her gaze on the dead mother in the snow. "What happened here?" she asked. "Who killed these people?"

Verrigan smiled at her proudly. "We did. They are the last of the Bear clan. Very lucky we find them before other hunters. Kjarl will be pleased."

31: KEILAN

THE SHOP'S INTERIOR was as haphazard as the outside suggested, a jumble of ancient sea chests, rickety shelving lined with jugs and battered tableware, coils of rope, and rolls of sun-bleached sail. Dust swirled and eddied in the amber light trickling down from the high slatted windows, and Keilan had to pinch his nose to keep from sneezing. He didn't mind breathing through his mouth, as the air hung heavy and stale with the smell of old things carried in a ship's hold for far too long. There were other, fainter traces of more exotic fragrances layered beneath, though, as if that same hold had once contained rarer cargo: heady incense and sharp spices from faraway lands.

"Look at all this stuff, Kay," Sella whispered, running her fingers along one of the shelves. She picked up a ceramic figurine of a wizened little man with a hole in the top of his pointed hat. "What do you think this is?" she asked, trying to peer inside.

"He once held salt, and spent his days on a mandarin's table," said a voice from deeper within the store, and Keilan and Sella both jumped. "And please be careful, little lady, unless you have the funds to pay for it."

Sella placed the figurine back on the shelf with a guilty expression.

Keilan craned his neck, trying to see through the mounded clutter, but it wasn't until he wended his way around a few large wooden displays that he finally saw an old man seated behind an ancient and gleaming desk carved completely out of ebonwood. It looked like a piece of furniture that belonged in the home of a lord or a merchant prince, not a dusty shop on an island of smugglers and old pirates. Keilan glanced back to where Sella had picked up the salt holder, wondering how the old man had seen her, and then noticed for the first time the panes of glass spaced around the ceiling, each at an angle so that the man could watch his customers from his desk. Clever.

"Are you looking for something?" the shopkeeper asked, steepling his hands in front of his face. He was obviously very old, even though his dark brown skin was as smooth as the ebonwood desk he sat behind – the hair tufting above his eyes and in a ragged line around his bald head was white as the clouds on a summer day.

"Are you Arvik?" Keilan asked, coming to stand in front of the desk. Sella hurried to join him, but in her haste she accidentally brushed against a cage hanging from the rafters. Something feathered exploded within, batting its wings against the tarnished bars and chirping indignantly, and Sella gave a little cry of fear.

"Enough, Montezamas!" barked the old man, and, incredibly, the thing inside the cage quieted.

He turned back to Keilan and spread his arms wide. "I am Arvik, proprietor of this emporium of wonders."

Keilan glanced around skeptically at the piled sailcloth and lengths of wood, most of which looked like they had been scavenged from shipwrecks.

"My name is Keilan. I have a question, and someone thought you might have an answer."

The bemused smile on the old man's face collapsed. "Not a customer, then. Alas. Business has been a bit slow." He sighed, looking out at the glimmering dust falling like snow among the ruined cityscape of his piled wares. "Who said I had answers?"

"Chalissian ri Kvin's steward. We are guests at his manse."

A flicker of interest appeared in the old man's eyes. "The Bravo? I've never heard of him hosting guests before. And you must be talking about his hairless man, Gen of the Black Tide. What did old Gen say?"

"He said you knew my mother."

The sly smile returned. "I suppose I've known many mothers. Why would I remember yours?"

"Because she was different. She had long, silver hair, and she worked for Chalissian for a time."

The sudden change in the old man's expression was jarring. His face hardened, his eyes narrowing as he considered Keilan anew.

"I don't really know anything about her, though she came in a few times to buy things needed up the hill. We talked, but it was only idle chatter. The girl had an interest in old sea stories, I remember."

Keilan hesitated, unsure how to proceed. "Gen said that after she vanished, he heard you talking one night at The Haven. That there'd been others who had come around looking for her, even before she left. You hadn't told them anything, but you were worried they'd return once they realized you had misled them. I want to know about them."

The old man rubbed his chin, pulling on his few long wisps of white hair. He regarded Keilan with eyes that seemed to hold a hint of uncertainty – or was it fear? Could the old shopkeeper still be afraid of whoever had been asking about Keilan's mother more than fifteen years ago?

"You don't want to go looking for those ones, boy," he finally said slowly. "I know what they were – sailors tell tales of them. Most of the time they stay under the water, in their cities beneath the waves. Sometimes they come up to the surface, though, when a ship is sinking and bits and pieces of it are drifting down into the Deep. They'll find a sailor thrashing in the water and close their cold hand around his ankle, and that touch means he will be coming down below, where their goddess waits and hungers." The old man swallowed, and he seemed to be staring at something Keilan couldn't see. "And very rarely, they'll walk the sands and rocks of the islands, draped in robes that cover everything. They only come ashore when their goddess demands it. and it's a terrible thing if you're what they seek. Means you did something to anger them."

Sella's eyes were big as coins. "How do you know it was these things you saw?" she breathed softly.

The old man studied the shimmering whorls of his ebon-wood desk. "Because when they came here and stood just where you're standing and asked me in their croaking voices about the silver-haired girl, I peered into the depths of one of their cowls and I saw that what was here in my shop was more fish than man. Pale and white, with gashes in its neck. Gills, they were. The things had gills."

The sun had almost vanished by the time they left the shop, painting a river of gold from the sea's horizon to the docks. The few large ships at anchor in the harbor were reduced to silhouettes picked out against the brightness of the dying day. Keilan turned to start on the path leading up the hill, back towards the Bravo's manse, but Sella pulled on his arm and he let her lead him down towards the beach. The tumult of activity that usually swirled upon the docks and around the trading posts had faded with the light; most of the sailors and merchants had retreated up the slope, to find drink and company in The Haven or one of Ven Ibras's other taverns.

Holding his hand, Sella walked out onto the sand, almost to the edge of the surf. She shielded her eyes from the sun and stared out across the water, at the ragged line of rocks that reached out into the bay.

"Going out on the rocks with you, after a storm. Seein' what got thrown up from the sea . . . those were the best times I can remember."

Keilan gave her hand a little squeeze. "Yeah. It felt like we were explorers, finding something new. Looking for treasures."

"Do you want to go out on these rocks? See what's there?"

Keilan looked at her face, trying to tell if she was serious. He didn't think so, but he wasn't sure.

"You do remember those giant lizards?"

She stuck her tongue out at him. "I'm not scared. Are you?"

"A little."

Sella brushed back a strand of blond hair that the breeze had pushed across her face. They were quiet for a while, watching the ocean lose some of its luster as the sun continued to sink.

"Will we really go back soon, Kay?"

A small boat was rowing out to where the great ships waited, a pair of sailors straining hard against the tide. Watching them made Keilan think of his father, and fishing in the bay near his village.

"Yes. Nel said we had only a few days to ask questions before the boat she booked passage with sets sail for the Kingdoms."

Sella's fingers tightened, squeezing his hand. "Back to Chale? And me to the farm?"

Keilan nodded. "You have to go back, Sella."

"But I don't want to!"

"You must," Keilan replied, trying to sound stern.

"Please, Kay. Let me go with you. Nel isn't much bigger than me and no one ever says she shouldn't have come!"

Keilan turned to her, sighing. "Nel is one of the most dangerous people I've ever met. Do you remember how I told you about the big spiders we fought beneath the old city? They were swarming and she was slashing with her daggers and they were falling away, dead . . . "

"You said Nel protects a sorcerer in Dymoria? I can do that for you! Let her teach me how to fight!" Sella pleaded, gripping him fiercely. "I can learn!"

"Nel knows just like me that you can't come with us. You belong with your family, at your farm."

"No, I don't!" Sella cried, wrenching her hand from Keilan's. "And you know that, too. There's nothing for me back home. We were always the two outcasts, different, and then you left and I was all alone!"

"Sella . . ." Keilan began, reaching out to take her hand again, but she backed away. "Sella, I could never forgive myself if anything happened to you."

She sniffed, rubbing angrily at her eyes. "And what if something happened to you on your great adventure? Do you think I could forgive myself for not being there?"

"Sella . . ."

But she was gone, dashing back up the beach towards the path. Keilan watched her go, feeling something heavy settle in his stomach. She couldn't come, could she? But she was right – there was nothing back home for her. He stood there on the beach, watching the horizon and considering how unfair it was that it had fallen on him to break his best friend's heart.

By the time Keilan turned to follow Sella the only reminder of the sun was a purple glow where the black sea merged with the star-speckled sky. Lanterns had been hung on the ships in the harbor, and laughter drifted across the waves. Keilan kicked at the sand as he trudged towards the path. Perhaps Sella *should* leave her farm. Maybe he could bring her back to Herath somehow, convince Vhelan or another magister that she could serve in the Scholia. Would she be happier doing that? The more he thought about it, the more certain he became of what he should do. Sella could come with them on this journey, and afterwards he would find a place for her in Saltstone. It would be dangerous, and they would have to protect her. Now he just had to convince Nel.

He was so lost in his thoughts that he didn't even remember climbing the hill, and suddenly Chalissian's manse loomed before him, lanterns strung along the huge veranda that overlooked the beach far below. He paused with his hand on the door, for the first time realizing he was in the exact same spot his mother must have stood, back when she wasn't much older than he was now. A young girl alone in the world, desperate enough to beg shelter from a stranger. What had she been fleeing?

Before he could push on the door, it swung open and he stumbled inside, nearly colliding with Nel.

"Oh! You're here," she said. "I was going out to look for you." Her face was pale and drawn, and there was a wildness in her eyes. Something had happened.

"What is it?"

Nel licked her lips. She seemed about to say something, but then she shook her head sharply. "Come with me."

Concerned, Keilan followed her as she led him deeper into the manse. It seemed unnaturally quiet, like the house itself was holding its breath.

"Nel?"

She did not reply until they arrived at the entrance of the room where he had waited to meet Chalissian. The steward of the manse, the hairless man Gen, was outside the room. He also looked like he had seen a spirit.

"Go inside," Nel simply said, pointing within.

Keilan stepped forward hesitantly, wondering what could have unnerved the usually unflappable knife. He saw Senacus first, standing against the wall, his hand on the hilt of his sword. Sella was there as well, clutching at his shirt. They were both staring across the room, at the curtains which led out to the balcony.

"Senacus?" Keilan asked, coming to stand beside the paladin. "What's going on?"

The wind gusted, rippling the curtains, and Keilan glimpsed something dark on the balcony.

The Pure reached up and slowly removed the amulet of Tethys; as the chain passed over his head, the radiance of Ama spilled again from his eyes. His expression was grim. "They are asking for you."

"Who?" Keilan said.

"I don't know," Senacus replied softly.

Shapes moved outside on the balcony, coming closer, and then the curtain fell away as if thrust aside by an invisible hand.

Three shrouded figures, their faces hidden, glided into the room.

"Son of Vera Lightspinner," a voice rasped from the depths of one of the cowls. *"You are summoned."*

The prickling warmth of the Pure beside him was uncomfortable, but Keilan drew courage knowing that Senacus stood with him.

"Who summons me?" he said, with as much forced bravado as he could muster.

"The goddess."

"Why would your goddess want me?"

A white hand with unnaturally slender fingers emerged from a sleeve holding something long and thin. Whatever it was glimmered in the light, stirred by the wind.

A strand of silver hair.

"Because you are the last of her blood. And she loves you, as she loved your mother."

Keilan gathered his few belongings quickly, buckling on his sword and stuffing the books he had been reading into his travel bags. His thoughts were scattered, and the air seemed to have thickened, as if he were dreaming. He even drew his sword and touched the sharp edge of the blade, just to make sure he wasn't actually asleep.

He was so distracted he didn't notice Nel's approach until her hand fell upon his shoulder. Her mouth was set in a thin line, and her bag was already slung across her back.

"Keilan, are you sure we should go with them?"

He slid his sword back into its sheath. "No. But do we have a choice? We know they have some connection to my mother. This goddess they spoke of – she must be the sorceress we saw in the Oracle's vision."

"From what I've gathered, your mother fled when these things showed up the last time. She was afraid of them."

Keilan let out a long breath. "I know. But we came here to find the sorceress. Now she's found us. Whatever she is – whatever she's become – we have to convince her to help us stop what is coming."

Nel still looked uncertain, but she nodded. "Then we follow them."

"You don't have to," he said, his words tumbling out. "You all brought me here, but you heard what they said – they want me. It could be dangerous. You can return to Lady Numil or Queen d'Kara and tell them what happened –" He paused when Nel rolled her eyes.

"Don't be foolish, Keilan. We're going with you."

Relief washed through him. He thought that would be her answer, but he was still happy to hear it. Now to try and convince her about what he had decided earlier.

"And Sella?"

Nel's small smile twisted into a grimace. "She should stay."

"Here? On an island of thieves in the manse of an old pirate? By herself?"

Nel's shoulders slumped in defeat. "Fine. Bring her along. I suppose if Senacus and I have to defend you from an immortal sorceress, we can also protect her." She stood quickly. "We should go."

They passed out of the house and onto the veranda. Senacus was waiting beside the door, Sella still clutching at his waist. Gen was there as well – he held a long curving sword now, its point set in the wooden planks of the deck and his hands resting on the hilt. Down the steps and near the path, just at the edge of the lantern light, waited the three robed figures.

"Are you sure you will go with them?" Gen asked.

Keilan nodded. "Yes. This is why we came here. They can take us to someone who has answers."

Gen fiddled with the dark jewel at the end of his sword's pommel, his face solemn. "Then I wish you good fortune, and I hope one day to finally get answers about your mother and these creatures. The Bravo will want to know, as well."

"Where is he?"

"At The Haven, playing chalice." A hint of a smile tugged at the corners of his lips. "He will be wroth when he discovers he has lost you, like he lost Vera. So you have to promise me you will return."

"I will try," Keilan said, holding out his arm, and Gen clasped it.

"Keilan," Nel said, a note of warning in her voice. "They're going."

The shrouded figures had turned away from the manse and were moving towards the forest.

"Come on," Keilan said, motioning for the others to follow him. Their steps clattered down the stairs as they hurried after the creatures.

They passed into the tangle of knotted branches and hanging vines. In the darkness, Keilan couldn't see the serpentine roots that rippled the ground, and he stumbled a few times, nearly falling. He remembered what Seric had said about the giant lizards that lurked in the forest, and he hoped Sella had forgotten about that. He pushed the image of serrated teeth flashing from the shadows from his mind and concentrated on the slices of deeper blackness that were moving through the forest ahead of him. Could those things see without light? Was that why they weren't stumbling over the roots and rocks?

Keilan was so focused on not falling down or losing an eye to the thorned brambles that he didn't realize the creatures had stopped until he almost walked into one of their hunched backs. He peered around them; they had reached the edge of the forest. The rocky ground sloped down steeply to a small beach which glowed a faint white in the light of the moon. A long oblong shape had been pulled up onto the sand – a boat, Keilan guessed.

Without a word the figures glided forward, navigating the sharp decline without any apparent effort. Keilan put his foot forward and found the way treacherous, though the slope seemed to be veined with roots or vines.

"Be careful," he warned, pushing himself over the edge. His boot skidded in the loose dirt and he almost went tumbling forward. "Go slowly."

It took them quite a while before they were all standing on the sand of the beach, but the figures waited patiently while they descended. Then one of them held out his hand, motioning for them to climb inside the long rowboat. Keilan shivered as the tide swirled around his boots, soaking his feet, and he pulled himself up and inside the boat, just as he used to do before his father pushed them down into the water. Senacus lifted Sella, and Keilan helped her the rest of the way, and then the paladin and Nel climbed aboard. They found space on planks of wood, and for a moment Keilan thought the creatures that had brought them here wouldn't be coming with them. But then with surprising nimbleness the shrouded figures leapt aboard, two of them settling on seats beside where long oars rested. The last of the figures came to stand at the prow of the boat and raised his hand, the long sleeves falling away. In the moonlight Keilan couldn't see very much, but he noted once again that the fingers were unnaturally pale and long. The figure made a gesture, and the boat slid hissing across the sand and into the water. Nel cried out in surprise and clutched at the side, and Senacus nudged his leg. The paladin once again wore the bone amulet, and Keilan saw that he had changed out of his white-scale armor.

But the artifact of Tethys did not dampen his powers so much, it seemed, even as it hid them. "Sorcery," Senacus muttered as the boat was rocked by the surf. "Different than I've felt before. It feels . . . old."

Once the boat had pushed past the breakers, the figure at the prow lowered his hand. The other two robed creatures gripped their oars and silently began to row in strong, smooth strokes.

They rowed through the night, never resting, their pace never slackening. Keilan tasted salt on his lips as the spray reached up over the sides of the small boat. Beside him, Sella dozed into his shoulder, but Keilan couldn't even imagine sleeping at this time. Where were they going? What would they find?

The sky lightened, darkness giving way to tattered strips of pink and blue. A pod of dolphins passed the boat, their sleek silver shapes gleaming in the dawn light. Some great bird floated high overhead, then dove with jarring speed towards the water and plucked a wriggling shape from the waves.

Still the figures rowed, untiring. A mist descended, so thick and clotting that nothing was visible more than a few dozen span from the boat. The figure at the prow did not stir, staring ahead into the murk. Keilan shivered. These creatures seemed so unnatural, like simulacra of living things. He was reminded of the clockwork toys that Halix, the son of one of Seri's artificer lords, had shown him back in the Scholia. A few quick twists of the keys sunk in their backs and the automata would perform their tasks with mindless efficiency.

"Look!" Nel cried, pointing ahead. Something huge and dark loomed deeper in the mists, swelling as they grew closer.

"Land?" Senacus asked, standing up to get a better look.

"Yes," Keilan said, just as the mists swirled and parted. They gazed upon a beach, and beyond this curving scimitar of black sand a misshapen tumble of a mountain brooded. There were some buildings also, pressed up against the flank of this mountain, slender turrets and graceful archways built of black stone. But that was not what drew Keilan's gaze.

Upon the black sand a woman watched them approach, leaning against a staff of pale white wood. She wore a blue dress, and her long silver hair rippled in the fitful ocean breeze.

32: CHO LIN

THE FROSTLANDS. FOR the Shan, it was a place as distant and exotic as the dark jungles of Xi or the skirling wastes where the Qell hordes roamed. Once, a mighty sorcerous queendom had ruled here, but the same magical cataclysm that had fractured the south and flooded it with the Sea of Solace had wrapped these lands in endless winter, entombing the holdfasts of Min-Ceruth in black ice. The stories Cho Lin remembered spoke of ancient dragons nesting in lost ruins, mountains hollowed out to become lairs for the *gaitunpan,* and powerful artifacts infused with sorcery waiting to be dug from snowy barrows. The tales had stirred her imagination as a child, and she'd dreamed of one day visiting this realm.

Yet after days of riding north through the Frostlands, Cho Lin could only agree that the stories contained one incontrovertible truth: there was, indeed, a lot of snow. It stretched in every direction, a seamless white plain, until finally it would break upon a line of trees or mountains – both of which were also, inevitably, draped in snow.

By the afternoon of the third day since the warriors had rescued her, she was well and truly sick of it all.

The Skein captain Verrigan seemed intrigued by Cho Lin and spent much of the days riding close and asking questions about her homeland. What did her people wear? And eat, if not spiders? Was it true that the Shan king had his manhood removed when he took the throne? Had the Shan really sailed across the ocean on the backs of monstrous turtles? Why were their eyes not shaped the same as other people? How could a woman carry swords and travel on her own and fight a pack of wraiths?

Cho Lin answered as best she could considering the tenuous grasp Verrigan had on Menekarian – though he did show surprising improvement the more they spoke together. It amused her that the barbarians of these lands told breathless stories of the empire in the same way the storytellers of Shan spoke of the Frostlands. When she finally got questions in edgewise she asked about the massacre she had stumbled upon, and if war now gripped the Skein.

"War is finished," Verrigan said with obvious satisfaction. "A small war, really. Just one battle at Nes Vaneth."

"Nes Vaneth. That is the big city of the Skein?"

"Aye. It is where the king and his clan always live. Used to be the Raven held the city. They did for hundreds of years, then the old king went mad and many clans fight and throw him down. I was just a boy at the time, but old enough to come along with the warband and help the warriors put on armor and care for axes. The Bear thane became the new king after that, ten years past. Agmandur. Strong warrior – I saw him wrestle an aurochs to the ground at the . . ." The Skein warrior gestured with his hands, as if he could conjure up the word he wanted. "Happy time when fighting finished."

"The celebration?"

Verrigan clapped his hands loudly, the sound sending a white-furred hare bounding from its burrow. "Yes! Now the last of the Bear are dead, we can have celebration again. You and the skald are lucky!"

"Did the Bear thane become mad as well?"

Verrigan shook his head. "No. Much worse. He showed he was weak."

"What happened?"

The Skein's face darkened. "We are strong people. We want something, we take it. Beneath the mountains are many lands with fat sheep and soft women. We go over the mountains or the River Serpent and fight and take these things. It is the way." Verrigan shook his head, as if disgusted by what had happened. "A few years ago, the red queen of one land came into the north. She was angry because we had taken many cattle and gold things. Agmandur led clans south to kill her for this, but he lost the battle and many died and he ran back to Nes Vaneth. A coward, and weak." The Skein captain spat in the snow. "After that the clans are angry. The White Worm clan live far away, but they hear about this. Hroi send a message to my thane, Kjarl son of Kjartan. Join him to throw down the weak king, he say. So the Stag and the White Worm and the Crow come together, kill all the Bear. Now the Stormforger is pleased."

"And the Skin Thief," growled another of the Skein warriors who had been riding nearby and listening to their conversation.

Verrigan narrowed his eyes and his hand went to a silver hammer hanging on a string around his neck. He said something harsh and tumbling to the warrior who had spoken.

"Who are the Stormforger and the Skin Thief?" Cho Lin asked.

Verrigan rubbed the haft of the hammer and muttered something in Skein under his breath. Then he tucked the amulet under his roughspun shirt and looked at her again. "Stormforger is the strongest of the gods. Great warrior. Many clans give thanks to him. But the Skin Thief . . ." He shot a reproachful glance at the warrior who had mentioned him. "Only the White Worm hold him most high."

"Gundeschkal! Gundeschkal!"

Verrigan twisted in his saddle as another Skein cantered towards them. Cho Lin recognized this warrior as one who ranged far away from the warband during the days, hunting and scouting.

When he finally reined in beside them, his horse's breath misting the air, he unleashed a torrent of guttural Skein words and gestured back the way they had come. Verrigan listened, nodded, and asked a few pointed questions that the scout then answered. Finally, the Skein captain dismissed the warrior with a wave of his hand. As the scout galloped away again he turned to Cho Lin.

"Algren say we are not alone."

"What?"

"He say someone follow us."

Cho Lin glanced behind her, beyond the sweeping *li* of snow they had ridden through, at the Bones looming in the far distance. Could they somehow have passed Jan over the last few days? The Sword of Cho was still vibrating as they rode, though, which suggested he was to the north, in the direction they were traveling. But who else would be following them?

"Maybe someone from the Bear clan? Someone hunting for revenge?"

"Algren just see him once, quickly. But he say this man wears clothes from the south. He try to ride to him but the man –" Verrigan paused, holding up his hands and spreading them wide as if to show her they were empty. "– he not there. Like he is ghost."

A servant of the Crimson Queen? Surely Cein d'Kara would not let them escape so easily . . . but to send a single man? Could he be a sorcerer?

"I don't know who he is," she said truthfully, and Verrigan seemed to accept this.

"Very well. But I tell Algren, next time he see the man he put an arrow in him. Then we see if he is ghost."

The first indication that they were approaching the great city of the Skein was the haze of smoke smearing the cloudless blue sky. It drifted up from the shadow of a craggy mountain, and to Cho Lin it seemed there was something strange about the cliff-faces high up near this peak – they drank the sunlight rather than reflecting it, as the sheer rock walls of Red Fang had done. It was almost like a layer of oily blackness covered the stone . . . Realization came to Cho Lin, and she felt a little flutter of apprehension. This must be the black ice that had enveloped the holdfasts and destroyed the ancient Min-Ceruthans. How could sorcery remain so potent after a thousand years? And why would any people choose to live in such a cursed place?

Remnants of the lost queendom emerged from the landscape through which they rode. A circle of white stone pillars – some broken, others whole and soaring twice the height of a man – surrounded a great basin mounded with snow. They had left the plains behind, and perched atop the hills rippling around them Cho Lin saw the shattered remains of towers. Smoke trickled from a few of those buildings; apparently the Skein still made use of the walls that remained to keep watch on those approaching Nes Vaneth, as no doubt the Min-Ceruthans had also done long ago.

The mountain swelled larger and larger until it filled the sky, its peak shrouded by clouds. Black ice and snow swaddled the upper reaches, but below it was mostly jagged rock, though there were patches where hardy trees clung to the slopes. More ruins were visible here, clinging to cliff faces or secreted in rocky folds. Cho Lin wondered what secrets and treasures they might give up to those daring enough to brave the mountain's dangers.

Near midday, they crested a rise and saw the legendary ruins of Nes Vaneth spread below. The Empire of Swords and Flowers was littered with the vestiges of the Kalyuni Imperium, but the greatest of the Mosaic Cities were drowned beneath the Sea of Solace, and Cho Lin had never seen anything to approach the size and grandeur of the holdfast now before her.

The city filled a flat expanse ringed by the mountain to the north and foothills everywhere else – not the best placement for defensive purposes, perhaps, but if the stories of the Min-Ceruthans' sorcerous prowess were true, Cho Lin suspected they had little to fear from besieging armies. A frozen river meandered through the ruins, spanned by silver-glinting arches and dotted with tiny fishing huts. Most of Nes Vaneth appeared abandoned, tumbled buildings of white or gray stone half-sunk in snow or black ice, here and there pierced by the jagged remnants of pale green towers that looked to be made of crystal or glass.

The area inhabited by the Skein covered only a small portion of the ruins. Dozens of thatched longhouses clustered around the remains of Nes Vaneth's gates, and a well-trodden path led from this encampment through the heart of the city to an imposing building that looked to have weathered the long-ago cataclysms better than any other in the dead city. Smoke was coming from this mighty edifice, emerging through great rents in the domed roof. It appeared that many slim minarets had once surrounded the central dome, but most had been reduced to shattered stone.

"That is the Bhalavan," Verrigan said when he saw where Cho Lin was staring. "Heart of Nes Vaneth. The king and his warband are there. That is where we go to tell we killed the Bear who fled."

"Do you think the . . . skald will be there as well?"

Verrigan nodded. "Aye. Skalds from the southlands are rare. He will go before the thanes and king and they will give him gold and a place to sleep in the great hall . . . if he sings well."

Cho Lin's hands tightened around her reins. Jan would be surprised to see her, and perhaps even angry. But she had to impress upon him the danger the Betrayers posed to these lands.

And if he still refused to take her to the chest, she would have to compel him by force. How, she wasn't quite sure. She didn't think they could ride all the way to Menekar with him slung across his saddle. Hopefully she could convince him to abandon whatever had brought him to this forsaken place.

The Skein warriors descended the hill and approached the crumbled remnants of the city walls. They passed longhouses that bore scars of the recent fighting, such as blackened timbers or staved-in doors, and a few had even been gutted by fire. The corpses must have been cleared away, but Cho Lin could see a few patches of blood-stained snow, and there was even a small pack of gray and white dogs fighting over what looked to be a pile of entrails. A number of men moved among the houses, carrying armfuls of spoils that they dumped on the ground in a great heap: chests and barrels, iron tools and weapons, looms, and even a beautifully carved bed. Some of these men wore tined helms, and they shouted greetings to Verrigan and his band as they passed.

Just beside the shattered gate, Verrigan called for a halt in front of a large circular building with walls of tanned hide and no door that Cho Lin could see. He called out something in Skein and a few moments later a trio of older men in dark woolen robes emerged from within, pushing through one of the flaps of animal skin.

"Who are they?" asked Cho Lin as the men approached.

"Priests of the Stormforger. This is a holy place."

One of the old men came to stand beside Verrigan's horse, his face as craggy as the mountain looming above, and held out his hands. To Cho Lin's surprise, the Skein captain unslung his great war-ax and passed it down to the waiting priest. She twisted around and saw that all the warriors were relinquishing their axes and bows, and the three priests soon staggered under the weight of the weapons.

"You must give them your swords," Verrigan said, staring at where he knew she concealed her butterfly blades.

"Why?"

"Because only the king of Nes Vaneth and his warband may go armed in the city. For others to bring weapons within means war, and the punishment is death."

Cho Lin unclasped the sheath containing her butterfly swords, but she hesitated before handing them to the impatient priest.

"Will my swords be safe? They are precious to me."

"Very safe," Verrigan assured her. "Stealing from the Stormforger's temple is death, and worse than death. The doors of the High Hall would be closed to any who dared this terrible thing. No Skein would do it, I promise you."

Reluctantly, she passed the sheathed swords to the waiting priest. Verrigan gestured at her travel bags and the long keppa case where she kept the Sword of Cho.

"Nothing else, Shan girl? The king may order what you bring inside searched. You are a stranger here in a time of much death. If they find a weapon – even a dagger for cutting meat – they will cut open your belly and leave you on the mountain for the wolves to feast upon."

Gritting her teeth, Cho Lin pulled the keppa case into her hands. She hated leaving the Sword of Cho outside the walls, but Verrigan was right that the risk of discovery was simply too great. He seemed certain that nothing would happen to the weapons stored here, but still she felt a churning sense of dread as she handed the case to one of the priests. Find Jan quickly, convince him to leave with her, and reclaim the sword. If everything went well she would only be separated from the sword of her ancestors for a very short period of time – but still, she couldn't help imagining how aghast her brother would be if he heard she had willingly given up the sacred weapon to a wild-bearded barbarian.

Verrigan seemed to sense her consternation, his brow drawing down as he glanced from her to the keppa case.

"That's all," she said, forcing a smile. Well, except for the shuriken studding her belt, but she was sure the Skein had never seen the deadly, three-pronged throwing knives before.

After giving her one more curious look Verrigan grunted and snapped his reins, guiding his horse towards the wide gap in the tumbled walls that must once have contained the gates to the city. A pair of guardsmen flanked the entrance, watching them approach. These warriors looked different than the Skein she had seen so far: their cured leather armor was a mottled grayish green that looked disconcertingly familiar to Cho Lin, and black markings covered their faces. As they neared, she saw that these tattoos were meant to suggest the faces of other creatures, as on one man she saw lines drawn to make his eyes appear slitted, and a serpentine tongue extending down from his mouth to his chin. The other Skein's face resembled some forest beast, perhaps a bear.

One of the guardsmen called out to Verrigan. Cho Lin noticed there was none of the friendliness she had seen from the warriors with the tined helms.

Verrigan barked a guttural response and the snake-warrior's face twisted, as if he was not pleased about something. But still he stepped aside to let them pass. Cho Lin felt his eyes slide over her as they rode into the city, and she almost shivered.

"Who are they?" she asked Verrigan, and the Skein warrior grimaced.

"Hroi's warband. They all follow the Skin Thief." He glanced around him, as if making sure no one was listening. "Black god. Even other Worm fear them. They are called the Flayed."

"The armor they were wearing . . ."

Verrigan nodded. "Aye. Wraith skin. And that not all they have. Every strong thing they kill – animal, man, monster – they take a piece of the skin and wear it. They think they can take the power."

Cho Lin thought back to the gate guards. "Where do they wear it?"

"Most do not have so much. Maybe tie it to arm, or sow into shirt. But Hroi –" Verrigan turned and spat, as if trying to clear his mouth of this talk. "– he wear the skin he stole as cloak. Many souls there . . . including his father."

So the new Skein king had killed his own father. In Shan, such a deed would be considered the blackest of crimes. But here such a man could rise to lead his people.

She should be careful – despite Verrigan's friendliness, these were a dark and dangerous people. And now she was without her swords. Her hands itched at the thought of entering their great hall with no blades at her side.

To distract herself from her nervousness, Cho Lin studied the city through which they rode. As she had seen from the hill outside, a wide avenue ran arrow-straight from the gate to the great building the Skein had taken as their hall. The snow here had been churned by countless feet, and just as she had among the longhouses Cho Lin saw dark patches and bits of shattered iron and armor. A great battle had raged here not long ago. In her imagination, a host of Skein – some wearing tined helms, others clad in wraith skin – charged from the gate towards the Bear warriors as they boiled from the great hall led by their old king. She could almost hear the clash of metal and the screams of the wounded.

A hundred paces to either side of her were the remains of the buildings that had once hemmed this great avenue. Blocks of white stone, cracked and listing pillars, shattered archways. Many of those fallen structures must have soared several stories, at least, but the only ones still standing that high were the few wrapped in black ice, as if the ancient sorcery was all that was keeping them upright.

"That black ice, it never melts?"

Verrigan looked at her blankly, and she tried again.

"Melts . . . goes away when the sun is strong."

The Skein captain shook his head. "Never go away. It is cursed. I remember coming here after the death of Raven king, when I was young. We boys dared each other to run up to the ice and look inside. Then my father caught us and beat us, said the Stormforger watches over this road and the Bhalavan, but the rest of the city belongs to older gods."

Cho Lin stared in fascination at one of the great chunks of black ice wedged between several of the collapsed buildings. "What did you see inside?"

Verrigan's hand drifted to the amulet around his neck. "Is dark inside, hard to see. But I thought I saw woman within, looking out. Maybe it was the Pale Lady."

"Pale Lady?"

"A spirit many have seen drifting through the ruins. Death will follow when she is seen, they say." Verrigan touched the amulet beneath his tunic briefly, then glanced up at the sky, whispering a prayer to his god.

They came to the entrance of the great hall, a massive set of bronze doors covered in squirming runes. Great drifts of snow were piled against the doors, but one had been cracked open wide enough for a man to walk through, and from within Cho Lin heard sounds of revelry. They dismounted from their horses and handed the reins to a group of boys that had run up as they approached. Verrigan spoke to one in stern tones, and when the boy gave a fierce nod to show he understood, the Skein tousled his hair affectionately.

"My brother's son," he said to Cho Lin as the boys led the horses away to whatever passed for a stable here.

They slipped through the door and into the great hall of the Skein. Smoke filled the air, billowing from both the massive cook pits in the center of the huge room and the great iron braziers scattered about the edges. Several large animals were being roasted on spits over the open flames, and the rich smell made Cho Lin's mouth water. A hundred Skein, at least, sat shoulder to shoulder on long benches, laughing and bellowing as they tore meat from bones and drank from tall clay tankards. Deeper inside the hall, well past the celebrating warriors, she saw strange shapes looming from the gloom – statues, she thought, but she couldn't be certain. None of the Skein had ventured beyond the circle of warmth and light cast by the cook pits and the little sunlight that was trickling down through the smoke from the rents in the ceiling.

"Come," Verrigan said, motioning for her to follow him. "I take you to Kjarl, my thane."

They wended between the tables and the long benches, towards a dais where Cho Lin could see a number of seated figures. She glimpsed Jan through the haze, speaking to a man wearing a tined helm with a more impressive rack of antlers than she had seen before, and her heartbeat quickened. He was here.

A huge hand clamped down on her wrist. Despite her surprise, she reached down into herself, straining for the Nothing as a massive Skein warrior with long black braids and hair threaded with black feathers tried to pull her closer. He grinned and barked something to his companions seated with him upon the benches, and they broke out in laughter. For a moment she was off balance, and Cho Lin stumbled a step towards him, but she quickly caught herself before she ended up in his lap, then twisted free of his grip. More laughter from the watching Skein, and the warrior's face reddened. He surged to his feet, but Verrigan was there, his hand on the warrior's chest, spitting angry words. The warrior's mouth twisted and he shoved Verrigan back so hard that the Stag captain went stumbling into another bench, upsetting drinks and eliciting howls of indignation. The black-braided warrior's rage at his humiliation was evident, and he grabbed again for Cho Lin.

She knocked his hand aside and drove her fist into his face, sending him sprawling onto the table where he'd been seated. A rope of blood flew from his shattered nose as he fell, lashing his stunned companions. There was a frozen moment of silence as the Skein lay there, his hands clenching and unclenching, his eyes fluttering as he fought for consciousness, and then Verrigan was by her side again, putting himself between her and the still-shocked friends of the warrior who had grabbed her. He shouted something in Skein and then ushered her away from the table.

"I tell him you are guest of Stag, but he is Crow, he does not care," Verrigan said, and Cho Lin heard a hint of apology in his voice. "Not so many southerners come north. Most are thralls we take back. But you are not thrall. Not yet, anyway." He twisted around and said something to the tall Skein who had claimed to have saved her life from the wraiths, one of several of Verrigan's warband that had trailed them inside. The warrior's eyes were round with surprise, and he held up his hands as he replied to his captain with a string of tumbling words.

Verrigan snorted as he turned back to Cho Lin. "Kelissan say he no want you as thrall any more. Or wife."

Well, one problem taken care of.

Smoke swirled around them as they passed by the firepits, and Cho Lin coughed, closing her stinging eyes. She stumbled forward, trying not to trip, and walked into the back of Verrigan. Muttering a curse, she opened her eyes and found herself staring at Jan's bewildered face. He sat on a stool upon the dais she had glimpsed earlier, next to a finely carved wooden chair where the young man with the tined helm lounged. Three more wooden chairs upon the dais were empty, as was a larger and more impressive throne carved from stone.

"Jan," she said, blinking away the last of the smoke.

"Cho Lin," he said, his surprise quickly giving way to wary resignation.

The young man in the wooden chair glanced from Jan to her, and then posed a question in Skein to Verrigan. The captain of the Stag cleared his throat and launched into what must have been an exhaustive account of what had happened to his warband, because it wasn't until some time had passed that Cho Lin heard her name and Verrigan started gesturing in her direction. When he had finally finished, the young man asked several more questions, and Verrigan answered each with alacrity. Throughout this exchange Jan continued to stare at her, his face troubled.

Finally, the young man turned his attention to Cho Lin. He had a narrow face, almost vulpine, and from beneath his great helm a few red curls had escaped.

"Greetings, Lin from Shan. Welcome to Nes Vaneth and the great hall of Hroi, king of all the Skein. I am Kjarl, son of Kjartan, thane of the Stag."

Cho Lin did not bow in the northern style or show obeisance like she would before the Phoenix Throne – from what she understood, a thane was akin to a mandarin in the Empire of Swords and Flowers, which would imply little difference in their respective rank. Instead, she held the gaze of the thane with her chin held high, to show she expected to be treated as an equal.

"Greetings, Kjarl, son of Kjartan. I am Cho Lin, daughter of Cho Yuan and sister of Cho Jun, mandarins of the Jade Court."

A small smile curled Kjarl's lips. "You are far from home. What brings you to the Bhalavan?"

Cho Lin pointed at Jan. "I come seeking this man. I did him a great service, and he promised to lead me to something I must find. But he abandoned me south of the Bones and fled north. I came to insist that he carry out his part of the bargain we struck."

Kjarl turned to Jan with an expression of mild surprise. He spoke quickly in Skein, and Jan gave a pained nod, then responded in the same guttural tongue.

Whatever Jan said seemed to amuse the Stag thane, for he chuckled and shook his head. "I can tell there is more to this story than I have been told. And I wish to know more, Lin from Shan, for it is rare we get travelers to the Frostlands, and this interests me. But the skald has agreed to compose a lay about our great victory here, so he cannot accompany you now. I will make you a guest of the Stag, though, and put you under my protection while you wait for him to finish. Then, perhaps, he will go with you."

The Stag thane made a dismissive gesture towards her and turned back to Jan. Cho Lin opened her mouth to say more, but Verrigan shook his head and guided her away from the dais.

"Is good," he said to her when they had moved back beyond the cook pits. "Kjarl says you are guest, so you can stay in the Bhalavan and no one will dare hurt you."

"But I don't have the time to wait!" she hissed angrily.

Verrigan shrugged helplessly. "What can you do? Bash the skald over the head and run away with him? No, I don't think so. Kjarl likes the southerner, I can tell. He would not allow such thing."

Cho Lin made a frustrated sound and peered back through the smoky haze at the figures on the dais. Others had come, a tall man with dark hair who lowered himself into the stone throne. There was another as well who hovered at his side, a boy with unnaturally pale skin and a gaunt face. His bones were etched so sharp he almost looked skeletal, and she felt a shiver go up her spine as his pale blue eyes found her through the smoke.

"Who are they?" Cho Lin asked, and Verrigan turned to the dais. A little shudder of revulsion passed across his face.

"That is Hroi, thane of the White Worm and new king of the Skein."

"And the boy?"

"They say his name is Lask. He is shaman of the White Worm. Hroi found him in the snow when he was a babe, cast out of the Ghost clan. He never speaks, they say, except to the Skin Thief himself. He frightens me."

33: KEILAN

*"**WHY DOES THE** water turn red at sunset?" Keilan asked, watching the fiery horizon closely for the return of his father's boat.*

"Ah," his mother answered, stroking his hair, "that is a wise question. It is because when the dying sun falls into the sea it cracks open like the egg it is –" she made a clucking sound with her tongue, "– and the yolk spills out. It spreads across the waves and then sinks below, where the fish eat it and grow fat and strong for your father to catch."

Keilan pressed himself against his mother, his head resting on her hip. "If the sun breaks every evening, how is there a new one the next day?" He breathed deep of her smell, wanting to gather it all up into himself and hold onto it forever.

"Well, the great hen in the sky lays a new egg in the morning, just as our chickens do."

Keilan giggled and glanced up at his mother. "There's no great hen. The mendicants say the sun is Ama's throne, and the warmth we feel is his love shining down on us."

His mother's face turned sorrowful, but he knew she was only playing with him. "My son, you would believe a stranger to our village instead of your own mother? Oh, what sadness."

Keilan tangled his fingers in the long silver hair that fell around him. He twisted a glimmering strand around his thumb, careful not to pull. "I believe you," he said softly, and was rewarded with his mother's laughter.

The sun continued its slow tumble; the shreds of clouds remaining in the sky darkened, turning from pink to red to deep crimson. The sea glittered, as if strewn with tiny jewels. Upon the beach the waves whispered their secrets and began to creep towards where Keilan and his mother waited at the edge of the long scratchy grass.

"Ma," Keilan asked, his thoughts drifting in the immensity before him, "where did you come from?"

He felt his mother's fingers in his hair go still. She was silent for a moment, long enough that he wished he hadn't asked.

"Somewhere far away," she said finally, her voice as distant as the setting sun. "A place both wonderful and terrible."

Birdsong woke him, and as Keilan opened his eyes the tattered wisps of his dream dissolved in the light. Across from his tiny cot, on the ledge of a small square window that had no glass or shutters, a large bird cocked its head and stared at him. Its sleek feathers shimmered iridescent, flashing red and green and blue as it hopped upon the stone, and around its neck a few of these feathers tufted up to form an elaborate headdress. Its black beady gaze held Keilan's without a hint of fear, and then it opened its long, curving orange beak and trilled again, commanding him to get up. Keilan swung his legs over the edge of the cot. As if satisfied that its task was complete, the bird turned and leapt from the ledge, vanishing in a rush of flashing wings.

A place both wonderful and terrible

His mother's voice echoed in his thoughts, clear as if she had been standing beside him. Had he been dreaming about her?

He glanced at the other cot in the room, but it was empty. Senacus must already have risen, though his bags were still piled on the floor, including the wrapped bundle that contained the Pure's white-metal sword. What time was it? The sunlight pouring through the windows was burnishing the stones of the chamber a deep gold; it looked like afternoon light to Keilan. Had he really only slept a few watches since they arrived on the island?

Keilan quickly dressed, pulling his tunic on over his spider-silk shirt and buckling his sword around his waist. There were sounds coming from outside, and he thought he recognized Nel's voice. He pushed through the door, shielding his face from the bright sun. His companions were seated around a table that was partially hidden from his view by a thick curtain of vines hanging from an intricate copper trellis.

"Keilan's awake!" he heard Sella exclaim as he bent to slip on his boots, which he'd left outside to dry. He grimaced as he laced them up – still damp.

Sella appeared from within the veil of green tendrils and beckoned for him to hurry, the excitement clear in her face. "Come on, Kay! Come quick!"

He stepped forward but hesitated before he touched the vines – they were writhing slowly, almost worm-like, and tiny red flowers bright as blood-drops were opening and closing along their lengths.

Wonderful and terrible.

Keilan skirted the edge of the trellis and found that he was staring down at the beach where they had arrived. The waves were fiercer now, crashing with a fury upon the black sand. Of the figure he had seen earlier, there was no sign.

"How do you feel?" Nel asked from behind him, and he turned back to his friends. They had all found seats around a wooden table laden with food: there were slices of cheese and fruit, a brown loaf of bread that had already been ripped apart, and a haunch of glistening red meat, all fairly glowing in the bright sunlight. Sella was eating with the abandon of a hungry child, but Senacus and Nel looked to have barely touched what was in front of them.

"Rested," Keilan replied to Nel, sliding into an empty chair. "How long have I been asleep?"

"Half the day," Nel replied, rolling a grape between her fingers. "I didn't sleep. Someone had to keep watch."

"Watch for what?" Sella asked as she chewed, crumbs falling from her mouth.

Nel shrugged. "Spirits," she said, staring pointedly at Keilan.

"I saw her," Keilan insisted. "Standing on the sand, watching us coming closer."

"But no one else did." Nel's gaze softened. "You're exhausted, Keilan. We all are. I know you wanted to see her so badly, but we don't know yet if she's really here."

Keilan gestured at the feast spread before them. "Where did the food come from, then?"

Nel tossed the grape she held back on the table. "After the robed things brought us to these huts and told us to rest, I waited and watched to make sure they didn't return with axes to cut us into little pieces. Well, they did return, but they were carrying this table and the chairs and the food. They set everything up and disappeared again."

"So you haven't seen anyone else?"

"I did try and do a little exploring," Nel said, glancing at the stony path that led farther up the side of the mountain. Several larger buildings of black stone were visible on a higher ledge, pressed against the mountain's flank. "But one of those robed things blocked my way and told me to go back."

"She's here," Senacus said softly. "This whole island . . . everything I've seen so far . . . it thrums with sorcery. I've never felt anything like it."

"I can feel it too . . ." Keilan began, his words trailing away as he glimpsed something coming towards them down the path.

The distant figure was a woman, and even from far away he could see her waterfall of silver hair, shimmering in the sun. She wore the same blue dress he remembered from that morning, and she was using a white-wood staff to navigate the descent.

But that wasn't what made Keilan gasp. Following her was a creature unlike any he had seen before – though it bore some resemblance to the illustration of the Dymorian tiger he remembered from his copy of the *Tinker's Bestiary*. Like the tiger, it was also a huge cat, and its coat was similarly patterned. Instead of orange and black, however, the stripes this creature sported were red and white. A mane of strange russet tendrils fringed the creature's neck, each strand far too thick to be made of hair.

And its size. Unless the woman was shorter than Sella, the creature was as large as a pony – the sorceress leading it looked to barely come up to its shoulder. Keilan swallowed as he watched it descend the rocky path with fluid grace, its muscles rippling beneath its fur.

"Senacus," Nel said warningly, "perhaps it is time you went and got your sword."

"No," Keilan said, holding up his hand. "She'll know you are a paladin of Ama. We don't want to threaten her."

Nel jabbed her finger at the giant cat flowing like water down the mountain-side. "I feel threatened! That thing could tear us apart like we were mice!"

"Just wait!" Keilan said firmly. "This is her home. If she wanted us dead, she wouldn't have brought us here."

Nel subsided into her chair, muttering. Keilan saw her fingers playing with her sleeves, and he knew she was struggling to keep herself from drawing her daggers, Chance and Fate.

"I will not let her know what I am," Senacus assured him. "I agree that is best for now." His hand went to the fingerbone amulet he wore, as if making sure it still hung at his chest.

Keilan's heart quickened as the woman approached where they waited. This close, he could see that her face was the same as the sorceress in Jan's memories – slightly narrower than his mother's, but otherwise a perfect reflection. Her pale blue eyes matched the dress she wore, and the only jewelry he could see was a silver pendant shaped like a butterfly.

She stopped a dozen paces from where they waited around the table, leaning on her white staff. The great red and white cat settled on its haunches, watching them disinterestedly with eyes of liquid gold.

"Whispers have come to me on the wind," she said. "They say Vera Lightspinner is dead, and her son has come to the islands." A pang went through Keilan as he listened to her speak – so familiar, yet there was a hardness that he had never heard in his mother's voice.

The giant cat yawned, displaying teeth longer than his fingers. Steeling himself, Keilan stepped forward.

"I am Keilan Ferrisorn. My mother was Vera. She . . . she looked like you," he finished lamely, wishing he could have his last words back.

The sorceress pursed her lips and appeared to be studying him carefully. "I have thought she was dead for eighteen years." She moved closer, cupping his chin with her slim white fingers. Keilan flinched, but he did not pull away. She searched his eyes and face, as if looking for something. After a few long moments, she let him go and stepped back.

"You have little of her in you," she murmured. "But perhaps I do sense something of myself."

"I'm sorry?"

"Talent, Keilan. Vera had only the lightest smattering of the gift. But you have great potential. I can feel it roiling within you. Raw. Untrained and dangerous."

Dangerous? "Yes. I spent some time in a school of wizards, but I had to leave before they could teach me how to harness my sorcery."

"Talent alone does not make you my grandson," she pronounced, and there was an edge to her words, though her face showed no emotion.

Grandson! Keilan's breath caught in his throat.

"Perhaps," the sorceress continued, her eyes narrowing, "you are some clever ploy by the Weaver to infiltrate my sanctuary." As if sensing its mistress's thoughts, a deep rumble came from the great cat.

Keilan swallowed. "I have something she gave me. Let me show you."

The sorceress nodded slightly, and Keilan turned and dashed for the door of his small hut. The writhing vines clutched at him as he pushed through them, and then he was inside, scooping one of his bags from the floor. He undid the drawstring as he hurried back, pulling out what was within.

"These books," he said, holding one of them out for her to take. "They are written in High Kalyuni."

The sorceress accepted the book, some distant emotion trembling her face for the first time. Holding the spine in her hand she opened the book and began to leaf through the yellowing pages.

"I read her these stories when she was a child," she whispered, pausing to study an illustration of a great white hart perched on a rock in a forest glen, its silver antlers glimmering in the light of a swollen moon.

"The Folk Tales of the Middle North," Keilan said softly, knowing the book's title even though he couldn't see the cover. "She read them to me, as well."

A single tear trickled down the sorceress's cheek, but she ignored it. Gently, she closed the book and handed it back to Keilan. "I believe you are Vera's son," she said, letting go of her white-wood staff as she stepped closer to him; it did not fall over, remaining upright, as if it had suddenly set down roots. "Welcome to my home."

Keilan wanted to embrace her; it would be like holding his mother again, he was certain. His body ached for it. But he held himself back – there was a distance to this sorceress, a coolness that suggested she did not fully trust him yet.

She seemed to sense what he felt; perhaps she saw the struggle in his face. The tear that had trickled down her cheek was gone, as if it had never been, and she looked at him clear-eyed. "Strength, Keilan. You must rule your emotions, lest they rule you."

"Emperor Chalcedon, *Beneath God*," he said softly, recognizing the quote. "In the second letter to his younger brother."

"Vera taught you something," she said. "But what you truly needed to learn was beyond her knowledge. It is good you came here, for there are few in the world who can show you the way you must follow." She glanced up the path, at the buildings higher up the mountain. "Now come. I have much to teach you."

"I don't even know your name!"

The sorceress turned back to him as she took up her white staff again. "Niara. That is what the wise woman who pulled me from my mother named me. I was born in a yurt to the chieftain of the Devashii, in a place that no longer exists. When I came into my Talent, they called me Lightspinner and sent me far away, to the Star Towers of the Mosaic Cities."

"Niara," Keilan whispered.

"That will do," the sorceress said. "'Grandmother' would make me feel too old. Now come with me, Keilan."

"What about them?" he asked, gesturing towards the table, where his companions had watched this exchange with open-mouthed astonishment.

Niara seemed to notice them for the first time. She frowned slightly, as if they were an annoyance she would prefer did not exist. "You are my guests," she said without a trace of friendliness. "But you must stay in these huts while you are here. There are dangerous things on this island, and delicate experiments. Do not," she said, her voice hardening, "venture anywhere else, even down to the beach. Only here can I assure your safety. All your needs will be taken care of, I promise you, and if you wish to speak with Keilan while he is with me you may pass your message to one of my servants, and what you say will be relayed to him just as you have spoken it. Do you understand?"

She did not wait for their reply but turned away in a swirl of her blue dress. The great cat stretched languidly, its long claws carving furrows in the dirt, and then padded to her side as she started upon the path.

"Keilan . . ." Nel began, moving towards him, but before she came too close Keilan held up his hands and she stopped.

"I will be fine," he said, sparing a glance at the sorceress and the great cat. "Wait for me."

"Be careful!" Nel cried. Their eyes met and he saw her fear.

"Wait for me," he repeated, and hurried to catch up with his grandmother.

"What was this place?" Keilan asked when they reached the higher ledge and its collection of ancient buildings. They were all constructed of black stone veined with lines of quartz and in various states of disrepair – some had entirely collapsed, while others had been buttressed crudely with chunks of granite that looked to have been pulled straight from the mountain. Trees grew among the ruins, huge fruit unlike any Keilan had ever seen hanging pendulous from their branches.

"It was a monastery," Niara said as she guided him towards the most impressive structure still standing. "Before the sea flooded these lands it clung to the top of a mountain, and sorcerers made pilgrimages to beg for a glimpse of the hidden knowledge the monks had collected here."

They passed through a great square entrance and into a long, wide hall. Sunlight filtered down from narrow windows set the length of the building just below the peaked roof, illuminating the surprisingly homely interior. Couches and comfortable-looking chairs fashioned from wrought copper were scattered about, and beautifully patterned carpets covered much of the stone floor. Long tables held strange silvery instruments and other artifacts, and the very air seemed to crackle with sorcery. Recessed down the length of the walls and stretching almost to the high ceiling were shelves bursting with books and scrolls and even some of the Min-Ceruthan saga bones Keilan had first seen in the Barrow of Vis.

"This is my refuge," Niara said as they walked the length of the hall. Along the way, the great cat found an appealing spot on one of the carpets and sprawled onto its side, showing its belly to the sorceress as they passed.

"How long have you lived here?" Keilan asked, stepping carefully around the cat's lashing tail.

The end of the hall opened up onto a balcony that thrust out from the side of the mountain. Niara walked to the edge and placed her hands on the cracked balustrade of black stone, staring out at the sea. The ocean breeze played with her hair, pushing long silver strands across her face.

"For most of the last thousand years," she said, glancing sideways to see how Keilan would react to this claim.

He affected astonishment, not yet ready to reveal that he had known how old she truly was.

"After the cataclysm, the paladins of Ama led a bloody crusade against the surviving sorcerers. I searched for a place to hide and found this island, and I wove subtle spells so it would remain concealed from all but the most determined searchers."

"The mist?" Keilan asked, remembering the unnatural fog they'd rowed through as they approached the island.

"Yes," Niara said. "A powerful sorcerer or the Pure would sense something amiss, if they concentrated, but my sanctuary is remote enough that there is little chance of it being discovered."

Keilan studied her profile as she continued to watch the horizon – her hair, the shape of her jaw. Her lips and the way she tilted her chin when she was thinking. The resemblance was uncanny. He had to remind himself that no matter how familiar she seemed, he knew almost nothing about her. With some effort he tore his gaze away, concentrating on the sea far below as the dark water churned endlessly among the jagged black rocks.

"Why did my mother leave you?"

Out of the corner of his eye, he saw her slim white fingers tighten upon the stone balustrade.

"I'm sorry," he apologized. "I have to know."

There was a long silence, and then finally Niara sighed. "Vera . . . she was born on this island. When she was young, she played with my creations and was cared for by my servants – who, as you've seen, are not the most personable of companions. As a young child it was enough, for she knew nothing different. But as she grew older she began to explore the world through my library. She came to realize that the life she had here was far different than what others experienced. The island is my refuge, but for her it became a prison. She wanted to leave and travel and I forbid it. We fought and argued, and then one day I awoke and she was gone." Keilan thought he heard a trace of anger in her voice. "She had read the sea charts and realized she could reach Ven Ibras in one of the small boats I keep on the island. I sent my servants out to try and find her and bring her back to me. But she vanished from Ven Ibras, and by the time I had discovered which ship she had taken it was already at the bottom of the sea. For nearly twenty years I have thought she died, and that there was no remnant of her in the world except for what I keep in my memories." Keilan sensed Niara turn towards him, and her hand fell upon his arm. It was the first time she had touched him. "And yet here you are. Somehow you found me, and in a way it is like she has returned."

Keilan swallowed away the tightness in his throat. "Niara . . . all my life I wanted to know where my mother came from. Even in my wildest fantasies I never imagined anything like this, though. It feels like a dream."

"I have much to show you."

"And I want to see it," Keilan said, "but I have to tell you that I came here for a reason. I sought you out because . . ."

The sorceress made a shushing noise. "Not today, Keilan. That can wait until the morrow. Right now, I want you to share with me everything you remember about your mother, and then I will do the same."

34: ALYANNA

DEMIAN WAS GONE.

Cold fear washed through Alyanna as she entered the chamber where he had been convalescing and saw that the mossy dais was empty. Possibilities flitted through her thoughts – had his condition suddenly worsened while she slept, and the kith'ketan already removed his corpse? Had the daymo decided they should be punished for their failure and chosen to strike while the sorcerer was helpless? Or had Demian finally realized that binding himself to a weak abomination like herself was utter foolishness?

Calming herself, Alyanna tamped down her panic – chiding herself for such imaginings – and went to look for him.

She found the swordsinger in a large empty space not a hundred paces from their quarters. It was one of the rooms she had always thought of as 'the ossuaries' – walls soared up into the darkness, pocked with countless small niches, each of which contained the skull of one of the wraiths that had lived here thousands of years ago. When Alyanna had renovated this mountain fastness she had decided to avoid these chambers – while she personally cared little about the empty eyes staring down, she knew others would be more superstitious about such things.

Demian, apparently, was also unconcerned about the attentions of the dead. He stood in the middle of the room clad only in loose black trousers, his back to Alyanna, and with the grace of a dancer was slowly going through his swordsinger routines. One of the glass spheres filled with glowing worms had been placed nearby on the floor, and the light gave his skin an eerie bluish cast. She watched from the ossuary entrance as his movements flowed together, his cracked metal blade flickering out to strike before returning to a guard position. His entire body was twisting to some internal rhythm – it was beautiful, in its own way. Almost hypnotic. Even with her limited knowledge, Alyanna could tell his movements represented the pinnacle of swordfighting's art.

That had always made Demian an anomaly among the great wizards of the Imperium. The pursuit of power was so consuming and exacting that it was very rare for a sorcerer to achieve mastery in a discipline not related to sorcery. And yet he had been recognized as not only one of the greatest Talents of the Star Towers but also as one of the preeminent swordsingers of the Imperium.

"I thought you had abandoned me," Alyanna said with an affected playfulness, and Demian turned, lowering his sword.

"I would not do that," he said simply, returning his blade to its sheath and pushing back the sweat-damp curls that had fallen across his face.

Alyanna entered the ossuary, her slippers whispering upon the stone. She stared up at the pockmarked walls rising around them, wondering how far above into the gloom they extended. "You seem better."

"I am. I did not feel any sorcery when that physicker was attending to me, but the results are impressive. There is stiffness and some pain, but far less than I expected."

Alyanna moved closer to one of the niches set in the wall and tried to pick up the skull inside, but it crumbled to dust between her fingers.

"I was always curious – did you consider yourself first and foremost a sorcerer or a swordsinger?"

"Swordsinger," he answered without hesitation.

That surprised her. "Truly? But it is your Talent that made you one of the most powerful men of our age."

Demian went to where his black shirt was puddled beside the light sphere and bent to pick it up. "The reason is simple – we are born into our magic. Yes, we must work to develop unique spells, but that is simply a matter of lashing the sorcery already within us together into novel combinations. We cannot change the amount of strength we draw from the Void, since that was determined at our birth."

He slipped the shirt over his head, grimacing as it settled on the wound at his side. "Swordfighting is different. Everyone begins with nothing – it is only through discipline and willpower that one can achieve mastery. And it is this distinction between the two pursuits that helps explain the weakness of sorcerers."

"Weakness?" she scoffed.

"Yes. Those born with sorcery in their veins never had to struggle for their power. It was innate. And because of this, they do not truly appreciate what they have. They believe they are superior merely by virtue of their birth and the vagaries of fate. Everyone without sorcery becomes little more than a tool for their ends, and even other sorcerers can only be rivals in the pursuit of more power."

An accurate sentiment. The sorcerers of the Star Towers had been in constant competition. The strongest ascended, and the weak either served them or were destroyed. It was, in Alyanna's opinion, a perfect representation of how the world functioned. One was either a predator or its prey. She had promised herself long ago that she would never be prey again.

"The swordsingers," Demian continued, "they were a brotherhood. We learned the routines from those who had come before, bettered ourselves by practicing against each other. That kind of life fostered loyalty. Respect. A swordsinger would fight to the death to defend his brothers. What sorcerer could say the same?"

Any wizard of the Star Towers who had conducted themselves like Demian had just described would have been thought a fool, Alyanna knew. She certainly would have considered them one.

"In all the years we've known each other, Weaver, you've never asked me why I joined with you under this mountain to remake the world."

"I assumed you wanted what we all wanted: immortality."

Demian shook his head slowly. "No. You chose to believe that we shared this motivation. I will admit that the thought of having the time to explore the great mysteries unencumbered by the fear of death was liberating. But above all else I wanted to destroy the society in which I had grown up. I knew first-hand how the powerful of the Imperium treated the weak as mere objects, as only ends to their desires."

Alyanna sighed. "Revenge, Demian. However you are trying to justify what you did, in the final tally you were punishing an entire society for the actions of the few who abused you and your brother when you were slaves in the House of Hyacinths."

Demian smiled, but there was no humor in it. "My experiences as a child were not unique. It was the guiding principle behind the glorious Imperium – it has been, in truth, the principle behind every sorcerous empire, from the Warlock King's Menekar to the Mosaic Cities. The strong take what they want from the weak. But power unearned by suffering or discipline corrupts the soul. The Imperium was an ancient, dead oak in the forest, its rotten limbs blocking the light. Better to chop it down and give another tree the chance to grow and see if something more healthy can thrive."

"What you see as a flaw in sorcerers," Alyanna countered, with more than a trace of bitterness, "I see as a flaw in mankind. Sorcery is just one advantage men are born with. Are the kingdoms that have arisen today any more just than the old empires?

No. Wealth and nobility have taken the place once occupied by sorcery."

Something like sadness flickered in Demian's eyes. "Perhaps you are right, Weaver. But I have chosen to reject this flaw and hold other things to be above base self-interest. And I suppose you should be grateful of that."

His words were like a slap. Yes, he had risked his life to save hers – just as a swordsinger would have done for another of his order. "I . . . thank you. I don't understand why you came for me, but I am grateful."

Demian accepted her thanks with a slight nod. He opened his mouth to say more, but a shadow suddenly filled the ossuary's entrance.

"Undying One," said a kith'ketan with the dusky skin of an Eversummer Islander, "you are recovered. The daymo wishes to see you at once."

The last time Alyanna had stood in this chamber it had been in the daymo's dreams, and the darkness had been absolute. She remembered the fear she had felt, and how her racing imagination had tried and failed to give form to the presence she had sensed before her. The truth, as she discovered now in the radiance spilling from her eyes, was less horrific than the dark fantasies she had conjured up.

In the inner sanctum of the kith'ketan an old man sat cross-legged atop a great knob of what looked to be bone. His long beard was coiled in his lap, and his fingernails resembled yellow talons – clearly, neither had been cut in years. His robe was so black that it seemed to absorb what little light she had brought into this darkness, and a silken cord dangled near his shoulder. Suspended far above, where the walls curved together, she could just discern the shape of a great bell.

"Undying One," the old man murmured in his cracked and ancient voice. "You return to the mountain with the sorceress who brought you to my dreams. But she is a sorceress no more. Your enemies have bested you."

Demian held the daymo's unblinking gaze, and Alyanna could feel the crash of two great wills coming together.

"They are your enemies now as well," Demian said in a voice shriven of the emotion he had displayed while speaking with her earlier. "The Crimson Queen will not forget that your assassins invaded her home. And your kith'ketan also failed – Cein d'Kara and her school of wizards survived."

The old man shifted slightly, as if annoyed at being reminded of this. "Perhaps I should deliver to her both of your heads. A peace offering to settle this difference between us."

Demian chuckled dryly. "If you truly believed that to be your best course, you would have done this before I recovered my strength. An empty threat."

The old man leaned back, raising his face to the darkness above. He was quiet for a long time, and Alyanna was just starting to consider that they had been dismissed when he suddenly returned his attention to them. Now he looked different: his cheeks were flushed, and his dark pupils seemed to almost fill his eyes. It was not so much different, she thought, than when the other concubines in the imperial gardens had indulged in dreamsmoke.

Something had just happened, though she knew not what.

"I would have made you a gift to the red queen," the daymo said, his voice thicker than before. "But I am not the master here."

She felt Demian stir beside her.

"What are you saying?"

The daymo's lips pulled back in a ghastly smile. "I am saying, Undying One, that you and this once-sorceress have been summoned."

35: KEILAN

NIARA WAITED FOR him the next day on a faded velvet divan, the great red and white tiger curled around her feet. Morning light filtered down from the high windows, drenching her sanctum in warm shades of copper and bronze. The dress she wore reminded Keilan of the spider-silk shirt he had found in the ruins of Uthmala – it seemed to have been woven from countless fine gossamer strands, and it nearly matched in color her unbound silver hair.

"Keilan, sit down," Niara said as the shrouded servant who had brought him there turned and glided away. "Have you eaten?" she asked, gesturing at the slices of red melon and speckled yellow fruit arrayed on a low table.

"I have," Keilan said, finding a seat in a cushioned chair. In truth, he'd only managed a few bites at breakfast – the nervous flutterings in his stomach about seeing the sorceress again had robbed him of his appetite. That, and Nel and Senacus's questions about what he had discussed with Niara had made him feel guilty about not yet bringing up the reason they had sought her out. He'd admitted to them that he hadn't told her about the Shan children or the vision shared by the Oracle, and although Nel hadn't said anything about this, the annoyance in her face had been clear enough.

Then, as he'd stood to leave, Senacus had gripped his arm and pulled him closer.

"Don't forget what she did. We need her help, but she is dangerous."

Niara used a small fork to spear a sliver of the yellow fruit from its silver tray and popped it into her mouth. "Well, what did you think? Delicious?"

"Yes. I've never seen any fruit that looked or tasted like this."

A slight smile curled the edge of her lips. "That is because they only exist on this island. They were some of my first creations."

Keilan stared at the glistening fruit in surprise. "Truly?" How did someone make a fruit?

"Yes," she murmured, taking another bite. "Plants and fruits are much easier to work with than animals." She reached down and scratched behind the great cat's ear.

"And this tiger, too?"

Niara nodded, and Keilan thought he could see pride in her face. "I did. Surely you've noticed all sorts of strange creatures on this island. I've devoted myself to . . . improving life, let us say. Making it more beautiful. More intelligent, or fierce, or quick." She took another piece of the fruit. "Or delicious."

"Now, Chanevia here," she said, stroking the great cat again, "was born from a pair of Dymorian tigers I had my servants buy for me in Gryx. I tinkered with her inside her mother's womb, using sorcery to alter her nature."

"I didn't know sorcery could do such a thing," Keilan breathed, awed by the idea that a creature's very being could be malleable.

"What sorcery is capable of doing is limited only by our power and imagination," Niara said, watching him carefully. "You do not share the constraints of the merely gifted. You are a Talent, like me, and we can guide the very weft and warp of life's tapestry as it is being woven. We can remake the world to reflect our desires." She leaned forward, staring at him intently. "*If* we can draw enough sorcery forth."

He caught the emphasis she put on her last words. "What do you mean by that?"

"I mean, Keilan," she said, the passion now clear in her voice, "that I have been waiting for you for ages. I hoped Vera would be a Talent, so she could help me with my great work. Yet it was not to be. But fate is a fickle goddess, and now here you are, Vera's son, returned at last. And just in time. Together, we can do great things."

"What work are you doing here?" he asked softly, but she dismissed his question with a wave of her silver fork.

"Not yet, Keilan. First, I will help you to bring forth what is inside you. I can feel it – no doubt fragments of your power have squirmed loose in the past, yes? But you must learn how to summon your sorcery whenever you wish. At first it is like reaching into a basket of eels and trying to pull one out. There will be times, and do not be dismayed, when the strands of your power wriggle away and you are left clutching at nothing. But it will get easier, until it becomes as natural as breathing." She offered him a crooked smile. "You will be my apprentice."

"Niara . . . there is nothing I want more than to learn from you. But first I must tell you why I've come. It is of tremendous importance."

The sorceress sank back on the divan, studying him with guarded eyes. "Tell me, then."

And so he did. He told her how the servants of Dymoria's ruler had kidnapped him from the Pure, how he had come to study for a short time in the Scholia of the Crimson Queen, and how, when visiting Lyr, he had been summoned to the coral temple of Lyr's Oracle. He spoke of the twisted children – the ones the Shan scholar at the Reliquary had named the Betrayers – and how he had seen her, Niara, alight upon the ruins of

Menekar's imperial palace and challenge the demons. He did not speak, though, of how he had seen her before, in the memories of the sorcerer Jan, as she and others fashioned immortality from the souls of the countless dead. It was not the time to reveal that he knew she was connected to the cataclysms that had shattered the world.

When he had finished describing his journey from Lyr along the Iron Road, and the scattered clues that had led him and his companions to the manse of the pirate lord on the island of Ven Ibras, Niara stood abruptly and went over to a cabinet of golden wood. From a drawer she pulled forth a carved box and then returned to her divan. Her fingers drummed a pattern on the lid as she placed the box on the low table between them.

"What is that?" Keilan asked as she continued to stare at the intricate patterns decorating the lacquered red wood.

"Tell me of this dagger you say I wielded," she said.

Keilan strained to recall the details of that terrible vision. "The blade was curved and black, and there were red runes down its length."

The calm certainty in Niara's face never wavered, but Keilan thought he sensed the briefest of hesitations before she slid back the lid to reveal the dagger he had just described, nestled among folds of purple cloth.

Its hilt was plain silver, unornamented with any decorative flourishes, though a single line of strange characters spiraled above the circular pommel. But the blade . . . it was not a metal Keilan had ever seen before. Gleaming and black like obsidian, but slightly translucent, and beneath its surface darker lines like veins or roots threaded the metal. Runes that looked similar to the tiny spidery characters that wrapped the hilt were incised along the blade, glimmering red as if they had been coated with some special resin.

"The vision was true," Keilan whispered, unable to tear his gaze from the dagger. There had always been some tiny niggling doubt that the Oracle had pulled the sorceress from his memories and fashioned what they had experienced because of some unfathomable madness. He wasn't sure whether he should be relieved or terrified.

"It would appear so," Niara said, lifting the dagger from its box. "This was created to be their doom," she said softly, twisting and turning the dagger so that the morning light caught the blade and ran like water along its curving length.

"Those children?"

"Yes," said Niara softly. "I forged it, centuries ago."

"Then you knew they would come?"

"No," the sorceress said, laying the dagger down again in its bed of cloth.

"Then why . . ."

"You are not the first visitor to my island, Keilan. Some have washed up along the shore by chance, others have heard of my legend and come to beg for something. Your own grandfather was one such shipwrecked sailor." She pushed the lid closed with a click. "A Shan warlock came here long ago, searching for me. He brought with him a pouch of bone dust and dried blood flakes scraped from the edge of a knife. The last remnants of the Betrayers from before they had brought down the Raveling upon the ancestral lands of Shan. Pai Xin was his name. An ambitious man who wanted to make a name for himself in the bone-shard towers by finally banishing the spirits of the Betrayers into the beyond. He had been told about me by another of his order as that warlock lay dying, a man I had once saved when his ship foundered in a storm. Pai Xin wanted to use the blood and ashes of the Betrayers' physical form to forge a weapon that could destroy the demon children, but such an act was far beyond the abilities of the warlocks now. Once, they had their own Talents, but just as in our lands none had been born since before they fled across the World Ocean."

"And that is what you made?" Keilan breathed, staring at the box.

"I did. The blade is infused with their essence, and if my sorcery is true it can slay them – it might be the only way to forever end their cursed existence."

"But he did not take it back to Shan?"

Niara's mouth twisted. "He tried to, along with a few other items that had caught his fancy during his stay with me. In the end, he did not depart these shores, and I kept the dagger I had made."

"Then we have a weapon against them! We have to find them before –"

Niara held up her hand to quiet him. "And where are they, Keilan? Pai Xin told me the spirits of the Betrayers were bound within a chest that is protected by ancient wards in the bone-shard towers of Tsai Yin. Should we try and sneak inside, past these mysterious defenses and an entire order of sorcerers, and open the prison that has kept them locked away for a thousand years? Then hope this blade can truly dispatch them forever? What if I am wrong? Perhaps such an attempt is how they escaped in the Oracle's vision to bring doom down upon these lands." Niara sighed. "Prophecies are tricky things, Keilan. Sometimes, by trying to avert what has been foretold, the seeds are sown for that very future to come about."

"Then what shall we do?"

With her finger, the sorceress traced the patterns carved into the box's lid. "I will think on it. In a few days, you will have your answer. Until then, I want to begin your instruction in sorcery."

"Your schooling until now has been lacking," Niara said, after they had finished their lunch of flat-bread and dates drizzled with honey.

"In the Imperium, a student would have been given a foundation of knowledge about the nature of sorcery long before it ever manifested in them. But here you are, nearly a man grown, and yet ignorant of the simplest facts."

Keilan thought back to those days along the Wending, listening as Vhelan had tried to explain how the magisters of the Scholia believed sorcery to work.

"I was told that within all sorcerers there is a connection to another place. And along this thread sorcery travels, and gathers within us, and we can twist this power to do wondrous things."

"Wondrous and terrible," Niara amended, and for some reason those words tickled at his memory. Where had he heard them before?

"But you have the basics of it. Sorcery is an energy from elsewhere, a realm beyond our conception. It is sometimes referred to as the Void, though I doubt its inhabitants would use such a name. The Void implies emptiness, and this place is most certainly not empty." She took a quick sip from a silver goblet. "Now, the simplest use of this energy is to project it outside of ourselves and make it manifest in the world. That is why all sorcerers, even if they have just a glimmer of the gift, are capable of summoning light and fire. Wards – defensive shields formed from hardening this energy – are also one of the most basic uses for sorcery."

"What about other spells? Like seeing into another's memories, or the sinking of these lands beneath the Broken Sea?"

"Only the most powerful among the gifted, or a Talent, can shape sorcery in such ways. But if you are that strong, then nearly anything is possible. Sorcery is infinitely pliable – it just requires enough imagination and will."

"And strength," Keilan added, remembering what Niara had said earlier.

"Yes," the sorceress agreed. "And strength." Niara twisted a strand of hair around her finger, something his mother also used to do when she was thinking.

"One of my old teachers," she continued, "once described the difference between Talents and the merely gifted as being analogous to a master metalworker and a man who just wanders into a smithy. Give the man a heated piece of metal and a hammer and he can pound it into a simple shape – a sword, say. It may not be beautiful, but when he swings it the edge will still split open flesh. Most sorcerers are like this, wielding sorcery with the clumsy skill of the untrained man. But a master metalworker could take that same lump of metal and fashion something wondrous. A sundial that can track the watches as the sun moves across the sky. Or a delicate piece of filigreed jewelry. Or even – if the smith is very highly skilled – one of those automata filled with gears and wires that stumble about when a key is wound in its back."

She reached out to pat his arm. "You are many years away from crafting that kind of sorcery, Keilan. We shall start with the simplest of spells."

Niara raised her hand, and blue energy coruscated like lightning along her fingers. It came and went in the briefest of glimpses, but Keilan thought he actually saw the lines of sorcery as Niara lashed them together.

She seemed to notice this. "Good, Keilan. You saw what I did?"

"I think so . . . but how could I see it?"

"It means you have come of age. It is one of the things that makes Talents different than the merely gifted, along with not needing gestures or incantations to shape spells. The sorcery so saturates our very being that at about your age it actually becomes visible, and we can learn simple manipulations of energy from merely observing."

"Yes!" Keilan said excitedly, remembering the Kindred he had encountered along the Iron Road. "I met an old man who could shape fire, and as he was doing this I could *see* the spell being formed! I was able to imitate what he had done later, though I could not control it very well."

Naira extended her hand towards him, palm upraised, and a sphere of crackling wizardlight flared into existence. For a brief moment Keilan again could glimpse the lines of sorcery twisting together, but they flickered past too quickly for him to see clearly.

"Did you notice what I did?" she asked as the wizardlight vanished.

"No," Keilan admitted. "It was too fast."

"Watch carefully," she told him, summoning the glowing sphere again. This time she seemed to have slowed the twisting of the sorcerous strands . . . but still he couldn't quite tell what she had done.

"How about that time?"

He shook his head, frustrated.

Niara frowned. "Concentrate, Keilan. Pay attention to what I do."

Again, the wizardlight appeared. He thought he could see now how she had managed it . . .

Keilan reached down into himself, into the churning sea where his power waited. He grasped at the roiling sorcery, feeling it flood him with cool strength, and tried to twist it the same way as she had just demonstrated.

Light swelled in the air before him, and Niara smiled, applauding. The shock of seeing the wizardlight form from nothing except his will and what he had drawn from within himself made his concentration slip, and the light dissipated into a few glittering motes.

"That is good, Keilan. You are ready to learn."

"Will you teach me more?" he asked softly, watching as the last few drifting sparks winked out of existence.

"I will."

36: SELLA

AMONG ALL THE tasks on the farm that Sella hated, churning butter was by far the worst. Half a day or more of standing over a barrel of cream, moving the plunger up and down and up again, until her back ached and her arms felt like they were about to come clean off. And always on the days her ma had grabbed her to do some churning the sun would be shining, maybe poking out after a storm had come and gone, and Sella just knew there'd be all sorts of things to find down on the beach or in the forest . . . if only she had been able to escape her ma's quick hands. And as she was standing there in the barn her thoughts would wilt away like flowers at the end of summer, nothing but numb emptiness inside her as she churned and churned and churned and prayed to Ama and the Deep Ones and every forest spirit Mam Ru had ever told her about that this cream would hurry up and magically turn into butter.

Sella didn't like waiting.

By the fourth day on the island she'd done near everything she could think of: she'd thrown rocks at the strange colored birds that roosted in the trees near the huts, till they finally flapped away and hadn't returned; she'd placed twigs and rocks among the hanging vines and watched them curl and grasp like the hands of babies; godspit, she'd even pulled out Keilan's books and leafed through looking at the few pictures. When she did that, she knew she was bored beyond all reason.

The angry woman and the quiet paladin didn't seem to be enjoying the waiting very much, either. Senacus spent most of the day inside his hut – she'd peeked inside, once, and saw him sitting there on his knees, his head bowed and his hands on his legs. Praying, Sella guessed. For Kay, maybe? Or his home, which Sella had overheard he'd seen all ruined in some dream. Or perhaps he was just asking Ama how he'd ended up the guest of a sorceress on an island in the middle of the sea. Sella had listened to enough mendicants to know that this was probably gnawing him up from the inside. They didn't like sorcery at all.

Nel, on the other hand, was always moving around, restless as a cat trying to get inside a cupboard. She'd pace back and forth, flipping those daggers to herself and muttering, pausing every once in a while to scowl up at the buildings Kay disappeared into every day. She'd look more and more haggard and nervous as the watches passed, until the time when he'd come tripping down the path in the evening. Sella had started to look for that shiver of relief that would cross her face when she caught sight of him, though it would be gone by the time Kay arrived – the anger would be back then, and it would stay the rest of the night while she talked to him crossly about what he should have been doing all day. More important things than learning magic, apparently.

On the afternoon of the fourth day Sella decided to go have a look around. That sorceress had said there were dangerous things on the island, but Sella hadn't seen anything that scared her. Except for that big cat, maybe, but it looked like a pet, not something that hunted and ate people. Well, and the robed things, but they didn't seem so fast. Sella was pretty sure she could run away if one happened to see her out and about. She wasn't worried. And anyway, Niara was Kay's grandma. She wouldn't let anything bad happen to his friend.

The rear of the huts brushed up against the edge of a rocky slope, and at its bottom was the beach where they had arrived. No one seemed to be paying attention to her, but still Sella made sure the paladin was busy with his praying and Nel with her worrying before she slipped around the back and half slid, half scrambled down to the black sand. Then she followed the curve of the beach, keeping to the shadows thrown by the higher places so that no one up above could see her. Eventually Sella came to the spot she'd picked out – a steep bit of cliff that soared up to a higher ledge than where they'd been staying. She couldn't see it right now from so far down below, but she knew there was a building up there, too. As she'd hoped, the rocky wall looked pretty easy to climb. Lots of crevices and ledges to hold onto – really, it didn't look much harder than the rocks she and Kay used to climb out in the bay, and those had been slicked by the sea.

She gave a final glance at the huts where she'd left Nel and Senacus, hoping not to see them pointing and screaming at her – they weren't – and then she started to climb. It was easy going, so long as she didn't look down. She did once, and then she'd felt dizzy and had to hug herself a bit closer to the stone. But she was never in any real danger of falling. Her mother had called Sella her 'little gibbon', after those forest apes, since she had gotten to the top of every tall tree round their farm. Felt good, actually, to climb again. The sun on her shoulders, the feel of being up high, going somewhere and doing something.

By the time Sella pulled herself up over the ledge, her hands were scraped up and her hair dirty from when she'd managed to knock a bird's nest onto her head, but still the exhilaration of the climb was rushing through her like lightning. She did feel a bit of disappointment, though, when she saw that the ledge she'd climbed up to wasn't all that interesting – just another hut, not much bigger than the one she was sleeping in. She'd just have a quick look inside and then hurry back before Nel realized she was missing.

The door looked rotten and about a thousand years old, but it didn't budge when she pushed. Sella circled the building – there had once been windows, but someone had piled rocks in them pretty tight. There were a few little gaps where the stones came together, and so she stood up on her toes and tried to peek inside. Shapes loomed in the darkness.

One corner of a wall had crumbled, and there was a hole Sella thought she might be able to squeeze through if she sucked in her tummy. Pushing down that little nagging voice of caution she got down and wriggled her way between the jagged bits of stone.

Once inside, she climbed to her feet. She couldn't hear the waves anymore, or the wind, so her breathing sounded loud in the silence. Didn't smell as musty as she'd have thought it should, so maybe Kay's grandma came here pretty often. But what was here?

Slowly, Sella's eyes adjusted to the little light trickling through the chinks between the stones filling the windows. Looked to be a few long tables scattered around most of the space, with something larger hunched along the far wall. Maybe a bookcase or a cupboard. She stepped closer to the nearest shape and ran her hand along it – yeah, it was a table, smooth and hard. Her fingers bumped against something lying on the table, and she felt its edges. Small pieces of wood, little knots where they joined together, cloth . . .

It was a doll, she'd wager anything. But what was it doing here? Holding the doll in one hand, she kept moving her fingers over the table. More dolls, sprawled out like someone had been playing with them. Her eyes were pretty good now, and she could see that the other shadowy shapes in the room were tables as well, and that they were also strewn with dolls. Twenty, thirty at least.

How strange. Sella stroked the bristly hair of the doll she held with her thumb, wondering if this was where Kay's mother had once played. She remembered Esme, the doll Mam Ru had lent to her, and how that fat fool Malik had used the doll to lure Kay out into the forest. That memory made her smile – watching Kay beat those boys had made her heart feel big enough to burst.

Kay's grandma certainly wouldn't be angry if she borrowed one of these dolls to play with while they waited for her to finish teaching Kay. Maybe Kay would even be interested to see a doll that had probably belonged to his ma. It'd be tough to climb down the rocks with only one hand, but Sella thought she could do it. Or maybe she could tuck in her shirt and stuff the doll down the front. Yeah, that was a good idea.

Gripping the doll tight, Sella made her way back to the hole in the wall. Then, squirming through the little gap, she emerged again into the brightness of the day.

37: CHO LIN

AFTER HER BRIEF audience with the Stag thane, Verrigan led Cho Lin over to a table where she recognized some of the warriors who had brought her to Nes Vaneth. She wanted to confront Jan again later that night, but Verrigan counseled firmly against it – if the Skein king summoned her, then she must approach the dais once more, but otherwise she should avoid the White Worm thane's attentions. Cho Lin was about to inform the Stag captain that she feared no man, but the look on his face stilled her tongue. Best to wait until the morrow, he advised, and corner the skald when he was not seated beside the most dangerous man in the Frostlands.

So instead Cho Lin choked down a blackened chunk of unseasoned meat carved from the creatures turning on the spits. As the Skein around her feasted and drank, she kept her eye on the king and his entourage through the smoky haze, but they seemed to have settled on the dais for the evening – more warriors had joined them, and it almost looked to Cho Lin like they were all listening intently to Jan as he regaled them with a story. Or was he singing? Could he truly be a skald? She had thought it just a clever ploy to explain his journey to Nes Vaneth, but perhaps not.

As the evening waned, the Bhalavan began to empty. A few of the Skein warriors slumped forward on the benches, finding space to sleep among the spilled ale and scraps of meat, while others stood and stumbled towards the great hall's shadowed recesses. The great cook pits were extinguished, and the thralls stopped replenishing whatever was used for fuel in the iron braziers. Shadows draped the hall, and through the rents in the Bhalavan's roof Cho Lin could see the distant glimmer of stars, visible now the smoke from the cook pits had cleared. A heaviness had begun to press against her eyes, and even the thought of staying the night in such a cold and cursed place could not keep her from yearning for sleep.

"Is that where the bedchambers are?" she asked, pointing to the end of the hall where she had seen the Skein warriors drifting.

Verrigan blearily looked in the direction she was indicating. She was actually quite impressed that he was still conscious – from the amount she had watched him drink, she was certain there was more ale than blood flowing through his veins.

"Bedchambers?" he slurred, blinking as he tried to focus on her. "Just one chamber. Big enough for hundreds to sleep. Warm, but smells terrible." He stared into her eyes intently, as if to impress upon her the seriousness of what he said. "Terrible."

The thought of trying to find sleeping space among countless drunken Skein warriors passed out cheek to jowl made Cho Lin shiver with revulsion. But where else could she bed down?

"Thralls," she said, catching sight of an older woman who was collecting tankards from a nearby table. Most of her hair was gray, but she still had a few of the red curls that Cho Lin had come to associate with Dymoria. She was moving with exaggerated care, so as not to wake a sprawled Skein warrior.

"Thralls?" Verrigan said in confusion, swaying slightly as Cho Lin rose beside him. "You want to be a thrall now?"

"No. I want to sleep with them."

"That's a good idea," she heard him mumble as she moved towards the red-haired thrall. "If you see a pretty one, send her to me."

The woman started as Cho Lin laid a hand on her arm, nearly dropping the half-dozen tankards she had collected from the tables. She turned, letting out a little squeak of terror when she saw who had touched her.

"Do not be afraid," Cho Lin said, forcing her most comforting smile. "I am a guest in this hall. I . . ." She hesitated, realizing that what she was about to say would be considered absolutely horrifying to any other daughter of a Jade Court mandarin. "I want you to show me where the servants sleep."

The woman stared at her blankly, and for a moment Cho Lin thought she must not speak Menekarian. But then she shook herself, as if making sure Cho Lin wasn't some spirit, and set the tankards down on a nearby table.

"You want to sleep with the thralls?"

Cho Lin nodded, relieved that she had been understood. "Yes. I do not want to sleep with the Skein."

The woman glanced in the direction of the warriors' quarters. "Wise decision," she said, motioning for Cho Lin to follow her. "They've been feasting and drinking for days, ever since they killed all the Bear."

"You were here before the battle?" Cho Lin asked as they threaded their way among the tables, towards a small archway set in the far wall.

"I've been here since I was a girl, more than forty winters ago," said the thrall. "First it was the Raven, then the Bear. Now it's the White Worm. I can feel it in my bones that bad times are coming. The Bear and the Raven, they were not cruel. Sometimes even kind. But these new Skein from the north . . ." She shuddered. "Three girls have disappeared in three nights. Some are saying they ran off, scared by this new king. But I don't think so. Where would they go?"

The thrall led Cho Lin down a short passage, to a large chamber scattered with piles of rushes and small mounds of furs and clothing. There was a fire burning in a pit in the room's center, and the only furniture were a few ancient looms and a stool where an old crone hunched wearing filthy rags.

"You can sleep where you wish," the thrall said, gesturing at the bedding. "The other kings didn't allow it, but these feast days most of the pretty girls are getting dragged off to warm some warrior's bedroll. Some might come back before morning light, but there's still enough space for everyone."

"Thank you," Cho Lin said, and the woman blushed and looked away.

"Ain't nothing," she murmured. "The Bhalavan is a bad place, but this room here is safe. No Skein warrior would ever be seen going where the thralls stay. Just be careful everywhere else in this cursed city."

As the Dymorian thrall had said, there were plenty of empty piles of rushes when Cho Lin awoke the next morning. She wondered whether more girls had disappeared during the night, or if they had been forced into the bedrolls of the Skein warriors in their sleeping hall. Perhaps she'd slept in too late, as a few of the women were already moving about the chamber. One was stirring the embers of the fire, while another was pouring water from a bucket into a metal container. Two more of the thralls were seated on the ground slicing up vegetables, while the crone on her stool didn't seem to have moved at all since the night before.

The woman wrestled her heavy container sloshing with water over the flames, then noticed Cho Lin watching her from across the room. She nudged the shoulder of the other thrall who was trying to coax the fire back to life and murmured something softly into her ear. Cho Lin climbed to her feet, brushing dirt and clinging bits of stale straw from her clothes. By the Four Winds, she'd give anything for a hot bath and a few pieces of crispy fried *yautiao* right now.

She tensed as she noticed the woman who had been poking the embers approaching her. Tentatively, the thrall held out her hand, avoiding looking at Cho Lin directly.

"Breakfast," she said softly, and Cho Lin saw that nestled in her palm was a small speckled egg. "It's cooked."

Cho Lin murmured her thanks as she accepted the egg, and the thrall scurried back. The other women in the room watched this exchange with mingled awe and trepidation.

"Thank you," Cho Lin said again to the entire chamber, feeling a tightness in her throat. The actions of these slaves reminded her of how the servants in the Cho house had treated her when she was a girl. Why was it that those with the least often showed the most kindness?

She peeled the egg as she passed through the corridor to the Bhalavan's main hall. Most of the benches were empty, which suggested the warriors had not yet risen for breakfast. Verrigan was there, though, nursing a tankard in the same place he'd been seated when she had left him the night before. Cho Lin suspected he'd never made it to the sleeping hall.

"Good morning," she said, sliding onto the bench across from him. The Stag captain blinked bloodshot eyes at her, as if he was still having trouble focusing, and grumbled something unintelligible.

Cho Lin ate her egg in two quick bites, glancing at the empty dais.

Verrigan noticed where she looked and shook his head.

"Too late," he mumbled into his tankard, and Cho Lin felt a chill go through her.

"Too late?"

"Already left before dawn."

"*Tsanme*?" she cried, leaping to her feet.

"What?"

"*What*? Where did Jan go?"

Verrigan motioned for her to sit again, his face suggesting that just watching her jump around was making him nauseous.

"Hunting. The king and the thanes and their favorites left this morning on a hunt to celebrate the killing of all the Bear."

"You told me to wait until the morning," Cho Lin said angrily, restraining herself from grabbing the Skein and shaking him.

"I did, I did," Verrigan said with a hint of an apology in his tone. "The hunt is – how to say? – tradition. But I did not think they would leave so soon. Or that the skald would go with them."

Cho Lin glanced at the hall's great bronze doors, which were permanently cracked open, gauging the time from the color of the light. It looked to her to be mid-morning, which meant that the royal hunting party had left at least a few watches past.

Verrigan waved his hand, as if to dismiss what he knew she was thinking.

"No. You can't go after them. They went north, into the wilds. There are wraiths and bears and yerclaws in the forests – even the strongest Skein warrior would not go unless with many others."

"I cannot let Jan get away –"

"He not getting away," Verrigan assured her, taking a swallow of his drink. "Where would he go? And if he does, better for you. If they return with no skald, you can go chasing him again, and there would be no thanes to stop you from catching him at that time."

There was some wisdom to his words. Jan had come to Nes Vaneth for a reason, so likely he would return. And if he did not, then Cho Lin could continue her pursuit without the interference of the Skein.

Verrigan seemed to sense her resignation. "Sit. Have some drink. Hunts only last a day or two."

Cho Lin licked her lips as the Stag captain took another swig from his tankard, realizing how thirsty she was.

"What is it?"

Verrigan belched contentedly. "Drink of the gods – mead."

Cho Lin grimaced and turned away from the Skein captain, the memory of the last time she'd drunk mead making her gorge rise.

"What? Is delicious."

The hunting party did not return that day, and Cho Lin kept her impatience at bay by wandering the Bhalavan and the small section of Nes Vaneth that had been settled by the Skein. Like the city, much of the king's great hall had been abandoned – passageways curved away into darkness, the dust of many years undisturbed upon the stone. She considered exploring a ways, but then wondered if this would violate some law of the Skein and bring down punishment upon her head. Also she had to admit to a trickle of fear staring down the empty corridors – who knew what lurked in the recesses of this cursed place? Did some dark magic still linger? Surely the Skein avoided these hallways for a reason.

Cho Lin did discover that the vague shapes she had seen looming at the edge of the great hall's light were indeed statues: men carved from gray stone in intricate detail unlike she had ever seen before, their elaborate armor strangely ornamented. Incredibly enough, in one of the statue's open mouths she could actually distinguish individual teeth. A snake coiled around the arm of that statue, scaled with strange designs, and on the shoulder of another perched a bird, its head a nub of chipped stone. The fear and anger etched into the warriors' faces made Cho Lin shiver. Who would carve such things?

She also spent some time visiting the horse Verrigan had gifted to her after the wraith ambush. Despite the Stag captain's admonitions about the horse, she'd found herself growing fond of the shaggy fellow.

A hundred tents of hide and bone had been pitched beside the Bhalavan around a long, wide building of crumbled stone that looked to have been used as a stable in Min-Ceruthan times. The owners of these tents must have moved inside the great hall, as the camp seemed populated only by boys and large dogs which looked to have more than a little wolf in them. They snapped and snarled as she passed, and Cho Lin was glad of the leashes that kept the dogs from trying to savage her. She found her horse pressed in with dozens of others inside the stables, and she refilled his water trough from the well outside and carried several armfuls of hay over to him from where it was mounded near the entrance.

The revelry that night in the great hall was much more subdued, and Cho Lin attributed this to the absence of the king and the thanes. It may have been her imagination, but she thought that the other Skein were giving her a wide berth – perhaps the story of how she had felled a Crow warrior had spread. She ate quickly, ignoring Verrigan's attempts at conversation, and retired early to the thralls' quarters.

The next morning, she found a stream of Skein warriors rushing from the sleeping hall towards the Bhalavan's great doors. She glimpsed Verrigan among the tumult and fought her way to his side.

"What is it?" she asked, loud enough to be heard over the excited babble.

"The hunt has returned," he replied.

They joined the throng and pushed their way outside; Cho Lin blinked and shielded her eyes from the dazzling sun, blinded from spending so long in the Bhalavan's gloom. She gasped when her vision finally cleared, clutching at Verrigan's arm.

Dozens of Skein warriors and their horses were approaching up the broad snowy avenue that led to the Bhalavan, light glittering upon spearpoints and helms. The dark-haired Skein king, Hroi, was in the lead, clad in the same gray wraith-leather armor that Cho Lin had seen the Flayed wearing earlier, a twisted black crown upon his brow. He wore a patched and mottled cloak – it looked like something a beggar in Shan might wear, but she remembered what Verrigan had said, and she shivered. Beside the king on a smaller pony rode the shaman of the White Worm, and he looked to be only sixteen or seventeen winters old, hardly more than a boy. Behind this pair came the rest of the warriors: Kjarl and his warband, the tines of their helms flashing; a contingent of the Flayed; and a host of Skein with black feathers threaded in their hair. And there was Jan riding among them, a sword of much finer make than the one she had bought for him outside Herath at his side. Apparently the king had decreed that he at least could bring his weapon inside the walls of Nes Vaneth.

But Cho Lin had not gasped because of anyone in the hunting party. No, it was what they had returned with.

On a makeshift sled drawn by two horses lay a head unlike anything she had ever seen before. It resembled a great lizard, as it was scaled and horny protrusions encircled its dead eyes, but its face was longer and more tapered than the smaller lizards she had seen in Shan. A forked tongue the length of her arm dangled from its slack jaws, and the fangs Cho Lin glimpsed more resembled daggers than teeth. That mouth could have easily crushed a horse's head in life, she thought. It looked like something no one in the Empire of Swords and Flowers had seen for a thousand years.

"Is that a dragon?" she whispered, and beside her Verrigan chuckled.

"Nay, lass. That's only a wyvern. A big one, though, to be sure. Dangerous."

A wyvern. She had learned about them in her studies – the spawn of true dragons, stunted and mindless. For every egg that contained a dragon, a hundred more hatched wyverns.

Hroi shouted something in Skein when he reached the swelling crowd outside the Bhalavan, and the warriors bellowed back a cheer. He was younger than Cho Lin would have thought to already be king, not yet close to his middle years. His hard eyes scanned the gathered Skein as he cried out again, then he lifted something he had been holding.

It was black and bulbous and curved, almost like the stinger of a scorpion, though much, much larger. Mutterings rippled through the warriors around Cho Lin.

"The end of the wyvern's tail," explained Verrigan. "It brings great luck."

The king threw it into the gathered warriors, and chaos erupted.

The grizzled Skein warriors had become a mob of excited children, scrambling over each other as they tried to claim this prize. Cho Lin was nearly knocked over as the crowd surged around her, and when she'd recovered her balance she saw that Verrigan had abandoned her to join the melee. Steel flashed and a gout of blood arced through the air, followed by a pained scream. The thanes and their entourages were laughing at the mayhem Hroi had caused, but the Skein king and his shaman watched without expression.

Cho Lin backed away, almost to the great bronze doors of the hall, and was just about to slip inside again when a hand grabbed her arm. She turned, reaching for the Nothing as she readied herself to fight.

But it was Jan.

"Come with me," he said, and she let him lead her inside the Bhalavan. The noise of the quarreling warriors receded as they entered the now empty hall.

She shook herself free when they had gone a dozen steps. "You left me," she said accusingly, and he grimaced.

"I did. I'm sorry."

"How could you?" she hissed, wishing now that she had struck first before seeing who had seized her. "I told you I must find the Betrayers. Everyone is in danger while they are free."

He held up his hands placatingly. "When last I saw them they were bound in the service of a powerful sorceress, and as wicked as she is, she has no cause to let them work whatever foul deeds they want in the world."

"They must be captured again! No wizard is strong enough to control them."

"Alyanna is," Jan said. "She might be the greatest sorceress in the world."

Cho Lin clenched her fists, her nails digging into her palms. She wanted to strike that condescending look from Jan's face – he had no idea what the Betrayers were capable of doing, and the danger they represented.

"You came here . . . to write a song about the glorious Skein king?"

Jan sighed. "No. Of course not."

"Then why? Tell me!"

"Do you remember what I said that night before I left? You were very drunk."

Cho Lin made a face. "On your northern tea."

"Yes, well, I told you that for a long time my memories were hidden. But on the night the assassins attacked Saltstone Cein d'Kara helped me to recover them – all of them. And there was one memory I cannot ignore, and it was that which drove me here, to this dead city."

She eyed him warily, but her curiosity was piqued.

"Long ago," he began, seeing that he had her interest, "but still many years after Alyanna first took away my past, I began to remember something of my old life. I was here," he said, gesturing with his arms to encompass the great hall, "in the glory days of Nes Vaneth, when the fire wardens burned the sky with blazing streamers and the silver trumpets pealed the arrival of the queen astride her dragon."

"That is not possible," Cho Lin said. "This city has been a ruin since before the Thousand Sails entered the Sea of Solace."

"It is possible," Jan insisted, and the intensity in his eyes surprised her. "You must believe me. After many years, the memories of my old life began to seep through the barriers Alyanna had constructed in my mind, and so I journeyed here. This was before the Skein had settled in this city, and it was empty save for the ghosts of my lost people. I entered the Bhalavan and, remembering the way, I followed the hidden paths to the ancient throne room. There are corridors, you see, that extend from beneath the Bhalavan and into the mountain. There I found something I cannot forget, and I must return to."

"What was it?"

"In the throne room I discovered the greatest heroes of my people encased in stone, and a great wall of ice filling the dais where once my queen had sat upon the dragon bone throne." Jan looked away from her, as if momentarily overcome by the memory. "We were lovers. Her name was Liralyn, and she was a sorceress as powerful and as glorious as Dymoria's Crimson Queen. I walked up to that wall of ice as if in a dream, wondering if I would still be able to see her, my lost love, entombed inside forever. But instead there was something else – a babe, hanging in the ice as if it had been placed there."

"A Skein warrior told me he has seen the Min-Ceruthans trapped within the black ice elsewhere in Nes Vaneth."

"No!" Jan said, dismissing her words with sharp gesture. "It was not the black ice from Kalyuni. This ice was summoned by Min-Ceruthan sorcery, I could sense it. Which means it had been created to protect what was within."

"You mean . . ."

"Yes. The child might still be alive."

"You think the child is the queen's?"

Jan's face twisted. "I . . . believe it could be. She was with child, and I was her lover. It was why I left the north and journeyed south – the other lords were enraged that she had allowed a lesser noble into her bed. We quarreled over this, and she exiled me."

"So the baby could be yours as well," Cho Lin breathed softly.

"Yes," Jan said, and she could hear the raw emotion in this admission.

"Why did you not do something before?"

"I did at the time! As I said, my memories were not complete. But I remembered hints about a great sorceress named Alyanna, and I sought her out. I begged for her to help me craft a sorcery that could free this child in the ice without killing it."

"And she refused you?"

His jaw hardened. "Worse. She robbed me of the memories that had returned, so I forgot entirely about what I had found in Nes Vaneth. Until that night in Saltstone."

"And so you have come here to find the child again."

"Yes," Jan said, his expression suddenly pleading. "But I need your help, Cho Lin."

38: ALYANNA

Round and round
They spiral down
Bare feet upon the stones
A winter chill
That lingers still
Did creep into their bones
Mother wails
And father pales
To see their girls so cold
While beneath the ground
They spiral down
Never to grow old

IT WAS A fragment of a song from her childhood, and Alyanna could not get it out of her head. On the darkest night of the year, when the moon had vanished from the sky, an old woman dressed as the Crone of Bones would sing about the dead to the children who clutched at the hem of her shawl. Spirits wandering lost on battlefields, new born babes drawing in shuddering breaths even as the light faded in their mothers' eyes, cold fingers closing around a woodsman's heart while he worked alone in the forest. But the song that had made Alyanna shiver the most as a child had told the story of two sisters who had wandered away on a winter's night and been found by their father the next day clutching each other in the snow, pale and lifeless. As their parents mourned, the girls' souls had descended into the depths of the world, terrified by what they would find but unable to turn away from the path that drew them below.

She was one of those girls now. Dreading every step that brought her deeper, yet still she continued on.

Spiraling down, into the darkness.

They had left the passages carved by wraiths and men far above. Here, stony fangs dripped from ceilings that sometimes brushed their heads and sometimes soared beyond the reach of Demian's wizardlight. The tunnel they followed would constrict so tightly that they had to squeeze through narrow openings, and then widen into great caverns where black water tumbled from above to splash into pools swarming with phosphorescent fish.

"Are we lost?" she asked Demian when he paused at the juncture of two passages.

"I remember the way," he replied, sending his wizardlight skittering down the left branch.

She watched the glow vanish far too quickly. There was something strange about the blackness down here – it clotted in the air like a physical thing, hovering just beyond where the radiance spilling from her eyes and Demian's sorcery faded. And it felt as if from the dark something was peering back at her.

Time lost all meaning. They might have been descending for half a watch, or half a day. When Alyanna was hungry she ate the dried mushrooms the kith'ketan had given her. A few bites and her stomach was full again, as if by sorcery. When she was thirsty she drank from her water skin. She did not feel tired, but then again, she did not feel entirely awake, either. The laws that governed the world above had been growing weaker as they descended – it was almost as if they were infringing upon an entirely different realm, one with its own set of rules.

Demian's drifting wizardlight suddenly sputtered and went out. In the moment before it vanished, Alyanna saw a gap illuminated in the stone ahead, an entrance to what looked to be a larger space beyond. Then they were plunged into darkness, save for the muted light shining from her eyes.

"Why did you extinguish your wizardlight?" she asked, with some effort keeping the edge of panic from her voice.

"I did not," Demian replied, turning towards her. "We have arrived, Weaver."

"What is down here?" she asked again, as if to delay the moment when she would have to step forward and face what dwelled beneath the mountain.

"As I said, I do not know its true nature. Only that it is very old, and very powerful. But despite its age and strength, it can be bargained with."

"Are you frightened?"

"Of course."

"As am I," Alyanna admitted, swallowing away her fear as she stepped forward. "Let us see what it wants from us."

The cavern was vast. She and Demian were a drop of light in a great dark sea, and for the first time Alyanna was grateful for what the mendicants had done to her, as it at least kept the oppressive blackness at bay. The scrape of their footsteps on the stone sounded strange, far too loud.

Something crunched beneath her boot – a shard of glass, perhaps? She bent down to examine what it was, and then recoiled as coldness blossomed where her fingers brushed the substance.

"Demian," she said warily, "do you see what we are walking on?"

"The fragments of the soul jewel. It must have been brought here and shattered."

"Why?"

Before the swordsinger could answer, a sound came from deeper within the cavern. It was rasping, like scales scraping against rock. The darkness roiled – something vast moved within its depths.

Dost thou admire thy handiwork?

The words exploded in her mind, and Alyanna staggered backwards. Slivers of pain stabbed behind her eyes, making her head spin. The force of the looming presence was almost overwhelming, and Alyanna felt a compulsion to drop to her knees. Gritting her teeth, she fought back this urge and faced the blackness with all the strength she could muster.

She had peered into the Void before and glimpsed the beings that drifted in the endless dark. Gods and demons, men called them.

She knew she now stood in the presence of one such creature.

"It seems you appreciate what we did under this mountain," she called out, her words echoing. "Was the jewel what brought you here?"

Silence. Something churned, a shadow shifting in the darkness. Coils unspooling, slithering closer.

Aye. Thou hast the right of it. For an age it hath sustained me as I lingered on the border.

"The border?"

Between existence and nothing, sorceress. It drew me here, a beacon in the dark.

"You were injured?" Demian asked, coming to stand beside her. She saw his hand was on the hilt of his sword, though she doubted there was anything here that could be harmed by metal – even the spell-steel of his ancient sword.

Grievous are my wounds still. I fled a war ye could not comprehend and found solace here beneath this mountain. Long have I sucked the marrow from this gem, persisting on the tattered remnants of the souls ye filled it with. But its power fadeth, and soon only the worship of my servants shall remain. And that is not enough.

The darkness seemed to be encroaching on them, the circle of light thrown by Alyanna's radiance shrinking. She swallowed away her fear. "So you are dying."

I do not die, because I do not live. I exist or I do not. But now I am an echo of what I once was, fading into oblivion.

This thing – this creature of the Void – it must want something. Otherwise why summon them here?

Aye. And thou knowest what it is I desire. For a bargain was made.

Alyanna had not spoken – it had listened to her thoughts. She would have to be careful. "The kith'ketan served me, and in return they wanted the boy Keilan. Is this what you mean?"

A hiss came that chilled her blood, and to Alyanna it sounded like affirmation.

"I wanted the boy as well," she continued, "to help me craft again the spell that granted us a thousand years of life. But I have no use for him now. My own sorcery has been stolen away."

Thou art mistaken, sorceress. Nothing can sever thy connection to the realm beyond. The stream still runneth into you, but it hath been diverted and a different kind of power floweth now. But the stone that did this could be removed.

Alyanna's throat was dry. "How?" she managed hoarsely.

Such a feat is within my power, if a vessel was brought to me.

"A vessel?"

One that could contain my essence and let me realize myself fully in this world.

"And this boy Keilan could do this?"

He is what thou calls a Talent. Bring him here, and spill his blood upon this stone, and as his life flees I shall fill what is left behind. And then I could bring back what thou desireth most, sorceress. That is the new bargain I offer thee – sacrifice a Talent to me, and I shall return thy sorcery.

She could be whole again. The thought was dizzying, and she felt her legs weaken. Before she could fall, Demian's hands were on her shoulders, holding her up.

"We can do this, Weaver," he said excitedly, staring into her eyes as she tried to focus on him. "He cannot escape us twice. We will bring Keilan here and offer him to this creature and you will be restored –"

"No," she heard herself say, her own voice distant to her ears. "I cannot take the risk of failure."

A moment of confusion passed across his face, and then she plunged her dagger into his chest.

Demian's eyes widened. She pushed the blade in deeper, searching for his heart.

Please, die quickly.

Demian shook his head slightly, as if in disbelief. "Alyanna," he whispered, and then he coughed, blood darkening his lips.

He crumpled, his hands fumbling with the jutting hilt. With a pained grunt, Demian pulled the dagger from his chest. Slicked with his blood, it slipped from his fingers, clattering on the stone.

His breathing rasped, loud and wet, as he twisted to look up at her. Their eyes met. His face was pale, his jaw clenched from the pain. He struggled to say something, but when he opened his mouth there was only blood. A spasm went through him, then he gave a final rattling cough and was still.

Tears burned Alyanna's cheeks as she faced the darkness again. "Do what you promised!" she screamed, her bloody hands clenched.

A cold wind arose in the cavern under the mountain, lifting Alyanna like she was a leaf and tossing her backwards. She struck the ground hard and rolled, the back of her head smashing against rock.

As she slipped into unconsciousness she saw a glistening tendril emerge from the darkness, wrap itself around Demian's body, and drag him out of the light.

Alyanna awoke to darkness. Utter, seamless darkness.

She mewled in terror and pain, lightly touching the back of her skull with shaking fingers.

There was no wind now. No sound. No light? She blinked – yes, her eyes were open. But there was no radiance leaking from them . . .

She felt it then, coiling inside her. "Oh, thank you," she murmured, tears that did not glow or scald wetting her face.

She was a sorceress again.

Raising a trembling hand, she reached down for the squirming lines of sorcery and lashed them together into the first spell she had ever been taught. Wizardlight blossomed, a silver orb emerging from the blackness.

Alyanna screamed, scrambling backwards.

Demian sat cross-legged not a half-dozen span from where she lay, watching her. His sword lay across his knees, its strange cracked metal shimmering iridescent in the light she had summoned. His black shirt was shredded and stained darker where she had stabbed him.

Shadows pooled in his eyes.

"Demian . . ."

"Sorceress."

It was the voice of the swordsinger, but she knew it was not Demian with whom she spoke.

"It is done, then."

"Aye, our bargain is complete. I have shed my dying coil, and thou art a sorceress once more."

"He is dead?"

Demian's thin lips twitched. "I entered him before the last of his life leaked away and preserved what I could." He ripped wider the rent in his shirt, showing her the puckered flesh where the wound in his chest had closed. "Some fragment of the Undying One still resides within me. Would thou like to speak with him?"

"No," Alyanna said softly, climbing to her feet.

Now the creature before her did smile, showing bloodstained lips. "Understandable."

She compelled her wizardlight to drift closer. The sorcery was singing in her veins; she wanted to sob in relief. She was whole again.

"I am free to go?"

Demian watched her with eyes of liquid black. "Aye. My servants will not stop thee."

Keeping her gaze on the creature, Alyanna began to slowly back towards the cavern's entrance. It continued to watch her, until her wizardlight had moved far enough away that the thing that had been Demian was swallowed again by darkness.

She had nearly reached the passage from this place when the voice of the swordsinger came again, echoing in the vast emptiness.

"Sorceress, a warning. Five abominations are loose again in the world. Children of man tainted by the realm beyond – thou knowest of what I speak, and of thy role in freeing them. They will come for thee once you leave this mountain."

Alyanna clenched her fists, feeling her roiling power rise within her. The air around her trembled, hazed by the force of her anger.

"Let them come."

39: SELLA

"**WHAT ARE WE** doing here, Keilan?"

Nel's raised voice brought Sella grudgingly awake. She groaned and buried her face in her pillow, knowing what was coming next.

"We are waiting."

"Waiting for what?"

They were outside, probably around the small table the shrouded servants of the sorceress set with meals every day. Sella turned her head so that her cheek rested on the cool fabric and glanced at the window – it was very early, the sky just starting to lighten. Keilan must have tried to slip away to see his grandmother before anyone got up, but Nel had caught him. The argument that usually happened in the late morning was now being played out at dawn.

"Waiting for Niara to decide what we should do. She knows about the demon children. She has a weapon that can kill them."

"Then it seems obvious what the best course is."

"And that is?"

"We all go together to Herath. We bring the sorceress and her – what did you say it was? A dagger? – to Queen d'Kara. Let them decide the best way to oppose these creatures. Because by ourselves we cannot!" Nel fairly yelled these last words, and Sella flinched. She didn't like it when people were angry, even if it wasn't because of her. She'd learned from experience that anger at something else – like when Teneal Gundersorn had moved her father's boundary stone in the southern field – often still resulted in her getting beaten later. "This is a war between the great and powerful, not us! We did our part by finding the sorceress and telling her what is coming. We can do no more!"

"I can help them!" Keilan replied, his own voice rising. "Niara is teaching me how to control my sorcery. Already I can summon light and harden it to make a shield. Yesterday I learned how to create blue fire from the air itself."

"That is the simplest kind of sorcery, Keilan. Apprentices in the Scholia can do the same after their first year." Sella heard a heavy sigh from Nel. "She isn't teaching you how to fight these demons, I promise you. Anything that can cause the destruction we saw cannot be stopped by a novice sorcerer who still struggles to control his wizardlight. So ask yourself, Keilan – *why* is she developing your sorcery now? What does *she* want?"

"Niara is my grandmother! She is teaching me because we are family, and unlike every other sorcerer I've met, she knows I'm ready to learn!"

"Keilan," Nel said, and it sounded to Sella like the emotion had suddenly drained from her voice. "I know it feels like your mother has come back. But remember, she was running away from Niara. This sorceress was part of a ceremony that brought about the death of countless innocents."

"She wouldn't have done that knowingly," Keilan replied with firm conviction. "Jan was tricked, and I think most of the others were as well. Only the leader, Alyanna, knew what would happen to fuel the spell."

"Are you so certain?"

"Yes."

"Ask her, then. Because if she *was* aware of the first cataclysm when it was approaching, she might not care very much about stopping the next one."

Sella heard the scrape of a chair as someone stood.

"I'll see you tonight." There was a hardness in Keilan's voice now. Sella had never heard that edge before in his words, and for some reason it made her frightened.

"Keilan –"

Nel did not finish, and from the sound of footsteps Sella guessed Keilan had started on the path up to the sorceress's house.

Nel continued muttering loudly to herself long after the steps had faded, colorful curses that Sella listened to with interest and squirreled away for later use.

Finally, she lapsed into silence, and Sella heard her get up from the table. She didn't come back to the hut they shared, so she must be starting her wandering early. Nel had spent the last few days pacing around the small space the sorceress had confined them to, restless as a caged animal. Like Sella, Nel didn't seem to enjoy waiting very much.

Sella's thoughts began to fragment as she drifted towards sleep again. The strange birds had started singing to the rising sun, but rather than bringing her fully awake the sound was drawing her back down into the soothing darkness . . .

Pressure on her pillow – it was like something small had alighted behind her head. She tried to fight back towards consciousness, but her body wasn't responding. Was this a dream? Had one of the birds fluttered into the hut through the open window? She struggled to come fully awake.

"Sella."

A tingling panic washed through her. The voice was small and reedy, barely a whisper.

"Sella, listen to me."

She tried to turn her head to see who else was in the hut – in the bed with her, even! – but she could not move no matter how much she strained. Who was talking?

"Can you hear me?"

Suddenly Sella could move her head, ever so slightly, and she nodded.

"Good. There are things you must know."

And the voice told her. When it was finished, Sella's blood felt frozen in her veins. Her thoughts whirled – she had to tell the others.

Her fingers twitched. Then the grip on her body seemed to loosen, and she could move her tingling limbs again. She turned her head, and as she suspected, the doll she had brought out of the ruins lay on her pillow, unmoving. This terrified her, but she forced herself to remain calm as she slipped from the bed. The small painted face stared up at her. Had it been a dream? Could what the voice had said really be possible?

Fighting back her fear, Sella reached down and picked up the doll – nothing but old, weathered wood and tufts of straw for hair. Holding it gingerly, fervently hoping it would not twitch in her hand, she carried it to the door. Dream or not – and it felt more and more like it had been a dream the longer she held the doll – she should tell Nel or Senacus about this.

She pushed open the door, then stumbled back in surprise, the doll falling from her slack fingers.

A shrouded figure glided inside, its pale white hands reaching for her.

40: KEILAN

"COME SIT," NIARA said distractedly as Keilan entered her sanctuary. "I'll be with you in a moment." The sorceress was examining a large ceramic sphere perched atop a stand of dark wood, running her hand over the pearly surface as if searching for imperfections. "You are even earlier today than you said you would be."

Keilan flopped onto one of the divans where they usually conducted his lessons, careful to avoid the great red and white cat sprawled on the floor, its tail twitching. "I'm sorry."

She glanced over at him, catching his tone. "You sound angry. Something has upset you?"

Keilan shook his head, not wanting to share what he had been discussing with Nel. "Just a disagreement. It's nothing."

Niara drifted over from the sphere and sank down across from him. She gestured, and the shrouded figure that had escorted him here turned and shuffled away.

"They want action, I imagine. For the hunt to begin. Patience is a rarity in the young."

Keilan watched the robed creature vanish back through the old monastery's entrance.

"What are they?" he asked, nodding in the direction the servant had gone. It was a question he'd been meaning to ask for days . . . and he also wanted to change the subject.

Niara sipped from a porcelain cup decorated with twining blue flowers. "What do you think they are?"

"I think they must be something you made. Like the animals on this island." He remembered his first impression of the creatures – that they were like the clockwork toys he had been shown back at the Scholia. Mindless automata.

Niara set down the cup and dabbed at her mouth with an embroidered cloth. "They are not."

"Then . . . I don't know."

Niara stared at him with pursed lips for a long moment. Finally, she sighed, as if she had reached some decision.

"You could say, Keilan, that they are the very reason I started my great work. They were the inspiration."

"They inspired you?" How could these strange, silent things have done that?

"Yes." Niara rose and glided over to the balcony that overlooked the sea. She clasped her hands behind her back, staring out at the rose-colored water. The great cat rose and padded up beside her, nudging her shoulder with its massive head.

"How old do you think the one that brought you here is?"

"I . . . have no idea."

"He is older than this sea," she said, her voice distant. "Older than the mountains. Older than anything alive at this moment except for the Ancients themselves. And he may be older even than them."

Keilan remembered that great eye sliding open in the darkness, far below the waves. Vhelan had told him about the Ancients, the impossibly vast and terrible creatures that slumbered in the hidden places of the world, and how Keilan had for a moment disturbed the rest of one of them. That was what had first brought him to the attention of the Crimson Queen, and perhaps also to Demian and his allies. The thought that these cowled, silent creatures could be older than the presence he had encountered under the Broken Sea seemed impossible.

"Where do they come from?"

"I found them," Niara said, turning away from the dawn. "In a ruined city clinging to the walls of a canyon at the bottom of the ocean. That city had not even been built by them, but by another species that has since vanished into obscurity. A temple had been erected around where they slept, and I believe they were at one time worshipped as gods. I woke them and brought them here to study."

"How can they be so old?" Keilan whispered, awed by what she had said. "And why do they serve you?"

"They serve me because there is nothing left inside of them. Their will has atrophied after all these eons. But once, they were the masters of this world." Niara twisted a strand of silver hair around her finger as she spoke. She seemed to be struggling with what to tell him first.

"Let me start at the beginning. The cataclysm that destroyed the Imperium and Min-Ceruth was a thousand years ago, Keilan. The Warlock King was slain another thousand years before that. The earliest writing of mankind, scratched on turtle shells or on the walls as our ancestors huddled in caves, was only a few millennia old when Menekar was founded. How long is our history as a species? Five thousand years? Ten? That is only a tiny sliver of time – if your life until now represented the entirety of our world's history, the span since mankind's emergence would be the same as since you entered my sanctuary and sat down. Can you conceive of that, Keilan? The immensity of what has come before?"

He shook his head mutely, trying not to show his confusion. Niara's speech was becoming more impassioned as she spoke.

"We are not the first race to develop language and art and sorcery, or to build cities and empires. A hundred have come before us, perhaps a hundred hundred. But the length of time is so vast that all remnants of their civilizations have crumbled into dust. Only the most recent of these elder races have left evidence for us to find that they once straddled this world – the others have vanished without a trace. In the Frostlands there are creatures known as wraiths –"

"I know them!" Keilan interrupted. "A pack of them attacked a caravan I was traveling with."

"Then you know how far they have fallen. But at one time they ruled these lands, carving magnificent kingdoms from the flesh of mountains. Now they are little more than beasts."

"What happened?" That horrible ambush was seared into Keilan's memory – he remembered the scabrous skin and flaming red eyes of the wraiths as they flowed through the long grass, slaughtering the merchants. Could those things have once been like men?

"As I said, they fell. It would be comforting to think that the story of our species will be one of constant progress. Perhaps a few missteps here and there, but when the dust settles our civilization will continue its march ever forward." Niara traced an ascending line in the air, and a silver thread hung in her finger's wake. "Sorcery, mathematics, art, philosophy – always improving, until we arrive at a golden age." She stared at the glimmering line for a long moment with a slight smile, as if imagining such a future. "But that is never what happens." With a cutting motion, she obliterated what she had drawn. "This is the story of almost every race." She sketched another line in the air, one that rose until it reached a peak, and then descended again until it had returned to the starting height. "Most species are like wraiths – they begin as animals, and they end as animals. The glorious epoch in the middle becomes just a faded race memory lurking somewhere deep in their bestial minds."

"And you think that will happen to men?" Keilan whispered, staring at the glittering arc suspended before him.

Niara again wiped away what she had drawn. "I do not. I said most species, Keilan. A few of the elder races mastered sorcery to such a degree that they were able to achieve the great dream of every sentient creature that has become aware of its impending death – they made themselves immortal."

"Which you have done," he said quietly.

The sorceress pursed her lips. "Yes. Although recently I have begun to suspect that the spell that rendered me ageless was in fact flawed." She held up her hand and stared at it as if searching for something. "I believe I am again aging." She sighed and shook her head. "But no matter. Events are finally coming to a head."

The silver light sprung from her finger once more as she drew a new shape in the air. This one ascended like the last, but after it reached its peak it descended only slightly before leveling off.

"This is the history of the few elder races who mastered the secret of immortality. They could live forever, but the sacrifices made to achieve this great feat permanently stunted them. The genthyaki were like this."

"The genthyaki?" That name tickled Keilan's memory.

"They were another of the elder races that persisted into our own time. Only a handful of them achieved immortality, the greatest sorcerers of their kind, and they did it at the cost of the rest of their species. The few that remained could not sustain a true civilization, and they instead retreated into the shadows as new species emerged, lurking in the fringes of the cities and empires that arose, secretly feeding on wraith and man. We wiped them out a thousand years ago when we discovered them living among us, cloaked in human skin."

The shape changer! Niara was speaking of the monster that had attacked them along the Wending Way! And she thought them all to be dead . . . so she was not allied now with Demian and the other sorcerers who had brought down the cataclysms. Keilan felt a tingling relief at this.

"And my servants here are another of the elder races that achieved immortality, though long before the genthyaki. Their name has been lost to history, but I call them the Ashen, for they are the cold ashes of what once must have been a great and powerful people who burned very, very bright."

Her expression grew serious as she searched his face, but for what he didn't know. "So do you understand, Keilan? What I am doing here?"

He shook his head, utterly baffled.

She reached out and clasped his hand with her own. "I am trying to save us from the fate of all the other species that have come before us. In the end they disappeared, as if they had never been, and that is what will happen to mankind unless I can complete my great work."

"What is your great work?" he whispered.

She clutched at him, her nails digging into his skin. "To change us! To elevate us above the wheel of history, so we are not ground to dust as it turns!" Niara paused, taking a deep breath.

"Ascension, Keilan. I am speaking of ascension."

Keilan leaned back, his thoughts whirling. Ascension? What did she mean by that?

He started as one of the Ashen silently glided past him and bent to whisper something to Niara, the hem of its cowl brushing her hair. She listened, her face clouding as it spoke. Then the creature straightened and drew back a few paces.

Niara blinked rapidly, as if trying to come to grips with what she had been told. When she finally turned to Keilan again, she looked troubled.

"Keilan," she said slowly, "something has happened to your companions."

"What?" he cried, coming to his feet.

She waved at him to sit again. "They are alive and unharmed. But they have been taken to the cell I use as a prison on this island."

Slowly, he lowered himself back onto the divan, though his body was thrumming with nervous energy. "Why?"

Niara sighed. "I warned them, Keilan. Not to leave the huts and explore the island. But one of them – the little girl – she crept away and stole something very, very important to me. When my servants found out, they did what I had instructed them to do in such situations and imprisoned them all."

"She didn't know any better," Keilan said quickly, almost babbling. "She's very young and I'm sure she meant no harm –"

He paused as Niara raised her hand. She looked sad, he thought.

"I know, Keilan. But this incident has demonstrated that I cannot have them here. They could accidentally destroy centuries of my labor. I will have my servants return them to Ven Ibras shortly, and you will remain with me."

41: SELLA

HUDDLED IN THE corner of the small chamber where the shrouded creature had left her, Sella hugged her knees to her chest and sobbed. The tingling numbness that had spread through her when those spindly fingers had grabbed her had finally faded, but the memory of the horrible paralysis wouldn't leave. She had tried to scream, but her mouth would not open, then attempted to will unresponsive legs to kick and arms to flail as she was carried deeper into the island. She had been sure the creature was going to kill her, maybe feed her to another of the sorceress's monstrous cats, but instead it had dumped her unmoving body in this empty building and then departed, the sound of a key turning in a lock telling her that she was now a prisoner.

Gradually feeling had seeped into her limbs and she'd managed to crawl to where she was now. The chamber was empty of any furniture or decorations, and the only light came from narrow slotted windows that were no wider than a span. Others had been kept here, though – someone had scratched strange runes into a wall, and also many small marks that Sella supposed were the numbering of days. She tried to count, but she kept losing track as the lines became more uneven and faltering.

How was she going to tell the others what the doll had told her?

She jumped at the heavy clunk of a key in the lock, and her breath caught in her throat as the door swung open. One of the cowled creatures glided into the chamber, Nel limp in its arms, and dropped her unceremoniously on the floor. Sella moaned as the back of Nel's head hit the stone with a crack. As the creature retreated, Sella crawled closer, and she felt a rush of relief when she saw the knife's eyes darting about the room. Whatever these things had done to her they had also done to Nel. A fractured groan escaped Nel's lips, along with a little bubble of spit.

More of the shrouded creatures entered the cell, a pair of them supporting Senacus. The paladin's feet dragged upon the stone, and his head lolled like he was unconscious – but from his eyes Sella could tell he was aware of what was happening. The creatures released him and he collapsed like a sack of meal beside Nel. Then, without a second glance at the prisoners, the sorceress's servants filed from the chamber, the door slamming shut behind them.

"Nel," Sella whispered, trying to push down her rising panic. "Are you all right?" She shook the knife's shoulder gently, close to tears.

"Hng," Nel murmured, and Sella saw her fingers twitch.

"Oh!" Sella cried, feeling lightheaded from the flood of relief. "Oh, thank you, Ama. Thank you."

"You are a follower?" Senacus slurred as he struggled to push himself to his hands and knees.

"My mother is," Sella said, clutching at Nel as the knife slowly began to move again. "Just old habit."

"No," Senacus said, with effort shaking his head. "No, it is good. We will need the Father's help today."

"Why . . ." Nel began, then swallowed hard before continuing. "Why are we here?"

A wave of shame washed through Sella. Nel must have seen the guilt in her face, because her hand grabbed Sella's wrist.

"What did you do?" she hissed.

Shame burned Sella. "I . . . I snuck away from our huts yesterday. I just wanted to see something else on the island!" Tears prickled her eyes.

"And what did you see?" Senacus asked. Sella turned to the paladin – she did not hear anger in his voice, only curiosity hardened by grim resolve.

"Just an old house. But I went inside and there were tables with dolls scattered around. I didn't think the sorceress would care if I borrowed one! So I took one back with me."

Senacus blinked in confusion. "Dolls? Surely they can't be why we were brought here."

The tears were running freely down Sella's cheeks now, and she wiped them away. "No, it is why those things grabbed us. I'm sure."

"Why?" Nel's dagger had appeared in her hands as she struggled to her feet with a pained grunt. The knife approached the door and bent to examine the lock.

"Because they're not just dolls," Sella said, the horror of what she had been told rising up.

"What do you mean?" Senacus asked, his hand falling upon her shoulder as he gave her a comforting squeeze.

Sniffling, Sella drew strength from his touch. "They're people. Or they were. The doll I took from the house talked to me just before those bad things came."

Nel turned away from the lock she had been peering inside to stare at Sella like she had gone mad. "People?"

"Yes. They . . . they were the sorceress's daughters. Before they get too old, she does something to them and puts their souls inside the dolls."

"Monstrous," Senacus whispered.

"Keilan's mother found the dolls and that's why she ran away. She knew the sorceress would do the same to her soon."

"Are you sure this wasn't a dream, Sella?" Nel asked, pulling a thin piece of metal from her hair.

"I don't think so. It sounds terrible, though. How could anyone do that to their own daughters?"

"She is immortal," Senacus said softly. "And has already done terrible things to achieve that."

"She is insane," Nel said, sliding the metal into the lock and jiggling it around.

"But why even have children?" Sella asked.

"I don't know," Senacus said. "We have to warn Keilan."

The click of a lock turning sounded, and Nel let out a triumphant cry. But when she tried the door it was still shut tight. "God's blood," she cursed as Senacus stepped closer.

"There is a magical seal on it as well," the paladin said, laying his palm flat upon the wood.

"Then we're trapped?" Nel asked bitterly.

"No," Senacus said, closing his eyes.

A tremendous crack sounded and the door exploded outward in a maelstrom of broken wood and iron.

Sella screamed and shrank away, but the paladin only turned back to them with a slightly sheepish expression.

"My apologies. I do not always know how Ama's blessing will react when it touches sorcery."

Nel dashed to the edge of the destroyed door, shielding her eyes against the light. "I don't see those creatures. But I know where we are – look, we're around the other side of the mountain. The sorceress's home is that way."

Senacus motioned for Sella to join him.

"You two should find a safe place to hide," said the paladin. "Sorcery cannot hurt me – I will go find the boy."

42: KEILAN

"I CAN'T STAY with you!"

"You must, Keilan," Niara said calmly. "Great forces are at work right now in the world. I need you here, by my side."

"I saw the future!" Keilan cried, rising to his feet again. "Cities in ruins. The sky broken open. We must stop those demons from bringing down this doom!"

Niara's expression hardened. "And how would we do that? Did the Oracle tell you where this cataclysm will come from? How it can be averted?"

"No, but –"

"Then we should remain on the island. Continue your lessons. So if what was foreseen does happen, you will be ready."

"If we wait, we might be too late!" Keilan leaned closer to Niara, his hands clasped together. "Please, Grandmother. Give me the dagger you made if you will not join with us, and let me take it to Cein d'Kara. She is a mighty sorceress as well."

Niara waved his words away. "Impossible. I will need the weapon when I confront the Betrayers."

"So you are going to destroy them?"

Niara frowned, as if she was unhappy with what she had just said. "I am one of the great powers, as are they. If they truly mean to bring doom to the world then our conflict is inevitable. But now is not the time."

"Then when?"

"Sorceress!"

Surprise shivered Niara's face as Senacus's voice filled the long hall. She rose, twisting around just as the paladin strode through the entrance, his hand on the copper hilt of his white-metal sword.

"How are you free?" she asked, holding up her hand to halt the Ashen, because the shrouded creature had begun to glide in the Pure's direction when he'd appeared.

"Your cell could not hold me," he answered her, and then his gaze settled on Keilan. "She imprisoned us."

"I know, she said Sella stole something –"

"A doll. The girl found a doll in the ruins."

"Quiet!" hissed Niara, and Keilan saw her lash together a complex spell and send it hurtling towards Senacus.

The sorcery melted away as it reached the paladin, evaporating into nothing. Niara gasped, her anger giving way to shock and horror.

"What . . . what are you?" she asked numbly.

Senacus ignored her and continued speaking to Keilan. "The girl said there was a spirit inside the doll. The spirit of one of this sorceress's daughters. She said she had been murdered so that her mother would never have to watch her grow old and die!"

"Do not listen to this madness, Keilan!" Niara cried, her voice shaking.

"It was why your mother fled this place," Senacus continued, still talking to Keilan as he strode forward. "She did not want the same to happen to her."

"Enough!" Niara flung out her hand and a river of green flame erupted. Keilan had seen this sorcery before – it was what he had summoned when Nel was threatened by the shape-changing monster in the ambush along the Way.

The fire carved the air, hissing and crackling, only to dissolve just as it reached the paladin. Senacus ignored the flames while he crossed the hall, intent on the sorceress.

"A paladin of Ama," Niara said, spitting the god's name with hatred. The green fire subsided, but she did not lower her arm. With another flicker of sorcery, she compelled something to lift from one of the tables and flash across the room to her waiting hand. It was the dagger of black metal, the red runes carved into its blade burning.

"Stop!" Keilan pleaded, stepping towards Niara. "Both of you, please stop this madness!"

His grandmother turned on him, her face twisted in anger. "You brought the Pure into my home?"

"This is not what I wanted!" Keilan cried. "You must believe me!"

Senacus had nearly reached the sorceress when a massive shape rose from where it had been curled behind a divan. The red and white tiger stalked forward to come between the paladin and the sorceress, its tail lashing the air and its ears pressed flat against its great head. A rumble like distant thunder came from the cat, and a primal fear swept through Keilan at the sound.

The paladin's face showed only grim determination as he drew his sword, but he did back up a few steps to put some space between himself and the tiger.

"Did your children accept what you did to them?" Senacus asked the sorceress as the cat crept closer, the thick tendrils around its neck writhing.

Niara's face was a mask of rage at the Pure's words. Keilan saw her weave another web of complex sorcery, and a hardened golden light suddenly appeared, sheathing her body like armor.

"You dare speak to me of child murder?" she screamed, the sorcery she had gathered to herself making the very air in the hall tremble. A row of glass flasks on one of the tables burst asunder and a wind rose, pulling books from the shelves and scattering papers like leaves. "I have seen what you do in your temple! How many have died under the knife in the name of your vicious god?"

Keilan pushed through the roiling power surrounding the sorceress, desperate to stop this.

"Niara, listen to me!" he said, but she ignored him.

He reached out for her arm to try and get her attention and she whirled on him, slashing with the dagger. It grazed his hand, opening up a line of fire just below his knuckles.

"This is your doing!" she cried, and then he was tumbling backwards, thrown by a great force.

He struck something cold and hard and fell to the floor in a heap. Whatever it was he had collided with had seemed to shift slightly, and as he struggled to steady his spinning head he heard something shatter. He glanced over his shoulder – he had dislodged the great pearly sphere Niara had been examining when he had entered the hall, and now opalescent shards were spread across the stone. A dark object had been nested inside the sphere, and Keilan struggled to make sense of what it was before a roar from the great cat returned his attention elsewhere.

The tiger lashed out with a massive paw and Senacus stumbled backwards, away from the flashing claws. He swept his sword in a wide arc, trying to keep the cat at bay, but the beast kept creeping towards him, and it looked to Keilan like the paladin's back would soon be up against the wall. Niara was moving closer as well, brandishing the dark knife, swirls of light coruscating across the golden armor she had forged. She braided more sorcery together in an eyeblink and a light blossomed near Senacus's head – the paladin flinched, momentarily distracted, and the tiger did not hesitate. It leapt, enveloping Senacus as he tried to meet it with his sword's point, bearing him to the ground.

"No!" Keilan yelled, stumbling to his feet.

The muscles under the tiger's red and white fur rippled, the long tendrils of its mane shuddering. He couldn't see Senacus beneath the great cat . . . Those claws and teeth, they must be tearing him to pieces . . .

Keilan rushed forward, dreading what he would see, but gasped in relief when he realized that the tiger had gone limp.

It wasn't moving. Senacus must have impaled it with his sword.

And there he was, his head so close to the unmoving jaws of the great cat that he could have looked between its great fangs and down its throat. The claws of one of the tiger's paws had savaged Senacus's left shoulder and still rested there, but his other arm was free and his hand was desperately scrabbling at the ground. The agony he was feeling was evident in his face, and he panted in short, pained cries.

Niara screamed in wordless rage and stalked forward, the sorcery she was holding making her silver hair twist and writhe. Senacus saw her approaching and strained to lift the massive cat, his face darkening with the effort, but it was too heavy.

"Niara, stop!" Keilan yelled at her, willing his legs to move faster. He was too far away, though, and before he'd crossed half the distance she was lifting the dagger over the helpless paladin.

A flash of movement from the doorway to the hall: Nel, ducking around one of the square stone pillars, light glinting off the dagger she had just sent tumbling towards the sorceress. Niara hesitated as the blade struck her armor of golden energy and skittered away, then gestured contemptuously towards where Nel had hidden herself again.

A lance of purple lightning erupted from the sorceress, striking the pillar with enough force that a large chunk of it exploded. Without this support, the lintel and part of the ceiling near the entrance collapsed in a rush of dust and shards of stone.

"Nel!" Keilan yelled, his heart in his throat, but he couldn't go to Nel as Niara was again poised to bring the dagger plunging down.

He knew he couldn't hurt Niara through her wards, but perhaps he could distract her long enough for his pleas to penetrate her anger. Reaching within himself, Keilan grasped for his sorcery, twisting the strands into the pattern she had taught him only yesterday. Blue flame billowed from his hand, arcing towards the sorceress. It splashed harmlessly against her golden armor, melting away into wisps of smoke. But it accomplished what he had hoped, as Niara turned to look at him. Her arm was still upraised, the curving shard of black metal suspended over Senacus.

"You would strike at me, Keilan?" she asked bitterly, disappointment and disgust twisting her face. "And to protect the paladin? This abomination? Do you know what his kind has done to those like us?"

The holy radiance of Ama suddenly filled Senacus's eyes – he had pulled the bone amulet he wore from around his neck.

"You finally reveal yourself, creature," Niara spat, and raised the dagger again.

"No!" Keilan cried, in desperation unleashing another wave of blue fire.

Senacus watched the dagger descend with calm acceptance. At the last moment, his hand flashed out holding the artifact of Tethys and pressed it against the sorceress's bare leg, just above her ankle.

The golden armor vanished a moment before Keilan's spell struck.

The force of the sorcery lifted Niara from her feet and tossed her against the wall, the dagger torn from her fingers. She struggled to her feet, screaming in agony, blue flames crawling along her shimmering dress and silver hair.

Oh, gods.

Numb disbelief flooded Keilan as Niara stumbled away from Senacus. Her arms flailed, beating helplessly at the fire that was consuming her . . . and then she was running through the hall, a blazing blue torch, each step leaving a smoldering mark on the floor . . . Her screams stabbed at Keilan's heart.

"I'm sorry," he whispered to himself. "I didn't want . . ."

Niara Lightspinner, the ancient sorceress who had survived the cataclysms and built this island of wonders, staggered out onto the black stone balcony and toppled over the balustrade wreathed in swirling blue flames.

His grandmother.

What had he done? Everything had happened so fast . . . he'd just wanted to stop her from killing Senacus . . .

Keilan was in such a daze he barely felt any relief when he noticed Nel crawling through the collapsed masonry at the hall's entrance. Her skin looked in places to be a bit blackened, and her hair was definitely frizzier than last he had seen her, but she seemed otherwise unhurt. She saw him looking at her and pointed towards where Niara had vanished, as if telling him to go see what had happened.

Keilan nodded jerkily and moved unsteadily out onto the balcony. He put his hands on the black stone balustrade and peered over the edge, to where the dark water gnawed at the rocks far below.

There was no sign of Niara.

It was like she had been swallowed whole by the sea.

Keilan's gorge rose. He staggered back a step from the balustrade, trying to keep himself from being sick.

He had killed someone. He had burned his grandmother to death.

He glanced back inside, trying to focus on anything other than what had just happened. His eyes were drawn to what had been revealed when the giant pearl had been shattered. His mind tried to come to grips with what was lying there among the wreckage of the sphere.

It was a great faceted jewel the color of the sky at dusk, flowers of purple and blue light blooming and then wilting within its roiling depths. Keilan found he couldn't look away from the pulsing colors.

He had seen a jewel just like this before . . . in the chamber under the mountain, when the sorcerers had fed the souls of the recently dead into it to fuel their dark sorcery.

Why was it here?

Keilan stared down at the churning water, his thoughts as agitated as the sea below. He remembered things Niara had said, pieces sliding into place.

Fate is a fickle goddess, and now here you are, Vera's son, returned at last . . .

Great forces are at work right now . . . I need you here, by my side.

We can remake the world to reflect our desires . . . if we can draw enough sorcery forth.

Ascension, Keilan. I am speaking of ascension.

Events are coming to a head.

A soul jewel. Niara must have been planning some great act of sorcery, and this jewel would have helped her to augment her power. But if it was like what had happened long ago, something terrible would have had to happen for enough people to die . . . Nel's words, spoken just this morning:

If she had been aware of the first cataclysm when it was approaching, she might not care very much about stopping the next one.

What if Niara had known that the doom they had seen in the Oracle's vision was coming? What if she *welcomed* it, so that she could finally complete her great spell and the transformation she had spoken of? That would be why she hadn't wanted to help them find and stop the Betrayers.

Keilan shook himself, chilled by the thought. Surely that couldn't be true. He was exhausted, traumatized, his mind clutching for purchase after this madness. And yet . . .

He heard the scrape of footsteps and turned to see Nel and Senacus limping out on to the balcony, the paladin leaning heavily against the knife. Senacus's face was pale, and a strip of silk torn from somewhere inside was wrapped around his shoulder. That binding was already darkened by blood, but otherwise the paladin looked to be whole. His eyes blazed again with the holy light of the Pure.

Anger rose up in Keilan. This had all happened because the paladin had come charging into Niara's sanctuary claiming she was a murderer . . . and what Keilan had done, he had done to save the Pure's life.

"Is she dead?" Nel asked as they came to stand beside him, staring over the balustrade.

"I don't know," Keilan whispered.

"She is," Senacus said, raising the arm that had not been savaged by the tiger and gesturing down towards the beach. "Look."

A line of shrouded figures were gliding down the path to the black sand. Remembering that one of Niara's servants had been inside the hall as the madness had unfolded Keilan twisted around to see if it was still there.

Senacus saw where he was looking. "It is gone," he said. "The thing must have left after the sorceress threw herself into the sea."

Keilan returned his attention to the beach. The first of the Ashen had reached the water's edge. As he watched, it shrugged out of its dark vestments, letting them puddle in the sand. Beneath the robes the creature was the sickly white of a fish's belly, its limbs long and knobby. Even from this great distance Keilan could see the sharp ridges of the ancient creature's spine thrusting up from the flesh of its back.

"Where are they going?" Nel asked as the lead Ashen waded out into the waves, quickly vanishing beneath the surface of the water.

"Back where they came from," Keilan whispered.

One after another the rest followed, not hesitating or hurrying, until the water closed above them and they abandoned the world once more.

43: CHO LIN

"**THE PASSAGE TO** the old throne room is behind this door," Jan whispered, and she heard the scrape of his fingers against wood.

Cho Lin stepped towards his voice and reached out, groping blindly into the darkness. She brushed something soft and warm and scratchy . . . his cheek, she realized with a twinge of embarrassment as she jerked her hand away.

"Sorry," she murmured, suddenly grateful for the complete lack of light in these corridors, since it kept the blush she felt rising in her cheeks hidden. They were within the deepest recesses of the Bhalavan, far from the halls occupied by the Skein, and the blackness filling these passages was absolute. He'd brought a torch, she knew, but hadn't lit it yet.

"It's fine," Jan said, his hand finding hers and then guiding it to touch what was obviously an ancient and pitted wooden surface.

She restrained herself from pulling away – to be grabbed like this would be a gesture of extreme impudence in Shan, but as she'd learned many times over on this journey, the customs of her home differed greatly from those in the northlands.

Cho Lin allowed him to bring her hand lower, until she felt what seemed to be a massive block of cold iron.

"The door is barred," Jan said quietly. "It's too heavy for me to lift on my own. But I can make it shift slightly, so perhaps we can do it together."

Cho Lin shook free of his grip and traced the edges of the iron. Yes, it did seem to have been placed across this wood. But there was something puzzling her . . .

"Why would they bar it from this side?" she asked, already dreading the answer.

Jan was silent for a moment, as if deciding how to respond. "The Skein must have feared what was within."

"And what *is* within?"

"The way to the throne room where the old queen of Nes Vaneth once held court. If the Skein have discovered that chamber, they might have been frightened of what they saw inside."

"Is there something to be frightened of?"

"No. But the Skein are superstitious. I promise you, there's nothing that can harm us."

Cho Lin wasn't sure if she entirely believed him, but she found the bottom of the iron bar and braced herself. "Very well. Are you ready?"

"Yes," he replied. "Just remember: do not drop the bar after we raise it. Set it down silently."

For a moment the bar did not budge, and then Cho Lin felt the cool strength of the Nothing flood her and it lifted smoothly.

"Slowly, slowly," Jan said, his voice strained, as they carefully lowered the bar to the corridor's stone floor.

"Good," he said, and she heard his hand on the wood again as he sought the handle in the dark. Then came the scrape as the door opened slightly, though Jan hesitated before pulling it wide.

"Thank you, Cho Lin," he murmured, and she could hear his nervous excitement. "I could not ask you to continue past this point. I don't think I will need your help anymore."

Cho Lin gave an exasperated sigh. "I am not letting you out of my sight again until we are in Menekar."

"You know," he said, and from his tone she could tell he was grinning, "if you chase the demons with the same tenacity you have me, they're as good as caught." With a grunt he pulled the door open, its hinges squealing.

They slipped within, and he shut the door behind them.

"Wait a moment," he said, and then she heard the sound of a stone striking flint. Sparks flared in the darkness, and soon after a larger flame kindled.

Cho Lin blinked as the torch's light revealed their surroundings. They stood within a large room that looked to have been a bedchamber. There was a pile of ancient rushes and several fur blankets scattered about, as well as a tarnished copper urn that might once have been a chamber pot. On the far side of the room was a hole surrounded by fragments of stone and tile, as if the floor had been shattered to reach something beneath.

Jan hurried closer and crouched down, holding out his torch so that some of the darkness below was revealed. "There was a hidden entrance here," he said, picking up a sliver of tile and tossing it aside. "But it looks like they simply hacked through the floor."

"Who did?" Cho Lin asked uneasily, unable to tear her eyes from the hole.

Jan shrugged. "The Skein, I suppose. Otherwise why seal off this room? Somehow they found the passage to the throne room." There was an edge of worry to his words now. "Come," he said, sitting on the edge of the hole so that his legs dangled within. He passed her the torch, then lowered himself down into the darkness. It was not even as deep as he was tall, and soon he was beckoning for her to join him. She ignored his outstretched hands and gestured for him to move, then leapt into the hidden passage.

At first they had to crouch, but the corridor soon expanded until they could both comfortably walk upright. Empty wall sconces carved into the faces of demons leered down at them as they passed, their gaping, fanged mouths clotted with spiderwebs. It felt to Cho Lin like they were descending into the tomb of some forgotten emperor.

"Why would the Min-Ceruthan queen hold court down here?" she asked as she pushed through a web that had grown to span the width of the corridor.

"Tradition," Jan replied, brandishing the torch as he led the way forward. "In the earliest days, my people lived in the shadows of the great wraith kingdoms. Those creatures tunneled vast labyrinths out of the mountains, endless spiraling passages that twisted and turned, all in the hopes of protecting the king and his harem at the maze's heart. When the holdfasts of Min-Ceruth eventually arose, we adopted this practice. The passage we are following now is actually leading into the mountain that rises beside the city. If Nes Vaneth was invaded the queen could collapse this tunnel, and she and her favorites would be safe within."

"And there they would slowly starve, sealed inside the mountain?"

Jan chuckled. "No. There were other passages leading away from the throne room, secret exits the queen could use to escape."

"Look!" Cho Lin suddenly hissed, a wave of cold surprise washing through her. Up ahead, far beyond the edge of the flickering light of Jan's torch, a blue glow was creeping from around a bend in the passage.

"We are there," Jan said simply, his pace quickening. Cho Lin followed, wishing that she had something other than just her shurikens to protect herself from whatever had been entombed down here.

"By the Four Winds," she murmured as she rounded the corner. They stood at the entrance of a vast chamber nearly as wide as the Bhalavan's great hall, and the ceiling soared even higher, vanishing into the darkness above. Cho Lin wasn't certain how deep the throne room extended into the mountain, however, as atop a nine-tiered dais a great wall of ice spanned the width of the chamber, completely sealing away the rest of the room. As Jan had said, this was not like the black ice she had seen in Nes Vaneth – it was infused with a pale blue light, though she did not know whether this glow came from something recessed deeper within or from the ice itself.

In the lower level of the chamber, below where the broad steps climbed up to the dais, several dozen statues were scattered. There was something unnatural about these figures – they were men and women in intricate armor and beautiful dresses, but they were not striking the sort of poses that sculptors usually carved. Instead of standing tall and wearing expressions of calm certitude, many of these statues were holding out their arms, as if to shield themselves from something terrible. Their faces – rendered in excruciating detail by some artisan of otherworldly skill – showed surprise, anger, and fear.

"Why are they like this?" Cho Lin asked softly as she moved between the strange statues.

"They saw their deaths approaching," Jan replied as he reached out to brush the cheek of a stone maiden. "Even the bravest of men cannot accept their end when it finally comes swirling down."

"They were alive?" Cho Lin whispered, peering closer at the strange coiled designs emblazoned upon a warrior's shield.

"Many of the greatest heroes of my people are in this hall. I knew them, and they knew me. If I had not quarreled with the queen, I might have been here when the doom arrived."

They had nearly reached the base of the steps that ascended to the dais, and Cho Lin found her eyes drawn away from the statues and to the seamless wall of ice looming above them. "How are you going to free the babe? Surely that would require some spell, yes?"

Jan shook his head as he started on the crumbling steps. "When my memory returned in its entirety I remembered something that eluded me the last time I stood in this chamber. While I do not recognize this particular sorcery, I know of others like it, spells of preservation. One common aspect between almost all of them is that magic is not required when it comes time to break the spell – sorcery is a rare thing, and it could not be relied upon that the rescuer would be gifted."

"So how are you going to break the ice?"

Jan had nearly reached the top of the dais, and he turned back to Cho Lin and raised the torch he still held. "With this," he said, then touched the hilt of the sword at his side. "And this. I am lucky the king gifted me this sword because of my valor on the hunt, and then let me bring it inside the Bhalavan. Otherwise I'd have to chip away at the ice with a rock."

He stayed for a moment where he was, looking out over the cowering stone figures, his expression unreadable. Then he sighed, shaking his head, and faced the wall of ice again.

Cho Lin lost sight of him as he approached the wall. She waited at the base of the steps, uncertain if he wanted her to join him, until the length of the silence from above made her feel a trickle of unease.

"Jan?" she called up, but there was no answer.

The trickle became a flood, and Cho Lin took the steps two at a time until she stood upon the top of the dais. She found him standing next to the wall, his palm pressed to the ice.

"What is it?" she asked, hurrying to his side. "Why didn't you answer me?"

"She's gone," he said, his voice distant as his fingers stroked the blue-tinged ice.

And then Cho Lin saw it: a hole cut into the otherwise smooth surface of the wall. It wasn't more than a few span deep, barely large enough to reach inside . . . but it was certainly large enough to hold a newborn babe.

If there had been one within.

Jan turned to her in disappointment and confusion. "Where did she go?" he murmured, clutching at her arm as if he needed help to steady himself.

"I remember this place!"

The shout came from across the great chamber, and the surprise Cho Lin saw in Jan's face must have been mirrored in her own. They turned away from the wall, back towards the cursed stone heroes of Min-Ceruth and the mouth of the tunnel that had led them here.

They were no longer alone.

A score of Skein warriors had entered the chamber and spread themselves among the statues, swords and axes in their hands, clad in the mottled gray armor fashioned from the skin of wraiths. They were the ones Verrigan had named the Flayed, and like outside the city gates the face of each was tattooed with the visage of some fierce creature. They stared up at her, wolf and bear and lynx, silent and unmoving. Among them was one who was different, a man whose face was not tattooed but burned, and he wore clothes more suited to the southern lands. Cho Lin felt a small shiver of surprise when she noticed that he was staring at her with an expression that made her think of intense hunger.

The king of the Frostlands was walking among the statues, pausing occasionally to peer closely at the tortured expressions of the doomed Min-Ceruthans. At his side was Lask, the young shaman of the White Worm, pale and silent as a ghost.

"It has not changed since I first came," Hroi said loudly, his voice echoing in the vast chamber. Then he glanced up to where Cho Lin and Jan stood upon the dais. "Except, of course, the ice-child is no longer here."

"Where is she?" Jan asked warily, descending the steps. Cho Lin followed him, reaching for the Nothing as she considered what she would do if the king ordered his warriors to attack. She wouldn't be surprised if they had committed some great sin in the eyes of the Skein gods by coming here, but she hoped they hadn't. Cho Lin doubted very much they could escape this chamber if the king desired their deaths.

Hroi shrugged. "I do not know. A priest of the Stormforger cut the thing from the ice. I still remember its cries when it sucked in its first breath. I would have dashed the thing against the stone, but the priest took it from this hall and vanished."

"When was this?" Jan pressed, and Cho Lin heard the desperation in his voice.

Hroi chuckled dryly. "Such audacity to demand answers from a king."

"Please, Northlord," Jan implored, "I must know." They had reached the bottom of the steps just as the king and his shaman emerged from among the statues, and now they faced each other only a few paces apart. Hroi was younger than Cho Lin had first guessed; she doubted he had even seen thirty winters. The hardness of his eyes and the confidence with which he carried himself had made him seem older from afar. He was also slighter than most of the other Skein she had seen, lean strength instead of burly muscle, but she sensed that he knew how to use the sword at his side. Like his Flayed warriors, he was cleanshaven, though there were no tattoos marring his pale face.

Even if her senses had not been heightened by her grasp upon the Nothing, Cho Lin would have known that this was one of the most dangerous men she had ever stood before.

Hroi studied Jan with an enigmatic expression, then turned his gaze to the wall. "That thing was what put me on the path to this." He reached up to touch the black circlet upon his brow.

"Ten years past, the old king of the Frostlands, the thane of the Raven, descended into madness. His dreams were haunted by images of this city as it once was, before the ice came down.

Somehow he knew that these visions were seeping up from this place, and so he cut into the stone beneath his bedchamber and found the tunnel that led here. He discovered the child hanging in the ice and worshipped it. He tried to turn the Skein from the old gods to join him, and so the clans came together to cast him down." Hroi paused, his eyes traveling around the great space, as if he was reliving that moment. "I slew the champion of the Raven upon these steps, but it was Agmandur the Young Bear who claimed the blackbone crown then. And the priest who had guided us here cut the child from the ice, commanding us never to speak of what had happened in this cursed place."

"This priest," Jan said softly, "who was he?"

Hroi grinned mirthlessly. "I tire of your questions, skald. And I have some of my own." He stepped closer, his eyes narrowing. "Who are you?"

"A traveler from the south. I heard of the treasures of Nes Vaneth and came to explore –"

"Liar."

The voice was soft, barely more than a whisper.

"The Skin Thief has told me what you are," murmured the shaman as he came to stand before Jan. "A sorcerer."

Cho Lin had never seen anyone as emaciated as the White Worm shaman – his cheeks were hollow, his eyes sunken deep in their sockets. If it were not for his thatch of pale hair and pale blue eyes, it truly would seem like there was a skull perched atop his brown robes.

"A sorcerer?" Jan repeated, followed by an uneasy laugh. "Then where is my magic?"

The shaman did not answer, but he reached up to touch the iron torc around Jan's neck. Cho Lin saw Jan stiffen and his sword hand twitch, and she knew he badly wanted to draw his blade. But he restrained himself as the shaman's skeletal fingers stroked the dark metal.

She remembered what Jan had told her on the road outside of Herath:

> *'There are only two ways it can be removed – with its key, which is probably somewhere back in Saltstone, or if a sorcerer stronger than the one who placed it on me attempts to unclasp it. And since that sorcerer was Cein d'Kara, I'll likely be wearing it for quite a while.'*

The boy-shaman pursed his bloodless lips, his brow furrowing as if he was straining hard to lift something.

The collar snapped open.

For a moment, no one moved. Cho Lin could see the surprise etched in Jan's face, and then motes of light began to swirl around his head . . . only to wink out of existence as suddenly as they had appeared.

"What –" Jan gasped, falling to his knees before the Skein king. He looked to be struggling, trying to rise, yet some invisible force was holding him down.

Cho Lin grasped the Nothing, the strength deep within her Self flooding her muscles as she prepared to leap at the shaman. Lask was distracted, his face contorted with the strain of keeping Jan from rising.

She couldn't move.

It was as if impossibly heavy chains were wrapped around her limbs – even her throat seemed frozen, and when she tried to scream only a thin mewling escaped her lips.

Jan managed to put one foot on the stone and rise slightly, trembling with the effort, but then the shaman's face darkened, a vein in his temple throbbing, and Jan cried out in pain and could go no further.

Cho Lin strained against the bonds binding her, but they would not give in the least. The strength granted by the Nothing was helpless before this sorcery.

"The Skin Thief's servants told me about you," Hroi said to Jan, apparently unconcerned by the struggle being played out before him. "And they knew you as well," he added, turning to Cho Lin.

What was he talking about?

Movement behind the king, in a shadow cast by one of the cowering statues. A pale child in tattered gray rags stepped into the wan blue light, its face veiled by tangled black hair.

No.

Terror sluiced through Cho Lin, and she fought frantically against what held her.

The Betrayer approached them, and the shaman moved back so that it could stand in front of Jan. It looked past the struggling sorcerer and smiled at Cho Lin, black lips curling back from yellowed fangs.

daughter of cho xin, it whispered in the ragged voices of many children. *you are far from home*

On his knees, Jan was the same height as the demon child, and the Betrayer reached out to cup his chin.

we are not alone here. another watches

Viper-quick the Betrayer released Jan's face and raked its clawed fingers across his eyes. Strips of flesh were torn away, although a single long shred still clung to the Betrayer's curving talons, and Cho Lin watched in horror as it brought it to its mouth. A dark lump rolled out of the creature's palm and fell to the stone.

The keening that rose up from Jan did not sound human.

Cho Lin tried to scream as a wash of black blood flowed down Jan's face, but an invisible hand was crushing her throat, driving the breath from her body, and she felt herself falling into darkness . . .

A crash like thunder, but the flash was black instead of white.

Blinded, Vhelan was lifted from his feet and thrown backwards; his head struck stone, his spine cracking as the force of the explosion sent him rolling across the floor.

Groaning in pain, he struggled to his hands and knees, trying to blink away the darkness clotting his vision.

"Your Majesty," he said, fearing the worst. "Are you all right?"

"I am."

Vhelan sagged in relief. Thank the gods. The room slowly came into focus – the scrying bowl had been shattered, golden fragments strewn about the small chamber. Cein d'Kara was already on her feet, crouched among the detritus, examining one of the larger pieces of the basin that remained.

The Crimson Queen slowly rose, surveying the mess. Then she turned to Vhelan.

"Summon every sword in and around Herath. Every ranger, every soldier, every Scarlet Guardsman. We are riding north."

44: KEILAN

IN THE COLD and black she waited.

Once, she had been alone, a sliver of a soul drifting in this abyss. Lost. Confused. Uncertain about everything . . . everything except for the need to keep the thing in the darkness asleep. That was all she knew – it must not wake. So when it twitched, she stroked the tiny segment of its vastness that intruded into where she floated, soothing it until it sank into a deeper slumber. In the darkness, she crooned lullabies that had once been sung to her, long ago.

For a time, that was her purpose.

But change had come. Now others were here – she had never touched them, but she could sense their souls out there, elsewhere in the dark. They were not of her blood, but they had become her brothers and sisters with the kiss of a knife.

Sometimes she strained to reach them, but always they receded as she grew closer. Her desperate cries for them to join her returned to her like an echo, unanswered.

But then everything changed.

A new brother had entered this place. He was different. Stronger. When he was approached, he did not pull away.

And, most importantly, he remembered.

Keilan returned to himself. He was sitting on a wooden plank in a small boat, his chin resting on his chest. He raised his head, grimacing in the harsh light. Had he fallen asleep? He didn't feel groggy, but for a moment there it had been like he was somewhere else. A dark and cold place. It reminded him of when he used to slip beneath the waves to hunt for fish – his dowsing trick, as his father had called it. Floating in an endless blackness, with presences lurking deep below.

Keilan shook himself. Just a daydream. The horror of what had happened back on the island was weighing on him, that was all.

He rolled his neck, trying to get rid of the stiffness. Across from him Sella sat cross-legged, intent on the doll she was holding. Its painted eyes returned her attentions blankly. That must have been the doll Senacus had spoken of when he'd burst into Niara's sanctum. It certainly didn't look like there was a spirit bound up in it. Maybe when Niara had died the soul had finally been released . . . or perhaps Sella had imagined it all. Beside her on the floor of the boat was the red lacquered box they had taken from Niara's sanctuary. Had the dagger been worth what it had cost?

Keilan twisted around, to where Nel and Senacus strained at the oars. The paladin's face was ghost white and covered with a sheen of sweat, and it looked to Keilan like the wound in his shoulder was bothering him. Good. He deserved to suffer after the madness he'd brought down on all of them. If it wasn't for Senacus his grandmother would be alive, and there would still be hope that she would help them in hunting down the demon children. Senacus might have doomed the world with his rashness.

Keilan blinked. Where was this anger coming from?

He tried to push it aside. What had happened wasn't Senacus's fault, as he had only been trying to protect them.

His hand itched, and Keilan scratched at the cut below his knuckles. Strange – the flesh around the wound had lightened, turning almost as white as milk. There must have been some kind of infection, too, as the veins close to where the dagger had cut had started to darken.

Keilan shook himself – he was exhausted, because it almost looked for a moment there like one of his veins had moved, ever so slightly.

EPILOGUE

GREAT BLACK WORMS writhed in the crimson sky.

At first glance, Alyanna had thought the slowly drifting shapes were storm clouds. Then one of the creatures had lowered its head towards the dark plains below, questing blindly. A herd of striped deer with horns like scimitars had scattered as the monster moved closer, bounding through the long grass with panicked bleating. Somehow she could hear them even though she was many leagues distant.

Alyanna paused in her ascent of the barren hillock, watching the impossibly long worm as it slowly swung in her direction. Could it sense her? It certainly seemed so. A great ripple passed along its length, and then it retracted back to where its brethren formed the living lattice that obscured the sun and clouds. Lightning flashed even higher up, illuminating the moving coils in stark relief against the red heavens.

Almost no one else would have dared climb a hill like this in the middle of a great flat expanse with such monsters filling the sky. Perhaps not even her, if she hadn't known that this was all her dream.

She truly did have a strange imagination.

Sighing, Alyanna continued to trudge upwards, her boots sinking into the soft black earth. Green shoots speckled with bright colors were emerging in the indentations she left in the ground behind her. Alyanna wondered absently if this place would cease to exist when she woke, or if by dreaming it into being it would in fact persist after she departed. Of course, if that was true, it would raise the possibility that her own reality was nothing more than the abandoned sediment of another's sleeping mind. An interesting thought. Perhaps they were all just fragments spun from the dreams of drowsing gods.

Alyanna reached the top of the small hill and found it sheared flat, as if cleanly sliced by a giant's sword. A small stone table had been placed in the middle of this empty space, along with two high-backed chairs of black wood. She slipped into the closest chair, reaching deep within herself to grasp her roiling sorcery.

It had surprised her how quickly her mastery over her Talent had returned to her, but right now would be a test. She had learned how to dreamsend fairly recently, and only once before had she successfully pulled another into her own dreams.

Alyanna concentrated, braiding her sorcery into an intricate pattern. Far above her the black worms twisting in the sky mimicked what she was doing. She finished the spell and sent it hurtling away from this place, towards the sleeping mind of her far-away target. With Demian, she had known him so well that it had been relatively simple to find and draw him to her. This time it was far more difficult, as she did not have the same familiarity to rely upon. Just one brief encounter, though it had been inscribed deeply into her memories.

A pang of sadness rose up as she thought of the swordsinger. She shook herself, trying to put him out of her mind. He was gone, and she was restored. Now she needed new allies.

New allies, or – at the very least – fewer enemies.

A vague shadow gathered in the chair across from Alyanna, and within the span of a few heartbeats it had sharpened into the form of a young woman with pale skin and curls of bright red hair. A moment of confusion passed across the woman's face, and then her eyes narrowed as she realized who else was sitting at the table.

"Welcome, Your Majesty," Alyanna said to Cein d'Kara, allowing herself a crooked smile. "I believe it is time we talked."

ACKNOWLEDGMENTS

The second book is harder than the first, it turns out.

Thank you to Phil Tucker, Joe DiZazzo, Kareem Mayan, Pacific Smiley, Scott Smiley, Patrick Lechner, James O'Neal, and Jeffrey Hall, for helping me to bring this book together. Thank you to Andrew Rowat, for being one of my first big supporters. The fuel for writers is confidence, and your kind words were much appreciated in the early days. Thank you to the Terrible Ten and Sigil Independent, for bringing comradery into the lonely life of a writer. And thank you, of course, to Will Wight, for doing me an incredible act of kindness I never could have expected.

ABOUT THE AUTHOR

Alec Hutson grew up in a geodesic dome and a bookstore and currently lives in Shanghai, China. If you would like to keep current with his writing, please stop by:

AUTHORALECHUTSON.COM

and sign up for his newsletter.

SIGIL
INDEPENDENT

Made in the USA
Monee, IL
06 February 2021